# CITADEL 7

**EARTH'S SECRET TRILOGY: BOOK TWO**

# WAR AND LIES

# YUAN JUR

PROMONTORY
P R E S S

Promontory Press
www.promontorypress.com

ISBN: 978-1-987857-08-5

Typeset by Edge of Water Designs, edgeofwater.com
Cover design by Edge of Water Designs, edgeofwater.com

Printed in Canada
987654321

The Citadel universe is created for all those who feel that,
in reality, all beings are greater than the sum of their parts.

" Everyone always said we looked like father and son, in our dress sense anyway. It's obvious, though, that he's fairer skinned than the physical meat suit I chose—and there's thousands of standard incarnate cycles difference in our ages. I suppose our Jenaoin mentors Roland and Trever could be right about that. It's probably the only time they upfront agreed on anything ever.

"You once said our whole Texas lawman Wild West attire motif of hat, long duster, pants, belt, and boots gave us intercosmos wardens a sort of old world charm. Except, I'm a lesser god with a sword and he's … Well, he's … The jury is still out on that. He takes a whip and a hell of a right cross—and something else far darker with him.

"Anyway, Reader, my name's Unity, and I'm an Evercycle creation pattern assessor. I prefer just 'Uniss' from here on, though. My partner, Dogg—aka Tula—had the same rank as me, although she is a Filion priestess when she's not stuck in her present canine guise. Our partnership of a dozen millennia or so as Citadel profilers and wardens of the Continuum has seen us have some interesting times. She and I found him—or, rather, were manipulated into taking custody of him after our stitch-up. Ensnared in a Citadel Council conspiracy, we were charged with the task of training him as our replacement … and then everything went really south. It's way down the track from that now.

"We've returned to this parallel present with you by order of the Triporian Alliance to examine the life, parallel present, and escapades of our last protégé, Benjamin Albert Blochentackle, or as you eventually came to know him, Commander Bloch—but that's down the road for you yet. We must ensure nothing like it can ever happen again. For my part, and Dogg's, too, privately we are happy some of it did happen. So let's head planetside and bring you up to speed.

"Now, Reader, your soul stream is returning to synchronize with Ben's historical parallel present so that we can get to work. The north winds have started moaning and pushing through Yorr Pass in the forest behind us, and it will get bitter soon. Both half-moons make all the shadows dance with the wind. Don't be concerned, though; we are safe for now on this slope at the forest edge. No one knows our location. It will be dark soon. As an intercosmos Continuum profiler and warden of the Superverse Citadel Council, I have seen many things on many worlds—but nothing like Commander Bloch's story. A master of fiction would struggle telling a greater tale of a hero's escapades.

"Okay, now look down the slope. See how the wind bends the long golden straw-grass in front of the Yorr Forest line here? Its nature's comment on the endless struggle of warring factions here. The Scarzen of this land say: 'Learn from Tora's nature. She displays the hearts of those in her care everywhere.' Malforce, the High Keeper of the Scarzen Talon East Bunker, said that to me when this all started. To be sure, this Toran continent has lands as diverse as a dozen other places along the mild rain belts of Planet Earth. Right now, we're in the season that locals call 'leaf fall.'

"Now that we've regrouped after the need to scatter earlier, I hope that, as we rejoin the parallel present here to continue our interactions and observations, we can prevent as many needless deaths as possible. The reincarnation gateways are jammed with traffic. It is because of the unrest—and is getting worse.

"I still remember how cautious you were the first time you arrived here with us to watch Dogg and me show the ropes to a young Commander Bloch—or Ben, as we all called him back then. I know it turned out quite

< 8 >

a tangle, but decisions already made set us on the path to set the future right. You said as much yourself. Don't worry, a war is coming and one likely to press beyond this planet's boundaries if my gut is right, but we are still ahead of the pack.

"Traversing one Continuum timeline thread to another can really scramble your present, Reader. So I'll give you some background to jog your memory of some of the details now that you're shifted from your own present to this one. Look there, away southeast to your left in front of the foot of the Lyran Mountain Range: the Gantry Road is quiet tonight. It's good to see the natural onset of early night unaccompanied by hurled kinetic barriers, sounds of advancing military columns, and the pounding hooves of war drommal, isn't it? It is somehow a surreal quiet, though, like the calm before a terrible storm, I think. Maybe nature is giving us forewarning because she feels it too. It's colder since we last spoke, and some time has passed. I thought it better we start out here in the wilderness away from any of the Flaxon's greater populated areas, or the Scarzen city bunkers—less likely we'll have prying ears and eyes out here. I hope you can remember more this time, Reader; we are going to need you, I suspect. Your part in all of this helped turn the tables last time, for sure.

"Throw some more timber on that fire, would ya? Tea's nearly ready. Ya know, Reader, although he never said directly, I'm sure Commander Bloch sincerely appreciated the help you gave him in his past. After our first big event together, the Jenaoin have had the human race recorded and honored in the karmic commendation files archived in the Fortress of Bach, I know that much. Fitting you know that upfront for what we have to do here as our soul streams continue synchronizing to the parallel present of Commander Bloch's young life and the paradox of how the Superverse was changed forever.

"In the present we are entering, there are billions of intelligent life pockets evolving across the Superverse. Still today, even after the first great Citadel Wars, there are ethereal super-sentient races and great mortal space-race empires that interact and trade with one another.

"But where Commander Bloch's present begins here, it is amongst the less technologically advanced but more arcanely gifted Scarzen of Tora that

< 9 >

we merge with his history.

"Now, I know what you're going to say. Humans are the center of the universe and any idea that ethereal races could even exist, let alone work and trade, alongside mortal ones, is a flight of fancy. You always say that before your soul stream merges and you start to remember. Humans are an important evolutionary species, yes, but by no means the center or remotely the most advanced of even the galaxy your planet's star system exists in. At least now, you should remember your universe is one quadrant that makes up what the greater administrators of the intercosmos call 'the Superverse.'

"After the last intercosmos Citadel Wars, of which a large proportion of the mortal races were ignorant, Citadel admin thought we'd patched things up pretty well. That was until we realized Evercycle Herrex—you might remember—with some help, had found a way to escape his dual-planet prison of Earth and Tora. After the clues we found here on Tora last time, and from what our personal nemesis Starlin let slip during our last scuffle, we discovered that Ben—or, rather, the secret he carries—was part of the key to Herrex's escape and more beyond. We now know Herrex has full intention to make good his promise of subjugating all existence and breaking the Evercycle Council. We are sure that his worse-than-crisis-bringing mother, Evercycle Three, Lord of Chaos, is manipulating circumstances to make that happen.

"Do you remember now, how Ben, Dogg, and I ended up in a tangle with Starlin, Three's corrupt agent who served as the former chief karma accountant for the Citadel Council? He tried to take Ben from us to implement the next step in the plan to free Herrex on Tora. But we got the better of him and left Starlin screaming to the heavens like a struck cow after Dogg grabbed Ben and jumped through a teleport right in front of him after I'd hit him with a wrap field. He didn't see that comin', the bastard. While Starlin was blinded, I extracted the tracker bug they'd planted on Ben and transferred it to myself. Then, before Starlin could break the field I wrapped him in, I teleported in the opposite direction, across the mountains, to lead Starlin off the scent. He tracked me out here in the scrub before I set our meeting point—knew he would. So I formed a clone field and circled back. While he focused on the clone, I went to take him down with a sleep field before

< 10 >

I took him off-world. But there was a lull in the dark-matter life force feed we wardens draw our power from, and my soul power ability failed. So I hit him on the noggin with a rock. Low-tech answer, I know, but I had to get primitive. He squealed like a pig with a hernia before he hit the dirt. Worked, though—he didn't see who did it and he still thinks Ben has the bug. He'll be max angry with the dent I put in his favorite hat and prob'ly blame it on the lad too. At least he'll have no idea where Dogg's taken Ben—and I stuck the tracking bug on a passing asteroid.

"I am a bit worried about them, though, Reader. It's another reason I got you out here. I've had no communication from Dogg since the jump, and in the present we're synchronizing with Ben, who's in his early twenties now. We both know there's a wider, far more dangerous intercosmos conspiracy brewing out of the Council's activities, and Ben's mixed up in the middle of it in a big way somehow. Herrex's and Three's minions are pushing hard to make Herrex whole again on this planet, and just to make things interesting, an interspecies war of epic proportions is thundering toward us, playing right into our enemy's hands. For each death on this world, Herrex will siphon off part of the karma and life force of those passing before they transition, I'm sure of it. See, that's his fuel source. The more dead occurring by unnatural and karmically unbalanced causes, the stronger Herrex gets. Now, Herrex's luck is turning positive here on Tora, with the Scarzen gearing for all-out war against the Flaxon, whose regent, Trabonus, managed to recover the *Tome of Zharkaa,* which contains the incantation capable of resurrecting Herrex. Good thing Dogg managed to snatch that book away before Trabonus did his worst.

"I reckon Dogg was right about Ben, Reader. In that moment when I realized what Starlin was really up to and how he wanted to use Ben all along, I knew Ben had far more importance than any of us realized. My mission became to find out who Ben really was and what his secret power truly represented. More important than that was who really stood behind this whole mess! Besides, I've grown to like the kid; he sort of reminds me of me, way back when. I couldn't let Ben be used like a key to suit their ends and then be thrown to the darkness of the Echaa Realms to get rid of

< 11 >

the evidence, no matter what he's done in past cycles. And there was you watchin' over our shoulder while all that went down. Do you remember yet? You did well, Reader: played your part and helped the cause—well, at least until that catastrophe in Yorr Fields, which we'll have to revisit later and see if we can't fix. Funny thing is, Reader, if I had erased Ben soon as we brought him to Tora as I first intended, well then, none of us would have been around to tell how it all ended up. Paradox and hindsight make you smile, don't they? Don't tell Dogg I said so. Wouldn't want her gettin' ahead of herself again, okay?

"We're almost in Ben's present, Reader. He's getting closer, and the Continuum threads are almost synchronized. Can you feel your soul stream beginning to merge with the Toran atmosphere here? Good. Soon, your present and those who live in Ben's parallel past will become one, so remember: when Ben rematerialized, he and Dogg had jumped from Talon East Bunker to the wilderness of the southern Yorr Fields, amidst long grass and tall tilby trees west of here. By the time he regained consciousness, it was hours later since he and Dogg had left Talon East near sunset, and the temperature was dropping. Ben realized quickly he'd arrived alone, and unfamiliar with his surroundings, he became frightened. I didn't know that, when Dogg hit Ben at a gallop in front of Starlin to escape through a short jump teleport, their soul streams had been deliberately separated before rematerialization on the other side. We know now it was much more than just a timeline glitch. Even I didn't suspect the hand that interfered, let alone its true nefarious intention. Ben was totally disoriented, having no idea where he was or even if he was still on Tora. At least Starlin is on a wild goose chase, for now. Looking back, I realize that our rebellious free will and our refusal to hand Ben over was something our nemesis never predicted. That action was the first of several such extraordinary anomalies to come that brought everything to a head and changed the Superverse forever.

"So, here we are and right to go, Reader. All we have to do is stop the greatest Superverse threat whoever existed from becoming whole, and prevent an intercosmos war that will destroy the Superverse and existence as we knew it. We'll split company from here, Reader. I am going to try and locate Dogg

< 12 >

and Ben. You're going to the Scarzen bunker of Talon East to eavesdrop on the planning for the coming war and the revenge assassination of an autocrat called Regent Trabonus of Flaxor, which we sparked into action last time. I'll fill you in from a distance at times via mental script, as I'm tapped into your thought waves now that your soul stream is synchronized. See what you can find out and tell Dogg or Ben if you find them before I do."

< 13 >

# CHAPTER 1
# PLANNING FOR PAYBACK

A t the foot of the Lyran Mountains, inside the black glass-stone walls of Talon East Bunker, for Quall assassins Sooza and his brother Cezanne, the recent day's outcomes had been … unexpected. Both were certain they would never see their families again. They had completed their two-part mission of theft and assassination before being discovered by a Scarzen sellenor aerial patrol while trying to exit the bunker.

The bunker alarm was raised, and thus began a relentless hunt over several days across Scarza. The strengths of the two Quall were uniquely adapted to the night, so they hid by day, unable to outrun their eight-foot-tall tireless pursuers. They were finally caught—first Cezanne and then later Sooza—near the Scarzen northern border, heads bagged and all four arms painfully bound, then forced to march back under duress to be interrogated. Both Quall were convinced their capture meant a slow and torturous end, as it typically did for any unauthorized outsiders who entered a Scarzen bunker. Further sealing their fate was their inability to return to the Flaxon city of Weirawind, where the extortionist Regent Trabonus held their clan elder, Makayass, captive.

Then, during separate yet equally vicious interrogations in which each thought the other dead, the Scarzen offered an alliance with the assassins. The whole show turned out to be a deception by their interrogator, Commander

Titarliaa, bunker security chief. Typical of a Scarzen master war strategist, Titarliaa saw an opportunity to use the Quall as an asset when reasons for their infiltration of the bunker emerged. Sooza's wounds were healed using the blue demon crystal called trilix, which the Scarzen guarded so fiercely. The interrogation door swung open, and there stood Sooza's perfectly healthy brother, with three original arms and one new re-grown one, courtesy of the power of Scarzen trilix. Sooza and his brother now had the unprecedented fortune of being inducted into service of the Scarzen military. Specifically, they had willingly agreed to be sent on a mission to assassinate Regent Trabonus of Flaxor, and to thereafter rescue their clan elder, with full support of Scarzen special forces, no less. Their ascent from their former prison felt liberating indeed.

At five feet and some fingers tall, Sooza strode alongside with Cezanne at a quickened march to maintain pace with their purpose-driven escort and new Scarzen employer, Commander O'Rexuss Titarliaa. Sooza and his brother were again clad in their mission-ready clan grays, much to their comfort, and the Scarzen commander had also permitted the return of their throwing blades, blade belts, and all leg and arm Quall assassin tools. The Scarzen felt no threat from them, but then, the Scarzen feared no one. With the Quall happily covered from head to foot, only their large eyes showed through a slit in the head wraps they wore. Sooza felt whole again—even his wife, Selika, had never seen him fully naked as Commander Titarliaa had. His topknot ponytail swung in an easy pendulum, barely higher than Titarliaa's hip as they headed toward their meeting with the Talon East ruler, High Keeper Malforce.

Sooza took the time to remember every detail of Titarliaa's image. He realized that all Scarzen took pride in their appearance, and though their general dress style was similar, much diversity in color and dress style could be found amongst their ranks. Hairstyles, such as Titarliaa's for instance, had a far greater and fixed significance. Sooza noted that Titarliaa had braided hair pulled back into a ponytail, where Sooza noticed a teardrop blade woven into the base. But, unlike the others in his escort, Commander Titarliaa wore two decorated braids that trailed off from behind each ear to lap over his

< 15 >

shoulders and then almost to the center of his chest. Each braid bore several gold and silver bands, with colored thread above and below. The others in their escort had no such adornment, and thus Sooza concluded this was the Scarzen manner of rank.

The two Quall now felt strangely secure as they exited the irregularly patterned sandstone security building. The scent of the fresh early evening air uplifted them further. Moving down a cobbled lane and then out into a paved thoroughfare, still led by Commander Titarliaa, Sooza spotted a wall keystone marked with one of the writing symbols of the Scarzen Chicaa script. He looked higher and saw a statue of a gargoyle-faced obi mounted on a building wall facing the keystone. Sooza knew the correlation of the two meant that this stone would activate a sliding wall that would seal off the road as part of the Scarzen defenses against invaders. He recognized it only because of a previous example he had seen used much earlier.

"Much nicer being welcomed as an honored employee of Scarza and guest of Keeper Malforce than your earlier option, don't you think?" asked Commander Titarliaa, casting a glance to Sooza.

"Out of life's greater struggles often emerges something worthwhile," replied Sooza.

Titarliaa paid his answer with a tiny curl of a smile and marched on. They passed other moonlit buildings along their route, seeing manicured gardens covered in shadow. As they continued along the paved street, it was the ambiguous detail of things happening around them that interested Sooza the most.

Although a heavy military presence could be felt everywhere, the troops roaming the streets blended into the background more as shadows than bunker residents. They moved about in virtual silence as if they were part of the shadows cast from one building to another. Most ordinary eyes would have missed the hidden guards and traps designed to blend in. Now, without being under threat of capture and death, to the Quall's sensibilities, the Scarzen bunker emerged as a living environment, sophisticated both in culture and function. Not only were the Scarzen a remarkably well organized and disciplined warrior race of war tacticians, but it was also now clear to

< 16 >

Sooza they had advanced logistical planning. Sooza now recognized that the Scarzen wielded their politics every bit as well as one of their deadly blades.

"Your Talon East is a masterpiece of engineering and planning," said Sooza.

"Yes, we know," said Titarliaa.

The group left the main thoroughfare and proceeded up a rise to where the street narrowed and to what appeared to be a dead-end. In front of them stood a wall nearly eighteen-feet high, barring the way. Sooza noticed on the left, running parallel with the adjacent wall, a two-story building was secreted amongst some natural stone.

"That is the precinct officer's house," Titarliaa said, noticing Sooza eyeing everything. "A brave Scarzen if ever there was one, as I might expect of one in my clan."

The building's façade only offered two narrow windows on the second story. Some illumination dimly highlighted one window's outline, sealed with outside shutters. An occasional soft sound from within suggested the occupants were still awake. Titarliaa gestured to one of their escorts, who walked over to the wall on the right where some bushes grew flush against it. They reached behind the foliage and pressed a keystone. The sound of a heavy rolling millstone inside the wall disturbed the night silence. Speedily, the dead-end wall disappeared to ground level to expose a beautiful fragrant garden and broad cobblestone pathway. At the pathway's end stood a huge multiple-arched, two-story residence. Before entering, Commander Titarliaa turned to the two Quall guests.

"Before we continue, Quall clan," Titarliaa said, "there are some things you should know for your own safety. This place is sacred to all Scarzen. It is known as the supreme navigator's residence. Every high keeper is regarded as the supreme navigator of the bunker's future; their word is law. Challenge it at your peril. Bear in mind where you are at all times. Wait for Keeper Malforce to speak or inquire. Speak the truth at all times. Keeper Malforce is supremely empathic and as good a lie detector as Minnima Clan's Queen Yazmin herself. Incorrect observations can be fatal to an ignorant visitor. Now, let us continue inside."

< 17 >

\* \* \*

They all proceeded forward, and a short way in, the wall behind them rose to its original blockade position. In the surrounding garden, no guards could be seen, but the Quall felt eyes close by. As they drew closer to Keeper Malforce's residence, moonlight brought out all the mother-of-pearl hidden in the black glass stonewalls and arches. Its sheen reflected the moonlight very well for one whose eyes were well suited to the night such as the Quall.

"It is a beautiful sight to behold," said Cezanne.

Sooza nodded in agreement. All about, the Quall saw the garden's shaped hedges and statues of Scarzen heroes and gods. Some stood in poses of combat and strength, and others in contemplation or gazing at the stars. The entrance to the high keeper's residence felt daunting. Deep stone steps to fit the stride of a Scarzen showed the way through tall arched double doors. Broad hexagonal black granite pillars rose high to support the roof overhead, each with ornate reliefs bearing Scarzen history. Two enormous sentinels stood on either side of the entry doors just inside, each cradling a double-bladed poleaxe.

Inside, they found themselves in a large foyer of white and bronze marble, offering several exits to the rear, left, and right. The space was softly ground-lit with scented lamp oils. Sooza waved a hand past one just to see the shadow. With the assistance of skylights projecting sun or moonlight, the lamps imbued the entire space with a subtle natural beauty. Rugs and decorative hangings from the walls represented a convincing masterpiece of design. Natural light was amplified by polished metal plates mounted on walls. As they walked on, at their feet, the tiles presented the most exquisite frescoes, each one telling some history of Scarza. Looking up, they saw centered on the cathedral ceiling a backlit fresco showing Scarzen in a great war—around it, in Chicaa, was written: *Living legends from the Battle of Yorr Pass.* Heavy stone arches supported the multi-domed convex roof design, from which hanging baskets of brilliant trumpeted flowers perfumed the air.

Walking through this powerful heart of Talon East, Sooza and Cezanne could not help but be impressed.

"This way," Titarliaa said, guiding them to the left and down a corridor

< 18 >

that eventually led out into a private courtyard.

* * *

They stepped through a tall archway and into the enclosed space, then Commander Titarliaa stopped.

*It's so peaceful and serene here,* Sooza thought, then said, "Not at all like I imagined it would be."

Looking around the perimeter, which appeared circular, Sooza saw high, lush green hedges blossoming with pink and crimson flowers, obscuring the bulk of a stonewall behind. The perfume of the flowers filled the air and smelled sweet and distracting. Sooza noticed gold- and silver-armored sentinels uncharacteristically wearing battle helms, standing in the recesses of the hedged walls.

*No one attempting to gain entry covertly would have noticed them after dropping to ground,* Sooza thought.

Anchored from the walls, suspended above the courtyard, almost spanning the entire opening above, hung an overlapping set of triangular sails. Each glossy-black sheet glistened in the evening light, billowing in a gentle breeze.

A servant approached the stationary party. They paid respects to Commander Titarliaa, saying, "Sir, please wait while I inform the keeper of your arrival."

Titarliaa nodded and the servant went to the other side of the courtyard, where Malforce, High Keeper of Talon East, stood near a still pond in exquisite rose-red and orange leather armor. The servant spoke to Malforce, who turned to look in their direction. He gestured, and the servant returned to the waiting party.

"My Keeper requests Commander Titarliaa speak with him alone for a moment."

Titarliaa nodded. "Take them to the address point. Stay with our guests. They have highest priority for the navigator's future plans.

The servant looked down at the Quall, both of whom responded by folding all four arms to strike a pose of confidence.

"As you wish, Commander," said the servant.

< 19 >

Titarliaa dismissed the other escort and moved away to speak to Keeper Malforce. Sooza nudged Cezanne. "Not quite the solid build of one of those maximum sentinel Scarzen, but as tall," Sooza said in a whisper, ignoring Titarliaa's request to use common tongue and instead using Quall dialect.

Titarliaa strode away, crossing the carpet of short green grass. The servant then led the Quall to an assigned address point, stopping to the right of the pond that took the shape of a figure eight.

"Sir, the beauty of High Keeper Malforce's armor … I've not seen matched anywhere," said Sooza to the servant.

The servant cast a considerate eye down to his left upon Sooza. "My Keeper's armor is one of a kind, imbued with the spirit of his ancestors."

Sooza noticed fine embroidery of the house emblem for Talon East on the keeper's raised collar: the image of a sphere balanced on the center of a crossbar over a set of scales that rested upon an anvil—to emphasize the precariousness of life according to the moment.

Sooza then saw large rainbow-colored fish swimming in the crystal-clear water. The pond had a wellspring infusing the water with small bubbles from beneath, near the center. It made the air around smell somehow … fresher and uplifting.

Casting an eye upward, Sooza watched as Titarliaa greeted the keeper and waited for Malforce to speak. Malforce sat casually on the capstone shoulder that formed the lip of the pond and began feeding the fish some bread from a silver plate beside him, speaking to Titarliaa quietly. In the shallows a short distance away, Sooza saw a tall black-and-pink ibis lazily probing with its beak to fish for morsels. Two attendants brought a seat for Commander Titarliaa. Malforce gestured for him to sit and then waved to the servant with the Quall. The servant escorted them over. Malforce raised a hand. The servant halted, and Keeper Malforce spoke to the commander in High Scarzen while occasionally glancing suspiciously at the two Quall. Watching and listening in silence, neither one of the Quall could understand this new Scarzen tongue and wondered what would unfold next.

"Most interesting, Commander," Malforce said, looking to the two Quall. "They showed courage and commitment to their cause during our

< 20 >

consultation, my Keeper," Titarliaa said.

Being in close proximity to Keeper Malforce, Sooza felt a palpable aura from this leader of Scarzen. Hearing the strength in their voice for the first time, Sooza thought, *He surely must have descended from the heavens.*

"You don't look your relaxed self, Commander Titarliaa. What importance carries such weight?" Malforce asked in common tongue so the Quall could hear.

"As reported to you earlier, my Keeper, these two Quall came to our jurisdiction as a result of coercion and as the enemy of Scarza."

"Then why are they not dead and feeding the slaa groves?" asked Malforce.

"Because, my Keeper, they were sent by our old adversary to the north and have since revealed that one of great worth to them is held hostage to force their compliance."

"Unwilling arrows, then?" asked Malforce.

"Just so, my Keeper. After a thorough consultation, I now believe their story to be without deception. They have agreed with full heart and signed life bond to now give their service solely to Scarza. In return for sanctuary and assistance to Scarza, I have agreed to help them retrieve their most beloved leader ..." Titarliaa looked to Sooza.

"Makayass, Scarzen Commander," Sooza said.

"Yes, the Quall clan leader, Makayass, is to be retrieved from the clutches of the Flaxon tyrant Trabonus. I have given permission for our Quall allies to exact revenge and illuminate the Flaxon tyrant as payment for our assistance."

Malforce looked at the Quall, who both placed their four palms across the center of their sternum and bowed respectfully.

"Trabonus," Malforce repeated bitterly. "How do we know they are completely truthful?" he asked calmly.

"It was a third-level consultation, my Keeper, conducted by me," Titarliaa said.

"Really, and they are still breathing. Hmm ... impressive," Malforce said, sitting back and brushing the water with one hand while looking straight at Sooza and then Cezanne.

Sooza didn't know if he should take Malforce's comment as a compliment

< 21 >

or something else.

"Tell me, Master Assassin," Malforce said, "why change your position and ally yourself to the hellspawn Scarzen? Quall are not known for such resignation even on pain of death. Recalling your edict, which I regard as honorable, I have seen that without exception, captured Quall would rather suffer a brutal and slow death than give up their source. Surely, there is a loss of honor for you in this turn of events. What say you to this?"

Titarliaa went to speak, but Malforce gestured for him to wait.

Sooza knew the edge being walked. He answered in a respectful but confident manner: "Great Keeper, I regret that extortion forced us to comply with such unscrupulous wishes of Regent Trabonus. It is clear that you know our clan well. Our work and its expertise, though repulsive to some, have been in Ludd since before written histories. Our storytellers repeat over and again of one of your own great clan, Trilix, unifier of all Scarzen, enlisting our aid. We are sought by many, sadly with the exception of Scarza, until this latest unusual occurrence to our mutual benefit."

Malforce cast Titarliaa a considering glance.

"Our services are often requested at the behest of those promoting themselves as pious. The risk to us is always high, but is always negotiated fairly. In this last case, it was not. Regent Trabonus has no honor. He forced our hand in the matter regarding your clan. After the retrieval of our elder—the Great Makayass—my brother and I intended on treating Regent Trabonus for his disgraceful act," Sooza said, looking to Cezanne, who nodded.

"Is that so?" Malforce said, his expression remaining unreadable to his visitors.

"Yes, Scarzen Keeper," Sooza said. "In this case, Regent Trabonus's contract is not forfeit but reversed according to Quall law."

"And if such occurred between us, would the same apply?" Malforce asked.

"We would be bound to it, Great Keeper," said Sooza.

"Go on."

"We previously declined the contract to infiltrate this bunker, telling the envoy that doing so would mean failure and incur the Scarzen wrath upon our entire clan of Black Mountain. The regent's envoys offered valuable

< 22 >

spices and safe passage in Flaxor until the regent's passing. Our elder still refused to sanction the contract. With negotiations closed, the envoy and his soldiers took our elder at poisoned knifepoint. Our best assassins tracked them for days. They had warriors who practiced the dark arts. We lost many good warriors attempting to rescue Elder Makayass, but we failed. We entered the Flaxon city of Weirawind to find Great Makayass chained to Regent Trabonus's throne. Trabonus ordered the successful completion of the contract on pain of Elder Makayass's death."

"What specifically did the Flaxon regent ask you to do?" Malforce asked.

"Regent Trabonus intends to raid every Scarzen bunker and steal all the reserves of the crystal you call 'trilix.'"

Malforce looked at Titarliaa as if this might be some kind of joke.

"It gets better, my Keeper," said Titarliaa. "Go on, Quall Sooza."

"Our first task, after securing the personal notes of the alchemist Ereedaa and then assassinating him, required us to map this bunker, identifying all possible entries and main streets. We learned of your moving walls—and the difficulty of locating and recording each keystone. It took us weeks of comings and goings."

"Weeks?" Malforce said, sounding surprised. "Commander, you are going to have to do something about your security."

"Scarzen Keeper, your security is supreme in Ludd," Sooza said. "Even with our skills, our work proved treacherous, and it was almost impossible to move about inside your walls—and that is why we were detected during one such foray."

"Did you see any of our trilix reserves or send any information of their location to your employer?"

"No, Scarzen Keeper. Our information is kept up here," Sooza said, tapping his head with one finger. "And we intended to mislead Regent Trabonus in the hope that, if we could not deal with him, you surely would. We were captured before any advantage could be gained."

"It was by Senior Scout Hellexaa's unit they were captured, my Keeper," Titarliaa interjected.

"See that a commendation is awarded to him and his unit," Malforce

< 23 >

said. "Go on, Master Assassin."

"Regent Trabonus is desperate for us to acquire some of your crystal."

"Isn't everyone?"

"I overheard Regent Trabonus say he wanted to further what he called his 'experiments,' saying no force in existence would prevent his end goal of revealing the true ruler of this world. Before we left Flaxor, Regent Trabonus promised us that, after killing Elder Makayass, he would send his armies to crush our entire clan at Black Mountain if we failed."

Malforce sensed the Quall's truthfulness and understood his position.

"We humbly apologize for our intrusion, Scarzen Keeper; there was no honor in it."

"Indeed," Malforce said, his face turning to a balanced calm expression.

Titarliaa internally elevated his level of respect for this Quall Sooza and his brother. Malforce tossed a few torn crusts of bread in the water to the fish, thinking.

"It would seem the heavens bring us together in bond for a common goal, Master Assassin," Malforce said, still looking at the water. "Your account matches my officers' own, which sits well with me. The upstart Flaxon leader is naught more than a steward of his people. He has never proven his grit on the battlefield and stands in my mind as a devious politician of the worst kind. I neither respect nor see him as an honorable enemy." Malforce looked squarely at both Quall. "I feel we have an accord. You may rest at peace and feel welcome here under my protection, as outlined by my commander's treaty."

"Thank you, Scarzen Keeper," Sooza and Cezanne both said in unison before the softest sigh of relief passed their lips.

"I will have the navigators of other bunkers informed of the regent's treachery. Your names and clan shall be recorded amongst us as trustworthy. A rite of free passage shall be issued for your movement in Scarza from this day on."

"Scarzen Keeper, with your permission, I would address Commander Titarliaa," Sooza requested.

Malforce accepted the request and looked on.

< 24 >

"Commander Titarliaa, as you were our judge and potential executioner, on seeing the true motivations behind your actions toward Quall Clan, we feel you have turned your enemy with wisdom. By negotiating better terms, you have shown yourself to be a true strategist and warrior of great integrity. You have our pledge as guardians of Quall Clan. Should you ever independently require our services, we will support and honor your request as best we are able. Only service to Scarzen Keeper Malforce shall override such a request. We hope this commitment is acceptable," Sooza said, placing his top two palms together in respect.

"Jikaa arune," Titarliaa said, giving a nod of agreement.

"We are honored, noble Commander, and may I say to you, maatulac. This contract by word bond will be supported by our clan elders." Sooza shifted focus to address Malforce: "You shall see us worthy of your trust, Great Keeper. Such a permanent alliance is a first for the Quall. We are honored the Scarzen have presented such an opportunity."

"That you have already picked up on some Scarzen protocol bodes well for our future alliance," Malforce said.

"My Keeper," Titarliaa said. "There's more!"

"More?" Malforce said in a concerned tone. "And that would be?"

"Sooza mentioned the theft of Ereedaa's personal notes: the Flaxon tyrant also sent these two to steal the stabilization formula for trilix."

"Of course he did. How could we expect any less?"

"Yes—and any information allowing them to turn the trilix compound against the Scarzen nation. Apparently, Trabonus intends to poison our aquifers and has begun to implement his plan."

"Now that act of stupidity I didn't expect! Why would he put his entire race in such jeopardy?" Malforce said, his agitation showing through.

At that moment, Sooza was sure he saw the keeper's eyes change to a deeper shade of blazing orange and the pond's water surface shudder with ripples. Malforce called his servant, who held a tray with a goblet and crystal carafe. The servant lowered the tray and Malforce calmly took the goblet, then sipped its contents casually. He placed it down softly on the stonework with a sigh before speaking in a perfectly normal tone.

< 25 >

"Ushtaa," he said, addressing the servant, "bring some seating for our guests, and parchment and writing instruments." He looked to the Quall. "When did you take your last good repast?"

"Before entering this bunker under duress, Scarzen Keeper," said Sooza.

"Some acceptable sustenance to suit their diet, and the usual for the commander and me, Ushtaa."

"Yes, my Keeper," the servant replied, leaving smartly.

"Now, Master Assassins," Malforce said to the Quall, "you will sit and tell me every fine detail of your communication with Regent Trabonus and a full layout of his city. The Flaxon regency is about to live in interesting times."

* * *

Their long conversation went late into the night. At its end, Malforce sat back, looking to the stars.

"Well," he said after a sizable exhale, "it is rare for the Scarzen to take allies from outside our clan. In this case, I am pleased it is done. I sanction with aid the expunging of Regent Trabonus, who is neither innocent nor defenseless in many crimes across Ludd and against his own people. This order, I imagine, is one you will not find disagreeable?"

The Quall brothers craned their necks skyward and, in perfect harmony, nodded in approval.

"It is all we could have hoped for, Great Keeper. It will be done with all of our skills and focus," Sooza said. "May I ask, what of our elder?"

"He is to be extracted on the same mission. I will have my best Brasheer unit assigned to your operation," Malforce said.

Sooza knelt, prostrating in front of Malforce, his forehead touching the ground. Cezanne followed suit.

"Now, go. My adjutant will escort you to quarters assigned. Do not wander about until the watch has general knowledge of my sanctioning your residency here. The gate master is not a patient Scarzen," Malforce said.

Sooza and Cezanne paid respects and left Keeper Malforce's courtyard as allies with a new purpose. Malforce turned his attention to Titarliaa.

"This will crack everything wide open, Viceroy," Malforce said plainly.

< 26 >

"And it is welcome."

"Shall we draw them to neutral ground to avoid bringing others in, or should we just invade and sweep them from the face of Ludd? I can have an assault force ready within three standard hours of the bunker's clock," Titarliaa said, not hiding his enthusiasm to get rolling.

"The latter would have been preferable in the past, old friend, but there is more to this—I feel it in the air, like pairs of eyes watching over our shoulder to see how we might proceed. Mistress Farron will not release her Brasheer even for me without good cause."

"What could be greater cause than we have just heard?" asked Titarliaa.

"Her reach is beyond this world and my understanding, and she has prophecied such an event as this on our present horizon. She contacted me recently using her personal sellenor to courier a message to my observatory."

"What message, my Keeper?" asked Titarliaa.

"It foretold of a great disaster sweeping across Ludd that would affect us all—originating in Flaxor. 'All is not what it seems,' she said."

"Surely, a good war is healthy for all concerned. My unit's last good exchange was months ago. They are in need of a purpose."

"Our enemy had made some surprising advancements in their projectile weaponry of late, so our informants report."

"Cowards."

"Indeed, to counter this, I have asked my armorer to consider a solution."

"I ask for the days when wearing of protection would have been dishonorable."

"Now it would be foolish not to," said Malforce. "The Flaxor matter will take some steady planning and gathering of information." Malforce pressed his lips together in thought. "In two passes of the moons, I will call all bunker navigators to a full-mobilization war council."

"I was just out of cadets when that last happened. The ancestors will be pleased," said Titarliaa, clearly elated.

"Then you see the weight of it," said Malforce. "Before this occurs, gather all information you can that has to do with the Flaxon's latest developments. In the meantime, send your swiftest sellenors with a message to each bunker

< 27 >

navigator and give warning to raise security around water access."

"Consider it done, my Keeper."

"Let's have this tight in the top circle for the time being, O'Rexuss, until we have jointly concluded what is to be done."

Titarliaa acknowledged the order.

"From today, raise background security in the bunker to midsummer," Malforce said. "The lunar games approach in ten passes of the sun. All non-Scarzen merchants must be outside our walls after the last day of games. At that time, have our chief physician send word of an outbreak of Scarzen flu and scale rash in the bunker via the security patrols. That should change the minds of any guests wishing to remain beyond their welcome. Meanwhile, I'll request Mistress Farron send our Brasheer units to covertly hamper any further Flaxon stockpiling of arms. Her Majesty Queen Yazmin of the Minnima should hear of this too. Ask her to come up from her sanctuary in the jungles of the south; her empathic abilities could prove useful, yes? Tell her Mistress Farron requires her counsel. The queen hates the male-dominated Flaxon almost as much as we do, and you know how High Keeper Jallanaa likes to make Keenas bite. After the last stunt they pulled on her envoy at the Bon City trade negotiations, I imagine she will be eager to assist."

"I will see to it immediately, my Keeper."

"Good, now ingest some of my finest brew," Malforce said, offering up a mug of Meelow wine. "I believe it to be the best we have produced yet."

\* \* \*

A stream of light invisible to the mortals of Ludd spilled into a space nearby Malforce's pond with a faint ringing sound. Malforce looked about suspiciously.

"Pssst ... Reader, over here! It's Uniss again. I'm back with you now. What did you find out so far? Did you see Dogg or Ben? I went to the original present timeline start point and they weren't there. This isn't good. We agreed to meet where she found Ben on the original present timeline. I had half a garbled short-area comm message from her planetside, and then she dropped out.

< 28 >

"Look, there goes Titarliaa. At least the original present still seems correct here. Someone of great influence is interfering in the Continuum's stability, Reader, I'm sure of that now. The Triporian administration reported nothing about a flawed Continuum thread when I checked in off-world. My last stop was to see Farron Bach in the Brasheer Mountain southeast of here. I followed your thread here when your open thought channel communicated they were speaking about her. Farron is a close associate of Dogg's and mine, and she did a lot to influence Ben on the old timeline. Good thing he's agreed to a memory wipe for our investigations, so all his reactions are spontaneous. Farron is Honan Lord, former Abbess of the Fortress of Bach. She elected to stay behind once the three of us had shut down Herrex's last resurrection attempt after he managed to manipulate the old commander of the Scarzen Brasheer, Zharkaa. Anyway, she sent a short-area comm message that she's on her way to Talon East. No word from Dogg and Ben to her, either. Always had a nose for trouble, that one. I thought to make my presence known, but held back. We need to speak to Farron. None of this is adding up to a happy end for the Continuum.

"Now, Reader, for the Scarzen, war functions like a trade or economic negotiation, with use of logistics and the implementation of skillful means. There's a Scarzen saying: 'Consider your obstacles and objectives wisely. Have your enemy comfortable in the belief of his victory and strike him down as he sits to celebrate.' What a mess this is working up to be—and my last conversation with Dogg, at odds over what to do with Ben, doesn't help. See, Ben developed an association with two Scarzen who were instrumental in changing not only his life, but the ripple effect of their decisions affected the whole Continuum. Their names are Beetaa Pinnaraa of Talon East and Thorr, offspring of Tralldon—both of whom you saw before, remember? It's at about this time in this present that those two over in Talon West started effecting change in Continuum outcomes. That is likely where Dogg has headed with Ben.

"Ben, we knew, represented something terribly powerful to our enemies, possibly for another attempt to resurrect Herrex. Reality shifts have started occurring different from before, and unauthorized memory wipes are

< 29 >

reported across the Continuum. I've even received reports of agents going missing here on Tora without a trace. I have to see what I can find out. This all has to do with Herrex's getaway for sure. I told you things weren't good, and standin' hear listenin' to this, none of it happened in the other parallel present last time, which tells me the Continuum is losing integrity—fast.

"If you experience being caught up in an unnatural cosmic wind, it's likely an unstable reality shift. There are some odd things occurring here. Just plant your will and wait for it to pass. Find the Scarzen Beetaa and Thorr, and you'll likely find Ben."

Toran days and weeks passed after Malforce received the warning from Titarliaa and the Quall. Across Scarza, all bunker high keepers implemented maximum-security actions. All squads ordered that tactical exercises be increased twofold in preparation for what became whispered as "The Great Assault." Finally, a Scarza-wide decree that no bound couples should engage in attempts to bring new pups into the world was handed down. Any Scarzen who were in term of production cycle were to suspend further pregnancy evolution until further notice. Prior to having had the privilege and blessing of giving birth, all Scarzen referred to one another in the masculine. Being an Otutt was held as one of the highest honours a Scarzen could achieve off the battlefield. Being born of neutral gender until electing to choose gender bias post being lifebound to another, all Scarzen had capacity to suspend a pregnancy through a meditative procedure called the Warb. Times approaching were not for the joy of birth; they were for the ecstacy of victory in battle and the cleansing of the soul through engagement with a worthy foe.

Exercises in kinetics, camouflage, battlefield shock circles, and combined pair unarmed combat … all high keepers commanded that troops go beyond previous assault efficiency benchmark expectations. Setting another precedent, torso body armor and gorget for standard troops was issued and worn night and day. All officers took on added studies in the latest enemy Intel, and officer cadets due for active service were promoted to full field duty without delay. Flaxon field tactics and information on all Flaxon strongholds, including Weirawind City, became compulsory knowledge for all officers. Some special units, like the Brasheer assigned to Talon North, developed specialized incursion plans for Weirawind City. A buzz of excitement filled the air that a united Scarza intended to take all of Flaxor and the city of Weirawind for their own.

In Talon West Bunker, as anticipation and pressure mounted for the largest battle Scarza had seen in generations, cadets Beetaa and Thorr's bond as friends and potential lifelong battle allies had become strong. Both found a natural empathy in most activities and liked each other's company. When their Rite of Passage was authorized, advancing their deployment by several months, Thorr for one had made the decision to ask Beetaa to be his lifelong battle ally. One particular night exercise saw the two isolated from the rest of their Blue Squad in an assessment mock battle against two seasoned Scarzen battle circles. The ratio meant they were two against ten, all unarmed. The ferocity the two pressed their opposition with ran close to true battle conditions. As the zeal for battle escalated, a war exercise instructor had to step in because seasoned troops began incurring serious damage from the duo. A horn blew the call to order even as Beetaa used potent kinetic fields to pick off encircling adversaries and pin them against one another, the ground, or a hard vertical surface. At the same time, Thorr shoulder-charged a pair of opponents into a wall, rendering them both unconscious. Thorr's combat assessment registered him as shock troop capable, besting a five-against-one odds critical hot spot convincingly. It was noted Thorr also went back to revive each of the opposition he had knocked out, after the war instructor released him. Beetaa received an award for skilled heavy-support ally and again for best kin field-defense warrior under pressure in battle-circle formations amongst galloping drommal. The two were declared battle-fit after that. Their movement caught the eye of Commandant Zaastaa, who recommended them as a pair for the ranks of Special Forces. The pair bonded tighter with each passing of the sun.

< 32 >

"I liked your thinking when it came to ambush tactics on foot or mounted drommal," Thorr told Beetaa at a field lunch, chomping on some kambaa root and a slab of blue-vein drommal cheese. "I'm sure I can wind that drommal if I charge it harder next time."

"The beast threw its rider and wet itself when you hit it with both legs like that. What more do you want?" Beetaa asked.

"Better poteen to celebrate with—cold with a good froth ... not like the warm brew you bunker dwellers sling down. Downing six of those tankards makes my butt cheeks clench in the night. My morning ablution is a dramatic affair."

Beetaa thought of Thorr as a bit of an uncut precious stone: the real deal in need of a little cultural upgrading. Soon, privileges were narrowed. There were two compulsory meditation sessions a day in both standing and sitting postures, which they did together. All troops ate lean and were allowed only a few pleasures, such as sharing a bolt of tobacco weed leaf for smoking. Even Thorr's beloved practice of chewing kambaa mushroom jerky after hours was refused. Beetaa told Thorr the lack of it appeared to improve Thorr's reflexes, which Thorr told him was not comforting.

"Well," Beetaa said. "We still have our potato jump brew."

"That's no consolation; it's still warm. On our first liberty break, I'll introduce you to my Otaa Tralldon's finest brew. In our village, potato jump is respected. It is distilled and turned to a rectified spirit before being mixed with distilled turnips and corn juice." Thorr laughed. "One mug of my otaa's silken elixir, Beetaa, by the ancestors, your head will turn into a corn-fried broznick before the last drops are swallowed. It always helped relax me after battle practice at our lair."

In those times, to alleviate anxiety, Thorr let off steam some days through wrestling matches. The "Sentinel," as Thorr became nicknamed, quickly shone as the warrior none wanted to tangle with, rarely losing a match, with Beetaa often making a clear profit for both of them while acting as Thorr's second. Everyone knew, however, the sun would soon set on these mostly carefree times.

< 33 >

\* \* \*

In the south grounds of Talon West, just before sunset one day, Beetaa and Thorr were at rest under a large ginkgo tree, chatting casually before late-night maneuvers began. While engaged in a debate over comparative battle tactics, Beetaa noticed a huge, familiar figure in black gloss-satin battle dress emerge from a cluster of trees at the other end of the compound. Their hair braids were in formal ceremony style, crisscrossing their head into a ponytail that lapped the breast with a bronze battle ball braided into the end. His red and gold commendations and special service bands on the ends of his officer braids glinted in the early evening light and swayed with his steps.

"What is he doing here?" Beetaa said softly, beginning to stand.

"Who is it?" Thorr asked, peering at the sentinel-sized officer approaching. "Do you know them?"

"Yes … I do," Beetaa said with his expression changing to concern. "It's my otaa—Maximum Sentinel Spanaje Zealnaa."

Thorr stood at the sound of the familiar name. "Sentinel Zealnaa," repeated Thorr.

As Beetaa's surrogate otaa drew closer, Thorr could see that, though he was no longer in service, Spanaje still commanded an imposing presence. Thorr also noticed the reverence Beetaa had for this living legend. His traditional military tunic displayed two red lanyards of tribute, and honor bands served as piping on his collar. A Scarzen ceremonial dagger sheathed itself neatly in the scabbard of his battle belt. Any Scarzen who knew their history understood this to be the highest battlefield decoration any warrior of Scarza might achieve. Thorr felt dumbstruck.

Further, on Spanaje's tunic, pinned on the right pectoral, were three red horizontal bars encrusted with a stone of tiger-eye, representing his participation in the Ludd Crusades war campaign. They glinted in the evening light. Unconsciously, Thorr took a half step forward, stopping beside Beetaa. Spanaje came to a stop in front of them. Beetaa and Thorr paid regulation respects and waited for the maximum sentinel to speak.

"Stand easy," Spanaje said.

"Otaa, it is an honor to see you," Beetaa said. "May I ask what concern

< 34 >

has brought you such a distance from Talon East?"

"You did. Wanted to see if your assessments produced the potential I'd hoped for. I have a reputation to uphold still," Spanaje said with a dry tone.

"Otaa, how did you gain bunker access? We understood all the bunkers were in lockdown for the coming war," Beetaa asked, noticing Thorr shuffling a little.

When Beetaa ignored the subtle action, Thorr gently nudged Beetaa on the elbow.

"Oh, yes. My apology," Beetaa said. "Sentinel, Commander of Special Forces, Spanaje, late of Unit Jin Gung Myst, may I present my intended battle ally, Thorr of the Southern Shandaa Clan, offspring of Tralldon."

Spanaje looked the younger Scarzen warrior squarely in the eyes. After a long breath of silence, Thorr began to wonder if something should be said.

"Tralldon," said Spanaje, thinking back. His eyes lifted, remembering. "Tralldon Wall Ram! Battle of Western Tealg Hills and the Sinking Sands Desert War, correct?"

"Yes, sir. I understand some in his field shock unit called him by that name," Thorr said.

"Harder to put down than a charging bull drommal, I heard tell. He made his mark well there." Spanaje looked at Beetaa. "You have chosen good stock for consideration." A faint smile curled at the corner of his mouth, and he looked back to Thorr.

"We have stood well under pressure together so far, sir," Thorr said proudly, his comment trailing off.

Beetaa gave a glance, suggesting, *Was that the best you could do?*

Thorr nervously cleared his throat. "Ah ... it's my honor to make the acquaintance of such a decorated officer of the field," Thorr said.

"We are not at a dress rehearsal for march-out, drommal nuts," Spanaje said. "Get that protocol pole out of your arse before it breaks your spines."

Thorr shuffled with a little nervousness, not knowing what else to say.

Spanaje slapped Thorr on the shoulder. "Relax, warrior, just me having a look at you," Spanaje said. "Your accent suggests you come from the Eroin Mountain Clan?"

< 35 >

"Your linguistic skills serve you well, sir. On the northern hip, in fact," Thorr said, straightening with a little pride that such an officer would know of his home outpost. "Your clan's name is heard across Scarza and on our mountain in song and around our campfires, sir."

"Enough of that. The songs they now sing satirize something they know nothing of—and I was never that tall. Pedestals of any kind only offer a sharp stop at the bottom when those who put you there no longer think you fit and drag you off it. Other warriors far finer than I remain unknown," Spanaje said, dismissing the compliment with the wave of a hand. "Now … let us talk plainly. There are still some things I can request of command. Your commandant is an old carrack adversary of mine. Never met a finer strategist, except for your blood otaa, Beetaa. We shared many a battlefield in times past." He broke his stony exterior and laughed. Then everyone relaxed. "The bards have their work and we had ours, I suppose," he said. "Everybody must do their part for the clan."

"Then, will you sit with us, Otaa?" Beetaa asked, gesturing to a stone seat under the tree.

"Mmm … yes, I think we should."

"If it is a private matter, respectfully I will take my leave," Thorr said.

"No, given the pending commitment I see stirring, you are part of what is to unfold," Spanaje said. "Come."

When the three sat down, Thorr passed Spanaje a water skin, which he accepted gratefully and then returned after taking a draught.

"So, how successful has your training been?" Spanaje asked.

"You will have already seen our assessments," Beetaa said.

Spanaje feigned a slight annoyance. "Ah, you still jump to conclusions. You give me too much credit, but … alright, I have spoken to Zaastaa. What she had to say was pleasing."

There was a breath of silence. Nearby on the other side of the thick tree trunk, an unseen stream of silver light spilled upon the ground as Thorr finally broke the silence by saying, "Sir, if I'm not imposing, one of my favorite subjects is battle history. Beetaa's clan history is most important to me from a battle ally heritage perspective. Verbal and written accounts say you were

< 36 >

in the fray at Yorr Pass. Beetaa, in fact, confirmed you are one of only two survivors of the legendary unit Jin Gung Myst who retrieved the Tears from the Flaxon conflict. I wonder if I might press you to give your account—in brief, of course. Your perspective about Myst Commander Benat—"

"Thorr! You go too far," Beetaa snapped. "Otaa has no time for such campfire tales."

A flash of tense feeling swung between Thorr and Beetaa. Spanaje considered the question.

"Beetaa has some difficulty with this subject," Spanaje said. He shuffled in his seat and blew a breath through pinched lips.

Beetaa went to speak and Spanaje raised a hand. "Perhaps it's time to set things straight," he said, looking at Beetaa. "There has been much exaggerated nonsense of that time. A full account given by me never left High Keeper Malforce's private inquiry. Your blood otaa was a warrior, the likes of which Scarza has never seen, Beetaa—even greater than Trilix the Unifier, some suggest. There were none more proud to serve at his side than I."

"Sir, the other survivor was a scout from Talon East. Is that so?" asked Thorr.

"It is true. Scout Hellexaa—he must be toward retirement now. He was only a pup back then."

"You never spoke of Scout Hellexaa to me before except with scant reference," Beetaa said.

"Hellexaa and I preferred to keep their part in the battle quiet, out of respect for your Otaa Benataa. Memory and a change of politics have blurred the edges of truth. So, in telling you what I saw then, I may perhaps help to remove wounds of the past and have you understand why your adoption was necessary."

Clearly, Spanaje felt it was time Beetaa knew the hidden truths of Beetaa's true otaa. As for Thorr, well, given that the bond of battle ally had been announced, it was only fitting Thorr knew the truth of the legend too.

\* \* \*

In that moment on the other side of the tree, Dogg's canine body took

< 37 >

solid form. Beside her, in a crouched position with a hand on her shoulder, twenty-three-year-old Ben Blochentackle appeared in the gray travel garments of a warden's apprentice. Invisible to three Scarzen in council nearby, a faint ring and rustling leaf sound could be heard, drawing their attention for a moment. Nothing seen, they went back to their conversation.

Dogg stood and shook the dust off from nose to tail, unaware at first of the Scarzen group nearby. She heard Ben sigh as he fell sideways in a slump and then groaned drunkenly, pressing himself to a kneeling position.

"I feel like someone filled my head with concrete," Ben said.

"Ben, look at me. Are you all right? Focus on me," said Dogg.

"Where are we, Dogg?" Ben asked. "Still on Tora?"

"Yes. At Talon West … I hope. We've made the jump, but our soul streams took a shunt!" She reached out with her senses. "Still no comm ability with Uniss. That struggle with Starlin left us in a right mess. Is your universal translator working? Can you understand those three on the other side of the tree?"

Ben looked past the broad tree trunk to see the three large figures. He touched the small skin-colored device that Uniss had implanted behind his left ear—as if it might help.

"Yes, I think so," he said. "There was a bit of a fizz, but it's fading now."

"Good, it's just recalibrating. But it should be quicker than that. Our soul stream direction was taken from me in the transition, and we were redirected here, causing us to miss the rendezvous with Uniss … again … and then …"

The Scarzen conversation stalled her words and made the now alert Ben snap his view in their direction. She listened carefully to what Spanaje was saying.

"Spanaje!" Dogg exclaimed. "Well, at least we've found Beetaa and Thorr again." She checked her timeline chronograph. "My stars, he is about to tell the truth about Yorr Pass."

"And that is important because …!" asked Ben.

"Ben … Yorr Pass is the most significant turning point in all Scarzen history, and your other reality played a significant role in the redirection.

< 38 >

This could be the break we have been looking for."

She thought hard for a moment and began her own plan to get involved. Nevertheless, after the scrap of words with Uniss over Ben's reintroduced future, she knew her next step would stress their friendship, possibly to breaking point.

"It's the only way to solve the next thread," she muttered.

"Dogg, what about Starlin? Couldn't he follow? He was plain evil," Ben said, still woozy from their ethereal transfer.

His question drew her away from her musings. "And then some, Ben. But Uniss will have led him astray by now. Uniss could have been erased, pulling a stunt like that to save your life." She turned and looked at him squarely. "Something you must always remember, Ben: the past affects the future, and the future is a reflection of past deeds—and now we have a hell of a mess to clean up. Remember when you saw the Scarzen cadets tested in the mountains?"

"Yes."

"Well, you are about to witness another connector. Its importance will be revealed in the unfolding of events told by that very large Scarzen dressed in black with all the honor bands in his braids. I know your memory is still foggy, but it was at this juncture that Uniss sent you back home before to grow a little older in your own time. You were then eighteen by Earth standard years. I am now altering that timeline."

"For what? I'm twenty-three, so how big a difference will that make?"

"Immense, Ben. A thread will develop soon, and as soon as it does, we have to jump aboard. Someone is interfering with Tora's Continuum, and they are much more potent than Starlin. The old timeline is being rewritten to be irreversibly changed. This time, you must think and take responsibility for what you see on Tora—focusing on the responsibilities you have as an apprentice to us and what you must separate from in your Earthly life. Remember, a minute of time in one part of the Continuum can be years in another part. Don't forget that there are nine points of reality, Ben, and seven major planes of existence in the Superverse."

"I get that now, Dogg, but it was only a minute ago you dragged me

< 39 >

away from where I was sitting with Ann under the willow on Earth—again. That was a damn important moment for me—us, Dogg. She was lookin' at me like she really loved me. Then, without warning, you, me, and Uniss end up kickin' shins with Starlin, who wants to snatch me off to somewhere unknown for reasons you can't tell me why. Hell, I wanted to break everyone's knees at that point for screwing up my big chance at loving someone special."

"Uniss told you what would happen if circumstances were forced the other way."

"Yeah, I know. Ann told me not to worry if it happened again. She said you'd come back. She kinda has a sixth sense about you two."

*And something far greater than any of us can realize, is my guess,* thought Dogg.

"She's the only one I feel connected to now, apart from Mum and Sal."

"Thanks," said Dogg. She listened to the Scarzen conversation again, waiting for the new thread to begin.

"You know what I mean, Dogg. Never expected to see you come to the farm. Remember all of us sitting around the dining table—Ann too? She nearly turned inside out when she saw you and got my attention. I nearly choked on my roast potato and fell off my chair. After that, she accepted everything I'd ever said about Superverse stuff."

"Well, at least you can't say my entrances are dull. I liked your family, Ben. Each of them are good for the Continuum."

Ben began to cheer up. "Hey, remember the first time you told Ann about Earth and how it and Tora were the original prisons for Herrex the Destroyer? Boy, did you make her beautiful eyes turn big as saucers. Then you explained about the tiny strings that hold everything together in folding space, and damn if she didn't get what you were talkin' about straight up. Wow, she had a hundred questions. I remember the debate you both had when you talked about the Continuum and why religions and spiritual traditions emerged in the minds of everyone on both planets."

"Y00, she was irritatingly pushy about that. But once she understood that such pursuits were to stop Herrex from having any chance of resurrection, she calmed down."

< 40 >

"Nothing created, nothing destroyed, right, Dogg?"

"Right, things only move around from one state of existence to another. It's how all karmic substructure is evolved."

"So why won't you talk about my past lives, then?"

Dogg's ears dropped in sadness. "Because, for now, what we know would not benefit you. I will tell you in time. I promise. Show Uniss you are studying hard. You need to show Uniss you grasp warden's profiler theory—things like the meanings behind where numbers come from and their connection to the Evercycles. You must become a competent scholar of Citadel history, and understand clearly why humans and Scarzen cannot stray too far from Earth or Tora to join the other interstellar races anytime soon."

"I get it now, Dogg, really. When you first told Ann and me about the Citadel Wars, the struggle for power of the Evercycles, it confounded us both. Well, me more than her. Hearing how some angels do the work of demons to uphold the principles of balance and justice bent my brain."

"Mmm, yes," Dogg said with a nod. "All gods, angels, and demons have their place, just as the super-sentient races do on the mortal Continuum. Each has free will and their own purpose."

"But you know what I liked most, Dogg?" Ben asked, taking a quick lean sideways to see what the Scarzen were up to.

"What's that?"

"Your own history: how you got stuck being a dog and why we have to find your missing ear tip. I knew those statues in the bunkers were of you. Uniss always fobbed it off. The Scarzen love you, Dogg. That story about you and Uniss and that Honan Lord Farron, what's her name ... wow! I wish I had seen that. Fighting Herrex and the Dark Scarzen side by side! You guys are mad!"

"Okay, Ben, put all that aside and look sharp. Spanaje has finished the formalities and is about to speak the truth of what happened in Yorr Pass. That's our thread."

< 41 >

## CHAPTER 3

# DUBIOUS HISTORY

S panaje gathered his thoughts in silence for some moments, and then he began:

"For what I am about to tell you, may our god scribe of fate, Gul-ses, hear my words and approve. As I have said, many of the events surrounding the engagement have been blurred, becoming campfire folklore. The truth of it was left with your otaa's ashes, Beetaa. There would be those amongst ranks who would dispute what I say to you now, but I was there. Glorified fiction I leave to the storytellers. The memories are in my mind as though the warmth of my battle ally's blood still covers my hands.

"High Keeper Malforce summoned me to sit in council with himself, Queen Yazmin, and two other keepers after the end of the battle and subsequent burial honor ceremonies." Spanaje's expression shifted to something grim, and he said, "There, as I gave my account, I learned of the poisonous Flaxon politics and twist of events that changed the face of Scarza and Ludd forever."

\* \* \*

Dogg watched Spanaje with a keen stare as he focused completely on Beetaa, the fur on her neck on end. She watched him, thinking of that time so long ago.

"Ben, put your hand on my shoulder."

"What for? Is something wrong?"

"No. Not yet. We are about to memory watch. Some parts of the experience can seem very real. Keeping in contact with me will stop you falling into unreality. You will see everything in Spanaje's memory as if it were your own. We may have to take it further. You may ask questions, but keep your hand on my shoulder and do not let go, clear?

"Yes, Dogg," Ben said.

Ben placed his hand on Dogg's shoulder and gave his full attention to Spanaje. He then felt a subtle vacuum as the gravity of Spanaje's emotions and memories encapsulated him. In the next breath, Dogg and Ben sank into Spanaje's mindscape, and his memories poured into theirs.

* * *

Spanaje looked at the eager Beetaa and Thorr, and took a steady breath to begin: "The season of leaf fall was past the midpoint—one of the coldest and bleakest in living memory. Cold, dry winds had been scouring the countryside for the third turn of the season in a row. The land stood in drought. That year, Beetaa, you were only in your fifth life cycle, living with your surrogate otutt, Mazaak. Your Otaa Benataa's squad had been on the long march back to their base camp at the foot of the Brasheer Mountains for many days. We had been in a guerilla war fighting the Chou clans in the north, where they had attempted, to their detriment, an advance on Talon North. At that time, I served as Myst company second officer alongside my commander and battle ally, your blood otaa, Benataa."

Looking at Beetaa, Spanaje had a grunt of a chuckle.

"What?" said Beetaa.

"You look so much like a skinnier version of him—and that thing you do with your jaw when you're concerned, when he thought none were observing, he did the same. The two of you remind me of us when we first set out."

Beetaa and Thorr glanced at each other.

"We were all looking forward to going home after being out in the field for a little over two years," said Spanaje. "Near Gantry town, north of our base camp, a scouting sellenor landed with a message from Talon East

< 43 >

containing new orders. At that time, just to the northwest of our position stood the entrance that led back through the Yorr Pass and into Flaxon territory. So we changed direction and headed for the Yorr Pass entrance. There, we were met by High Keeper Malforce himself, accompanied by the Mistress of the Mountain and leader of the Brasheer, Farron, along with then-Commander Titarliaa and a small elite escort. There was tension for all of us, seeing such prominent individuals gathered in that isolated place."

"That is a long campaign," Thorr said.

"Yes, they are rare now," Spanaje said. "Before the change in orders, there was the promise of new offspring for some, and others badly needed rest. That hope all came to a stop at Yorr Pass entrance with the mountains of Trilix Di and Trilix Tian at our backs. If your otaa had his way, Beetaa, we would all have continued home. But when I heard Mistress Farron and Keeper Malforce tell our commander what had occurred with a recent theft of the Tears of Heaven on the Gantry Road by the Flaxon, I knew that would all change. Since we were the most experienced unit in the area—skilled in infiltration and extraction—they said our return home would be delayed indefinitely until we recovered the prize. We were ordered to go to the enemy Flaxon city of Weirawind and retrieve the Tears of Heaven. A unit of our scouts tracked the raiding party there. Those orchids have been in our guardianship almost as long as our trilix and are of the most beautiful and rarest kind. Keeper Malforce said that the Tears protected by our Brasheer priests were on a caravan going to the Celeron city of Bon, to aid King Karnor, but they were intercepted. The contingent of disguised Brasheer and Gantry militia had traveled from Gantry town as a merchant textiles caravan. It was thought they would be less likely noticed that way."

Spanaje leaned in close as though to tell a secret and so too did everyone listening.

"The Tears' real value is that they produce an element that is one of only three known substances that combine to stabilize trilix. King Karnor, ruler of the Celeron, had been suffering a terrible disease of the bones, and it was threatening to end him, his line, and stability in the west. To protect him, the Mistress of the Mountain sanctioned that the Tears and some trilix be

< 44 >

taken there to make an elixir for King Karnor. On their way south, though, they met one of previous Flaxon Regent Straxus's second cavalry detachments on the neutral zone border of Yorr Fields and Flaxor. Outnumbered, the caravan halted and hoped to be let past. The Flaxon commander said they had crossed the Flaxon border.

"The caravan leader—a Celeron royal court official—protested that they were at the crossroads leading to Weirawind and the western hills there in the neutral zone. Although there was a Celeron delegation waiting for the caravan at the crossroads within eyeshot, the Flaxon patrol commander insisted on searching the caravan ostensibly for contraband."

"Broznick!" grumbled Thorr.

Beetaa shook his head. "Why do they always cause so much trouble?"

The other two nodded in agreement.

"Anyway," Spanaje said, "the royal court official protested again and was immediately placed under arrest for obstructing legitimate Flaxon border protection duty."

Thorr balled a fist into the palm of the other hand.

"I heard Mistress Farron say that the Flaxon and Celeron governing bodies had not been on good terms over some water disputes in recent years," said Spanaje. "Malforce believed the reason for the chance intercept and subsequent short foray was they thought to take some hostages for bargaining chips. The Flaxon took the court official, leaving the caravan to go on its way. Then things turned nasty. The following early morning, another Flaxon raiding party returned and ambushed the caravan in a secluded part of the Gantry trail not far from the end of Broken Tooth Mountain. Mistress Farron said that the patrol attacked with confidence, not realizing three of the guards charged with protecting the caravan were her Master Brasheer."

"Good! So they lost the limbs they deserved," Thorr said.

"Shush! Stop being a broz and just listen," Beetaa said.

"Brasheer protocol would dictate they travel in disguise," Spanaje said. "The Flaxon struck our caravan campsite from three sides. At first, instead of gaining a decisive victory, all that most Flaxon troops found was a fresh start in the afterlife. Mostly, that was thanks to the efficiency of the three

< 45 >

Brasheer guarding the Tears. Unfortunately, while the Brasheer were trying to save the lives of the Celeron officials, two Flaxon horsemen roped and took the chest containing the Tears. They probably thought it was some monetary treasure.

"Malforce and Mistress Farron said they were sure the Flaxon did not know the contents of the chest, nor their true purpose. If Regent Straxus discovered the actual value, and found a way to use it, his armies would have gained the potential for immeasurable strength in Ludd. Don't forget that the Flaxon, while in denial of the use of kin or the arcane, have a small but very strong contingent of their own conjurers. For those reasons, we were ordered to infiltrate Weirawind."

\* \* \*

"Dogg," Ben said, "if the Scarzen are so tough, why didn't they just march up to the city and take back what was theirs?"

"Because, dear boy, the Scarzen are smart enough to realize the long-term effects of such harsh action. If they fight, they fight to win the war, not just the first battle."

As Dogg finished her words, somewhere far away on the wind, she thought she heard a nasty little chuckle.

"Keep listening, Ben, this is shedding new light for our task."

\* \* \*

"It was a tall order," Spanaje said, "in that it was supposed to be done covertly. The Flaxon had improved their security at Weirawind substantially according to our agents in recent times—and changed tactics in the field, too. They were no longer so easily routed. In hindsight, some of us have agreed that it appears the gods had plans of their own back then."

*At least one or two I can think of,* thought Dogg.

"Both sides suffered dearly for their part in it," said Spanaje. "At that time, no is the case now, the balance of numbers held in favor of the Flaxon. We learned then that assassinations of a leading Celeron official and members of a Scarzen envoy had taken place too."

< 46 >

During Spanaje's explanation, Dogg compressed several events spoken of into snapshots and living visions for Ben.

"Often, during our directive to infiltrate Weirawind," Spanaje said, threading his fingers together and remembering, "bitter cold wind and driving rain swept the central lands. Conditions made us eager to get the task over with. It made the going slow for our seventy-strong column. A party of three entered the city, recovered the prize, and left the stronghold without incident. Your otaa said that our supreme god Naught had smiled upon us for a time. It didn't take long, however, before the city alarm bell sounded and search patrols were out looking for us as we retreated at double-time toward the pass. The game was up.

"They must have lit every watchtower in Flaxor across the mountaintops. Our unit could see them frantically signaling one another across the land. Some hours out from meeting up with the main column, our raiding party got obstructed when we ran into a random Flaxon patrol of about fifteen horsed archers. Three of the front-runners were downed quickly, but two of their scouts turned tail and galloped off from the skirmish without engagement. Shortly after, we could hear Flaxon trumpets calling for help on the wind. The signal fires in the watchtowers perched on the ridge tops began signaling, sending white smoke into the sky to other detachments in the area."

"They wanted you bad," said Thorr.

"They did. Our unit managed to coax the archers into part of a young forest where they were foolish enough to follow and dismount. Two of our warriors took flight and, using their blur capacity, removed the Tears from harm while the others continued to engage. It took longer than convenient for the remainder to be cast to earth, dragged off, and hidden. Another good while passed before our raiding party could meet up and carry the Tears on to safety across the Yorr Fields. Your otaa chose the Yorr Pass as the most likely secure route through to neutral grounds of Yorr Fields in the south. He intended to then cut east toward the Lyran Range and up into Hidden Pass, which opens over Talon West's rear entry. Yorr Pass at that time of year is always treacherous, but Commander Benataa wanted to avoid being routed

< 47 >

by the Flaxon swift light-horse companies he knew would soon be sent."

"Do they ride their mounts well?" Thorr asked.

"They do. In such negotiations, they make formidable enemies," Spanaje said. "So, at our best pace, we made for the pass. Going through there meant at least we could not be overrun, plus the steep walls would protect our flanks. As you know from your land studies, the breach is a narrow corridor that cuts straight between Trilix Di and Trilix Tian mountains. The pass is usually only open in the warmer months because of the rockslides and earth falls known to be common in leaf fall and the white months. On some older Scarzen maps, the two mountains were marked also as the Mirrors of Yorr."

"Why?" Beetaa asked.

"To be honest, I do not know," Spanaje said. "Look at this."

Spanaje took a map from inside a concealed pocket of his battle dress. He opened the parchment to reveal an old battlefield map of the Yorr basin and mountain areas. He began to point to the landmarks surrounding Yorr Pass, showing their position at the time.

* * *

Just at that moment, Dogg released Ben's mind. He stood, feeling the need to take a deep breath, and shook his head as if to clear the cobwebs. He put his hand back on her shoulder to immerse himself again.

"See the map? The two mountains he's talking about sit opposite the Lyran Dragon Spine to the north of our position, Ben. Right of where Spanaje is pointing," said Dogg.

"Between the two is a large natural basin called Yorr Fields. Some in Ludd teach that it was once an inland sea," said Spanaje. "Scarzen history scholars tell that the two mountains Trilix Tian and Trilix Di—which mean 'Heaven's Life Giver' and 'Earth's Life Taker,' respectively—are the bones of the spirit of balance. They say the spirit of balance's blood was frozen to crystal when the Great Spirit perished after losing a battle of epic proportion against cosmic forces intent on destroying our world. Legend says it is the Scarzen reason for being: to protect the spirit of balance's last remnants we now call trilix."

< 48 >

"Now, how do you suppose they got to know that?" said Dogg.

"I don't know," Ben said.

"Can you hear it?" Dogg asked, looking about as if there was something to see.

"Hear what?"

"Herrex: it's his whispers creeping softly closer on the wind to any who will pay attention. I think we have to reexamine all the way back where this story is buried. Spanaje tells an unembellished version—typical Scarzen forthrightness," she said. "Interesting to see how Scarzen culture has transformed the implanted story of Herrex's imprisonment into their own histories. Spanaje is telling what he believes is the truth. When reality collides with hindsight, Ben, the threads of truth commonly distort."

"How?" Ben asked, not taking his eyes off the three on the other side of the tree.

"Remember your history, Ben? After Zero created Earth to incarcerate Herrex, Tora was the site for final passing of judgment against Herrex. He stood in the intercosmos surrounded by a cavion field direct from Zero's heart center docked on the top of Trilix Di. After a unanimous vote, including Herrex's mother, Three, and the combined efforts of all remaining Evercycles, Zero divided and sealed Herrex away."

Ben and Dogg both turned their attention to Spanaje's voice, which coincidentally added, "And at one time, their peaks were the transition point for Shizaa, the great bridge to the beyond and the seat of judgment and to our Halls of Ancestors."

"See what I mean?" Dogg said. "The Continuum thread occurred, and for the Scarzen, it was the beginning of all things, but not accurate by a long shot. I'm beginning to think we are up for a field trip."

"What?"

"Just listen."

* * *

"Our rank moved fast up the slopes to the mouth of the pass," Spanaje said, finding his rhythm as a storyteller. "On entering through the north gap

< 49 >

as night closed upon us, we were slowed by a landslide a short way in. Two of our squad were almost buried alive when they tried to climb around some fallen loose stone. I tell you," Spanaje said, with a grunt of a chuckle, "that old Regent Straxus must have been furious at how easily we infiltrated his stronghold … and such small doorways, too—for a Scarzen. He honored us by sending three full Gagan light-horse companies straight off at the first war bell. One of our scouts climbed to the upper ridges to see how far behind our pursuers were; said horsemen two hundred strong were closing fast. I still had good legs and arms back then. Asked your otaa if I could take some clan and give them something to think about."

"That's what I would have done," said Thorr.

"You think like a sentinel, as is our caste," said Spanaje. "But my battle ally was not a sentinel. He said, 'Spanaje, temperance and steady steps avert the shadows of mind's conspiracy. I have a special consultation in mind for our tenacious pursuers.' And he did. Yes, pups, oh how he did."

"So how was Otaa's consultation presented?" Beetaa asked, leaning forward.

"He ordered we hasten to a part of the Yorr Pass called 'the Choke.' Our speed was hampered because of the delicate nature of the Tears, plus rockfalls from above. Seemed like old Naught himself intended we not succeed. There appeared to be an unusual amount of falling hazards, even for that time of year. At one point, your otaa, who always led from the front, called us to a halt to get a bearing. He went to take a step forward and a large boulder fell from above, with only a faintest sound of wind as company. Had Hellexaa not shoulder-charged him, Commander Benataa would have been crushed where he stood. We knew the Flaxon were prepared to sacrifice anything to get those Tears back, including open war with Scarza if necessary," Spanaje said, looking at them both. "Flaxon have excellent wilderness skills and tactics, though I'd not admit it to them. As well as being competent trackers and archers from horseback, their heavy cavalry is strong and maneuverable. They are particularly adapted to open-ground assault. It's why your otaa wanted to avoid the faster, more southern route that swung round through the rolling meadows of Lilarwa on the west shoulder of Trilix Di. It's a place the Flaxon have used as a killing field for many generations.

< 50 >

"So Otaa wanted them in a good tight spot?" asked Beetaa.

"Your otaa was an exceptional tactician, Beetaa—with small units, the best I ever saw. Keeper Malforce uses his tactics to this day. He was known for his unorthodox thinking, commitment, and consideration of his troops, and we loved him for it. As our column's feet pounded hastily through the northern end of the pass, the smell of many horses coming met our noses well before the hooves were heard."

"Back home, my brothers and I used the undomesticated horse beasts that the Flaxon are said to use. But we used them for throw-and-catch and kin barrier practice. They are good for on-the-run drills," Thorr said.

Spanaje gave Thorr a wry look and continued. "Sending the column on, your otaa and I left the column and went back toward the northern gap to see what might be done about our pursuers. From our position, we could see in the distance a forward column of some seventy Gagan light horsemen closing at a canter. They were separated from two other columns a short distance farther back. We thought the rest would be moving equally as fast to keep up when the front-runners increased speed up the slope toward our position, but they didn't. Instead, they just maintained a steady trot, leaving the first column to break away."

\* \* \*

"Okay, it's time for some parallel present perspective," Dogg said.

"You mean jump again? Will it be like the last time—dangerous, I mean?" Ben asked with a frown.

"You're training to be a profiler, Ben. We go where the next thread leads us."

"What about Uniss?"

"Still can't contact him. I get the feeling someone has been timeline meddling. Our jump will bring the past to us so we can stand in it as the present.

"If we don't come unstuck, you mean," Ben said, looking unconvinced.

"It could be dangerous … possibly. But that's in the profiler's job description. Now grab a handful of my shoulder fur and don't let go." *Uniss*

< 51 >

*won't like this direction,* Dogg mused, *but I have a feeling that being there will answer more than we can ask here. Tora's Continuum balance is tilting further off axis by the minute. The strange distortion around these events doesn't match the archive report. It's possible two alternate presents were overlapped.* "Don't worry, Ben. You'll still be able to hear Spanaje's voice in the back of your mind. But we'll see the rest for ourselves."

Their forms shimmered in a silver light stream, and they evaporated from that present.

< 52 >

## CHAPTER 4
## HORSES TWO BY TWO

The experience of a soul stream jump felt like being swept along in a celestial wind. Two silver ribbons of light fell on the shoulder of a cliff in Ludd's midlands, and Ben's head cleared quicker this time. "Oowa! That was a bit close," said Dogg. "Mind your step."

Beside her, Ben shuffled back and brushed a long blond fringe out of his eyes. His long gray denim travel coat and jeans blended with the coming shadows. At least this time, he'd arrived with proper walking boots.

"Wow!" Ben said. "Look over here. Did you see that eagle, Dogg? It's huge! We can see the whole world from up here." Ben stepped back from the cliff edge. "Goodness, that's a bit of a jump."

Dogg looked up. "Oh … Reader. Good. Wasn't sure if you'd make it. Have you seen Uniss? … You haven't, either. Hmm … Okay, well, stick with us, and I'll keep trying. Maybe he'll catch up with Farron."

"Who're you talking to, Dogg?" Ben asked.

"Never mind, Ben. Just keep a lookout below. Tell me when that forward horse column gets to that bend in the road where that rockslide fell. See, near that cliff … on your left?"

"Scrape a bone! These mountains are mad, Dogg."

"Yes, well, don't get too close to the edge. It's a long way down. Now, give me a minute, Ben. So, Reader, two questions for you: do we live in the present, or just one form of it? How much does anything we do or intend impact everything else? That's what this is about. I can tell you that what happens now has the ability to creep into our beds another time far into our future, even following incarnations. Remember that."

"They're nearly there, Dogg. I can see the Scarzen below now moving about too."

"Righto, Ben. Watch what they do below and start focusing on Spanaje. Let the gravity of his thoughts and voice draw you in. I'm braiding in his parallel time's timeline now."

"I can hear him, Dogg, I can hear him! He sounds like he's in a radio play."

"Yes, and you're going to miss most of it if you don't shush. Eyes peeled, just watch and listen."

* * *

"Commander Benataa," Spanaje's voice said as Ben watched events unfold below, "knew that without the burden of carrying the Tears, it would still take almost a day in fair weather and a strong pace to cross into the Yorr Fields neutral zone. He also considered that Flaxon cavalry would probably be sent to enter that region from the west to cut them off. In short, he knew outrunning them was virtually impossible."

"What Benataa didn't know," Dogg said, suspending the audio signal in Ben's head for a moment, "is that on this occasion, the advanced column of Flaxon horsemen was commanded by a newly commissioned young Lieutenant Waldon, and it was his debut hunt for Scarzen. For most of his troopers, Yorr Pass rose up as a rare sight as well."

The audio signal to Ben's mind phased back in, and he could hear Spanaje once again: "Once surrounded by enormous shoulders of Trilix Di and Trilix Tian, the horseman slowed their pace, now a substantial distance from the following forces. Approaching the entrance, enough room existed for the horsemen to ride twenty abreast. Entering the mouth of the pass, that quickly diminished to live with any real comfort, and as the cliffs closed in, riding narrowed down to pairs. Swiftly, the path degenerated, becoming less and less horse worthy, winding away like an outstretched scribble on

< 54 >

parchment even as gray clouds skyward began to form."

"He remembers good for an old fella, Dogg. Can't see the Scarzen now."

"Shh, Ben, just listen and watch."

"After a short way farther in," Spanaje said, "the path narrowed to nearly a track, shouldering against steep ascending cliffs on the left bank. To their right, a wide crevice stretched nearly seventy-five spans long and showed no suggestion of a bottom looking over the edge. On the crevice's far side lay more ascending jagged terrain that would reject any boot or hoof."

"And within that horse company," Dogg said, breaking into Spanaje's story, "the only soldier with any real field experience is the sergeant of arms, Rictor, who's well past his prime. The rest of the men are untried, fresh out of basic training. Rictor is the second horseman behind the commanding officer who's leading."

"Got 'em," said Ben.

"Sergeant Rictor wants a quieter life away from the military now. Somehow, I think he will be disappointed. This mission, in his mind, will be his last field assignment before he retires quietly to work with his brother Jeb in their family city brewery in Weirawind."

Ben nodded as Spanaje's voice phased back into his mind again: "Up ahead of the horse company, at some distance inside the pass, your otaa considered splitting the column into a forward and rear guard, but decided against it. There was only one other option: a small township allied to us. That was Gantry settlement, but it lay a considerable distance beyond the southern exit away to the eastern border of Yorr Fields. He knew there was small hope of getting the Tears to Gantry unseen without airlift from a sellenor, and none he knew of were in range. Although the Brasheer and Mistress Farron herself protected Gantry, it boasted little fortification against a serious assault. The commander knew that breaking the column could cripple us. He also knew that eventually we would have to make a stand before the north exit spilled into the central region of Yorr Fields."

"Sounds like a situation tighter than a drommal's dump hole," said Thorr.

"A bitter cold snap of wind smacked everyone's face as Benataa crouched on an elevated stone ledge ahead of the squad, planning his next step."

< 55 >

"Be a night fight if I had my choice," said Beetaa.

"Your instincts are good," said Spanaje. "I heard Mistress Farron specifically stipulate the day they met us to return the Tears to Talon East. 'Do not approach my lair with it,' she ordered. I thought it a curious thing since the Lair of Bach is the Brasheer stronghold."

"Before that time, Ben," Dogg interjected, "the Flaxon could bring a force straight up the center of Yorr Fields to overrun the column and the Tears could be stolen back or lost for good in a skirmish. Spanaje is holding true to what happened …"

"Traveling by night in Yorr Pass is always treacherous," Spanaje said. "There is never a safe place to sleep or rest anywhere along its pathways. Something to remember. If you ever need to pass through there, a traveler can be buried or crushed to death by falling debris in the early hours if sleep takes him. Benataa intended that danger be turned to an advantage."

"Yes," Dogg said. "In fact, at the same time Benataa is concocting his plan, so too is that young Flaxon, Lieutenant Waldon, stirring ideas of his own."

Ben nodded at Dogg's passing comment, but continued maintaining vigil on the fading images below and the sound of Spanaje's voice in his head. It was odd to be sure, but Ben adapted quickly to watching the events in real time while hearing them narrated by someone in the future.

"Slowly, a strategy to turn things to our advantage emerged in our Ruhe Benataa's mind," Spanaje said, falling into using titles of honor. "Our squad tramped on through the pass as the weather threatened to turn for the worst, knowing the Gagan horsemen were closing steadily. Sitting up on that rock, Ruhe moved several pebbles around like carrack pieces … thinking. He concluded that, by moving ahead of the other two columns, his Flaxon adversary had already made the first critical error. If Ruhe could force his hand to make one more, the ancestors might smile on us."

Dogg nodded and stopped the voice feed.

"Karma is like a sand scale, Ben, and that young Flaxon officer was about to chalk up quite a karmic futures debt, let me tell you. The three companies had been ordered by the commander of Weirawind garrison to herd the Scarzen thieves into the Yorr Pass—then, to ensure that they did

< 56 >

not speed east to more difficult terrain where the Scarzen have advantage. By flushing the enemy slowly through the pass, another stronger force would take a route from the west and lie in wait on the Yorr Fields. Once the enemy was annihilated, they would secure the stolen bounty. Strategy first, Ben, always have a sound strategy."

"Mmmm," Ben said with a nod, watching the horsemen ride forward.

"The Flaxon officer showed himself to be a right broz," they heard Spanaje's voice say in the background. "He was overly ambitious, which suited us fine."

"Yes, headstrong, just like his father," Dogg muttered.

Ben's attention swung in heightened interest back and forth as Spanaje spoke in colorful prose and Dogg filled in the details.

"We discovered much later that the young Flaxon pup officer turned out to be the son of one of the most powerful figures in Weirawind. Someone called Magistrate Waldon," Spanaje said. "Some kind of Flaxon justice enforcer, I think, and elder brother to the current regent, Trabonus."

Ben looked saucer-eyed at Dogg.

"Yes," Dogg said. "And that young officer's arrogance aims to finish the job early; he wants to stand above the rest today."

"Does he know how Scarzen fight?" Ben asked, like somebody watching a chess game unfold.

"Theoretically; he thinks he could finish it in the Yorr Pass in time short enough to have him back by sunrise, and get a medal in the bargain. Had he listened even a little to his field sergeant, Rictor, he would have known such child soldier views invited certain suicide. Instead, he feels being the *dux* of his military class just this year for theoretical battle tactics affords him some dynamic advantage. Something else far more dangerous underpins his brashness. He wants to return to his new bride. A difference between them has his head back in Weirawind."

"So his mind's got a kink in it," said Ben.

Dogg sighed. "Something has. Honestly, why Evercycle Seven approved that aspect of the male raw sex drive still stifles me. The previous pattern-makers upgrade proved more than sufficient."

< 57 >

"Dad used to look at Mum like a kicked chook sometimes. I asked him about it once when I found him in the kitchen with Mum. Dad just coughed and made me wipe the dishes. Mum turned his head a lot too, I reckon," Ben said, looking a little flushed.

"Don't miss much, do you?"

Ben shook his head, folding his travel coat's collar against his neck with a shiver.

"Hearts wear no clothes and say what they think no matter what moral parameters have been established," said Dogg. "Hand on my shoulder, Ben. Now, listen to what Spanaje has to say."

"Every third pair of mounted soldiers carried a burning torch," Spanaje recounted. "The temperature dropped quickly with the setting sun and filled the pass with shadow. Gathering mists manifested as a fine rain fell. It made the place most unwelcome."

* * *

In two flickering silver streams, Dogg and Ben appeared on the pass trail.

"Whooooa, that felt weird," Ben said, his head spinning, looking about.

"Yes, it did. Our transfer signals nearly unbraided again from something beyond my control," Dogg said, internally concerned at what or who could have caused the danger.

Ben folded his arms against the deepening cold. "Wish I had a hat. My head's colder by the minute. I liked it better up top, Dogg. Down here gives me the creeps," Ben said. The sound of some gravel falling from up higher across the way made him lift his view. "Look at all the dead tree trunks and fallen stones on the pass floor."

Suddenly, they both heard the clomping of many horse hooves. Ben snapped his view left to see a column of musketeer-looking soldiers on horses approaching.

"Quick, over against the wall!" Dogg said. "When they pass, we'll follow them."

Ben looked harried as they both darted quickly to the side just in time to be passed by the Flaxon column. His mouth dropped open wide as horses

< 58 >

snorted, trotting by and carrying tall men with straight backs and wearing brown and red leather armor and triangle hats. The tinkling and rattling of bridles and knocking of military equipment aboard the mounts filled the air. Allowing the Flaxon several yards' grace, Ben and Dogg followed the horsemen at a safe distance as Spanaje's words filtered into Ben's mind again:

"Gagan horsemen's standard issue weapon at that time was the short trident and straight skinning blade," Spanaje said. "The former was oil blued and hard to see at night. The knife, though, reflected light. The trident business end was narrow with a shaft nearly half my arm long. Looked like something more for cooking than for battle. The center spike extruded to be longer than the two flanking it. A cold-forged small heavy bulb was formed at the head of the shaft for blunt trauma blows. The Gagan soldier's skinning knife had a three-sided blade from tip to one third for puncture wounding. Hurt if it hit you in the eye."

"How do you remember so much detail, sir?" Thorr asked.

"He tells a good story, Dogg. Not sure I need the color, but ..." said Ben, looking about at the cratered stone cliff formations, expecting something to jump from the shadows.

"Details are a Scarzen's duty, as is economy of words," Spanaje said to Thorr, the tone of his voice suggesting there was a lesson there. The skill of memory is vital, so everything is turned to advantage." Spanaje picked the story back up. "Both blades were sturdy and easily wielded. They should have stuck to them; those lead spitters they now use are far too unreliable and obscure their vision allowing counter ... when they miss."

"I have heard of such weapons. Dishonorable instruments of war—likely helps to make them feel taller," Beetaa said.

"Flaxon lance-jacks carried tall lances and a long knife, while the officers and sergeant of the company carried a saber and a black-powder pistol."

"There goes one," said Ben, watching one rider resting a long-shafted spearheaded axe into a saddle nook.

"Like all Flaxon forces," Spanaje said, "under their lightly studded leather gambeson, they wore a shaped metal chest-plate that saved them against some blade strokes. On their hands, leather gauntlets, and brown thin-

< 59 >

skinned boots to cover their feet. The Flaxon armor of those times did not travel quietly," Spanaje said with a chuckle. "We could hear them coming from their home city well before we saw them. The Flaxon, however, knew this; in fact, they often felt it to their advantage. They thought it suggested a formidable cavalry's approach. To most other adversaries, it might have been menacing, I suppose. For us, it just made it easier to time our attack. Flaxon fight well when morale is high and superior numbers are in their favor. On this mission, both seemed to be present in their command's mind."

"Not on this day, I think," Dogg said, padding along. "The Scarzen misunderstand. The Flaxon's truest strength has always been their religion, as shown by a rune emblem on the heavily stitched shoulder leather and the gorget guarding their soldiers' necks. Did you see it?" she asked Ben.

"Yes, I did."

"It represents their one god. The zeal for their religion also serves as their greatest weakness. Superstition is fostered by their churchmen. Their church often interferes in matters of war, attempting to govern politics and giving unwanted forecasting of good and ill omens for victory. Their church teaches that Flaxon are born in the image of their god. They are taught that their regent is the supreme example of guidance in the world. They think they are god's representative on Tora, which gives them the right to rule the land. What Spanaje couldn't know back then was that Magistrate Waldon the Elder—father of that lad leading up front—ordered Sergeant Augustus Rictor next to him to protect his son. Rictor's karma took an ill turn there."

"Why?"

"Rictor's orders say the column that we now follow must be the first to apprehend the enemy. Unwillingly, Rictor prompted the lad into action. It's Waldon the Younger's first command. He must prove himself. Waldon the Elder wanted to see first honors bestowed upon his family." Dogg's voice suddenly sounded eerily like some older man's. "'Give him his first victory in the field,' Waldon told Rictor. That Magistrate Waldon is one of the most single-minded vindictive males of his race. Both he and Rictor had amassed a sizable karmic debt through their combined efforts, one difficult to repay."

"Bugger," Ben said.

< 60 >

"On the day before the Scarzen infiltrated Weirawind, the magistrate's son received a prophecy from a priest. It was one of ill omen, to which he should have paid heed. Generally, most Flaxon are superstitious to idol worship of the god of Flaxor. But the young officer was dismissive of the priest's warning. Silly boy; this time the priest spoke true. Dismissively, young Waldon said he would see him for wine and bread on the morrow. 'Keep the prayers for those in true need, priest,' he said. With a forlorn expression, the priest bid him to carry a small embodiment of protection from the church and handed young Waldon a small sacred statue bearing the face of the present regent, Straxus."

"Did it help?" asked Ben.

Dogg cast him a doubting look. "The young Lieutenant Waldon tucked the thumb-sized unremarkable effigy in his saddle purse and left to do his duty. Flaxon culture has many stories about the Scarzen, Ben—most portray them as physical demons. Few ordinary Flaxon, though, have even seen a living Scarzen up close. Imagine on Earth if there was a second equally powerful but separate humanoid race."

"That would be just insane," said Ben.

"In more ways than one. Now, in your mind, make that race bigger than you and give them differences in culture, purpose, and belief. What do you get?"

"Enemies ... fear, too, I suppose, of being dominated."

"Yes. The first and most potent struggle would be over species dominance— the very thing Herrex used on Earth to pit the Homo sapiens against the Neanderthals. The latter race was chosen initially to keep Herrex in check by using their hard-to-manipulate free will as a kind of super combination lock."

"What happened?"

"Herrex had the more easily influenced and faster-learning humans do it for him. We found out too late to save the Neanderthals, but managed to have the Jenaoin recalibrate the strength of human free will before Herrex jumped free. On Tora, the parallel is similar. Uniss and I believe Herrex has tried and failed to do the same thing."

"Supporting the Flaxon," said Ben.

< 61 >

"Yes, but he had help—off-world help—and a lot of smoke screens covered the tracks. That's why the Triporian Alliance sent us back. But something new is happening. Somebody is trying to reset the Continuum clock to recalibrate existence reality; we are sure of it, and you are a key factor. Scarzen have a very strong free will, subtle body design, advanced language, and a sophisticated, structured culture. Their kinetic barrier abilities and capacity to jump three times their height combined with unmatchable battlefield prowess have kept them ahead of the Flaxon. But the Flaxon are catching up. Flaxon are much more like humans, Ben. They have complex writing, gunpowder, and agriculture. They build stone fortresses, have good intellect and reasoning, and are ruthless in their aim for dominance over all they survey. Flaxon and humans have the same string pattern design, and soul stream emotional values are similar."

"So Herrex is treating the Flaxon like humans and the Scarzen like the Neanderthals to do the same again?" asked Ben.

"We think so. In many Flaxon minds, Ben, Scarzen are the stuff of other-worldly dark influence and must be purged by whatever means available—something Herrex will play for all it's worth."

"But if the Flaxon win, they'd get the trilix, which keeps Herrex locked away—and he could get free."

"You're catching on very fast. We now know that Herrex did his best to manipulate circumstances in this original timeline to give the superstitious Flaxon a cause. In Flaxon church view, Scarzen are only worthy of being purified through death or slavery to the church, and the latter has never occurred. I tell you this because, when the bell tower alarm went off, these Flaxon were presented two quests: one, to cleanse the land of the demon; the other, to retrieve one of god's prized possessions and return it to the rightful custody of Flaxor."

"The Flaxon sound really screwed up, Dogg."

"When was the last time you studied human history? From the beginning, humans have aspired to stand with the gods, and all they achieved was to twist points of view to suit one's political or religious stance once Herrex loosened your grip, Ben." She saw Ben give her a bemused look. "Learn

< 62 >

fast, Apprentice."

Spanaje's voice volume again drew Ben's attention: "Early night came. The Gagan continued to follow us deeper into the pass as the cold tightened grip."

* * *

For the soldiers on horseback ahead of Ben and Dogg, things began to resemble more of a path into a crypt than a winding mountain trail. Dogg sensed the first creeping of fear and discomfort penetrate their bones. The tortuous curves of the pass became more difficult to navigate as the first sprinkling of rain fell upon the ground, forcing riders to keep closer ranks.

"Ben, time to jump ahead. Take hold."

Their forms became a soul stream, and they left the Flaxon behind. Materializing not far from where they had been, they found that Benataa had brought his rank to a halt after receiving an update on the Flaxon progress from a scout.

"The forward company is closing," the scout told him. "It is separated from the other two. Only fifty horsemen armed for cavalry assault."

Ben noticed now that the vests, cloaks, and trousers of these warriors were rugged and tri-colored, in contrast to the Scarzen he'd seen in Talon East. Only their shin-high boots looked similar.

"What's happening, do you think?" Ben asked, looking at Benataa talking with another familiar-looking Scarzen in front of all the rest. "Hey, is that Spanaje? Scrape a bone! He looks 'break ya in half' tough in those battle duds. Are we going to see him punch on too?"

"Yes, it is he, in his prime," Dogg said. "And Benataa has just decided that, soon, they will set an ambush. He wants to challenge their pursuers directly. If he knew of the inexperience of the commanding officer, Benataa would charge back and strike them down instead of what he is about to do."

"Cripes!" Ben said. "Is it going get rough?"

"Very serious, very soon, my nose says. Look, Benataa is getting ready to move again. Come on. Let's move up the track to the original vantage point; we'll be safe there."

< 63 >

The bulk of the squad pressed on hard, passing Ben and Dogg, who had to dive against the wall to keep clear. Then Ben placed his hand on Dogg's shoulder for the soul stream. This time, as the transition began, the stream glitched like a flawed film before they disappeared.

## CHAPTER 5

# KILLING SHADOWS

B en and Dogg's soul stream manifested not where she intended at all, but barely a few yards behind the trotting Scarzen. A growing wind pushed through the pass from the south, which made Ben's spinning head feel worse.

"This isn't right," said Dogg, raising her view ahead to a ledge some twenty feet aloft on the right. "We should be up there."

"No kidding! My head feels like wet socks." Ben's vision cleared. "Dogg! There they go—and this doesn't feel safe, especially with those horsemen chasing."

"Come on. We'll have to keep up the old-fashioned way." They both started running after the Scarzen. *What in Naught's name is going on?* she wondered, frustrated with the inconsistency of powers that for her should have been innate. "Uniss, can you hear me? My profiler powers are degrading." There was some garbled syntax, sounding vaguely like Uniss and then with a static crack … nothing. "Uniss! Farron! Anybody! Tula calling on C7 priority SAC channel 1." She broke from her contact attempt. "Come on, Ben, we're on our own again. Get those legs working or we'll lose them."

The two set off at a strong run after the Scarzen, who'd quickly begun to fade in the distance. Anxiety built for Ben as his arms and legs pumped like pistons, unable to keep from looking behind for any Flaxon horsemen.

After an exhausting run, they finally caught up, with chests heaving, only because Benataa had ordered the squad to a halt ahead. Night's gloom now blanketed everything as a quarter-moon pushed through thickening rain clouds. Dogg and Ben crept closer, keeping to the pass shoulder.

"Fortunately, Scarzen eyes are far more suited to the dark than the Flaxon," Dogg said.

Ben leaned against the ravine wall, trying to catch his breath. He felt cold pushing through his coat.

"Crikey, those guys can run!" Ben said. "Why have they stopped? The walls feel much closer than behind us." He looked back to where they had just run from. "Shouldn't we be higher up?"

"Couldn't, I tried," Dogg said. "Something hampered my abilities again, and it's getting worse it seems."

"Could it be Starlin?"

"Not likely. Besides, he doesn't have the pull or the clearance to be manipulating soul streams. Only an Evercycle can authorize such things. If he had a fix, we'd be in a mountain of trouble now. Look, the Scarzen are preparing to act here. I think this is it," she said, looking about.

"An ambush," said Ben.

"Scarzen style, kiddo." She looked up to a ledge about fifteen feet off the ground to the right. "Up there on the ledge. Right, hold on. Let me try this again."

"If we materialize in midair, I'm gonna make a hell of a dent in the deck from up there," Ben said as his stomach tightened.

The pair evaporated and rematerialized upon the single ledge that Dogg had indicated, quite near where Benataa talked with some of the squad.

"Careful, there's not much room up here, Ben," Dogg said, peering over the edge.

"Just happy we made it, Dogg! How do we get down if you can't zap us down?"

"Right now, you don't get down at all." She looked at the Scarzen close by. "I was right: Benataa intends to strike right here, fifty yards short of where he did it last time."

< 66 >

"Does that matter?" asked Ben.

"An inch of difference can matter, Ben. Farther along we were safe … You still don't remember, do you?"

Ben shook his head.

"Blasted memory wipe," said Dogg. "We watched it all unfold quite safely over there. The light rain that has begun will make the rocks slippery, so be careful. The Scarzen archive file records that Benataa Pinnaraa is an accomplished tactician and highly skilled in kinetic element manipulation."

"He's a badass?" said Ben.

"Crude but correct," said Dogg. "Keep your head down; you'll see a true master of elemental manipulation at work tonight. He has history with our colleague Farron Bach in the Brasheer Mountain, too."

"Benataa Pinnaraa: the otaa of Beetaa Pinnaraa who Spanaje was talking about?"

"Yes, that connection is important. If things hold true, you will meet Farron in due course. After Benataa left the mountain, he spent many years in the field as Jin Gung Myst commander. Until his death, he was never scarred."

Ben looked at Benataa carefully. In the moonlight, his braided hair, pulled back into a ponytail, offset Benataa's strong facial features. The two braids separated from behind his ears and had many commendation bands that glinted now and then. It was clear he was only of average height compared to the others, but with a muscular build, all the way to his heavy black boots. Benataa called for some of his column to gather as he and Spanaje spoke about his plan.

"He is a source of admiration for all in Scarza," Dogg said. "When he was given command of a Myst squad, Benataa quickly rose in recognition amongst the ranks of high command. A statue of him now stands in the public arena of Beetaa and Thorr's present in the Talon East residence of Keeper Malforce."

Hanging from Benataa's battle belt, Ben saw the Scarzen's ends of peace—the arcs that Beetaa had carried into training at Talon West.

"Dogg, he's carrying the same weapons I saw Beetaa wearing on his

< 67 >

own battle belt in the parallel present Spanaje was telling the story from."

"Correct. They were handed to Beetaa per Benataa's wishes for him to take Rite of Passage. Benataa is a patient and tenacious warrior, Ben, and his squad regards him very highly. Benataa calls his warriors 'Heaven's Dark Crusaders.' The squad calls him 'Ruhe,' meaning 'Nemesis of the Enemy.'

"I heard the old Spanaje say that title," said Ben.

"You did. Such a title can only be bestowed upon him by members of the squad. It is a title not officially sanctioned by Scarzen high command, but not openly frowned upon when the title is deserved."

Below them, Benataa's voice drew their attention.

"Where is the responsibility?" Benataa asked Spanaje.

"Torjiaa and Rayaxx still carry it, Ruhe." Spanaje gestured to the two large unit members sitting by a mesh carry-box bearing the Brasheer emblem of light and darkness.

Benataa glanced left. "Rixaa, get my scout," he ordered.

"Immediately, Ruhe." The attendant stepped away from the gathering and called back down the line: "Hellexaa!"

Ben watched a lean dapple-complexioned scout lope up from the back of the squad.

"I hope those legs of yours can match the task I have for you, Hellexaa," Benataa said in his smooth husky tone.

Hellexaa's orange eyes burned bright with determination as they stood there awaiting orders. "They will carry me like the wind, Ruhe."

"Then hear me clearly, Scout. I need you to break ahead. After exiting the mouth of the pass, head east to the settlement at Gantry. Stay out of sight. Should circumstance disadvantage you, enter Gantry. There is help there, but remember, spies also reside. So watch your back. Go to the Lotus Inn and ask for Madeline. Tell her I sent you. She will have a hiding place for you to go till the threat has passed. If you are seen, make the Flaxon think you are heading for the east mountain range. With Naught's luck, they will turn back to report the sighting and your direction, then you will be able to travel on unhindered round the eastern shoulder of the range. Head to the Tillinaa Bog Flats and on to Talon East. It's hard going for horse or wheel

< 68 >

through that path, and they would not expect a slower, more treacherous avenue taken."

"Yes, Ruhe."

"Once at the bunker, speak first to the gate master, Kalfax. Tell him I sent you. Get him to send his best sellenor to our position. The distance will be a stretch for the sellenor keeper to hold the mind-tether, but it should not break the keeper's tether. We will await the sellenor inside the mouth of the pass and set a signal. Clear?"

"Ho!" Hellexaa said.

"Then, speak to Commander Titarliaa at once. When you see him, tell him, 'We face a force of some superiority in number. We have the Tears.' If his old bones still have the stamina and he is in the mood to consult, there is a Flaxon force that is in need of serious chastisement and he should bring his biggest stick. He should arrive by way of the Mustard Fields. Tell him that he will need to ride hard to reach us by the fourth day's end. After that time, our options will be few. Tell him we are being flushed into a stoning pool and that's all the time we have."

Hellexaa paid respect and without a word stepped off at a strong pace. Benataa turned to see Spanaje standing close by.

"Should Ruhe's shield know what he is thinking?" Spanaje asked.

Benataa considered his second-in-command's question. "We must stop the pursuing horsemen here. They are not pressing us hard enough."

"It could be inexperience," said Spanaje.

Benataa shook his head. "They are herding us."

"So you think they have a noose to tighten?" Spanaje asked.

"A much larger force, I'd lay odds," Benataa said. "I think they want us bottled up just beyond the exit onto the Yorr Fields."

Benataa turned his head toward the southern exit and nodded.

"If we don't stop our pursuers here, many could perish without deserved combat honors," Benataa said, looking around at his warriors. "We have created about two full hours of advantage before our hand is forced. Set a full corridor crush. It will give us the best control over events," he said, walking farther ahead. "No time to waste—get to it!"

< 69 >

Spanaje gestured to the squad and they set to work.

"Spanaje," called Benataa.

"Yes, Ruhe?" Spanaje said, facing him.

"The first twenty must crumble at the head of the charge."

"We will make it so, Ruhe."

Ben heard old Spanaje's voice overlap and filter back into his thoughts.

"While the traps were being prepared, your otaa thought through his plan in detail. We Myst were no strangers to a tight fix, but something made him uneasy. He knew this pass well, and we were not too far from the southern exit. The ambush point was about seventy standard strides and eighteen wide. That's why it's called the Choke. It is the narrowest point along the pass. Several rockslides recently had littered the ground nearby with piles of debris everywhere. The sides of the pass walls are vertically sheer with shallow ledges and cavities here and there, making good places for concealment."

Ben looked on while the warriors of the squad set traps by drawing tightly strung, braided slaa wire at horse fetlock and knee height, and then at rider neck height.

"That thread they are using is stronger than steel from your earth, Ben," Dogg told him. "Strung very tight like that between two points, it has an incredible strength. Struck at velocity, the slaa thread cutting power will sever bone with the ease of a laser-scalpel."

Below, Benataa looked to the sky as a light soaking rain increased. The air had a penetrating dampness and worsening chill to it, with an occasional gust as windblown debris began to whistle and whip through the pass.

"The Flaxon horsemen are closing," said Benataa.

Ben saw Benataa call for two of his warriors. Those who approached wore a sort of poncho and hood. Benataa ordered them back in the direction of the pursuing horsemen. As they departed, their images seemed to blur and become hard to follow.

"They are going to cut any retreat of the advancing Flaxon," Dogg said. "Preventing any reinforcements. The lead column of Flaxon is in deeper than they know."

< 70 >

* * *

Running back to meet the threat, silent as living shadows, the two warriors chose a place where the pass road was hemmed in tight by jagged sheer cliff faces on either side. That part of the trail ran around the shoulder of a deep gully, big enough to swallow a whole company of drommal riders. There was no way to return or re-route it if a slide blocked the road here. There, cold falling rainwater already dribbled down the cliff crevices from above, making the road slick with mud and offering unsteady footing. One Scarzen warrior nodded to the other.

"We will create the separation here."

In the distance, they heard the snorts and clomping hooves of approaching horses. The warrior in charge gestured for them to begin. Maintaining their body blur barrier, catalyzed by an arcane force of will, both moved closer to the foot of the bank opposite the gully. There, they lay between some fallen debris and stones to become invisible to ordinary eyes, and waited for the Flaxon company to pass. Onset of dark would force the horsemen to see by torchlight from here, drawn on as the trail curved away out of sight between ever-steepening banks of jutting stone, poisonous razor grasses, and the waiting ambush of their Scarzen commander. Soon, they saw the first mounted soldiers.

The Flaxon came at a steady amble into the warriors' line of sight. As horses passed the Scarzen, some of the beasts became agitated and skittish, although nothing could be seen. Most soldiers just thought the wind responsible. Still, some soldiers grew nervous while shadows played tricks with their eyes in the flickering torchlight and their minds brought back stories told of the demon Scarzen and this place. Flaxon knew the Scarzen camouflage capability well.

Using the ability to change their exposed scale to match their surroundings completely, the warriors lay there, still as the submerged crocodiles of Ludd's northern rivers, waiting to seal the enemy's fate. When the plated tails of the last pair of horses disappeared around the bend, the two Scarzen peeled away from their hidden positions and stood.

The Scarzen in charge looked up the cliff face close to them. Six standard

< 71 >

arm spans above jutted a loose boulder of considerable size. It hung precariously from under a larger ledge of stone and earth. Both warriors stepped shoulder to shoulder and combined their minds and kinetic strengths while raising their arms. They focused on dislodging some smaller rock from under the larger boulder. Suddenly, with an earthy groan and rumble, the boulder and a great mass of rock and dirt slid downward. They darted away to safety as an almighty crash echoed back inside the pass. In the end, hundreds of tons of debris blocked the passage north. The two warriors nodded to each other with satisfaction. Avalanche echoes sped deep into the pass, alerting all of the danger. Quickly, the two Scarzen concealed themselves as two Flaxon soldiers returned. Trotting up to the wall of earth to investigate, they halted. Even in the dim moonlight, they could see that the way back was shut.

"It'll take days to dig around this," one rider said.

"All the lieutenant will say is he's happy to be on this side of it. I prey our regent's grace is with us in this quest. I for one have no interest in facing the demons alone. The faster we push them out the other side, the happier I'll be," the other said, holding up his torch for a better look.

The horses became skittish again, raising the soldiers' apprehension. Both felt that bristly sensation of prey about to be eaten.

"I've seen enough," one said, pulling his horse's head round sharply.

Both riders spurred their mounts into a canter to rejoin their company and make the report—unaware that two Scarzen warriors silently followed close behind. As rain increased to a consistent downpour, the scouts met the Flaxon company's commander to deliver the bad news. As predicted, Lieutenant Walden replied, "Then we are in the advantage and able to finish our task. Column, ride on!

\* \* \*

At a point where the trail bent gently left, the Flaxon commander ordered the company to stop. His sergeant looked at him, hoping they would move in quickly from this blind spot.

*Feels like they're breathin' down our necks already,* Rictor thought.

Perhaps ten good minutes passed as the mountain fell silent again.

< 72 >

"Sir, if I may," said Rictor. "This is an easy part of the track to be buried from rockslide. We should continue with caution."

The lieutenant shifted his weight back on the saddle and looked at the sergeant, then spoke in a condescending tone. "Have no fear. I have studied maps and notes of this area with great attention. I'll have you back for retirement with commendation to boot before the morrow."

Lieutenant Waldon turned away to view their path forward. Prior to the ground shaking from the rockslide behind them, Waldon had fully convinced himself that breaking ahead would help him achieve victory and stand above the rest. Now, though, the pit of his stomach felt uneasy, accompanied by a dryness of mouth.

"We have the advantage and must prove our worth, don't you agree, Sergeant?"

"Absolutely, sir," said Rictor, not believing in his commander for a minute.

That said, a crack of thunder broke overhead followed by a dump of rain. The lieutenant wiped the water spatter from his face and waved the advance forward. He nudged his mount, and the chestnut stallion plodded forward. Out in front, speaking with his back to Rictor and the company, Waldon mustered some confidence and made a last comment before falling silent: "We shall have these vile animals pressed into the trap by dawn, men. Be not concerned: the one god is with us!"

"They are all the same, fresh out of school, using their stones instead of their brains," Rictor muttered to himself. Then Rictor trotted his horse up alongside his commander and spoke quietly, but respectfully: "Sir, you have my full support, but I've dealt with these jungle snakes before, sir. Scarzen are a hell storm on a close-quarter battlefield. Their tactics are fluid and don't appear in any of the command battle manuals. I've had the displeasure on several occasions and—"

"Well, Sergeant, in this case, fresh eyes and talent may bring unlooked-for victories. They are in retreat. We are pressing them into capitulation. If they are as strong an enemy as your now long-passed but distinguished career experience suggests, why have they not halted and met us head on?"

"Careful what you wish for, sir."

< 73 >

The lieutenant gave Rictor a disapproving glance. "What is your point, Sergeant?"

"This reminds me of when I saw a pack of dogs chase a bear once into a boxed wood."

"And?"

"Well, sir, at first the dogs seemed to have the bear spooked. It ran at speed all the way inside of a clutch of elm trees. Looked trapped like a maggot on a hook."

"Get to it, Sergeant Rictor," the lieutenant said.

"Well, sir, the whole pack followed that bear right inside, ready to tear it into a rug. They found the bear looking down, facing a steep embankment. The dogs all flew straight at his back. You could say it looked like the bear put his head in the sand, sir."

"Quite a bloody mess thereafter, I expect?" said Waldon.

"Yes, sir, there was. The bear let the first wave hit and then hunkered down."

"Defeat was imminent," said Waldon.

"Yes, sir. The bear suddenly turned with a maelstrom of teeth and claws. Killed every dog in the pack in less time it takes to down a pint, and ate three of 'em before it left the mess behind." Rictor saw Waldon's shoulders fall ever so slightly. "Scarzen don't spook, sir! Fear isn't in their thinking, and in twenty years of service, I've never seen one surrender or retreat out of fear—and they are meaner than a wonga baja when you get 'em in a corner, and sir, we have 'em in a corner."

Waldon slowed his mount and looked back at Rictor, speaking with a calm and soft voice: "Sergeant, I know your time in the field is near its end. If there's any *bear* in this match—it's us," the lieutenant said sarcastically. "It will be as simple as pressing a scorpion under one's boot once you have it cornered."

Rictor felt insulted at his inexperienced commander's comment and offered no reply. He had fought Scarzen in several campaigns and carried the loss of two fingers on his left hand to show for it. The generous scar down his right jaw was another memento. Rictor placed a hand on his hip

< 74 >

pouch, carrying the effigy of the protective saint.

"God give us safe passage," Rictor mumbled to himself.

At the same time, the lieutenant's mind ran through all he had learned of Scarzen tactics. Rictor's words proved unnerving, but they had no way back. Matching Scarzen troops on any field was dangerous enough work. Now they were in this narrow corridor with an unknown number of the enemy. He'd convinced himself these Scarzen were ordinary field troops. In any case, the recovery of Regent Straxus's valuables meant more than a couple of companies of men and horses—and Waldon was bound to his duty. The manuals said that Scarzen always took deliberate action, much preferring to stand their ground. This was clearly not the case.

*What was Rictor on about?* Waldon wondered.

To the sergeant, though, his instincts screamed "death trap." Many larger mounted forces had suffered heavy losses fighting Scarzen who were on foot. They had the idea that greater numbers and control of ground guaranteed victory too. Often, they were proven to be horribly wrong. The only way to kill a Scarzen was hit-and-run or heavy artillery, and Waldon had the capacity for neither.

*Arrogant prick,* Rictor thought.

Several of the men had served with Rictor in combat before, and the sergeant could see that they had little respect for the new commander Waldon.

"We'll all earn our keep this night," Rictor muttered, a stabbing pain hitting his ass from being in the saddle for too long. He guessed the others felt the same.

Being on constant high alert for many hours, hearing the exchanges between commander and sergeant, and being cut from the other companies had begun to erode the men's morale. Sleep was some way off, and there had been no time for the warmth of a fire or hot food in any bellies since early morning. Worse still, they knew their new leader was immature to say the least and looked on Rictor for true leadership. Waldon was straight out of officer school—and showing it.

*Debts to higher-ups be damned,* thought Rictor, cursing the day he'd become indebted to Magistrate Waldon.

< 75 >

A blanket of wind blew through the column from behind, making each man feel a foreboding of a very real danger in the making.

< 76 >

Ben and Dogg sat in silence after hearing Spanaje's last comments, watching an alternate history unfold in front of them. Privately, Dogg was worried about the irregularities occurring with all her greater abilities. As soon as this leg of their investigation had passed, she resolved to find Uniss and take herself and Ben to the Triporian Alliance base ship *Cagney* for a full checkup.

"Not long now, Ben. The Flaxon are quite close," said Dogg.

"Uh huh," Ben replied, distracted and leaning a little farther forward to peer over the edge at Benataa, who was now speaking to some of his warriors.

"Kill zone set, Spanaje?"

"We are ready, Ruhe," replied Spanaje.

The dull smatterings of moonlight filtered occasionally through the rain clouds, making it possible for the Scarzen to work faster. Slaa thread traps crisscrossed the Choke.

*How much worse could this be than that gruesome interrogation I saw in Talon East? Least we are at a distance and safe up here,* Ben thought.

"We will see the glow of their torches round the bend before we see them. Flaxon eyes hate the dark. Get everyone in position!" Benataa ordered.

"I will welcome them to the consult," Spanaje said with enthusiasm.

Benataa grinned. "No, my friend, not this time. The sight of you

standing here, beckoning the Flaxon, would surely scare them into retreat."
He pointed to a place directly under Ben and Dogg's position. "Crush their
flank from there. Break the spine of their rank's center."

"I can do that," Spanaje said, signaling for the others to move into position.

A feeling of anticipation prickled the nape of Ben's neck upon seeing
the Scarzen rush to position.

"Give the Flaxon shepherd and his sheep reason to reconsider their
position," Benataa said.

Ben craned his neck over the edge again, his eyes wide. He saw Spanaje's
image blur and then blend into a nook. Looking back at Dogg, Ben swallowed
hard.

"Back up, Ben. The trigger is about to be pulled."

* * *

Moments later, only Benataa stood in full view, as the rain ceased and
silence descended in the pass. A yellow glow of Flaxon torches preceded the
company around into the straight of the Choke. Just then, steady rain fell
again, increasing to a downpour, and the wind began to howl, muffling the
ability to hear well. The Flaxon torches burned just bright enough to offer
a close view of other horsemen. Above, sheet lightning ripped through the
sky, and the momentary flash of light illuminated the pass ahead, revealing
a tall dark figure standing in the distance. The chill of impending battle
washed over all in a saddle as a low clap of thunder and its shock wave caused
many Flaxon to cringe.

"'Tis the demon Scarzen come to challenge," one lance-jack said, winding
the rein of his mount around one hand.

Horses began to balk and whinny, feeling danger from in front and
behind. One or two of Waldon's men made their own noises of uncontrollable
dread. Some gave furtive glances left and right, the tide of doubt rising.

At the front of the company, Lieutenant Waldon and Sergeant Rictor
strained their eyes to see more detail in the bad light. Behind him, the
lieutenant felt the spirit of his men waning. Now faced with his enemy, and
dread filling him fast, Waldon swallowed and straightened in his saddle, forced

< 78 >

to a decision to show his mettle. Rictor anticipated Waldon's decision—and his heart sank as he felt the jaws of a trap expand.

"Hold steady, men," Waldon cried.

"No, not here," said Rictor.

"This is our time," said Waldon, drawing his sword.

"Gonads," Rictor muttered.

"Weapons ready!" Waldon shouted.

Every man held his weapon aloft, tightening their grip on the reins.

"CHARGE!" Waldon roared, pointing his blade over his mount's head.

* * *

Ben and Dogg both heard the war cry break the silence like a starter's gun. In that instant, Dogg tapped into Benataa's mind so that she and Ben could experience everything through the Scarzen's senses. Suddenly, Ben felt his point of view sucked along another mental tunnel way to emerge at ground level in heightened night vision color that added a slight infrared outline to all living in the pass.

The Flaxon rank charged, and Benataa smelled their adrenaline. The coming force felt euphoric to him, further supercharged by a flash of lightning as it lit the battle zone. He spread his arms like a wilted tree and began to spin like a top. Using his kin, he drew around him the falling rain, loose stone, and ground debris and channeled it into a whirling vortex. Gathering momentum like a skillful dancer while increasing the whirlwind's velocity into a destructive force around him, suddenly, like a hammer thrower, Benataa stopped spinning with an outstretched arm. His movement snapped to a frozen posture, releasing the mass of debris in a torrent into the path of the charging horsemen. Short strides away from Benataa, his projected wall of twisting refuse struck the charging with lacerating effect. The opposing forces crashed together with a shattering sound of solid matter mixed wind and heavy rain. Stone and other natural debris tore at flesh and broken bones.

The explosive beginning pressed Ben physically away from the edge. He jerked back so hard that he hit his head on a jutting stone behind, causing him to shout with pain, slamming his eyes shut. He opened his eyes to see

< 79 >

the forward group of mounts below begin to shy away, looking for retreat. Disarray overcame the charging company, causing an untidy division of the column. Men struggled desperately to hold their mounts as momentum carried them all forward. Like a tsunami striking a determined ship, the strong Flaxon mounts dropped their heads and put their shoulders into it. The initial blast that stalled them washed past, and the rank poured forward, determined to run down the single defiant Scarzen. Adrenaline rose, pumping courage into their veins, and the horsemen mustered a roar.

Ben's jaw dropped when Benataa turned to take off with the Flaxon almost upon him. With the speed and agility of a predatory cat at full pace, Benataa avoided every trip wire crisscrossing the corridor in front of him with a dive and tumble to his feet. He dodged sharp left behind a large boulder in the center of the Choke and stopped. The charging Flaxon, however, galloped on through the death maze with no such agility.

The rank split. Waldon led the charge, dashing left of the boulder and looking right and down for his enemy. Rictor steered right, leading the charge of the right column and passing a crouching Benataa. Half a breath later, Waldon's throat hit the first wire at full gallop. The removal of his head was so clean and effortless that his horse never broke stride and thundered on, leaving Waldon's head to disappear into the night.

The sergeant, knowing of such devious Scarzen guerilla tactics, rode with his body low and close to his mount's neck, taking only a bad graze on the side of his head. Opposite, the left column followed the headless rider. Ben gasped in horror as the scene unfolded.

Benataa held position as galloping horses stormed past on either side. He watched the lead horses fall with a dramatic drop of the shoulder, plummeting headfirst to the ground. Riders were launched like rag dolls—except the leader on the right, who had jumped to the ground when his horse fell. A pileup of horses and men ensued. Wailing animals hurled screaming riders forward, causing all manner of injury.

Looking down, Ben thought the mayhem appeared to form a threshing pile of terrorized upturned animals and panicking men with missing limbs.

On the ground, at the climax of the confusion, Benataa used his kin

< 80 >

ability to drive the rear riders forward, compounding the carnage. Any horse or rider that had survived intact tried frantically to get to their feet. With few lit torches still burning and producing little light, it proved difficult to know who was where.

From Benataa's view, Ben saw two men killed outright when thrashing horses struck the disoriented soldiers in the face. He heard the wet sound of cracked skulls and then their last cries of pain as they fell.

The few last riders at the back of the columns, less affected by the traps, attempted to turn and bolt, but were eliminated by the two scouts who had pursued them. The note of a war horn rang out, and the walls all around came alive with Scarzen warriors falling upon the Flaxon from both sides with horrendous force. Ben saw blue and green kinetic barriers crisscross all directions, striking horses and men with destructive force. Scarzen ends of peace whirled in savage cutting arcs, beheading and dismembering men as swiftly as they could stand or attempt to remount a horse.

Ben's eyes grew big as saucers at seeing a random blue field of energy rise and strike the ledge he and Dogg sat upon. A spray of stone shards hit his face. He rolled sideways in pain, crying out with one hand to his face and his other to the ground.

"Ben!" called Dogg. "Are you all right? Move back!"

Confused and in pain, Ben moved in the other direction, and the ground fell way beneath him. He slipped violently forward over the ledge. As he went over, Dogg's jaws locked onto his collar.

"Ahh! Dogg! Don't let me go! Don't let me go!"

Dogg pulled with a barrier that failed. She snapped with her teeth and managed to catch his collar with a better grip. She pulled Ben back for all she was worth, but when she heard his collar rip, the pit of her stomach tightened with fear. Ben dropped away down the bumpy stone cliff with cries of pain. He landed flat on his back with a thud.

"BEN!" Dogg shouted. "ARE YOU ALL RIGHT?"

Another random energy field struck the ledge, forcing Dogg back. She looked over the edge again but couldn't see Ben. She attempted to phase down there, but her powers failed—again.

< 81 >

"Stay out of the way!" Dog yelled. "I'm coming down, Ben! Ben!"

\* \* \*

On the ground, Ben's view became his own. He saw a Scarzen pair working in acrobatic tandem—one using cruel blades while the other hurled barriers. Together, they pinned, slashed, and cut through the enemy as though they were rice-paper dolls. The sound of slicing blades and grisly death cries filled the air as rain continued to pour down. Some Flaxon fought back, but barely made two thrusts of a sword before their much taller and more agile adversaries separated them into several untidy pieces. In their last moments, some soldiers called for their mothers, while others called to their god for mercy.

Sheet lighting strafed the sky overhead. In the mud and continuous downpour, Sergeant Rictor stood his ground, fending off a Scarzen while protecting a fallen wounded soldier. Rictor fell after being blindsided by a barrier and dropped his weapon, but before the enemy could move to finish him, he managed to dive out of the way. Extracting himself from between the body of a dead horse and the severed torso of its fallen rider, Rictor struggled to his feet and reached for a weapon buried in the chest of a convulsing horse. With a backhanded jerk, he wrenched the blade free and lashed out aggressively at his advancing opponents. Rictor knew his end was near. He heard a war horn as Scarzen closed in from several sides.

"Come on, you slippery bastards, earn your dinner!" Rictor shouted, snarling.

Then he felt a heavy boot between his shoulder blades. It drove him forward with his arms spread, skewering him on a blade of an oncoming opponent. Another Scarzen removed his head with one skillful stroke.

Finally, the sounds of carnage and forceful war cries ended with a last man atop an unsteady horse being beheaded by a leaping Scarzen. Benataa raised one arm, fist clenched, and his battle cry signaled for the victory horn to be blown.

"HO!" they all roared in a shout of victory, and the downpour slowed to a misty sprinkle as the wind dropped.

< 82 >

For a moment, Ben heard Spanaje's voice phase in as his eyes darted about, looking for Dogg.

"We sheathed our weapons and stood at ease. Ruhe ordered us to search for any Flaxon still breathing. After a few scants, one of us spotted a soldier trapped under a dead horse, struggling to get free. He squealed like a trapped piglet as two of us approached."

Spanaje's voice faded while Ben looked on in horror as one Scarzen warrior raised his short spear with two hands. Its two-foot-long spearhead hovered directly over the soldier's face. Ben's stomach churned at what would come next.

"Wait!" Benataa ordered. "Bring him here."

Ben breathed a sigh of relief. Two of the larger Scarzen grabbed the dead animal by the legs and rolled it off the soldier, who screamed in terror and pain. One Scarzen grabbed the Flaxon's gambeson at the sternum and wrenched the soldier to his feet. He stood with one trouser leg almost torn completely off, exposing the hem of an undershirt. The Scarzen grabbed him by the scruff of his neck and shoved him toward Benataa. Hat missing and face knocked about, the Flaxon stood there, trembling. Ben decided he looked about nineteen years old, obviously terrified—a state he empathized with. By the smell of him, even this far away, the soldier had shit himself. Benataa drew a long broad-bladed dagger from a scabbard on his hip and used its point to lift the man's chin.

"Stand straight and look at me square," Benataa said in common tongue. "What is your name?"

The Flaxon's eyes darted in panic from one dark form to another, and his reply amounted to incomprehensible blubber. The dull light of the torches and veiled moonlight made it look to Ben as if warrior demons surrounded the man.

"WHAT … IS … YOUR … NAME … FLAXON?" Benataa shouted, grabbing the man by the hair with his free hand.

The soldier started to speak but froze again.

"Listen to me, you pitiful maggot," Benataa said. "I'll have your name or life be forfeit."

< 83 >

The young Flaxon tried to shrink away but stopped with a dull thud as his head hit a huge Scarzen torso. Benataa looked at him with disgust, then noticed a small pendant around the soldier's neck. He pulled it out by blade point and took hold of it, then read aloud the common tongue inscription:

"*From Mara to Silix. May the one god keep you safe.*" Benataa looked at the man. "So, you are Silix," said Benataa.

The man nodded. "Y-yes," the soldier said with a cracking voice, not far from tears.

"Stand proud with that reputation your warriors are supposed to have!" Benataa said. "Is this keepsake from your mate?"

Silix nodded, dropping his eyes back to the ground. Benataa thumbed the pendant, considering its meaning carefully. He looked at Silix for a moment and then put the pendant back inside the soldier's shirt collar.

"Is she worth living for?" Benataa asked with a hint of compassion.

Silix looked up into Benataa's potent orange eyes and gave a short nod, then burst into tears.

"Look at me, you pathetic whelp!" Benataa said.

Silix cringed.

"Do you know who we are?"

Getting paler by the scant, Silix remained mute, staring at Benataa's strong midriff.

"We are called the Myst. You now see what happens once we are found. Look around you, Silix of Flaxor; remember this well."

Benataa had Spanaje pick up and present him the head of one of the dying burning torches. Benataa snatched at the flame as if to grasp it and with a backhanded flick of the wrist, then tossed some flame aloft. It stopped some arms' lengths above. He raised the palm of his hand to it, which caused the flame to grow brighter, filling the battleground with light. The scene looked horrifying to Ben.

"Tell your friends what you saw," Benataa said. "Tell your commanders that all these Flaxon warriors here had no chance against the Myst ... their bodies now only fit for the scavengers. Tell them to stay away if they love life, if they love their families, lest we come to fall upon them as well."

< 84 >

Benataa waved his warriors back. The circle parted toward the southern exit. The young soldier stood dumbstruck for a moment.

"Run, or breathe your last, Silix of Flaxor. Run until your legs will carry you no more!" Benataa roared, shoving the soldier with a broad sweep of his hand.

Silix ran several steps and fell, sprawling to the ground. He scrambled to his feet, then ran like a lunatic escaping a demonic nightmare. In his confusion, he hit the side of the bank before he melted away into the darkness.

"Set a picket," Benataa ordered. "I have some thinking to do. We are not done yet."

* * *

Unable to use her powers, Dogg's descent didn't come without mishap. She'd had to track along the ledge some thirty feet away from where Ben fell. There, she jumped and landed on her stomach, winded from ten feet high as Silix ran helter-skelter past her before disappearing into the night. Painfully, she got to her feet and made her way back toward Ben's last position, avoiding the patrolling Scarzen, and found him under a ledge huddled like a frightened rabbit. She could see he had been knocked about from the fall, with grazes on his face and hands.

"Are you all right, Ben?" she asked.

"You said it would be safe this time. I can't do this, Dogg. I thought I could, but I can't. I want to go back."

He had the expression of a kid whose fantasy had just run out. She thought a moment.

"We've been sent back to do a job—a job you participated in during another parallel that went horribly wrong. There are billions of lives on either side of the Continuum that depend on our making things right. Most important, it's a way for you to save yourself."

"What do you mean?" Ben said.

"There are things I can't reveal, things that must be your choice. It is your free-will choices that altered the course of events last time and got us across the line. Your actions were instrumental in saving this existence from

< 85 >

erasure."

"You keep telling me I'm important, but I don't remember any of that, Dogg. How can I be responsible for a whole other existence I'm not even sure I took part in? The Triporian Alliance is just a name. Evercycle Seven wiped my memory: you said as much yourself when you found me on Earth … didn't you?" Ben looked doubtful at his own question. "I don't even know what I'm supposed to do or even look for!"

"I know you don't remember, but the much older you said if we ever got to this to tell you that billions of lives depend on what you will do here on this planet and beyond. You carry a great power to set the Superverse on its right axis again, Ben. Only if things can run their course here to see where the thread was first corrupted can we make things right."

"I don't know, Dogg. I've seen enough killing to turn me inside out if I see another."

"If we stop, the number of dead and erased will be unthinkable. Herrex will get free. The Superverse will be plunged into endless collapse, and those twisted enough to want this whole existence to be erased will succeed. You will never see Ann again, and you will not live long enough for you and your older self to soul merge to erase the negative karmic debt that will allow you to live on in lives to come."

"Don't see what I can do."

"Let me get you out of here … catch your breath. I need you to be strong and stick with me, Ben. I've lost Uniss; I can't do this by myself."

"I don't know, Dogg."

"Ben, please. We need you." She cast a quick eye to the Scarzen moving about in the background. "Here, let me fix some of those ugly wounds."

Even as she said it, Dogg hoped her abilities would work. A transparent blue stream of mist drifted from her nose to Ben's wounds. All the cuts and abrasions closed up, then the stream of healing energy stopped.

"It still hurts," Ben said.

"Yes, I am sorry. It's all I have.

"Okay," Ben said, still sounding doubtful. "I'll help."

"Good lad. Come with me."

< 86 >

The two left in the same direction that Silix had fled, leaving the Scarzen behind and disappearing into the darkness while hearing old Spanaje speak in the background.

* * *

"Thirty minutes after leaving the site of the ambush, Benataa moved us closer to the south exit of the pass. Muddy ground splashed and squelched under the pace of pounding feet as water from the cliff shoulders glistened here and there in dappled moonlight. Reminded me of a dream I had back then. Ruhe stopped us about fifty spans inside the mouth of the pass. He and I then advanced to the mouth, which opened out onto the slopes of the Yorr Beech Forest and the fields beyond. We took up position beside some boulders to see down the slopes. The forest there is medium-density bleechenwood. A lot of thick bracken undergrowth, not the sort of ground lending itself well to organized mass assault for our enemy. From our elevated position in the moonlight, we could see across the canopy into the distance of the Yorr Fields. A considerable way across, campfires burned in both east and west positions."

"So they did intend a stoning pool. Otaa was correct," said Beetaa.

"Looked that way," said Spanaje. "The number of campfires suggested a considerable number of troops. Ruhe began to think the worst of Scout Hellexaa's chances of evasion. I looked at Ruhe and said, 'They will put up a worthy consult.'

"Ruhe coughed a laugh and said, 'Or they would have us think they will. Or there must have been a division in the area by chance. The gods are playing with us, I think.' He thought that a lot. I thought the odds just got better all the time."

"You looked forward to the engagement?" asked Thorr.

"Yes, of course. Then Ruhe slung me a casual glance. 'Ever the optimist, hmm?' he said.

"'Why do Scarzen exist if not to lock horns with a significant adversary?' I said to Ruhe. Flaxon methods are effective enough in numbers, so this could work out well and I had yet to reach my third century in squashing

< 87 >

the Flaxon heads.

"Benataa said nothing, just stared out from the side of the rock. 'We must play a waiting game,' he said.

"'Then why don't we use the dead of night to move from this position?' I said."

"I've heard Flaxon are weakest at night—sounds a good strategy to me," said Thorr.

"But doing so could hamper their object of returning the prize to Talon East," said Beetaa.

"Ruhe considered the ancestors were supporting us, allowing our initial victory and the cover of night," said Spanaje. "We could make the cliffs to the south before the sunrise and enter hidden pass or fight them there where their horse and infantry squares could not hold form or momentum.

"'No,' your otaa said. 'They will have small ambush groups with warning trumpets to call as soon as we are spotted. Once our position and numbers are known, they could just close to within arrow range and pick us off from a distance.' Ruhe knew we could not afford to risk our responsibility with continuous skirmishes."

"He would stick to his objective," said Beetaa.

"Losing the Tears was not something Ruhe would be happy reporting to Keeper Malforce or the Mistress Farron. Besides, they didn't know for sure we had it then. If they caught us with it … then it would be an open invitation to be crushed completely, which could have led to all-out war in Ludd."

"What's wrong with that?" Thorr said. "Better we wipe them from the face of Ludd. Many would thank us with blessings."

"I agree," said Spanaje. "But the problem with that, pup, is if you step on one ant, many more will come to replace it in ever-increasing numbers and ferocity. Such action would drag all the other regions of Ludd into hostilities due to obligation and the need to protect their borders."

"Undesirable bedfellows would come of it, not in our advantage," said Beetaa. "That would out the entire balance in Ludd."

"Good, you have been paying attention," said Spanaje. "Ruhe said he couldn't let that happen on his watch. Just when we were getting down to

< 88 >

some serious consult potential, your otaa got all philosophical on me, but he was right, as always. He said, 'Old friend, you'll all get your chance to remove some Flaxon arms and legs before too many days pass. But, as *my* otaa would say when engaged in a serious game of carrack: "The nature of achieving victory is about understanding the reality of the moment, then clear tactics and sound strategy follow naturally."'"

"I'm going to write that down," said Thorr.

"Ruhe said we would sever our enemy's core strength by destroying their logistics. Crushing their morale to fight would destroy their will to win. A short silence ensued while Ruhe made his final decisions. Then he gave me the orders: 'Set up a tight kill zone in the forest before us, a seventy-five standard-stride circle. Each pair stays concealed till the enemy is well inside.'

"His feeling was that they would come at daybreak, only a short time away. He wanted a one-way door. 'It will be done,' I said. He insisted the enemy be right inside the tree line, so those outside would hear, yet not know their fate. The undergrowth is thick and difficult for horse, which suggested they'd likely come on foot. Ruhe ordered that three remain behind inside the pass to guard the responsibility. The rest made their way forward to prepare to meet the enemy."

* * *

After Ben and Dogg left the pass behind, they went out into the Yorr Beech Forest on the slopes leading downward. Dogg now realized it was becoming continually harder to use her intuition. Spanaje's voice faded again. She felt a shift on the present thread.

*That's not good. Feel like this present is locking us in permanent. Have to find out what's going on,* she thought, leading Ben toward some rather sizable stendle trees.

"There is not a lot of time," she said. "I don't want you bottled up in case things turn nasty."

"Again? Are they going to start kicking each other's shins again?" Ben croaked.

"Yes, so do as I say. Hope you brought your tree-climbing legs. Right,

< 89 >

up you go."

"Up there? What about you?" Ben asked, reaching for a low branch.

"Don't concern yourself with me. You get to a comfortable position high up there. Don't move till I come back for you, understand?"

Ben nodded.

"One last thing," Dogg said. "Did Uniss tell you about all the capabilities of your universal translator?"

"Just that I'd be able to understand the language of just about everyone with it stuck there behind my ear."

Dogg shook her head. "Uniss does forget things at times. Well, the translator also works to turn your words into the local dialect—and, more importantly, it also functions as a communicator. It takes some practice, but if you think a message to me—or Uniss—we'll get it through our own device. Until you get the hang of it, just touch the translator and then say your message verbally while thinking about it."

"Oh. Yeah, that would have been nice to know about, eh?"

Dogg nodded. "When I return for you here, you must be able to tell me everything you saw. Now up you go."

Ben shinnied up the tree to a lofty fork. From there, he could see a considerable distance all around in most directions. He sat there, watching Dogg trot off into the undergrowth before disappearing. Silence set in, and he felt very alone.

\* \* \*

In the same present far to the south, after leaving the squad, Scout Hellexaa had moved through and out of the Yorr Pass, covering ground at a strong pace. Beyond the forest, he'd evaded a couple of advanced Flaxon patrols in places unexpected, heading east onto the rolling hills. The night and vegetation rising from the tall grasses allowed him to remain invisible to any eyes scanning the area. His present position lay just outside the borders of Sumra and was regarded as a neutral zone.

*Flaxon troops never came this far without some deliberate need*, he thought. Hellexaa sped along for all he was worth toward Gantry settlement. As

< 90 >

he crossed the landscape, the wind picked up and he felt a cold bite in the air, carrying pockets of misty rain. He could see the moon trying to push through from behind the clouds, spurring him to regularly check over his shoulder for sign of horsemen. Instinctively, he knew the way to Gantry regardless of the dark.

Just as the sun rose and the new day's light splashed the peaks of the Lyran Mountains, Hellexaa doubled back to take care of the mounted Flaxon scout he'd realized had picked up his trail. Near a lonely place called Craggy Hollow, amongst some large boulders, razor grass, and scrub, Hellexaa attacked his pursuer, leaping from the shoulder of a boulder and kicking the Flaxon off his horse. The two had a vicious but short exchange, resulting in the Flaxon scout being gutted from neck to pelvis. Seeing no other enemy, Hellexaa continued on unhindered to Talon East.

* * *

What Hellexaa didn't know was that a second scout in league with the first had also been tracking them. From behind some large stones farther back, the second scout watched his partner and the Scarzen finish their grim match. Not being a man possessing acts of valor as a strength, he remained hidden until the skirmish's end. Even when his partner screamed for help, he failed to stand. He watched his friend fall under the final vicious strokes of the demon, who leaped through the air and cut his comrade down the center. Watching the Scarzen head off to the south, he retreated with all speed to report to the Flaxon east camp commander some distance back.

< 91 >

CHAPTER 7
# MUTUAL RESPECT

At the same time, Benataa's squad was pursued through Yorr Pass, and another sizable Flaxon force camping near the shoulder of Trilix Di was ordered into the Yorr Fields. Colonel Ferdinand Hitex, commander in charge, force-marched his brigade to the southern exit of Yorr Fields and set up a net via two main camps. The east camp blocked the way to Gantry; the other to the west blocked the way to the Mustard Fields and the southern mountains.

On the edge of the Yorr Forest an hour after sunup, two experienced, mixed companies of standard Flaxon field troops were dispatched on foot. In standard field dress, they marched into the forest surrounding the pass entrance. Wearing open-faced helms with a gorget to protect their necks, their torsos and waists had leather-lined mail hauberks with external heavy leather ribbing around the midriff. Under that, they wore padded long-sleeved leather-and-linen shirts. They also wore long goatskin trousers and heavy hide boots with built-in greaves to protect the shins. The high brow of their helms was stamped with the Flaxon field unit crest, displayed as a hammer striking an anvil. With the colder months now upon them, they each wore a red weighted cape to cover the shoulders and back.

The approach to the forest in front lay choked with a thick morning fog, obscuring any details beyond the forest tree line. Watching from chosen high ground, Colonel Hitex sat on his white stallion. From there, he saw 250 Flaxon soldiers stalk warily into the forest through dense, long bead grass up to their breast line. The bulk of the troops carried the short trident in one hand and an oval forearm buckler in the other. A heavy long knife sat mounted on their right hip, and several units carried the standard black-powder lead shooter used by the Flaxon as a medium-distance charge breaker.

Privately, Hitex thought the field conditions poor for this engagement and hated running errands for his regent while a chaperone looked on. A member of the court representing Regent Straxus shadowed Hitex, observing all actions to recover the regent's property. There had been no sign from the pursuing light horsemen who had been ordered to flush the enemy from the pass.

*Where are they? Should have been some activity by now,* Hitex wondered. *A forest melee in unfamiliar ground I didn't want.*

His nose for a poor outcome was active, which made him feel very uneasy.

\* \* \*

Inside the forest, no breeze filtered through the trees, making birdcalls clear for some distance, and the previous night's rain clouds had almost gone. In the undergrowth of the forest, surfaces remained sodden and slippery. A fine shower fell sporadically now, making the smell of the grass stronger with the rising sun's influence.

Ahead, Benataa and Spanaje, like the other Scarzen, concealed themselves near the entrance to the pass, close to a cluster of older trees. All Benataa's warriors lay still as stones, completely hidden from the eyes of the closing enemy, and with their coming, all bird life and other animal sounds stopped. An unnatural heavy fog eerily rolled around the Scarzen kill zone in billowing clouds, showing no sign of lifting.

From their hidden vantage points, Benataa and Spanaje could hear the enemy's advance.

*"They approach, Ruhe!"* Spanaje said to Benataa in mind-meld.

*"And a dear price they will pay,"* Benataa replied.

< 93 >

\* \* \*

From his position in the tree overlooking the kill zone, Ben nervously watched events unfold. Earlier, he had seen some Scarzen arrive and dissolve into the setting below, totally camouflaged. He remembered how Dogg said that, unlike most other races on Tora, Scarzen could communicate without voices over many strides, using a mind-link or -meld. Via that meld, each pair in the squad could act silently with full combat synchronicity. One remained concealed, using kinetics, while the other acted as the duelist and forward target for the enemy to focus on. The members of this squad, Dogg had told him, had a motto: "I'll hold 'em, you fold 'em." A feeling of the calm before a storm blanketed Ben once again. Then, in the chill of the fog, it began.

At first, from different directions, men cried, warning sightings of the enemy, then screams of terror followed, then garbled noises, then silence. Grisly sounds of Flaxon being cut into pieces dressed every engagement. Sometimes, in a small break of fog, sparks from the end of a black-powder muzzle caught Ben's eye. Then, it seemed as fast as the flash would erupt, it would be extinguished with the howling war cry and blurred movement of a Scarzen warrior bringing their blade to bear, followed by a dull thud. As minutes passed, a gathering momentum of the skirmish struck Ben's ears. The sound of men being run through could be heard all about. For some Flaxon, the invisible exchanges were close enough to be spattered by the blood of a comrade. The noises and imagined visions of what was happening on the ground made Ben cringe. Flaxon morale quickly began to falter. Many soldiers separated from their units, losing one another in the fog.

Often, Ben had to be quick to see what was happening. Now and then, he caught a glimpse of action as a Scarzen nearby would appear and pick off troops who passed by, one by one. The forest quickly took on the scent of death, just as Ben had smelled in the pass. He wondered more and more where Dogg was. Below, he saw Flaxon troops treading cautiously over the ground strewn with thorn grass. He saw one Flaxon slip and cut himself to the bone as he snatched a handful of the tussock to halt his fall.

< 94 >

\* \* \*

On the west side of the kill zone, Scarzen eyes watched the second group of Flaxon cut through the center of the woods and separate from the others in the fog. One man's boot settled right beside the face of one camouflaged Scarzen. A moment later, with a unit member looking in the other direction, he disappeared within arm's reach, without a sound.

For many soldiers, like some ghoulish nightmare, a towering Scarzen would appear out of the fog right in front of them. The soldier would see only the thinnest flash of a blade, and then his head, arm, or lower leg would fall to ground. As quickly as they appeared, the Scarzen would evaporate back into the fog. When others approached the screams in number to assist, one of the Scarzen pair lying in wait would rise up and hurl a kin barrier. Taking momentary control of a soldier's gripped trident, the Scarzen would drive the weapon into the closest Flaxon ally. The other Scarzen then darted in and out of the space, striking hard and fast on the run. Feet were pulled out from under running soldiers, or ankles knocked about, sending them sprawling before their head or limbs were skillfully lopped off. Other soldiers were pushed into their comrades or a solid object before being leapt upon by a slashing scaled nightmare. Using these guerrilla tactics to great effect, the much smaller Scarzen force quickly and surgically decimated their rival.

\* \* \*

Heard from the fields beyond the forest, sounds of slaughter, demons, and dark predators filled the forest of Yorr. No one outside of the forest could tell who was doing what to whom. Although most of the high-pitched screams of pain were clearly Flaxon, every now and then a stranger, stronger shriek emanated from the forest. It was known that Scarzen had a war cry that resembled the wail of a beast not of this world. From Commander Hitex's observation point on the slope, his high-spirited horse shuffled its front hooves and twitched its ears with the sound of enemy war cries.

"Easy, Victor," Hitex said, patting his tall thoroughbred's neck.

Sitting next to his commander on a shorter well-groomed chestnut mare, a concerned young lieutenant frowned at the unnatural sounds emitting

< 95 >

from the forest.

"Sir, shall we send in more troops?" the lieutenant asked.

The stocky-built Commander Hitex straightened his back and leaned forward in his saddle. Maintaining a gaze toward the forest, he brushed a bit of loose grass seed off his sleeve and then glanced down and across at his subordinate.

"No, I think not. There has been enough fodder thrown into the fray for one day. We are getting to know our enemy's strength, and they appear to be very strong. Wouldn't you say so, Lieutenant?" Hitex said.

The young officer sat flush-faced and stiff on his horse. He advanced no reply, instead adjusting the nose plate of his helm to distract himself from the glare of his commander.

\* \* \*

The bushwhacking strategy of the Scarzen continued to punish the remaining Flaxon soldiers from every angle. No sooner would shots ring out than another chilling scream would follow. Bodies were found with gunstocks or barrels cleaved in two beside their users.

For Ben, the final straw happened near the base of his tree. Surrounded by unyielding clouds of fog, and getting more anxious as the minutes passed, he listened to the screams of executed soldiers, ferocious Scarzen war cries, and slashing blades. He now felt worse than in the pass, being trapped up in this tree. Where was Dogg to get him the hell out of there?

He began to scramble down, but then, directly below him on the ground, he watched a frightening exchange between a lost weaponless Flaxon soldier and a Scarzen warrior. The Scarzen appeared, walking out of the fog, and stood very close to the trunk of Ben's tree. The cold morning air made the Scarzen's breath visible as they waited to be spurred into action. From behind, the lone Flaxon soldier wearily crept out of the fog from the other side of the tree.

"Oh crap," Ben muttered to himself, gripping the tree branch tighter.

At first, the soldier advanced completely unaware of his enemy, who stood as still as cold stone on the other side of the large tree. It made Ben

< 96 >

shiver to think what would happen next. Looking cautiously from side to side, the soldier suddenly froze when he realized that only six paces away stood an eight-foot Scarzen facing the other direction. Ben knew that for the much larger Scarzen, the distance meant barely a step and an arm's reach away. The Scarzen just stood there, holding a gruesome-looking blade that had a vicious hooked end, but giving no indication that they knew an enemy stood so close by. As the Scarzen's weapon arm shifted his blade to one side, Ben saw blood from a previous victim drip from its tip. Ben looked back to the soldier, who now stood at the side of the tree trunk looking for some surprise opportunity.

Without warning, a bird darted out of the fog and past the Scarzen's eye line, breaking the creepy silence. The Scarzen's head snapped a few degrees left. With a horizontal stroke of his blade that had Ben doing a double-take to realize the speed of it, the bird dropped in two pieces at the Scarzen's feet. With his enemy distracted for that moment, the soldier bent down carefully and picked up a solid chunk of timber near his foot. Then, apparently thinking this to be his only chance, the soldier used the distraction to close the gap and swung with every ounce of strength he possessed.

The Scarzen made a half turn before the timber struck them on the elbow of the weapon arm. The Scarzen groaned with the pain of the impact, and the blade jack-knifed out of their grip, flying back toward the soldier before falling point first in the ground at his feet. The soldier dived toward the blade. With some effort—and bolstered confidence—he picked up the heavy blade and attempted to look threatening while brandishing it about. Ben thought he heard the Scarzen laugh. From the Scarzen's point of view, the expression on his enemy's muddy face showed a teeth-gritted, wide-eyed fool in a desperate situation. Facing their aggressor squarely, the Scarzen waited, seemingly quite relaxed, for the Flaxon to act. When nothing happened, they spoke to the would-be assailant in common tongue: "Die with honor, warrior of Flaxor," said the Scarzen, spreading their feet and arms, inviting the soldier to do his worst.

In an ignorant fit of aggression, the Flaxon managed to raise the big blade overhead as though to strike at his opponent, but the backward momentum

< 97 >

saw the blade slip from his grip. It flew lazily through the air and, with a *thunk,* lodged point first in the tree trunk directly below Ben, who felt the blade embed. He saw it continue to wobble several times.

Horrified, the Flaxon snapped his head around to see where the blade had gone. The moment his eyes lost view of his enemy—*SMASH!* He felt a strike from the Scarzen's fist that hit him so hard, his now stoved-in helm left his head and went skittering across the ground. The young soldier quickly followed the same direction, striking the ground with a dead thud and groan. The Scarzen stepped over the grounded soldier casually, seeming to ignore any possibility of retaliation, and grabbed the handle of their blade. Drawing the weapon from the tree, they turned toward the soldier, who was not trying to get up. With one graceful S-shaped stroke, the Scarzen sliced the soldier into four odd pieces. Blood and limbs fell about. Their adversary vanquished, the Scarzen walked away and disappeared into the fog.

Ben sat frozen, horrified at what he had just seen. Then a stray musket ball struck the trunk of the tree beside his head, spraying bark chips in his face. *That does it!* The shock of it all drove him to clamber down the tree in a panic as fast as possible. He jumped from a low branch and hit the ground awkwardly, rolled, and cracked his head on a stone not far from the untidy array of the dead soldier's bits. He felt dizzy, scrambling to his feet before staggering off in an aimless direction.

*Anywhere is better than this!* his mind screamed.

As his head became clearer, he ran harder, away. He continued until he found himself beyond the forest line, out in the open, and kept going, leaving the small war behind.

\* \* \*

Near the pass entrance, consultation on the west flank had not let up for Benataa and Spanaje. The fog lay thinner there and appeared to be fading fast. Benataa wondered if one his warriors perpetuating the fog had been wounded or killed. Working with Spanaje, Benataa played the part of kin shield while Spanaje, as always, acted as duelist and used his weapon of choice, called a reaper. Held vertical, its tall shaft stood to his elbow, with

< 98 >

a mace-shaped pommel, and its curved broad blade passed the tip of his topknot. With a twist of the shaft, the reaper could also be separated in two pieces to become a combination short scythe and mace.

Advancing directly toward them came a wall of twenty men, picking their way through the trees. Using a kinetic skill called "gripping field," Benataa reached for and wrenched a standing forty-foot dead stendle tree from its position. He threw it down across the advancing men with a huge crash and spray of branches and splinters. Soldiers unable to evade it were killed instantly, while many others became hopelessly pinned underneath. A few dove clear, only lacerated badly by falling branches.

Spanaje charged in to finish those pinned by running parallel with the fallen tree and using broad strokes like a woodsman trimming unnecessary branches. He swung at heads and limbs of the Flaxon—to the wailed pleas of, "Oh, please! Ahhh, god, no, please!" All were quickly dispatched. His last follow-through just finished, he looked to the other side of the tree to see many more soldiers forging ahead. Some had fearful faces, others vengeful sneers. Spanaje smiled.

"Yes! This is a sentinel's calling," he bellowed.

For Spanaje, it was the euphoric spark of life he lived for.

"Come, ugly pups—come one, come all! Let Spanaje lift your spirits!" he roared in common tongue. "The more the merrier!"

Benataa took Spanaje's flank, hurling Flaxon into Flaxon using grip barriers, thus making space for Spanaje to do his worst. In the clash, Flaxon began to retreat as soldiers in front fell and Spanaje stepped over crumpled messes. Only a dozen of the wave remained standing by the time the two Scarzen had finished. Spanaje bellowed a war cry, and like a changing wind, the last Flaxon lost all taste for further advance, turning in terror and fleeing.

With that wave repelled, Benataa looked about, considering they had made some headway, and then his expression turned grim. He suddenly realized their advantage was turning sour. The fog providing cover for them was retreating, and the sun had begun to assert itself, warming the air. He knew instantly the Scarzen producing the fog had lost the moisture elements in the air to keep it going. From Benataa's left, Spanaje walked across the

< 99 >

ground littered with dead and dismembered men, his blade still raised in the standard attack position.

"The broznicks have tarnished my blade, throwing their bodies at it!" Spanaje said, passing one soldier squirming on the ground facedown.

As Spanaje passed him, without looking, he upended his blade and punched it through the man's shoulder blades, then retrieved it with an effortless jerk and walked on.

"They'll need to up the ante if they are going to make this consult interesting," he said.

"Sound the gathering horn," said Benataa. "We are not done yet."

From his belt, Spanaje pulled a curved drommal horn, inlaid with gold and jasper, and blew a long, strong note. The deep-pitched sound filled the air, penetrating beyond the forest line into the field, all the way to the ears of the Flaxon officers watching from the slopes opposite.

\* \* \*

"Reader, this is Dogg. Can you hear me? Have you seen Ben? I've just come from the Flaxon command station watching from a rise beyond the tree line. When I returned to the tree I had left Ben in, he had scampered to parts unknown. My senses are dulled and have sporadic reach at best now, and I can't detect his soul stream. I managed to send Uniss a message, and I think it got through. None of this will hit his funny bone at all. No reply yet. I even tried an off-world jump a minute ago and failed. I think we are stuck in this thread: I'm sure I can hear Herrex laughing away on the wind.

"The Flaxon commander, Hitex, has just learned that his forest force sustained 90 percent casualties from the assault. The remainder fled for their lives. It all happened in less time than it takes to have a short nap. On the other timeline, I left Ben there and he reported back faithfully. He was younger in that timeline, though, and doesn't remember that now. I warned them that Ben's mirror present might not cope as the original Commander Bloch did. Even the Alushic archive warned of the danger. Damn. I hope he's all right. Now he's a random part of the circumstance—and that's bad, Reader. Now we are really winging it. Uniss will crack an asteroid over this. If

< 100 >

either Ben or Uniss don't turn up soon, my only avenue is to go find Farron. If you see Ben, Reader, tell him I'm looking for him and then come tell me!"

* * *

In the forest, Benataa examined some of his warriors. Only two dead of seventy so far.

*Each one a bitter loss,* he thought.

Looking in the short distance, he saw that one of his warriors lay there untidily beside a huge fallen tree. He had a broken Flaxon saber through his neck, and two dead Flaxon slumped across his chest, bloodied and missing an extremity or two.

"Luzaak is lying in a hollow of leaves and mossy rock over there, Ruhe," said Spanaje. "He died honorably."

Amidst a pile of twelve or more dead Flaxon infantry, Benataa saw the body of one of his best scouts. The sight disturbed Benataa; he hated losing good warriors.

"May Naught recognize their valor," Benataa said.

Warriors returned from all directions upon hearing the horn. All had released their blur ability to be clearly visible so their will reservoir could recharge. Some had wounds and lacerations; others stood unmarked but covered in the enemy's blood.

"We lost control of the fog when we were attacked on two sides, Ruhe. Takaa is badly wounded," said one of the four warriors responsible for the illusion.

Looking at his wounded troops, Benataa said, "Okay, use it!"

With that, five Scarzen each produced a metal flask from a pouch on their belt. Removing the lid, the musky smell of liquidized trilix stimulated their nasal senses, and a faint whisper could be heard on a passing soft breeze. Taking a cloth wad from the same pouch, they applied the milky liquid to it and then to their wounds. The healing began instantly, closing off lacerations and wounds with visible speed. All wounds disappeared, and their bodies returned to a supreme fighting condition once more. This time, though, some felt a strange momentary wave of fatigue pass over them and

< 101 >

then evaporate.

"What now, Ruhe?" Spanaje asked.

"Time to show broznick over there who has the high ground." Benataa gave a wink. "Time for something sunny, I think."

Spanaje raised an eyebrow. "Last time you did that, it decimated the land for weeks afterward and the Celeron lost a lot of good crops."

"True, but the northern tribes didn't return for another invasion attempt, did they? Something tells me the Flaxon commander will bring much more resistance now, knowing we must cross Yorr Fields. What I have in mind should hold their attention quite well and keep their commander on the back foot," Benataa said, looking skyward. "The environment is right for it." Benataa scanned the forest background, then nodded. "Right, this is how it will go. Spanaje and you four, you're with me. Bring a match," he said, pointing to his choice of warriors. "You guard my flank. Conserve your kin … you know the drill."

Benataa took a stick and sketched a rough map on the ground to lay out his plan.

"Two concealed pickets here and here, inside the pass entrance. Ten of you fifty spans inside with the responsibility, in case they break through from behind and attack our rear. The rest of you spread out and cover a standard fifty-stride circle. Consult with only those in maximum effect range. Xenax and Helldaa, you light a signal for the sellenor inside the pass after the next action has commenced. Hellexaa will be at Talon East very soon with Naught's blessing. Then sellenor will come to take the responsibility at all speed. Green is the signal color for this turn of the moon."

"The enemy will know their position, Ruhe," one said.

"So will the sellenor, and we will keep the Flaxon occupied on this side," Benataa said. "If the tactic fails, you all know what to do."

"Yes, Ruhe!" they all replied.

"Now, go! And shake our adversary till their ancestors cry for them."

< 102 >

## CHAPTER 8

# SWINGING ADVANTAGE

Benataa stood and headed down the slope for the edge of the forest, closely followed by his chosen group. They stopped where the long bead grass of the fields met the timberline of the forest. After gazing at the string of Flaxon officers astride their mounts up the slope in the distance, Benataa turned to his warriors.

"Once I get it rolling, keep an eye out for enemy projectiles and stay behind me."

"Yes, Ruhe," they all replied.

"Let's make this a day when the Flaxon came to unjustly consult with the Myst ..." Benataa turned a hard look toward the Flaxon commander he knew was focused on him and added with grit, "... and paid dearly for it."

\* \* \*

Some distance away from the forest to the west, Ben finally stopped running and sat low in some tall bead grass. With the feeling of being isolated and surrounded by all the warring mayhem, his anxiety rose like a rising tide.

*Dogg, where are you?* he thought, breaking a small stick into pieces.

He looked about, with the urge to flee again.

*This isn't safe.*

He touched the universal translator on his ear and remembered Dogg's instructions.

*Okay, think the message—and say it, too.* "Dogg, I need help. You said I'd be safe!"

Another scream in the distance caused him to jump and look about. He stayed low and moved on, heading farther west.

* * *

On the hill at the main Flaxon command point, the last short while had been a tense time for Colonel Hitex and his officers with him astride their mounts. The ground before them sloped down and away through a shallow depression before rising gently to the Yorr Forest tree line, where Hitex could see that a small group of enemy troops had emerged in plain sight.

"What manner of tactic is this?" he wondered aloud.

"Shall I have the archers take them down, sir?" asked the officer on his right.

Hitex raised a hand to indicate no, but said nothing. Directly in front, tall grasses wavered in a gentle breeze as Hitex watched the six figures, still wondering about their intentions. For a little while now, he had watched the remains of his decimated soldier units exit the tree line. All had expressions of defeat on their faces. Their hasty, disorganized retreat from the foray Hitex thought pitiful to observe. Looking over their shoulders as if being chased, many had lost upper limbs. He'd seen one soldier carrying his severed hand, following others with severe lacerations, slashed helms, and crushed breastplates.

"What a sorry lot," Hitex said, eyeing the remnants of the returning force in total discontent.

*This is not good for morale for my reports back to Weirawind,* he thought, glancing to the regent's representative who sat astride a gray mare just off Hitex's left shoulder. He also noticed the flushed faces and expressions on several of his officers.

"Sir!"

"Yes," Hitex said. "What?"

The captain sitting next to Hitex drew his attention back to the six

< 104 >

Scarzen who had emerged from the forest. One or two of the officers spoke muffled expletives at the sight of them and thought of further escalation of hostilities. Then they fell into an awkward silence. Hitex straightened in the saddle, annoyed at his officers' lack of discipline.

"Gentlemen, a straight back, if you please. I'll have no tunnel vision today!" Hitex said.

"Perhaps they intend to surrender, sir," said a young officer on Hitex's right.

The colonel glared at him. "How many Scarzen have you encountered, Lieutenant?" Hitex asked.

"None, sir! This is my first engagement," the officer said, steadying his mount.

"And what did you just observe over the last hour?"

"The enemy were unexpectedly resilient, sir," the officer said.

Hitex shuffled in his saddle, agitated and still glaring at the officer with steel-gray eyes. "Unexpectedly …" Hitex sighed and rubbed his jaw. He scoffed, finding some dark humor in the comment. "Observed without flaw, Lieutenant. If you survive this day, I'm sure your recount of events will elicit great interest. Tell me, are you married, Lieutenant?"

"Yes, sir, to a fine woman," he said.

"Then I hope you kissed her well before you left."

"Sir?"

"Scarzen don't surrender, lad. Weirawind command's squeeze has failed … badly. It has not impressed our enemy one little bit, as you have so bluntly pointed out. Unless I miss my guess, you're about to duel an enemy who regards our barring the way as inconsequential as crossing a shallow stream," Hitex said, swinging his attention back over his shoulder.

"Have we lost the advantage, then, sir?" asked the officer.

"Command's initiative has failed with the collapse of that last skirmish. Field command now falls to my discretion." He turned a steely look to the officer. "And I intend to balance the account. On your toes, gentleman." Hitex looked behind. "Sergeant Major! Something's up. These rats have another card to play. See that your soldiers keep their wits and work together.

< 105 >

It's time to force their hand."

The sergeant major saluted, then ordered his color sergeants to make ready. The young lieutenant beside Colonel Hitex blinked nervously, looking toward the enemy.

\* \* \*

"Well, they stand out for target practice. Couldn't I walk up there and ask the one in charge to make our work a little more challenging?" Spanaje said.

Benataa continued to stare straight ahead at the enemy. "I don't think your advice would be well received." A breeze cut across from the west, carrying the smell of Flaxon and much horseflesh to his nose. "He knows the clash is coming, and he'll want this consult to mean something."

\* \* \*

Back on the rise, Hitex issued orders: "Lieutenant, send in the rain."

"Sir!" the lieutenant acknowledged, looking to his rear. "Sergeant Major, have the colors for the archers made active. The rain, tight group, three hundred steps on my command."

"Yes, sir!"

Keeping entirely focused on the enemy, Hitex wondered what the crouching Scarzen ahead was doing.

*What are you up to?* he asked himself.

\* \* \*

"Spanaje, light the match," Benataa said softly, looking directly at the Flaxon commander on the rise.

Crouching down, Spanaje finished a knot at the head of a field-made torch and laid it across a flat stone at his feet, then struck some spark-stone over the torch's oily wad with a small metal tool. It lit easily. Spanaje picked up the flaming torch and handed it to one of the rear guardsmen.

\* \* \*

"What are they doing? Is that a torch they've lit? Do they intend to burn

< 106 >

us out?" asked the young lieutenant, staring at the Scarzen and straining his eyes.

"If they do, the wind blows in the wrong direction. It doesn't matter," Hitex said.

He took one last look, then gave a nod. "Lieutenant, loose now!"

The lieutenant signaled to the sergeant major.

"Range, three hundred steps north! Wind, two knots west, high drop!"

A long line of archers steepened the trajectory of their bows, and each drew their arrow to full tension.

"LOOSE!" the lieutenant commanded, dropping his arm.

The whistling sound of three hundred black needle arrows filled the air.

\* \* \*

The Scarzen looked to the sky.

"Here it comes," said Spanaje, hearing the arrows fly.

The Scarzen group formed a triangle, with Benataa in front, and lifted their arms, making circular motions with their hands while combining all their kin to focus in one place. Suddenly, a huge gust of swirling wind rose in front and arched over them in convex fashion.

The large volley of arrows descended, whistling through the air. As the accurate volley struck the twisting windshield covering Scarzen heads, all the arrows sheered harmlessly away in scattered directions. The projectiles clattered to the ground like joss sticks—except one black arrow, which scored Benataa's right boot and buried its shaft to one-third in the ground.

\* \* \*

Hitex watched the well-aimed volley made insignificant and groaned in frustration.

"What the bat shit was that?" a spotter said from behind the mounted officers.

The sergeant major turned sharply with a scowl.

"Sorry, sir!" the spotter said and stood to attention.

Then, through gritted teeth, Commander Hitex ordered: "Lieutenant!

< 107 >

Call the heavy infantry forward!" Then he looked at his officers and said, "Gentlemen, draw blades and bring me their heads!"

The officer beside Hitex sat motionless, staring with mouth open at the Scarzen's countermove. Seeing his lack of impetus, Hitex snapped, "Draw your blade, boy! That's an order!"

The other officers all sat up straight, elbow bent and blades vertical for the opening phase of the charge.

"Advance," Hitex ordered.

The lieutenant raised his blade high. "RANKS, PREPARE TO ADVANCE!" The sounds of many hundreds of blades being drawn rang out. "RANK, ADVANCE!"

The cavalry ranks advanced with several coordinating officers as Hitex looked on. Behind them followed two thousand foot soldiers.

\* \* \*

"Hmmm, we've drawn a crowd! Horse meat for dinner too," Spanaje said in a cheery voice. "Too many to count versus … us. A good day out, I think!"

"You always think the tighter the fix, the better," Benataa said. "Warriors, honor them with a precision death."

Seeing the Flaxon advance, Benataa said nothing further, but stepped forward and dug deep in his will to wield his most potent kin. In front of him developed a conical whirlwind that extruded quickly to twice his height before beginning to broaden. The twisting wind tore through grass and ground. Its increasing gravity vacuumed up all loose debris. Arms outstretched as though guiding a box kite, Benataa's will directed the whirling mass back and forth. Suddenly, it doubled in height and mass—again and again.

\* \* \*

"That's not possible …?" Hitex said, butterflies filling his stomach with adrenaline and the impetus to act. "We are not waiting for more arcane mayhem. Captain! All your strength. Sound the full battalion charge!"

< 108 >

* * *

Benataa's now enormous expanding whirling mass of grass and debris swung like a pendulum some forty strides in front. It made a frightening howling sound like a living thing ready to devour anything in its path. The war trumpets, thundering feet, and war cries of charging Flaxon pounded the ground toward the party of six waiting Scarzen. As the front wave of the Flaxon force charged toward their target, the neck of the whirlwind bowed, presenting the massive spinning head of what was now a tornado. The central ranks were pulled inside the nexus of the pounding debris, stalling the body of the charge to a standing panic. Many broke off into disorganized clusters as soldiers tried to evade the tornado.

Just as the ranks poured around the outer flanks of the tornado, Benataa stood the tornado up and commanded, "Light it up!"

A Myst officer stepped forward with the flaming torch in hand and then, using his kin, hurled it forward into the heart of the whirlwind. When the torch struck Benataa's storm, an enormous explosion erupted from inside. The transformed mass churned into a burning sphere, which seemed to expand as the flames grew hotter with a fine umbilical now tethered to Benataa. He rolled it back and forth over his oncoming enemies. Flaxon burst into flames, screaming in terror and falling in smoldering heaps. A thick smoke choked the air. All of the remaining ground debris caught flame around the Flaxon, and vision for those approaching the Scarzen dropped to almost zero. Mass confusion reigned as the fire began to create its own force and wind. Many began to cower and retreat in all directions.

* * *

In all the confusion, no one noticed the sellenor's approach from high overhead—except Colonel Hitex, who still sat at the top of the slope upon his stallion. It flew straight for the green ribbon of smoke now spiraling up from within the pass. Above, Hitex eyed the huge four-winged creature known to ally with the Scarzen. It descended right where the green ribbon had its origin.

"Why the messenger?" Hitex muttered to himself, then swung his vision

< 109 >

back to the battle.

Looking about, it was obvious that, for the second time in less than a day, a gross underestimation of the enemy's unconventional capability had been made. He called for the trumpets of retreat in disgust.

\* \* \*

In the pass, the sellenor instinctively landed near the smoking green signal fire with a whoosh of its four wings. Sitting on its haunches, the brightly colored feather-and-fur-covered predator still maintained a head height of just over eight feet. The Scarzen stepped forward with the mesh box containing the Tears and set it on the ground at the sellenor's banded talon feet. The sellenor stood focused on the box, rolling its owl-shaped face from side to side, its golden-yellow eyes locked on the two Scarzen warriors for a moment. Then the sellenor clamped one black talon foot upon the box. Without further pause, and with an explosion of beating wings, the sellenor carried the box with speed high aloft away into the distance. The warriors could hear its four large wings and the trailing sound of *womp, womp, womp,* before it became a dot in the sky.

\* \* \*

Out in Yorr Fields, the battle had subsided. Fifty or so Flaxon soldiers managed to evade the fiery sphere and closed upon Benataa's position. A short skirmish followed, and all the soldiers were quickly killed by Spanaje at close range.

Benataa let go of his focus on the fiery tornado. In its crash to the ground, it burst, spraying incendiaries everywhere away from the Scarzen. The last vestiges of the fire fell near the Flaxon commander's horse up on the rise. After that, random grass fires began to blow steadily east. In front of the six Scarzen, the smell of burning Flaxon flesh carried on the wind. Bodies, now featureless, smoldered amongst the ashes while others in the final throes of death rolled about in agony. As the smoke cleared, Benataa could see the Flaxon commander still atop the slope. The two seemed to stare at one another for a long moment. Benataa spread his arms and bowed

< 110 >

ever so slightly, saying as though the commander could hear, "Show's over."

Then Benataa stood, showing his palms and tilting his head as a sign of respect for the enemy. Familiar with the gesture from other battles, Hitex straightened in his saddle, felt patronized, and made no reply. Benataa watched him rein the head of his horse to the rear and disappear over the hill.

"Ruhe!" called one Scarzen warrior. "I saw the sellenor arrive."

"Mmm, I saw as well," he said, quickly moving to the next step in his plan. "Back to the squad."

The six disappeared back into the forest. It was early afternoon.

* * *

Earlier, over the Lyran Mountains in Talon East Bunker, Scout Hellexaa stood in Commander Titarliaa's room of focus, presenting the last of the verbal message sent by Benataa—having already spoken to Kalfax about dispatching a sellenor to Yorr Pass to retrieve the Tears.

"Hmm, in a bit of a snarl up there, is he?" Titarliaa said with bleached white smile. He looked upon the scout with hands clasped on his desk. He noted that the scout stood at attention, but was clearly exhausted. "To Yorr Fields. He dares order me to take a trek so far north?"

"Not my words, sir," Hellexaa said. "Just repeating things as ordered. I believe that Ruhe—uh, I mean, Commander Benataa—intends no disrespect, sir. He is aware of the commander's disdain for the Flaxon enemy's lack of honor. Commander Benataa wishes to convey that, under the present circumstances and value of the responsibility, a superior commanding presence such as yourself is warranted. The Flaxon have overstepped the mark, sir. They intend to make an example of Commander Benataa's unit inside the neutral zone … sir."

Titarliaa knew how much the common ranks respected Commander Benataa and the Brasheer he belonged to. Titarliaa had known Benataa for many years, and a bond of mutual respect existed. They even maintained a longstanding match of carrack in relaxed times, which at last count, Benataa was besting him two or three.

"I suppose if I leave him there, I'll never enjoy watching his face at my

< 111 >

next carrack victory."

"It would be a shame, sir," said Hellexaa.

"Flaxon are a scourge in Ludd, don't you agree, Scout?" Titarliaa said.

"A boil on the face of Ludd, sir."

"Well, we'd best lance it before it takes further root."

"You will be doing a great favor for all in Ludd, sir."

"Hmm. I suppose an afternoon's combat could provide some catharsis, even help my indigestion."

"Taking Flaxon heads amidst a lively consultation in mountain air will lift everyone's spirits, sir. And then there is the on-flow."

"Meaning?"

"A strong show of strength at this time will bring several victories, sir, and legitimize a consultation with our enemy who gather with intention to do harm in great number."

Titarliaa still sat, stonefaced. "I don't know it's incentive enough."

"When the consult is finished, Commander Benataa challenges you to a match of carrack while watching the Flaxon in full retreat—a contest our squad would relish too, sir."

Hellexaa watched Titarliaa stand slowly with that smile. Hellexaa felt a little nervous seeing Commander Titarliaa with a truly joyous smile—and it was scary. It usually meant something quite gruesome would occur. Hellexaa swallowed softly, thinking he may have displeased the commander in some fashion. The old commander's exposed white teeth combined with a sinister stare that made him look, well, very hungry—for something Flaxon, Hellexaa hoped.

"Yesss," Titarliaa said. "I think an honorable cause now exists! By Naught's hand, yes!" he said with enthusiasm, thumping his desk. "Norexx!" he boomed.

His office door swung open, with the long face of Titarliaa's adjutant Norexx filling its frame.

"You yelled, sir!" Norexx said from the doorway in his dry tone.

"Snap to! We are going to consult with some Flaxon needing a sound thrashing."

Norexx grinned with pleasure. "Oh, joy, I can't wait. Should I pack your

< 112 >

travel pillow, blades, and frontline attire, sir?"

"Without delay. Sound my regiment's call to arms."

"Yes, sir!"

Titarliaa marched straight past Hellexaa, then stopped.

"Don't just stand there, Scout! Clean yourself up. We can't go to a consult in sloppy attire. What will the enemy think?"

"Yes, sir!"

< 113 >

CHAPTER 9
## BAD COMPANY

In the west end of Yorr Fields, at Flaxon Mobile Command 1, a heated meeting continued amongst staff officers. Acting as arbiter, Magistrate Waldon listened to combative viewpoints, having only just arrived as Regent Straxus's new personal representative in the field.

"Don't you get it, Lieutenant?" Captain Holsworthy yelled. "No, wait, you couldn't. You hadn't finished your supper by then!"

Lieutenant Winterbottom shook his head. "I'll have you—"

"They finished cutting us down for the second time only two hours ago!" Captain Holsworthy shouted.

"Oh, I see," Lieutenant Winterbottom said. "So we should just let them ride right on through with the stolen cargo so aptly named 'the Tears!' Who's crying now?"

"Well, Rex, perhaps you think we should serve them a meal and ask for their blessing. No, no ... wait, I know: why don't we just all line up in a pants-down parade, bend over, and kiss our own arses good-bye!" Captain Holsworthy said, hand on his hip.

"Gentlemen, please! This gets us nowhere," another officer protested. "We suffered the losses because the enemy capacity was underestimated."

"Magistrate Waldon, sir, I appeal to your better judgment. We can't let this go," said Lieutenant Winterbottom. "We don't even know the nature of these Tears they carry off or their value, only that it is the property of our regent—your own father. Our honor and ability to be seen as a true threat is at stake here. These animals have handed us our arses twice in the space of half a day, sir!"

Waldon the Elder was a Flaxon in his fifty-seventh cycle and a man of strong character who didn't suffer fools. His slight build and gentle features and outward demeanor belied the steely will underneath.

"Yes, yes, so I've heard," Magistrate Waldon said, reclining in a chair. "And by all accounts, Lieutenant, I would say they did so quite decisively. First, I'll say to you that you are a professional soldier, Lieutenant. Not a member of the regent's Royal House Security. Whatever that cargo might be is none of your concern. Second, orders come from the top down. Right now, your orders are to reacquire the stolen cargo under the command of Colonel Hitex, Regent Straxus advised me. For the safety of your career, Lieutenant, I suggest you focus on that." Waldon turned to his aide. "Who is leading the Scarzen unit? Anyone we know of?"

"Well, sir, Scarzen security is very difficult to penetrate and—"

"If I wanted a commentary on how good their security is and how inept we have been, I would have structured the question so!" the magistrate said. "Do we know who?"

Swallowing, the aide shook his head. "There are only rumors, sir. But from the scant description of the Scarzen as identified by a scout patrol, which happened upon them much earlier, one stood out as their commander. He had red braids with gold bands. A significant rank for a Scarzen officer, like some of the dead we have seen in the past years. The same commander is identified as leading the Scarzen squad in other border skirmishes, sir."

"That's it! That's all you have? A Scarzen commander with red braids and gold bands?" Lieutenant Winterbottom snapped from his seat in the corner. "Wonderful. We are looking for a Scarzen with an outstanding hairstyle, wearing the latest in Scarzen braiding. How fashionable! This is to be helpful how?"

Waldon rolled his eyes in displeasure at the over dramatization. "Continue, Spence," he said to his aide.

< 115 >

"Y-yes, s-sir," the subordinate said. "Our ... our informants tell us that there is only one Scarzen leader wearing braids of that kind. And all Scarzen have quite unique markings, usually visible on the neck, sir. It's one of the only things we know for sure about their culture."

"Get on with it."

"Yes, sir," Spence said. "As you know, the Scarzen ranking system of gold bands is worn only on the braids of the officers, and the accompanying red bands are only worn by their elite warriors. So, identity is not too difficult once we can put a name to a marking. This officer over the past decade has given us considerable trouble, sir."

"And can we put a name to him, Spence?" Waldon asked.

"Yes, sir, we believe the name is ... Benataa, sir. A Brasheer commander—one who leads a Brasheer unit operating under the high keeper of Talon East."

"You believe?" Waldon sighed unhappily and sat forward. "Spence, how is it that the one god in his infinite wisdom chose us to represent his likeness when the best you can come up with is 'we believe'?"

Waldon's annoyance continued as he tapped the point of a pocketknife on the small sidetable next to him.

"We have more, sir. His unit terrorized some of our western border patrols recently during the attempted assault on Talon North."

"We lost a lot of good men for zero result there."

"Yes, sir. He—Benataa, I mean—was also seen at the conflict with the Celeron over the water supply treaty in the Western Plains a year ago. He has caused us a lot of trouble, sir."

"Yes. That became quite an untidy business," Waldon said, wanting to move on.

"We lost a lot of good men to that ordeal, too, and were unable to have the Celeron capitulate," Lieutenant Winterbottom said, seeming to have calmed down.

"I seem to remember that unit having another name," Captain Perry said from the corner. "What was it!" he asked himself, trying to remember.

"Myst!" said another officer.

The magistrate looked over his shoulder to where a field captain stood

< 116 >

in battle dress with his helm under his arm.

"Did you say something, Captain?" Waldon asked, adjusting in his seat.

"Yes, sir. Captain Gregory Dwain Soams, sir. Attached to Colonel Hitex's 3rd Army Field Regiment. Those Brasheer units are known as the 'Myst,' and they are the devil who walks. My soldiers have had the displeasure of engaging them on several occasions. I have filed many reports about this type of Scarzen unit, even put proclamations to high command. But I never get any formal reply," the captain said, stepping forward. "I know of this Benataa by the last whisperings of one of my scouts from the border lands. He died from severe wounds after tracking that Scarzen leader's unit for a time. The scout said one of the Scarzen even maintained pace with his galloping horse for a considerable distance, trying to catch him before they fell for some reason. The enemy managed to leave one of his blades in my scout's back as a memento. My scout described the same Scarzen you speak about just now, sir."

"Then what different news might you bring of this ... Benataa?" the magistrate asked.

"By evidence today, it seems the same Scarzen unit very recently engaged two of our assault companies near the forest of Blackwater one week ago. Three hundred of our best perished there. I conclude that a very high-percentage chance exists that the same unit infiltrated and stole the regent's property. They have been sighted near Weirawind before. Our city was struck at night and this Scarzen unit's preference is a night fight. They pick their dueling ground carefully and prefer close-quarters ambush in difficult terrain. These are not ordinary Scarzen troops, sir. Seventy of that commander's warriors decimated our two assault companies in as many days, leaving three to tell the tale. These are damn near unstoppable as far as I can see, sir, leading to only two possible outcomes."

"Those being?"

"Anyone engaging this commander's unit will have only one of two roads to choose. First is to fight to the last man. Second, withdraw and call for backup of three times as many as you had thought you would need. They hit and disappear without trace like the very mist that is their namesake."

< 117 >

The magistrate shuffled in his seat, clearly agitated.

"Normally, they kill every man and horse within the range of their vision," Soams said. "But, of recent times, they have been known to take the odd prisoner. After torture and interrogation, the prisoner is sent screaming back home for their clansmen to see. It's obviously a tactic designed to break morale, sir."

The magistrate scoffed in annoyance.

"Sir, may I venture an opinion?"

"Yes, you have something else to say, Captain?"

"My regiments of long muskets have fought standard Scarzen units also, sir, on several occasions. We've had some success at range. But only when we had cover and surprise, and poured a lot of shot into them.

"I see."

"Four generations of my family serving in Flaxon military have fought the Scarzen. I was raised watching my father's comrades return from their encounters stitched up in canvas burial sacks. Scarzen body scale will turn our super-iron blades even with the heaviest thrust, unless it's through the neck. It will stop a musket round at fifty paces. You have to shoot them square in the head for certainty. Hitting center mass at range always proves useless. Most men die while reloading if at close range. If you miss or your weapon misfires, they are upon you before you can drop your weapon to draw your long knife. And don't forget their healing dust. If they get away even mortally wounded, they use it and are back in an hour to finish the job as though the day had just started."

"You paint our enemy as all but invincible," Waldon said.

"Sir, their steel is better than ours. They are more agile over most terrain. The way they use a blade is not from this realm. Their speed and skill at close quarter is unmatched—and *some* suggest that the evil one himself guides their hand."

"That was quite a breath full, Captain," Waldon said.

"As I mentioned, sir, I've been trying to alert high command for some considerable time, but most have never seen the Scarzen's true capability."

Some officers began to shake their head in disbelief.

< 118 >

"So what would you recommend, Captain?"

"With every weakness we demonstrate, they become stronger, sir."

"Mmm. Indeed, so it appears."

One of the other officers stepped forward. "Ah, sir. May I?"

The magistrate raised his hand, pressing the officer to remain silent. "Go on, Captain," Waldon said.

Soams pinched his lips in thought. "As has been said, sir, these are not ordinary Scarzen. Many have seen them use their kind of magic. They can move and throw things, set them on fire using only their will."

A couple of the newer officers began to smirk.

"And turn blades upon the very soldiers that wield them, or the next individual closest. This news is not new, sir, but it has been dismissed from before we Flaxon separated from the northern tribes generations ago. It is something that command still refuses to face squarely. Because they cannot comprehend the abilities of the Scarzen, they constantly try to focus on other things, hoping the problem will be removed by some divine force our priests suggest they wield."

"That's blasphemy," Lieutenant Winterbottom said.

"I do not criticize god, only those who hide behind a veil of piousness, never having to personally stand against our nemesis. Magic or not," Captain Soams said, "they have serious strength that often devastates us in the field, sir. Using their devilry is the Scarzen's perfect instrument for breaking the fighting spirit of any soldier," he said with some chill in his voice, looking at the others.

"This is out-of-proportion madness, Captain Soams!" Captain Perry said. "You exaggerate with the color of a playwright. You speak as though Scarzen have league with the hell realms. Do you really expect us to believe this folly? It's just frightened Flaxon looking for excuses, I say."

"Do you?" Soams said. "And when was the last time you had cause to confront any Scarzen, Captain Perry? I understand the parade ground in Garrison Five is always pristine under your pedantic guiding hand."

Perry turned to Waldon. "Sir, give me one hundred men. I will have this settled by sunset," he said.

< 119 >

"I think not, Captain," said someone from just outside the tent's entryway.

"Now who?" Waldon said, rolling his eyes.

An arm pushed back the tent flap to expose its outer annex.

"It's me, Magistrate—Colonel Hitex. And that 'out-of-proportion madness' just killed seven hundred of my best men using the same very fictional abilities just spoken of. The Scarzen leader ended the melee with a finale of a fireball the size of our tallest building, burning each Flaxon soldier to smoldering cinders to seal an incontestable victory."

Hitex finished his statement looking squarely at all the other officers. Magistrate Waldon sat with a serious expression as Hitex gestured to the officer standing opposite.

"The young Captain Soams speaks accurately, Magistrate," Hitex said. "No doubt you have smelled evidence of the brush fires burning to the east?"

Another field officer tried to interject, but Waldon turned away to focus entirely on the colonel.

"You look like you've been busy this day, Ferdinand," Waldon said to Hitex. "We should have had this all in hand by now."

"Not long ago, I attempted to snare the very quarry we have all been sent here for," Hitex said. "Something went horribly wrong in Yorr Pass. None of our pursuing patrols have emerged. On the open battlefield, our casualties have been in the extreme. We have just received word that only one of the companies made it into the pass before a landslide sealed them inside."

"Which company? Did they recover the prize?" asked the magistrate.

"No, I am afraid not, sir," replied the colonel. "They are not an enemy that one tries to squash without respect. The magic is wielded as we might wield our most powerful siege cannon."

"Even a sabre cat is vulnerable if it underestimates the tree-cutter ant's capacity to overwhelm it," said Waldon.

"And today the ants ate us alive, sir," replied Colonel Hitex, taking a seat. "We used standard field procedure. We had numbers and position. They again used very unconventional responses and calculated their logistics well."

"Might I ask how many were on the field against you, Colonel?" Captain Perry asked.

< 120 >

"In the first battle, I cannot say," Hitex said. "They used the cover of the morning fog inside the forest to conceal their number and position, as we tried to do. In the case of the second engagement, I saw six Scarzen ... against seven hundred on the open field!"

"SIX!" the tent's complement all spoke up as one, horrified. For a moment, an awkward silence loomed. Then the magistrate stood and began to pace the room.

"Six individuals, you say?" Waldon asked.

"Yes. As I said, their leader manifested a fireball the size of our bell tower in Weirawind while the others covered his flank. It was pretty impressive, I must say!"

"Whose side are you on, Colonel?" Waldon said.

"Magistrate, I am commenting on the enemy's capacity, tactics, and ingenuity that we faced today. They were clear in their intention, used the terrain to maximum advantage, and their far smaller force trounced us. And one more thing, sir ..."

"There's more?" asked the magistrate.

"Yes. Before the mayhem began, the same small group also thwarted a full volley of war arrows from two of my best archer companies, using only the wind."

"The wind? How can they have such command over the elements?"

"Yes, Magistrate, the one with the red and gold braids was directing the force single-handedly."

"How do we stop such an enemy who has that capacity to repel our forces?" asked Captain Perry.

"Well," said Waldon, "I can only say, if the enemy brings a knife, ensure you have a sword."

"Ah, sir," Captain Soams said.

"Yes, Captain ... Soams, is it?" Waldon said.

"Yes, sir. My company gunsmithy has been working with the Weirawind bell maker, Screwman, and our master archer and fletcher, Mr. Gossling. Together, they have developed two new prototype weapons. One of those developments, a new type of small-unit field rocket, is ready to go. It is

< 121 >

light to carry and should prove more than troublesome to our enemy in a variety of theaters, sir. The other is a much larger rocket launcher on a rolling platform. Bell caster Screwman has a redesigned cannon, much more accurate. It's almost through final design."

Magistrate Waldon noticed Colonel Hitex whisper something quietly to his aide, who then left straightaway.

"And this has to do with now in what way, Soams?" asked Waldon.

"As you know, sir, we accompany Colonel Hitex's Third Column. I have some examples of the weapon with me that we have been testing in the field. The weapon packs a substantial wallop over a medium distance, sir. Two men can easily transport it. One acts as the loader and match, the other as the range-finder and trigger. A full unit consists of up to six. It fires a single rocket, its head casing filled with metal splinter and shot. There is no kickback when fired, and it's accurate over seventy-five spans. The shrapnel can spread up to twenty spans post-impact. It also carries accurate up to 150 spans on a still day. It's slower to load than a pigeon gun, but much more effective. The payback for the carrying effort is more than satisfactory, sir. I believe it could level the playing field for us. The Scarzen don't use firearms. Seems against their war code, which means a distance battle would strengthen our odds considerably."

"After what Colonel Hitex has just reported and your additional information, Captain, I think I agree," the magistrate said. "See to it! I want our property back in custody as soon as can be and to end here with an appropriate show of Flaxon military supremacy," he said with a thump of the table, looking at Hitex.

"Sir, let's not overshoot our mission objective," Colonel Hitex said. "They carry valuable empire secrets. The prize is delicate, I'm led to believe. Can't afford it damaged. Hitting them with too much power, we may win the battle and lose the objective. After today's losses, I took the liberty of calling for the other half of my full column. They should be here by early morning. I have a plan to hem in our adversaries and take back what is ours."

"Hmm. What do you have in mind, Colonel?" asked the magistrate.

"With the use of onega and net catapults, I believe I can subjugate and

< 122 >

contain the enemy. Once they are apprehended, we can negotiate for them to hand over our property or perish in defiance, and we'll walk over their bodies to get it. If you'll indulge me, I will provide details."

"Let's hear it then," replied Waldon. "Take a seat, gentlemen. We have some planning to do."

The officers all gathered around a map of Yorr Fields on a table in the center of the room. There, Hitex outlined his plan.

* * *

Meanwhile, in Yorr Fields beyond the Flaxon camp's northern picket, Ben had run until he was well clear of the entire skirmish. Wanting only to get away, he'd fled into the long-grass hills unwittingly toward the Flaxon west camp. Now he had no idea of direction, where Dogg was, or what other hazards may lie in wait.

*Anywhere is better than there*, he told himself. Finally, he collapsed in an exhausted heap in long grass near a small wild-apple grove and fell into a restless sleep.

* * *

Inside Yorr Pass, Benataa's squad gathered together.

"Did the sellenor take the responsibility?" asked Benataa.

"Yes, Ruhe, some thirty scats ago," said the warrior in charge of the responsibility.

"Good."

"Now, shall we break east and leave our sorry enemy licking their wounds, Ruhe? asked Spanaje, gripping his reaper. "Or shall we encourage them further?"

"No, we must keep them guessing. Warning patrols will be everywhere. Help will arrive soon." Benataa pointed to one warrior. "Assemble the spare mesh box. We'll need a misdirect. And you two there, gather reconnaissance until midnight and return to east and west camps. Go!"

"Ruhe, shouldn't we use the cover of night? And we could use the Gantry route now," suggested a scout.

< 123 >

"No. Their patrols will be many and the Lyran Pass lies behind the east camp position and Gantry. The moment we are sighted, horns will sound and the west camp will be put on high alert. Then our coming counterforce loses the element of surprise and cuts us off from their aid completely. I want as little focus on Gantry as possible. The Flaxon would level the town out of spite, or attempt to, if they thought we'd seek refuge there, which would force the Brasheer into engagement, something I was ordered to avoid. Gantry holds a secret the Flaxon must never discover. Lastly, Old Angry would get anger hives—"

They all laughed.

"Commander Titarliaa, that is, would be most put out, arriving via invitation to a healthy consult only to find himself with no quarry to engage. We would never hear the end of it. He owes me a carrack debt and would likely renege as protest."

Benataa bent down and picked up a small stone, then began tossing it lightly while in thought.

"They will not come back into the tree line willingly again, and we would fare poorly against a cavalry force in the open field. When the reconnaissance returns, we consult in the very early morn. Set a picket. Get some rest."

< 124 >

Passing Talon East front gate with his regiment, Commander Titarliaa received a dispatch reading:

> *Tears recovered. Now en route to sanctuary. Supporting regiment-scale consult approved to assist forces retreat, only.*

> *Signed,*
> *Malforce*

Sitting on his drommal, Titarliaa gave a guttural laugh and looked at Norexx riding on his flank. "Our assistance will be enthusiastically injected."

Titarliaa tucked the message into his saddle purse, then signaled his column forward. Traveling at a strong pace into the following late afternoon, Commander Titarliaa's company met up and merged with a force of twelve hundred strong medium assault troops at Talon West. Without rest, all continued north to Mustard Fields and onto the east road toward the Yorr neutral zone—unwittingly flanked by Dogg.

After missing Farron at two locations, Dogg found Commander Titarliaa in conversation with Scout Hellexaa about the dispatch from Benataa and decided to follow the emerging thread linked to Commander Titarliaa. It represented the only fresh lead she had since the debacle at Yorr Pass.

"This is the perfect opportunity to have my regiment tested," Dogg heard Titarliaa tell Norexx as he admired the passing majestic scenery. "We must be through Cragg's Gap and into the Yorr Fields by first light."

"We'll slap the Flaxon back to their senses, sir, and send them home wearing trousers of defeat," said Norexx.

\* \* \*

Early afternoon arrived with a cloudless sky over Yorr Fields. There, between clusters of trees, the topography spread over a combination of open ground, low hills, and shallow gullies. Only one dependable supply of fresh water was available in Yorr Fields. It emerged via a spring fed from an underground stream that had been traced along the southern shoulder of Cragg Mountain to the south. It was the first ground that Colonel Hitex commandeered. Overlooking Hitex's camp in the distance stood the derelict Flaxon stronghold of Fort Cragg. Near this spring circled Colonel Hitex's headquarters and the main body of Flaxon troops.

To the east, another smaller contingent, the second camp, blocked the way to Gantry. Patrolling camp sentries had no idea they were being watched by one of Benataa's scouts, who'd crept to a vantage point in some long grass on top of a hillock. Overlooking the Flaxon west camp, crouched low, he could see the camp movements clearly. Just behind him stood a wild apple grove that served as a windbreak from the chill of the building highlands wind. He munched on a tart green apple he'd taken earlier while looking down on the camp. He stopped his chewing when he saw, running at full gallop across the crest of another barren slope, a sight that filled his heart with joy: a sign that only the sages of Scarza spoke of when destiny and choice of actions meant victory. At full stride ran Tula, dog spirit protector of the Brasheer and all Scarzen. He watched her leap off a rocky ledge and vanish into thin air.

"Yes," he said, then nodded. "This day will be ours!

The Scarzen's heart filled with confidence. Then he saw one of the Flaxon sentries using a spyglass in his direction and decided to retreat closer to the

< 126 >

wild apple grove for a different view. There, he stopped and lay in wait for the early night to fall. During that time, one unfortunate Flaxon soldier on wide boundary patrol saw the same apple grove. Thinking a crisp apple would carry his stomach through to dinner, the rider dismounted to gather fruit from the trees, unaware of the eyes on him close by. He unknowingly moved ever closer to the concealed Scarzen. The Flaxon reached up to pull a ripe apple, craning his neck, when from behind, a large gloved hand covered his mouth and snatched him backward, running an eighteen-inch skinning knife across his neck to the bone. The Scarzen concealed the body and then lay in wait to near last light. It was then the scout heard a rustling in the long grass nearby.

*Too clumsy for an animal—definitely another Flaxon,* he thought, preparing for another kill.

* * *

When Ben had awakened on the brow of the hill, exhaustion still filled him. Sitting in the long grass, his stomach rumbled for something to eat, and in the far distance, he could hear faint sporadic sounds of people. Ben tapped his universal translator a couple times with his finger. Speaking low, he said, "Dogg! Dogg, are you there? … Uniss, it's Ben. Can you hear me?"

With only the sound of wind rustling through the grass, he sat back on his heels, wondering what to do next. Ben looked at his clothing, and he took some solace that Uniss had at least made it so that his exterior would look like a young Scarzen if he ever became visible to the locals—albeit a very small and fragile young Scarzen. Looking over the crest of the grass, he saw the treetops of the apple grove. Raising himself a little higher, he saw some low-hanging fruit and decided to investigate who was making the noise on the lower fields—and collect an apple or two to kill the hunger pains on the way. Staying low through the long grass, he made his way to the closest tree. Moving toward the gnarled trunk, he took an apple from a low branch and sat to eat, keeping an eye out for any movement. The fruit in his mouth tasted tart, something his expression mirrored. His hunger kept him eating anyway, and he forgot the world around him for a moment. He heard something

< 127 >

clatter to his left and snapped an alert look in that direction. Then his heart jumped when a large strong hand snatched at him from behind, dragging him backward to the ground. In the next instant, Ben saw a heavy-gloved black hand holding him fast, and he looked up into the face of a Scarzen. The frame of their hardened orange-eyed features, surrounded by a thick head of rust-red braided locks, held his full attention.

The devilish figure overhead had an arm raised with a gruesome long knife set to plunge downward.

"No!" Ben screamed, throwing his head to one side as the blade fell.

He gripped the Scarzen's wrist, struggling uselessly while attempting to shift his grip. The blade struck home in the dirt with a *thoongk*, nicking Ben's temple and severing a length of his hair to the skin on its way through. Ben felt a small trickle of blood run down the side of his head. Drawing his blade for a second stab, the Scarzen scout stopped when he saw that he was attacking a Scarzen newborn. The Scarzen's scowl changed to an expression of surprise.

He grabbed Ben at the sternum by a fist full of clothing and pulled him up sharply to a seated position with an agitated grunt, and then plonked him on his butt.

"You look like you're small enough to be just out of the chest cavity! Your braids have barely finished growing. What is a newborn doing so far from his bunker? Why are you covered in the smell of Flaxon? Where is your otaa?" The scout let Ben go. "Answer quick or the discipline will be harsh."

For a moment, Ben felt terrified. Then he realized that the earlier chameleon field cast upon him by Uniss was doing its job. The Scarzen saw him as one of them—and now Ben only hoped that the universal translator really would turn his words into Scarzen language.

Stammering a little at first, Ben spouted his best defense to the Scarzen's inquiry: "Forgive me, sir. I fell while riding my sellenor. She barrel-rolled, swooping the treetops, and I fell off. When I woke up, she was nowhere to be seen. I come from Talon Fact. I have been wandering for a while, trying to find my way back. My memory only extends that far. I don't remember my otaa's name," he said wearily.

< 128 >

"Well, you have wandered very far, newborn. Did you get that stink on you by wandering through the camp below? Naught will punish you if you lie, and you will be disciplined by your otutt for lack of integrity.

"You are correct: I came upon some Flaxon soldiers on horse and followed them. Then I lost my way and have been wandering ever since."

The scout looked at Ben curiously. "The ancestors chose a dangerous time to issue you with such misfortune, and I've no desire to have to field train a pup." The scout sighed. "My name is Raxx. You will be in my custody until safe passage can be issued for your return to Talon East. I field commission you to act as my temporary apprentice. Bear in mind, your every action will be recorded and handed to your otaa for review. Do exactly as I say."

"Without question, sir."

"Don't call me 'sir.' I am Raxx, scout master of the Jin Gung Myst under Commander Benataa Pinnaraa."

Ben's mouth fell wide open. "Benataa ... Oh, my ... I ..."

"Yes, do not be overawed. The ancestors have put you here for a reason, so ensure you do not disappoint them." Raxx looked at the wound inflicted on Ben's head by his blade. "Humph. Here. Let me fix the damage." Raxx pulled his field ration of trilix from a concealed pocket in his torso armor. "Stupid broznick, you nearly got a hole right between the eyes," he said, applying a thin smear of trilix liquid on Ben's wound.

The moment Ben felt the milky liquid on his flesh there was a brilliant blue glow. He felt strange, as if a piece of him went missing. The wound healed instantly. They heard a soft sigh on the wind, as though someone felt relieved.

"Kin in you is strong, little broz, I see that now. I have never seen the blue glow so bright in another. It means you are special and have hidden power."

"So everyone keeps telling me," said Ben.

The scout thought for a moment. Ben's heart pounded. He wanted to flee. But he knew it would be his undoing.

"We go for a closer look at the camp near here," Raxx said.

A noise from the camp drew Ben's attention. "The Flaxon camp ... down there?"

< 129 >

Raxx nodded. "You will play your part. Rejoice; it will be a story for your otutt to record in your life register. You may even get to kill your first Flaxon. That will bring some measure of kudos to compensate for your carelessness," he said, now with a voice of discipline.

"I will do my best," Ben said. *Beats a knife through the head,* he thought.

He wondered when he might ever see Dogg again—for now, though, this was his only option. Second, he knew the Scarzen were infinitely able to track him if he took off. Ben remembered that Uniss said he had to be out of sight—and at least seven feet away—for twelve seconds before he'd dissolve from the Scarzen's sight again. Then, with everything that Dogg said was going wrong with her abilities, he didn't know how that would affect him. He couldn't risk being caught in a worse position—and he knew the Scarzen would be on him in less than a clap of hands if he thought Ben was anything other than a Scarzen pup. Ben's muse was shunted by the feeling of the Myst officer shoving the half-eaten apple back into his lap.

"Stay here till I return. Eat—or they'll hear that stomach from a stone's throw."

Then, saying no more, the Scarzen left Ben where he sat. Casting a blur field upon himself, Raxx became almost transparent and then stealthily moved off. For about five seconds, Ben considered running.

*Won't work. He'll see me, then he'll make me into fish bait,* Ben thought. *I'm looking for the signs, Dogg. Don't know about timeline this or timeline that. The only ones I can find say, "Ben, for a sincere butt-kicking, walk this way." So, might as well see if this Raxx bloke can get me somewhere back to civilization where maybe you or Uniss can track me down.*

He sighed and resigned himself to stay put. By the late afternoon, the temperature dropped and the wind had picked up again. Uneasiness told Ben he was in for a bumpy night.

\* \* \*

An orange sunset signaled the close of day as Ben waited. In the short distance, he heard the sound of a plodding horse. Ben looked west to see a lone Flaxon soldier on horseback approaching the apple grove where he sat.

< 130 >

When the soldier saw the apple trees, his stomach grumbled. He thought for the first time about something other than salted pork and red-bean rice gruel that had been a staple the last fortnight. Ben sat dead still. Horse and rider stopped only feet away. Sitting on his horse, the rider pulled an apple. Before the rider could finish the first bite, Ben saw an approaching blur sweep in behind him. The shadow engulfed the rider like a silver-gray blanket. Ben heard a muffled cry of pain and the swift slice of cutting steel. The horse began to snort and stomp about. Then the Flaxon fell with a dull thud as his body hit the ground. The dead rider's horse settled and clomped around the tree, eating fallen apples. Then Ben saw the horse's head searching in some accessible branches for better fruit. In a blink, he saw Raxx become visibly solid and give the horse something. The horse eagerly snaffled up what was in Raxx's hand, and in moments, its legs gave way, leaving it to fall with an untidy thud asleep.

The scout moved directly to Ben, and in that moment, Ben knew that he had become visible again, probably from his reaction to the killing of the soldier.

"I gave her something to bring sleep, now we wait," said the Scarzen in his grave tone.

When the light of day was gone, Raxx reinstated his blur field.

"Stay on my heels, pup," said Raxx, moving off.

The two quietly descended to the camp perimeter. Observing the Flaxon camp, Ben and his newfound ally saw it was well lit in most areas. There were many pickets patrolling the perimeter, armed with what Ben thought were guns from Daniel Boone's time, making unseen entry difficult. To one side stood many tents in rows spaced to accommodate soldiers and stores. Groups of soldiers busied themselves with many duties. Some prepared sundries and tended the horses; others worked on assembling some kind of military apparatuses.

"They have brought artillery," said Raxx beside him.

In the dull light, Ben barely made out the blurred Raxx pointing to stacks of oil-soaked cane spheres on several wagons nearby.

In the short distance, smoke billowed from several fires, and Ben smelled

< 131 >

the beginnings of cooking on the night air—and thought it didn't smell half bad. That scent made Ben remember that he was still hungry. One large tent over to the right had a chimney where smoke spiraled out the top. Behind it, toward the back of the camp, several rows of horses stood tethered on a long line.

"That's where they eat," Raxx said, pointing. "That will be an important stop."

Ben wondered what Raxx wanted there. Raxx lay down on his belly, peering through the grass, thinking something through.

"I see two regiments of light horsemen and three companies of infantry, plus at least one heavy archer company," said Raxx.

He tapped Ben's shoulder and pointed out a fletcher sitting on a short barrel, making arrows. In one corner of the camp stood a line of flattop carriages not long arrived, each with an odd wheel standing vertically on the center of the wagon, along with a mix of other apparatuses. Alongside them, wagons carrying armor-piercing arrow racks for use in siege tactics stood by, ready for deployment.

"More heavy weapons. They are planning quite a party," said Raxx. "And who are they?" Ben heard Raxx add, noticing some oddly dressed soldiers arriving.

They escorted a number of wagons with strange sling-like mechanisms.

"I have no idea what they do," Raxx said, "but definitely some other kind of range weapon. Ruhe will not be pleased."

Looking across toward the center of the camp, they could see what looked like a command tent, identified by several royal flags stacked around it. It was heavily guarded and well lit.

"Assassination attempt there is out of the question—without alerting the whole Flaxon army, at least," said Raxx.

Ben relaxed a little, thinking they were about to retreat.

"Shortly, we move in," Raxx said.

\* \* \*

Raxx waited until mealtime had passed and then chose the kitchen

< 132 >

tent as his first target. With it now deserted, only one picket stood guard. Like snakes through grass, Ben and Raxx made their way around the back, keeping low via the shadows. Ben found it hard to keep up with Raxx at times. It amazed Ben how this large Scarzen could move so quietly for his size. Raxx even stopped once, giving him an odd glance. The pair stopped at the back of the tent near the chimney, coming within arm's reach of an unnoticed picket guarding the tent's rear. They slipped past him and then inside, using a loose flap without being seen or heard.

Inside the tent, low yellow lamplight filled the large rectangular area. At the back, the main cooking area was separated by trestle tables. Raxx moved straight to that area and found two water barrels marked *Officers Only*. A big smile appeared on Raxx's face as he pulled a small pouch from his utility belt. Raxx took two pinches of foul-smelling brown powder and sprinkled it into the water with an evil chuckle.

"This'll give 'em a butt storm they'll tell their pups about … if they live," said Raxx.

Ben thought the powder reeked while he watched Raxx quietly replace the lid. Raxx looked at him.

"In two scants, they won't smell or taste a thing," Raxx said. He then passed the pouch to Ben and pointed. "Do those other four barrels located around the perimeter."

Taking the pouch, Ben moved across to the barrels.

*He's mad smart,* he thought, realizing what was intended.

Ben took a pinch out of the pouch and sprinkled it in the water as Raxx had done. The pungent stuff smelled vile up close, and now it stuck to his fingers. He moved across to the next barrel, wondering if he'd throw up before he completed his task. He had just opened the pouch again to treat the next barrel when someone entered the tent up front. Ben froze upon seeing a guard carrying a lamp. Ben lowered his hand from the rim of the water barrel, staying still as stone, concealed in the shadows by the barrel. Several moments passed while the guard walked up the center between the tables. For a moment, he felt sure he heard someone whisper to him—but it wasn't Raxx. A splash of light from the guard's lamp exposed the lid

< 133 >

of the barrel Ben hid beside. He felt both terrified and exhilarated, and didn't know why the latter. Uniss's words echoed in Ben's mind: *"You can't walk through walls. If you bump objects, they will move or fall."* After a long moment, the lamplight drifted away. Leaving, the guard went over to the first contaminated barrel and drew a draught of water. Ben wondered where Raxx was and wished the guard would leave, but instead he sat down with the dipper cup. Ben caught sight of a faint blur moving toward the soldier and knew it was Raxx. He braced, thinking of what would happen next. Raxx closed in without a sound. The soldier drained his cup and stood to leave. Ben felt sure Raxx meant to do him in. Then, just out of arms' reach, Raxx stopped and nothing happened. The guard walked to the tent door, ignorant of how close he had come to death. For a fraction, he looked back and then left the tent. Ben relaxed and looked to the other end of the tent when he heard a small rustling sound, but seeing nothing, he breathed a sigh of relief. Then he almost wet himself as the vapor from Raxx's breath pressed on his cheek.

In a low ghoulish voice, Raxx said, "Finish the job, pup. There—that one. Quickly. We have little time."

Ben felt his protector nudge him toward one of the untreated barrels. *All right, I'm going.* Ben's legs moved before his brain finished. *When I next see Uniss, I want a new contract.* He finished his task, fumbling a bit with the powder on the last barrel. A good dollop of the stuff fell in with a small *plonk!*

*Ooo … bugger! Bit much, I think.* As soon as it was done, Ben looked over his shoulder for Raxx. *Where is he? Bloody hell.* He stood half up. *Where did you go?* Then he noticed a gap in the tent flap beside him. *One more look for Mister Creepy.*

He crawled under the flap to the outside. Fortunately, his exit placed him on the blindside of the camp. *Where to now?*

"Ben, Ben, pssst," came a familiar voice whisper.

He snapped his eyes right to see Dogg's vague outline secreted inside the hollow of a large fallen tree stump a few feet away.

"Get in here!" she said.

Ben scrambled over and crawled inside the big stump with her, kneeling

< 134 >

by her shoulder.

"Why didn't you stay where I put you? No telling who might have seen you," she snapped with concern.

"More than I was ready for," said Ben.

"What! Wait, your body field has crystallized. That means someone has seen you long enough for you to not escape their sight. Oh, Ben."

"Look, I'm not used to hearing people get their guts cut out and seeing bits get lopped off for real like a zombie movie, Dogg! And someone bloody well shot at my tree, nearly hit my head. Then I was caught by a Scarzen—Raxx. He was in the pass with Benataa. He's in there. Creepy as all hell," Ben said, pointing. "He's sure as eggs close by. Probably sitting in here with us," Ben said with a shiver to reinforce his defense.

"No. He's not. Let me try to destabilize your metta field."

Ben saw Dogg close her eyes in the dull light. He felt a wash of cold pass over him. Dogg opened her eyes.

"Right, at least I can still do that," Dogg said.

"What happened to you, Dogg?" asked Ben, sounding annoyed. "I thought you were never coming back. I called and called on the translator. Called Uniss, too, and no reply."

"No luck for me either there, I'm afraid," Dogg said. "I'm hoping he'll show up soon, although don't expect a cheery reception. Strange things are happening in a lot of places. Transition is becoming harder and harder, and there have been reports of agents here on Tora going missing. It's prob'ly Starlin interfering—could be someone worse, though."

"Well, as long as Herrex stays put, we should be okay ... right?" asked Ben.

"Even if we can contain him—and I'm beginning to have my doubts—others are equally as devious and powerful, should they choose to be," said Dogg. "We will have to be a lot more careful. Come on, we have to get out of here. I've seen a good hiding place till Uniss turns up. Stay close."

* * *

The time stood at two hours before midnight when a messenger from the Flaxon east camp galloped up. He pulled his horse to a stop in a cloud

< 135 >

of dust outside Magistrate Waldon's command tent. He dismounted and went straight past the sentry inside. There he found the magistrate and several of 3rd Army command standing around a table looking at a map of Yorr Fields. The messenger moved straight to the magistrate's aide and whispered. Waldon turned his head and saw the courier hand a dispatch to his aide—a dispatch with a black ribbon around it. Seeing it, Waldon knew that someone of significance had passed, and he raised an eyebrow of concern as his aide passed him the dispatch.

"Sir," said his aide, Spence.

Waldon took it, giving the lingering messenger a curious look. Breaking the seal, he began to read to himself:

*Attention to Magistrate Waldon.*

*Sir,*

*Regret to inform you of the battlefield passing of your son, Lieutenant Terrell Waldon the Younger, this day 2307-7-7 of Sun's Rise. Lieutenant Waldon's company bravely contested the enemy while being ambushed in Yorr Pass by the Scarzen unit pursued. An eyewitness account just to hand reports a 99 percent loss of Lieutenant Waldon's company. The individual surviving this reprehensible and murderous attack is presently in medical infirmary B camp Yorr Fields. With greatest respect and condolences, we now await your orders.*

*Signed Respectfully,*
*Commander Kollan*
*3rd Army, 2nd division*

The paper quivered in Waldon's hands before he seemed to almost faint. The officer beside Waldon caught him as he began to buckle at the knees

< 136 >

and then helped him into a nearby chair.

"Sir? What has happened?" the officer asked.

The magistrate bowed his head, covering his face with his hands. The officers looked at each other, frowning with puzzlement. The magistrate slumped back in the chair. The dispatch lay open in one hand. His bottom lip started quivering and his eyes shot with tears.

"My son Terrell … is dead," he said. "Dead! At the hands of thooosse!" His sentence finished not with words, but a balled-up fist.

He crumpled up the dispatch, his teeth gritted. A single tear ran down his right cheek. He wiped it away with an agitated wave of his hand. After some moments, he cleared his throat and straightened his posture. Then, feigning calm to focus on the officers who stood staring at him, he spoke with a voice beginning to crack:

"I want every one of those lizards caught. I want them ground to bone meal and fed to the pigs—except the one called Benataa. I want him alive. Bring him before me. That one is mine," he said, looking completely distraught.

An awkward silence descended upon the group, until flush-faced, the magistrate looked up at his quorum of officers.

"WELL?" he screamed. "DON'T JUST STAND THERE! PUT THIS ARMY TO WORK. BRING ME THAT SCARZEN!" he thundered. "And bring that eyewitness to me now!"

"Sir," Colonel Hitex said. "We each have the deepest sympathy for your son's tragic demise. He was a valiant soldier. But it would be folly to engage the enemy again so soon on their own terms. Night is their ally. We can affect a full victory in the early morning, when Flaxon can see what they should be killing!"

The colonel looked the magistrate straight in the eyes as he spoke. He hoped reason and better strategy would prevail. The magistrate stood slowly, a furious look in his eye. He went to speak sharply, then stalled and wilted in sadness.

"Very well," he said, more softly spoken. "Have them ready at first light."

Hitex saluted, followed by the rest.

"Now, leave me to my thoughts," said the magistrate.

< 137 >

They all saluted again and left him to grieve his loss.

< 138 >

## CHAPTER 11

# BROTHERS IN ARMS

Inside the pass entrance, the Scarzen gathered for the battle briefing. Muffled chatter surrounded Benataa as Raxx returned to report. Chatter stopped as the scout described the happenings at the west camp. Murmurs of hope rose upon hearing about the sighting of Tula, protector of all Scarzen. Raxx told Benataa about the curious find of Scarzen newborn—found and then lost—who helped in the sabotage during his time in the camp. That piece of news troubled Benataa. He eyed Raxx with concern for a moment, then patted him on the shoulder in congratulations on the bit of sabotage.

"If Tula and the luck of our ancestors are with us, we may yet get clear of this," Benataa said, looking around at his warriors.

"Seems to me the Flaxon intend on making an example," said Spanaje.

"Agreed," Benataa said.

*If we wait here much longer, their strength will have grown beyond our ability to contain or rout them. If that happens, Titarliaa's arrival could be irrelevant,* Benataa thought.

"Okay, hear me," Benataa said. "The enemy's first trap failed, and they have now fought us on our terms twice and been forced to capitulate. I think they are not likely to do the same again. Eyes on their camp suggest their next move will be severe. They would much prefer using distance weaponry to break our will and send us to the Halls of Ancestors without honor. No doubt, our pursuers are certain we still have the Tears and have hesitated only because of that fact. I now believe they have placed their recovery of their honor over retrieval of the Tears. They are wrong to think that way. Their anger and lust for revenge is their downfall. Blind with rage, their neck is fully extended and ripe to be severed."

"And so what strategy now, Ruhe?" asked Spanaje, looking beyond the pass entrance.

"The next question is how they intend to achieve that objective," Benataa said. "It is a Flaxon standard tactic to first draw out their enemy and then surround them, cutting off the retreat. In the next skirmish, I believe they intend a range weapons' exchange using those described by Raxx. They intend our utter decimation once we can no longer stand. But as long as they think we have the Tears, they will remain confused as to how far to take the carnage. Once they taste the end, their zeal for a slaughtering victory will drive them. They will rush from at least three points, making us fight on several fronts till it is done."

"I'll not die like a diseased womp rat struggling to pull free of a snare," said Spanaje.

"No. None of us will end that way. We go to meet them earlier than their preparations allow and bleed them before their combined efforts can be brought to bear."

"I'm for that," said Spanaje.

"The Flaxon east camp has several companies of mixed infantry from what Raxx says, mostly lightweight troops and only one heavy horse company that we know of."

Benataa walked away a couple strides toward the mouth of the pass and looked to the heavens. *Naught. Grant us this victory.* He turned around to face them.

"We go to the east camp to hit them in their beds and fill their dreams with nightmares. First, we eliminate the perimeter pickets from two sides. With that done, Moon Unit, you will go to deal with the officers." Benataa singled out two of his troops. "Raxx, Tanzaa: take the roving midfield pickets to suppress them being able to alert the west camp."

< 140 >

They nodded in acknowledgment.

"Sun Unit: Ajaa, Nixaa, Gorxaa, and Conax," Benataa said. "You deal with the heavy horse and supply company. Then poison the drinking water. And you, Enaxx," he said, pointing to another warrior, "you have the task of their commander. After that, improvise."

"Ho!" they all answered.

"We must decimate the east camp without a sound, inflict casualty that will break the enemies' will, and see that they cry a river of tears. Do it right and we achieve the larger objective: time for Titarliaa to arrive."

"Yes, Ruhe," they replied.

Benataa looked around. "It takes one hour for that exchange of patrols to make a full round. It's now two and a half standard hours past midnight. The Flaxon force will surely mobilize at the dawn." Benataa stepped back and raised a defiant fist. "Shine brightest in battle. Give our enemy something to write songs of lament about when word reaches Weirawind!"

"Oorah! Oorah!" the squad responded.

Everyone moved off to accomplish their tasks as stars pushed through the dispersing rain clouds. They passed beyond the forest quickly; a soft breeze cut from east to west as the Scarzen began their work. From both directions, all Flaxon movement seemed quiet as the assault party closed in on the east camp. It took little time for the Scarzen to take up positions around the camp. While a night bird called now and then, only the snoring of many sleeping Flaxon could be heard on the wind. It was dead calm when the nod was given.

\* \* \*

To the southeast of Magistrate Waldon's camp, Dogg led Ben up a slope and into a stone maze that sat proudly on a rise looking back toward the Yorr Forest.

*At least this feels right. Hopefully I can realign the thread and hopefully it will stay its original course. We keep Benataa alive right here in this place so he passes where he's supposed to during this battle, and finally we'll be back on track.*

"Ben, come on," said Dogg in a hushed tone. "It's alright; we are where

< 141 >

we're supposed to be."

"Why are you whispering? I thought no one else could hear us."

"Humph." *Damn.* "Because, my mind-link is fading in and out, and because, Ben, there are unfriendly ears on the wind. So keep your voice down. This will all be over soon." *I hope.* "Give me a minute while I try to call Uniss on the metta wave."

*"Uniss, can you hear me?"*

*Damn it, still nothing.* "Ben, stop here a minute."

Using her will, Dogg recalibrated the disc on her collar that served amongst other things as her universal translator. Ben saw three tiny pinhead lights flicker as she whispered an unintelligible password before speaking:

"Open encrypted channel. Trip log. Tula, person to person. Profiler Unity, voice print message: 'Uniss, I've uploaded this solid world mail through the *Cagney's* Triporian archive server. My metta-wave skill set is compromised. Herrex's strength is growing. He must have found a way to compromise the soul stream and metta comm planetside. Still no sign of Starlin. No contact from Farron for two standard days. We have made it to the crisis point time stamp: Yorr Fields 5.559, the stone maze, safe. Everything is in place. I think I can reestablish the thread stability here. End message.'" *Hopefully he'll access his solid world mail before this all goes down at dawn.* "Okay, come, Ben. There is a place in here where none will find us."

Walking along a natural stone corridor, it was damp, cold, and quiet amongst the huge stones. Wind whistled through the crevices, which made Ben shiver. As they moved deeper inside the maze, Ben noticed several other corridors just visible in the poor light. Now and then, he thought he heard a rustle, like soft steps nearby, making the place all the spookier.

"This is creepier than the pass, Dogg," Ben whispered.

"Shhh," she said, looking back over her shoulder.

He drew his collar up round his neck and hunched his shoulders for warmth. The stonewalls seemed like they were leaning upon him. Dogg entered a natural alcove on the right and Ben lost sight of her. Somewhere close by, Ben could hear crickets. He followed her cautiously. Inside, all at once the cricket sounds stopped.

< 142 >

"Bloody dark in here, Dogg."

Ben heard Dogg have a short shake. From her coat, tiny specks of light floated away like little glowworms. They settled against the walls, and slowly, a dim green glow filled the space.

"Wow, can you teach me that?" said Ben.

Now Ben saw water residue seeping in through the many cracks from outside, which fed orange lichen, following the moisture line from ceiling to ground.

Dogg turned to Ben and, in a sterner tone than usual, said, "Now. Sit and tell me everything you've seen, heard, and done. There is a trial coming and I want no surprises."

* * *

In tall grass midway between the east and west Flaxon camps, Scarzen intercepted the westbound Flaxon night patrol while the horse plodded along on return from the outfield. Raxx hid in long grass, watching the horse and rider amble past and then came at him from behind. Whirling a fine wire weighted on one end, Raxx flung the wire at the horseman. It wrapped around the soldier's neck twice and then Raxx gave a vicious yank, using the wire's anchor handle. The wire passed effortlessly through the soldier's flesh and bone, decapitating him instantly, leaving his head to fall and disappear with a thump in the grass. The horse faltered a little at first with a short neigh as the body slumped forward without falling from the saddle. Then, with the headless body spewing blood, the horse clomped on, following the rough trodden path toward the west camp. Using his blur field, Raxx trailed the horse and headless rider silently, and it was not long before the returning eastbound patrol could be heard approaching. The patrol made no change of pace or position, apparently seeing the horse and slumped rider. Instead, the soldier steered his horse closer to the other rider. *Fallen asleep again. Damn fool!* the patrolman thought and began to call softly: "Rance, you drunk again? Rance … sergeant'll have your stripes this time. I'll not cover for you again." *I'll shove him off his mount this time is what I'll do. Idiot could get us both killed.*

< 143 >

As the two horses drew adjacent in the darkness and wind whipped through the grass, the eastbound rider stuck his foot out to shove his counterpart, whose head appeared to be obscured by his mount's neck.

"Rance ... damn you. Wake up!"

As his boot touched the slumped soldier's shoulder, he felt a little cold sting at his throat and breathed his last, as his head, too, rolled off. Both horses became skittish and whinnied before scattering a few yards. Their noise carried some distance. Raxx quickly advanced forward and reined in both horses, then hid them in a cluster of trees nearby. Pickets on the edge of both camps stalled in their march momentarily when they thought they heard noises on the wind toward the center of Yorr Fields. But, hearing no more, both went on with their watch without reporting anything.

* * *

At the east camp, Benataa used a night bird call for the incursion to begin, and all Scarzen applied their blur fields. His units moved in from all sides, first taking down the pickets, then the officers in their beds, all to plan. One or two short squeals were heard, but they were only enough to disturb the lightest sleepers, who put on their boots and ventured outside. They found everything quiet. Benataa saw one soldier standing outside his tent in his boots and long johns, scratching his butt while looking about. One of the Myst appeared beside him and cut his head off, catching the severed orb before it had time to hit the ground, then tossed it away to the bushes. Each Scarzen chose a tent and cut through the back. Their weapons almost melted through the fabric, making only the tiniest sound. Then, one by one, they slit every Flaxon's throat.

* * *

When the patrols didn't return in their allotted time, the western camp duty sergeant sent two riders to see what had happened. These riders, too, were intercepted by Raxx, who had set the two horses of his earlier victims as bait.

*A little closer, broznick,* Raxx thought to himself, watching them approach.

< 144 >

*Come. Join your friends.*

His same tactic almost worked a second time when both new patrolmen halted and Raxx slung his garrote at the first mounted soldier. Having a higher neck collar with metal inlay, the slaa wire had more resistance, and instead of losing his head, the soldier toppled backward. He fell from his saddle, startling the other soldier, who raised his musket, ready to fire. The still-mounted soldier saw his opposite on the ground clutching at his throat. In puzzlement, he looked past him to see a tall shadow several yards away pulling on something in his direction and, with a hasty jerk of the trigger, yelled, "You! Halt!"

His weapon misfired with a *clack-fizz* of the striker and match.

"Turds!" the Flaxon growled and drew his dagger in time to see a dark shadow leaping toward him.

Raxx landed, planting one foot on the riderless horse's rump. The animal reared back as Raxx brought down a vicious backhand slash of his long knife across the nearby mounted rider's neck, and the melee ended.

\* \* \*

The sun would rise at the hour of 5.20. It now stood at fifteen scans of a Scarzen clock to 5.00. Camp awake trumpet sounded, and the western camp began to stir with activity. Water, dry biscuits, and corned beef were served to the officers on time. The general call to ranks for battle would come at ten strokes past 5.00. Most soldiers, though, had already assembled at the kitchen to receive rations early. Many men drew an extra draft of water from the drinking barrels in the mess tent while waiting. One officer with an acute sense of smell threw his water aside, thinking the problem lay in the tin of his cup, and then went on to have another draft. Trumpet call to order came, and all rallied to their posts. Readiness for battle was on everyone's mind.

\* \* \*

In the east camp, the bone-chilling sight of headless torsos still in nightclothes, stacked in tidy piles at every tent door, would shred the will

< 145 >

of the most hardened soldier intending reprisal, the Scarzen knew. Benataa had all the heads buried so the spirits of the dead could not ever be united with their ancestors. Only one terrified Flaxon was left alive. That came after a Myst warrior entered the medical infirmary tent to find six ill Flaxon in cots, along with the lone survivor of Yorr Pass—Silix—amongst them. Silix lay in his bed wide-awake, hearing the familiar muffled sounds of precision killing all around him.

*Oh no,* Silix thought. *Mercy, please not again. God in heaven, I'll be good. Let me live. I promise! Women and gambling—never again.*

His mind flooded with memories of the pass slaughter as he quivered under his cot blanket. Only hours earlier, he'd stumbled into a roving Flaxon patrol. Panic-stricken and chattering gibberish, the picket took him to the east camp infirmary, thinking him to be one of the soldiers from the earlier battle under Colonel Hitex's command. Now the horror had found him again. In the dim light of an oil lamp, in bed six, Silix lay there while everyone else appeared to be asleep. He closed his eyes hard and blocked his ears with the covers, feeling death and dismemberment creep his way. Then, just outside his tent wall right next to him, he heard a faint slice and gasp, then the collapse of someone falling to the ground. Breath held and teeth gritted, he heard another slice and thump just inside the front door of the infirmary. With the blanket up to his nose, he rolled his head to the right, eyes like saucers, and looked toward the entrance as the lamplight exposed a tall shadow. Then the flap was pressed back slowly, and through it, silent as moonlight, stepped a Scarzen warrior who moved from bed to bed, killing everyone. Finally, it was his turn. He cried but nothing came out.

*I'll be good! Cripes, I'll be good!*

The ghoulish Scarzen swiftly crept to the alert prey. Silix felt the black cold steel of a blade lay against his throat, and he resisted enough to pull the blanket off his face and neck, kicking his legs. The Scarzen stopped when he recognized the light-reflecting pendant around Silix's neck. Clamping a hand over Silix's mouth, the Scarzen put the tip of his blade under Silix's eye and said in a snarled whisper, "Be still." Silix lay there, still as a dead salmon. The Scarzen took keen interest in the pendent, thinking for several

< 146 >

breaths. He remembered standing next to Benataa when Ruhe gave this soldier a reprieve while holding this pendant.

Then, leaning closer and putting a rough finger to his lips, he said, "Shh!" *Lucky little hopper,* the Scarzen thought.

*God. Please make it quick!* Silix thought.

The Scarzen's bright orange eyes, cold in the faint lamplight, held no pity. He withdrew his bloodstained blade and whispered, "It is fortunate for you. You have protection of my ruhe. By his grace, you still breathe."

*Thank god! Thank you, god!*

"Go into the hills. Stay there till afternoon. Do not come out in plain sight. I will be watching and slit you in half if you do. Nod yes."

Silix nodded and began to blubber, and the Scarzen cupped his mouth and nose with one hand.

"Go! Before I forget my commitment," the Scarzen said.

Trembling and looking at the Scarzen, he swallowed slowly. He felt a long uncomfortable breath of silence. Then the Scarzen smelled the stench of urine from the Flaxon and gave the weak creature a shove to leave the tent. "Go."

\* \* \*

Lance Corporal Silix Tranor wandered into the west camp aboard an unsaddled mare at 5.25 of the morning. His ride plodded to an unassisted halt. Awkwardly he slid off his mount near a supply tent by some bushes. Grimy faced, hair a twisted mess, stinking of shit and fear, he froze with arms crossed in a nervous shiver, hearing the trumpet blast call to ranks. Wide-eyed, Silix's view darted left and right, watching soldiers urgently move to position. Most that did have eyeshot of him avoided the disheveled soldier. They wanted none of what was troubling him. Then, a corporal from his section who knew him saw the out-of-order soldier and hurried over to see what had happened.

"Oh, the gods have cursed you today, Silix!" said the corporal, looking at him with a concerned expression. "We are off to war and you look like you've been on the bottle and should be clapped in irons. Where have you

< 147 >

been? You know you've been listed dead?"

"Almost was—twice," said Silix with a crazy man's gap-toothed grin.

"They'll friggin' hang you this time, you damn fool," the corporal said. "Why did you fail to report for muster before we left Weirawind, Silix? Corporal Logan told me you were seen with Lieutenant Waldon's company, leaving the stables."

"The stables, I was at the stables. I like the smell of the stables."

"What! Have you got a friggin' death wish, balls for brains? Lieutenant Ichenstride'll have your arse digging shit pits forever. And the sarge said he was going to nail ..." The soldier slowed in his rebuke, then stopped. "Shit, Silix. What happened?"

Silix looked at his friend through bloodshot eyes. "He said if I went to the hills and stayed away, I could keep me neck, hee-hee." He raised a dirty finger to his lips. With the low, hushed voice of someone telling a secret, he only said: "Myst coming! Terrible Myst. Shhh!"

His friend frowned, then looked more closely at Silix. "Come on, old mate. Let's get you to the infirmary."

"Infirmary? No, no! It's not safe, not safe at all. They'll know I told you and slit me throat. They'll know I told and give me neck a smile." Silix began to sob uncontrollably. "I want to go home, Jacob. Don't want to be a soldier anymore."

Silix's friend took him to the infirmary tent and reported the situation to his sergeant, praising Silix's miraculous escape from Yorr Pass as his defense.

"He got away, Sarge, with all but his life."

As the corporal and sergeant were chatting by a wagon, Colonel Hitex walked past on his way to the latrine. He overheard a part of the conversation that slowed him, but nature's call forced him on. The contaminated water had started to take effect on all who drank it. Soldiers and officers experienced severe stomach pain and cramps with an urgent need to throw up or shit, sometimes both at once.

Back in his tent, reading the list of names in a report about Yorr Pass, Colonel Hitex remembered the sad, lost soldier being referred to as he passed the corporal and sergeant earlier near the infirmary. Their conversation referred

< 148 >

to men lost in Yorr Pass. It struck Hitex that the soldier in the infirmary must be the single survivor of Lieutenant Waldon's company lost in Yorr Pass. He hurried to the infirmary to find a broken Silix Tranor sitting there, arms around lifted knees on the edge of a cot, still in his dirty nightshirt. Hitex managed to get some scraps of information from the medic, who confirmed where he'd come from, and then he sent for Magistrate Waldon immediately.

Magistrate Waldon soon burst into the infirmary tent.

"This better be what I want, Colonel," said Waldon to Hitex, holding one hand on his abdomen, beginning to feel the crippling effects of the drinking water. Waldon looked at the decrepit individual sitting on a cot in front of him. "What can this maggot have to say? He looks as though he's lost his mind."

Hitex only gave a small shrug of his shoulders.

"Were you in Yorr Pass, Corporal Tranor, with Lieutenant Waldon's company?" Waldon asked.

Silix lifted his head slowly and stared at Waldon, then he nodded nervously. "Yorr Pass, yes—horrible things, dark things … happened there." He looked away before nattering on. "Demons let keep my arms and legs. The others lost theirs quick as choppin' corn." He looked up at Waldon. "My girl's hair is so beautiful. Have you seen her? Smells like wild flowers."

"He has battle shock, sirs," said the medic to the officers. "We know his identity for sure and that he was listed with Lieutenant Waldon's column. He keeps saying something about the east camp, but it's just gibberish. He is the sole survivor from Yorr Pass massacre, sir. His mind has broken."

"Well, what good is he like this? How can he tell us anything?" Waldon said in disgust.

Slowly, Silix pointed away to the east before whispering, "The camp, the camp, they danced all over the jolly old camp."

"HEY! IMBECILE!" Waldon roared. "Give me something pertinent or I'll have you strung up this very day and gutted!"

"Shhh!" Silix said. "Scarzen are here! They followed. Found me in my bed and cut up all the sleepy heads." He looked up with a slapped-face expression and stood slowly. "Can I go home? I really need to go home.

< 149 >

He'll know I told you. Don't want to be here when they visit."

"Oh. God be with us, NO!" Hitex exclaimed as he realized the meaning of the garbled words and gesture of pointing east. *The east camp! Saints alive, no!* "I need a scouting party right now!" Hitex ordered his attendant.

Waldon grabbed Silix by the collars. "You will die by my hands here and now if you don't start making sense, you miserable toe rag."

"Sir!" Hitex said to Waldon.

The magistrate ignored him. "Make sense, you blithering idiot!" he said, shaking Silix by the collars.

"Sir!" Hitex broke in, placing his arm between the two. "We must act now. All could be lost."

The magistrate flung Silix backward, and he fell on his cot.

"Do what you must, Colonel!"

Hitex rushed from the tent with all hope that he was wrong.

\* \* \*

Still some distance away, Commander Titarliaa's column had been on forced march since joining up with the Talon West contingent. Their final numbers came to just under three thousand foot soldiers and drommal-mounted troops ready to fight. Now they were less than two hours from the Flaxon position as the column marched through the southwest gap of the Mustard Fields.

< 150 >

## CHAPTER 12

# SHAKE THE GROUND

T he east camp taken care of, Benataa turned his attention to the west camp.

"My clan," Benataa said. "We must get their attention once more. It is time to draw their focus from the west so our allies can bring their welcome." *Perhaps we are yet to truly prevail.* "Come, we head west."

Covering ground at the strongest pace, Benataa moved his warriors to some raised ground where a tight cluster of young stendle trees grew.

*Here we can make a stand.*

The position stood not far from the midpoint between the two Flaxon camps, marked by a boulder cluster on another rise away to the south. Basic defenses had just begun when Benataa saw in the distance a unit of galloping Flaxon riders speeding toward the east camp.

*Soon, they will know. Not much time,* Benataa thought.

"Make ready, clan. The final consult dawns soon."

Benataa watched as the five Flaxon riders topped the rise a short distance from the east camp and stopped.

\* \* \*

The sight that met the eyes of the Flaxon scouts filled them with horror.

"They are all dead—every one of them!" the unit second-in-command said.

"Butchered, you mean. Come on, we have to report this right away," the unit commander said.

In the time it took to clap hands three times, they had wheeled around and sped back toward the west camp.

\* \* \*

As the horsemen passed within one hundred strides of Benataa's squad, he ordered his best archer to take down a single rider with an arrow. The warrior stood side on and drew upon a heavy reverse curve bow and loosed the shaft. The arrow whistled through the air and struck the second rider in the upper chest. He slumped and fell, passing under the hooves of the horses trailing behind.

"Nice shot!" said the archer's battle ally.

"I was aiming at the lead horse," said the archer.

The remaining horsemen looked in their direction while galloping on to report what they'd seen and the Scarzen position.

Once the patrol disappeared over the tree-littered rise, Benataa ordered his squad to split in two. One section stayed in the grove. The other moved wide and north of that position back toward Yorr Forest.

"Circle wide. Flank them from the north," he told them.

Benataa looked toward the Flaxon west camp position. *Splitting now is risky. Can't help it. Needed to buy time. Titarliaa will not be far away now. Then we will end them.*

\* \* \*

In the Flaxon west camp, a dark mood burdened command with the report of what happened to the east. Many held doubts over the best strategy to follow.

*How am I supposed to affect a sound victory now?* Hitex thought. *Better to retreat and gather true strength. Dysentary and illness afflicting most officers ... Issuing orders while their backsides are permanently in a latrine means almost no worthy chain of command. This is ludicrous.*

< 152 >

"Sir, we are nearly ready," announced an orderly.

"Very well," answered Hitex with a harrumph of frustration.

*Everything in chaos, ranks responding slowly. The stench alone is overwhelming.* He felt his stomach rumble and covered it with a hand. *What have I got to work with?* Hitex thought hard. *Wait! Soams's special unit. It's isolated. Surely they won't have been affected by the poisoned water.*

"Sir," the orderly said. "Ten minutes until the columns reach attack position. We still have many units without commanding officers."

"Then use NCOs, damn it!"

"Yes, sir."

The Flaxon army headed east to close on the reported position of the enemy. Hitex ordered a three-column split: two large forward columns and one smaller column to the rear for a standard pincer and ram maneuver on the Scarzen position. Two scout patrols went wide of the flanks to report any unusual activity and act as spotters.

\* \* \*

Though Benataa knew the Flaxon force would suffer thanks to the contaminated water, he had no way of knowing if damage was great or small.

*Will Old Angry get here in time? Scraa, not enough known factors.*

Benataa's section of the squad consisted of twenty. The second group had a complement of only thirty-eight to flank unknown odds, and a short squad of the remaining nine covered the pass. Benataa looked to the cloudless sky.

*Wind's slow and eastward. We won't be able to stall here for long,* he thought with an imperceptible shake of the head. *Hmm.* He looked to the ground. *The insects through the grass are restless. Maybe another weather change.* He closed his eyes and listened to the birdsong from the trees overhead. Then, suddenly, the singing stopped. In the silence, away in the distance, he could hear troop movements on a large scale.

\* \* \*

Several heavy onega catapults sat off to Hitex's right, ready to deploy from an elevated hillock in full range but beyond that of their quarry. The Flaxon

< 153 >

spotters on the steeper southern slopes began signals for the coordinated long-range attack.

"Sir. Sigs alerts from the spotters for the onega."

Hitex looked across his shoulder to the spotters' position. "Yes. Very well."

He looked back to the target zone.

*So, holed up in there, hmm?* Hitex glanced across to the regent's representative, who now sat on his blindside. *Bloody vulture.*

Waldon sat aboard a tall gray stallion on Hitex's right, looking very sour. Hitex ordered the battle-ready whistles blown. Quickly, the flag signals commenced for the barrage to begin. Each onega rolled forward, sitting on top of a flatbed wagon controlled by a team of five men and four draft horses.

"Unshackle the horses," ordered a color sergeant.

The horses were quickly unshackled and led to the rear.

"Place chocks!"

Troops chocked the wheels and threw on the locking brakes. Many races in Ludd used this kinetic energy weapon with a single torsion loosing post; the Flaxon onega, however, had two, which gave them capacity to hurl much heavier payloads.

"Begin targeting!" ordered Hitex.

Each onega's primary operator swung a long crank handle out to the side of a large clockwork assembly, locking it in position. Two soldiers then removed some rods from the center of the platform and, like a seesaw, the bed supporting the onega swung free, floating on a central pivot.

"Get lively, get lively!" ordered the color sergeant.

A trooper ratcheted a lever on the side of the platform, which tilted up several degrees at the front.

"Place lock pins!" the color sergeant barked.

That done, the men put their backs into winding the crank. Gears turned with clanks and latch-tapping sounds. As they wound the handle, a stressed noise rose as torsion developed in the onega launching arms. With full torsion reached, soldiers applied a neck latch, locking the loosening post in the ready position.

The team leader stepped away from the weapon, raising a red flag and

< 154 >

shouting, "READY!"

"Colonel," Waldon said, "I want those roaches crisp and well charred, understand? We'll pick the prize out of the ashes later."

*Blind vengeance. A first step to defeat,* Hitex thought.

"Sir," Hitex said to Waldon, "your father's orders are to retrieve the stolen artifacts undamaged. Acting to the contrary would be disobeying a directive from the regent himself should I neglect that!"

Waldon's expression hardened. "I'll tell you what would be more prudent, Colonel. It would be more prudent not to make an enemy of me, particularly since my father's health is rather fragile and I stand next in line for the regency. Do as I ask," he ordered in a bitter tone, glaring at the colonel.

Hitex stared at Waldon, then let out a slow breath. "Very well," said the colonel.

Colonel Hitex gave the color sergeant on the ground a nod. Another whistle blew. The last two men standing behind each onega moved into position: one called a triggerman, the other wearing a red cape and known as the match. The match positioned himself behind the onega's two hurling pod bays with a lit torch. Each onega hurling pod had been loaded with a terracotta urn filled with flammable oil and pitch. Then came the command ...

"LOOOSE!" the color sergeant roared.

For Hitex, things seemed to slow down while watching the nearest match man touch the common wick and the triggerman pull on the throwing lever. The projectiles flew skyward with a well-known deep *woodoomp* and *clatter* sound.

*What will you do with this, warriors of Scarza?* Hitex asked himself.

As the first burning spheres fell to earth just short of the target, the ground near the grove burst into flames.

"A good start," Waldon announced with a short laugh. "Hit them, Hitex! Burn them to ash."

*Stupid politician. Just let a soldier do his work!*

"Yes, sir," Hitex said.

The colonel ordered a company of heavy archers forward to flank the target position and hem them in.

< 155 >

\* \* \*

After the first volley crashed short, spreading fire everywhere against an eastbound breeze, Benataa's line of sight swung skyward again to the west. A second volley was already on its way. Each incendiary trailed with a thread of black smoke.

"DISPERSE BARRIER!" Benataa commanded just before the munitions crashed amongst the trees in front of their position, spreading more flames and burning pitch in all directions.

Soon, a thick choking smoke belched up from the grass. Another and another barrage crashed down upon the earth, progressively zeroing in with each volley.

"Ruhe!" a Myst officer called.

Benataa looked through the smoke. The officer pointed to a southern position where a spotter could be seen. He swung a trajectory flag for artillery back and forth.

"He's too far!" Benataa said. "INCOMING! BARRIER!"

*Boom! Crash!*

Incendiaries splashed sparks everywhere near the edge of the position now.

*Come on, Titarliaa! I'm running out of options. Get your hairy backside up here.* He looked northwest. *Where's my second unit? A sellenor to spot with would be handy now. Too much ground to cover to get amongst them …*

Fire now burned all around the Scarzen position. Warriors used their kin to bend the flames back with the breeze. Benataa knew their repelling efforts would not be sustainable for long under these constant barrages. Slowly, even his resilience was being tested. The incendiaries struck the trees with ever-increasing accuracy.

*Naught, put us back in grace.*

Benataa scanned for any alternative or escape, looking past the bodies of two dead clan.

*There—up the slope south. That collection of large boulders. It's in the open, but we could hole up there. If we could make it, the stone would afford a better defensive position. It's a two-hundred-stride sprint to make it … under full fire. That or we get burned out here. Thanks to Naught for small graces.*

< 156 >

*Okay. Time to go.*

"Unit relocation, on my command, the rock formation, south by southwest," ordered Benataa. "I need five volunteers to remain for the illusion until we have reached the objective," Benataa said.

He did not have to wait to press any into service. Five volunteered immediately. Warriors formed a Scarzen battle circle with Benataa and three others in the center. Those in the center focused their kin as a unit on the flimsy breeze to hold the smoke at bay. Other warriors tried to pick off an advancing Flaxon line with their bows.

\* \* \*

Under the cover of a blur spell, smoke, and flame, Benataa led his unit up the slope at a cracking pace against random volleys of musket fire whizzing past. Several Scarzen were wounded.

The Flaxon spotter on the hill near the southern ridge saw the small group unveil themselves near the stone maze and signaled command of the new enemy position.

Realizing that the Scarzen had split their force, Colonel Hitex responded by moving some infantry and heavy archers to be within range of the maze to pin them down. He ordered one onega repositioned to strike the maze and then sent widespread successive arrow volleys there to keep the Scarzen suppressed.

*We may yet win this day, even with all our troubles thus far. Yes ... I'll have you shortly, Scarzen commander,* Hitex thought.

"Don't lose them, Colonel. Not one of them, you hear!" Waldon said.

Hitex sighed. *Where's a good Scarzen archer when you need one?*

\* \* \*

Flaxon artillery continued to pound the burning cluster of trees at the first Scarzen position. Those amongst the burning trees tried to maintain a windshield defense against arrows and incendiaries. Most now stood injured. Some began to gather and project fireballs of their own back toward the enemy, but they all dissipated out of range. With their strength fading fast and

< 157 >

trilix exhausted, hope dwindled with still no sign of Commander Titarliaa.

From their sanctuary in the stone maze, Ben watched the exchange with Dogg through a small rock cavity as the Flaxon onega hurled incendiaries into where the Scarzen made their first stand; then, an incendiary crashed to earth in their direction.

"Thought you said it was safe here, Dogg?" Ben said, shooting her a glance.

"Well, it's safer than over there, which was my other choice."

"You also said the tree was safe—and the ledge! Look how that all worked out," Ben said.

"They were supposed to be, but things have changed. None of that should have happened," said Dogg.

"Yeah, but some of the warriors from the trees are coming here now," Ben said.

*Bloody hell. Is the fight coming here too?*

"It will be alright. Everything is mostly happening as it should, Ben," she said.

"Mostly! Well, it seems to me that we are about to get visitors—which means all the Flaxon are going to want to come here, too. I don't want to be barbequed like those guys down there, Dogg."

"I know, neither do I, but we have a task to perform and you're about to have to make a choice."

"Choice? What choice?"

"Don't worry, Ben. Everything is as it should be. You could try to leave, but if you go out there, things will greatly change again and we could all be in worse danger."

"Oh really? Worse than the last couple days? Scrape a bone, Dogg! I've already been shot at, had a Scarzen try to stab me through the head, and fell off a cliff. How could it be damn worse?"

"We have things to do here, Apprentice. Now, do as you're told. Sit down and observe! And watch the doorway for company. There's not a lot of room in here," Dogg snapped.

< 158 >

* * *

Just as he went to pass into the maze, Benataa's attention was caught by the sound of whistling incendiaries. He turned in time to see many smoldering black dots rising in a high-arching trajectory toward the clutch of trees they had just left. As the projectiles struck the treetops over his warriors, they burst, showering heavy burning pitch in all directions. On that occasion, the incendiary shower was dispersed by the Scarzen barrier.

Then Benataa noticed that Flaxon heavy archers had crept in closer. In significant number, they began to pick off Scarzen, which in turn weakened the defense shield. As more onega incendiaries struck through the trees at oblique angles, Benataa saw the Scarzen defense begin to fold rapidly. In that instant, he felt a great sadness for the inevitable loss of his warriors. He saw one of his warriors, a small figure in the distance, get struck directly by one of the fiery masses and burst into flame, trying to leave the position.

A large heavy hand fell upon his shoulder in that frozen moment.

"Ruhe, we must continue," said Spanaje in a deliberate manner. "They die with honor."

Benataa wrenched his line of sight back to his present position and went inside the stone maze.

* * *

Approaching the opening onto Yorr Fields from the west, Commander Titarliaa could see the smoke spiraling skyward in the distance.

"They have started without us, you lazy broznicks," he said over one shoulder. "This won't do! Time to run into the fray. There are Flaxon to be had! HAA!"

* * *

Crouched in the main corridor of the maze, Benataa tried to think through his next steps. *Where are you, Titarliaa?*

Over in the clutch of trees, good fortune had run out for the remaining Scarzen. Hellfire pressed on them from every side. Only two survivors held their ground as their kinetic barriers broke and random trees fell. They fled

< 159 >

by the north flank of the grove, only to be pin-cushioned by hundreds of armor-piercing arrows.

The tree grove unit was dead.

\* \* \*

Inside the stone maze, Benataa knew the Flaxon would close in soon. He looked at his remaining warriors.

*Several wounded. Their kin will be low. Spanaje looks unharmed; that's good. We must hold out, with Naught's grace. This place looks about fifty strides across and only thirty long. The west end of that corridor is a weak point.*

"Cover the west end, search for ambush advantage," Benataa said.

All the warriors spread through the maze for good defensive positions. *Fifteen spans high. That should keep most of the fire off.*

Then, on the wind, he heard the shrill call of Scarzen war horns.

*Titarliaa, finally! Still a ways off, though. Get your old bones up here, Titarliaa.*

He breathed a small sigh of relief as battle engagement outside turned eerily quiet.

\* \* \*

On the stone maze's west flank, Captain Soams approached with his three units of the 12th Stronghold Guard—or TSG. Colonel Hitex was right: Soams had kept his troops isolated and so the poisoned water in the camp had not affected their rations. Earlier, Soams had seen the stone maze from his camp position and planned to take up position there if things went in favor of his enemy. Soams wanted his TSG to use this war theater to show command what his unit could do. When his scout had returned ten minutes ago with news of the new Scarzen position, Soams rallied his soldiers to attack the maze.

"This is it, lads. Let's show command and the blasted Scarzen what the TSG splinter can achieve," said Soams, ordering his men to take up position. *Time to make a good account of ourselves,* he thought.

The TSG nicknamed their weapon the "Master of Ceremonies." Soams tagged it that way after an officer standing behind an unannounced release

< 160 >

of a rocket took fright during testing. The officer disgraced himself by defecating when the rocket backfired and the rear discharge removed his hat. General Fluge, commander of the 2nd Army and also an observer at the time, had said, "That made him stand to attention."

Now Soams intended for the Scarzen to do the same.

* * *

Inside the alcove, Ben sat, nervous with the growing calamity outside—and he now felt trapped. *Like being a snared rabbit. Have to sit tight and wait to be found with nowhere to run. Idiot! We're bloody stuck.* "Those fire bombs will be on our heads any minute, Dogg. You said we'd be safe."

"Our safety is relative to how much change we've brought to this thread, Ben, and you have interfered a lot. Things are changed, and now unpredictability will prevail. Many are dying at the wrong time and Herrex's strength is growing in the background because of it. We must now look for a way to change events for the better," she said.

"What are you talking about? I'm not going to touch anything." *Haven't I screwed up enough already?*

"You haven't screwed up, Ben," said Dogg, hearing that thread of his thoughts. "You just didn't do what you were told. Every bit of participation has consequences as we go along, Ben—learn that quickly. Now, stop feeling sorry for yourself and pay attention."

Just then, the tall frame of a Scarzen slid across the opening of their hide.

* * *

Up the hill through the rock seams to his left, Benataa could see a Flaxon flagman frantically signaling down to Flaxon command. Then trumpets for repositioning could be heard.

"They're coming," Benataa said to Spanaje.

"That's to be seen. It could be that our flanking unit has distracted some strength away," said Benataa.

"Ruhe. At least twelve hundred Flaxon swinging around into our position," said a warrior crouched on a rock ledge. "Including some heavy cavalry."

< 161 >

"Maybe not," said Spanaje.

\* \* \*

On the battleground's north side, Benataa's other Scarzen unit moved to antagonize the Flaxon flank, as ordered. The commander, Galaa, ordered his unit to skirt the base of a low hillock. Breaking right, Galaa and his unit ran headlong into a column of medium and heavy troops divided into three companies, accompanied by several Flaxon net catapults.

*The consult greets us early,* Galaa thought.

"Ready your ends of peace—weapons of Scarza," Galaa said. "Overlap battle circles. There's Flaxon on the menu."

The Scarzen slowed to a walk and formed three battle circles, each containing a defensive warrior in the center as they advanced.

Seeing the Scarzen, the surprised Flaxon force swung into attack formation.

"War chant!" Galaa shouted.

"JI-HA, JI-HA!" all chanted, weapons drawn.

\* \* \*

When the Flaxon commander between two of his ranks saw the size of the Scarzen unit, he filled with confidence, knowing the weight of numbers was in their favor.

"You have to give it to the Scarzen, lads! These bastards would charge a clutch of hungry crockengators with their bare hands," he told his men. "Trumpeter, set charge pace. Let's give them something to think on."

A single bar of trumpet call rang out, and the Flaxon began to run. The Scarzen quickened their pace to a steady run, and the defense began hurling repel barriers into the oncoming Flaxon. Earth and men flew. Neither force faulted in their trajectory. For many Flaxon, their view narrowed to a forward corridor, along which they ran with the enemy hurtling toward them. The commander called for full charge as a Flaxon soldier deep in the ranks screamed a war cry, spurring the Scarzen to high gear first. The two forces collided with a crash of mortal bodies, and all that was evil and merciless in war at close-quarter broke loose. With that eruption, from the flank one

< 162 >

of the net-gun crew panicked, tripped, and fell against the horse-drawn net-gun throwing lever. There was a whip and a *whoosh* as a whirling metal splinter-pierced net soared high through the air. It landed near the center of a large melee. Seeing the net launched, in the confusion the other net gunners fired their lot as well.

"GIVE 'EM HELL!" roared the Flaxon commander, charging at one Scarzen.

But the Scarzen vaulted over him like a high-wire acrobat and, on the tumble overhead, drove a blade through his spine and out his sternum. The commander fell and was trampled by his own horse threshing about amongst the whirling blades, musket fire, and energy barriers. Flaxon numbers pressed on the Scarzen circles like ants trying to bring down a great beast. The two remaining Scarzen battle circles tightened, one inside the other. The inner circle projected constant barrages of kinetic barriers to repel the masses as the outer circle cleaved anything that came within range.

"TURN 'EM TO CORN GRUEL, PUPS. COME ON, SAUCER EYES. TASTE THIS!" Galaa yelled, sounding euphoric while pulling his blade from a soldier's neck.

Scarzen were forced to use great reserves of kin to keep the ocean of Flaxon at bay. Stray Flaxon musket-shot found as many friendly targets as it did enemy, and some netting snagged ally and enemy alike. Things soon degenerated into a slash and club fest of angry figures bent on destroying everything in reach. The net's metal spines dragged against armor straps, flesh, and scale without bias. Frantic Flaxon with sword or spear often missed their intended target, spearing one of their own. Superior numbers against them, the Scarzen still made the Flaxon death count high, and soon bodies were being walked over to continue.

Five hundred and seventy Flaxon and thirty-eight Scarzen perished as those moments passed. When it was done and the Scarzen were all dead, the remainder of the Flaxon troops, bloodied and torn about with revenge and pride driving them, turned south, heading for the stone maze.

< 163 >

\* \* \*

Inside the maze, the last few moments for Ben had been very tense. The Scarzen warrior outside had not continued on; instead, they remained outside his doorway. *How will we ever get past now?* Ben thought. *The roof is low but they could still enter if they wanted.*

Then, without him activating his universal translator, it crackled with white noise and a degrading voice signal could be heard.

"Dogg! Ben! Can either of you hear me? I can't get a fix on your position. I'm being tracked."

"Uniss!" Dogg said, picking up the same signal. "We are at Yorr Fields, time stamp, crisis point three. Acknowledge."

The signal fell dead without her knowing if they'd connected, and activity outside drew their attention to more immediate matters.

"They know we're in here, don't they, Dogg?" Ben asked.

Then, for no apparent reason, the Scarzen blocking the doorway moved on. Relieved, Ben ventured forward for a look out into the corridor.

"Careful," Dogg said.

He went to poke his head out for a look, and another Scarzen walked up, close enough to touch. From the door shoulder, wide-eyed Ben saw the gold tabs on his braids that showed the Scarzen's rank as a Brasheer Myst commander—it was Benataa.

*Cripes, you're big up close!* Ben's heart jumped a beat as Benataa's presence saturated him. *It's like standing in front of a warrior god.*

"Ben, move back! The original thread is about to unfold," Dogg said.

Ben heard Dogg, but ignored her as all fear evaporated and he felt suddenly connected to Benataa somehow. Benataa turned to speak to one of his troops. At that moment, Ben turned his head to look out the other way to the end of the corridor. An expression of horror crossed his face. Without warning, two pairs of Flaxon soldiers stepped into the opening, shouldering black-muzzled cylinders. The weapon holders knelt while the other pair stood, each holding a small smoking stick, then set to fire the weapons. A double crack sounded as the trigger mechanism was engaged. The rocket left the cylinder, speeding toward its target as it spiraled down the corridor.

< 164 >

In that fraction of time, Dogg wasn't expecting what happened next.

"LOOK OUT!" Ben screamed to warn Benataa.

Benataa heard the screamed warning and swung his view around. Seeing the threat approach from the end of the corridor, Benataa began to lift a fist full of gathered energy to release a barrier, but it was too late. Prior to impact, he glimpsed the small figure in the doorway who had warned him. The figure pulled their head back just in time for the TSG soldier's rocket to pass his doorway, striking Benataa squarely in the pelvis. The kinetic shock wave drove Benataa backward, sprawling to the ground, mortally wounded.

Knocked down by the impact, Ben felt Benataa's blood spatter all over his face and neck. A shard from the shrapnel left a gash at the side of Ben's jaw, which should have bled profusely, but it closed up within seconds while Dogg looked on in amazement.

*Oh my, what in Naught's beard has happened?* Dogg thought.

Then she saw Ben look at her in a dazed manner, and his eyes showed a faint orange line around the iris. She went to move closer to examine him, but outside, other Scarzen began to charge past the nook exit when another rocket exploded, stopping them in their tracks. The shock and ground shudder sent Ben and Dogg to the ground again. As the dust cleared, Ben looked out to see Benataa lying just outside the nook, barely conscious. His eyes opened slowly as Dogg moved to Ben's side. For Benataa in that moment, all façades between mortal and ethereal worlds fell away, and he saw both of them as they truly were.

Benataa reached out, taking a breath and saying, "One honorable Flaxon …"

They saw Benataa's body surface glow faintly, and a fine mist gravitated toward Ben and passed through him. Dogg noted that the orange in Ben's eyes had not diminished.

"Oh dear. This isn't right," said Dogg. "His cycle didn't conclude here before, not right here. He was only supposed to be wounded here in the corridor. The timeline has permanently been altered."

Ben dragged himself to his feet and leaned against the alcove shoulder, feeling weak in the knees. He watched Benataa's body fall limp as he breathed

< 165 >

his last.

* * *

Into the west-end corridor, two more armed soldiers stepped up, splinters set ready. They fired, and several advancing Scarzen were cut down. Spanaje had been toward the rear covering the east-end corridor, remaining unharmed, and returned to see Benataa on the ground, dead. Fires of vengeance filled him.

*RUHE!*

He saw the Flaxon at the other end and propelled himself through a gap on the high side of the maze, then headed for the outside. With all determination, Spanaje made his way around to the Flaxon unit.

* * *

Inside the maze, another volley of rockets sped up the corridor, once more passing the alcove doorway.

"Come on, Ben!" Dogg said, bolting from the nook and turning hard left. "Follow me."

Ben didn't think; he just followed. A few yards down the corridor, Dogg darted right into a side exit that came out on the high side of the maze, as Spanaje had done. They ran and stopped at the end with Ben puffing so hard he thought he'd burst.

"Now what?" Ben said.

"Look," Dogg said. "Reinforcements."

In the near distance, they saw Titarliaa's force hit the west camp with awe-inspiring ferocity. Shouts from a skirmish nearby brought their attention around. Ben was staggered by what he saw. The Flaxon units had positioned themselves on either side of the corridor, firing in turn up the passageway, decimating anything inside.

"How do you like that, demon spawn!" yelled one soldier. Then he turned to face their direction. "Oh! Hell's bells! Look out, lads!"

Ben watched as Spanaje—after leaping twice his own height—fell upon them with all his wrath like a blade whirling hurricane. He cut two down before any could draw weapons. Spanaje's use of his halberd was with such

< 166 >

astonishing machinelike precision that, to Ben, he resembled a guided propeller.

"I will end you all!" Spanaje cried, splitting one enemy in half from head to pelvis.

Hurriedly, a Flaxon officer pulled a newly issued hand fire-iron from his belt, extended his arm, and took deliberate aim. There was a momentary sound of a whip crack preceding a short muzzle flash, announcing the release of powder and shot. The round clipped Spanaje's cheek and cut off one of his braids before he charged forward to slice the Flaxon into four parts with a short flurry of vicious strokes.

The next thing Ben saw made him gasp in disbelief. Uniss stepped from behind a large boulder. Using his own blade, which looked to Ben like a pirate captain's cutlass, Uniss cut several approaching Flaxon down as they ran up to assist their comrades. Attempting to flee, the last two remaining splinter unit soldiers dropped their launcher. Uniss ploughed through them without mercy too.

"Dogg! Uniss … He just … murdered them," Ben said.

"No, Ben," she sighed. "He's correcting the Continuum balance."

* * *

Standing in front of the opening, Spanaje looked up the corridor to see the carnage therein. It was then he saw exactly where Benataa lay on the ground. Not concerning himself with the last odd-looking Flaxon he noticed heading up the slope, Spanaje sprinted to his ally's side and hurriedly searched another Scarzen body close by for some trilix. But he found none.

"Ruhe has passed," a wounded warrior said, slumped on the ground close by before breathing his last.

Spanaje slowed, eyes wide, kneeling beside Benataa with tears falling.

"Every warrior has his time, my Ruhe," Spanaje said, closing Benataa's eyes with one hand. "This time is yours. It has been my honor to serve you. May the ancestors receive you well. You will not be forgotten."

As Spanaje's voice faltered, he took Benataa's personal ends of peace and stood. In the near distance, Scarzen battle horns and war cries sounded with

< 167 >

the thunder of drommal hooves announcing the charge into battle.

"The old wretch has not missed the day after all," said Spanaje in a quiet voice.

\* \* \*

Outside the stone maze, Ben watched a significant Scarzen force rise to full charge with a roar that shook the earth under his feet. As this happened, Uniss walked up to the two of them, looking furious.

"What in Naught's beard have you two done?" Uniss said.

"What have we done?" Dogg said. "You're the one who altered the timeline and wouldn't return messages."

"That was to lead Starlin astray—and I didn't get any messages until I accessed my physical mail!" Uniss said. "It took a miracle to find you two and not have him trace my movement. I had to go off-world to do both and then only half succeeded." Uniss glared at Ben. "What's that mess sprayed all over his face?" Then he looked closer. "And why does he have a fluctuating soul stream and orange eyes? What the hell happened, Dogg?"

"Benataa has passed."

"Yeah, that's right. He should be right over there and—where's the body?"

"In that maze! Ben attempted to save Benataa in the maze."

"He did what? And is that Scarzen blood on his face? Dogg, do you have any idea of the consequences that could have? Scarzen blood is unique. What happened to Benataa's soul stream?"

"It gravitated and combined with Ben's soul stream."

"It did what? Do you realize Herrex could have merged with it?"

"Uniss," Ben said, "I …"

"Shut it, Apprentice! Speak when you're spoken to!" snapped Uniss. "The whole timeline has been altered, two presents have collided, and now this time stamp is the present. Dogg, we are stuck until we see this thing played all the way through and the script has been thrown out the window."

"I know, I'm sorry. He did what he thought was right. He put himself at risk to help Benataa."

"He's put us all at risk—the entire Superverse! He wasn't supposed to

< 168 >

*do* anything, Dogg. Crackin' star systems, look around! Do you know how many mortals have had their rebirth destinations rerouted because of all that's happened? Do you know who told me where you might be found? Starlin! That's who. The smarmy mongrel left a message on my personal mail aboard the *Cagney.* How he even got the access is a mystery I haven't solved. He knows Ben's still here, and he has eyes on every soul stream corridor. He's closing in again, Dogg, and he's got significant help to do so. He wants Ben bad, and you two have just laid it all out on a platter for that to happen."

Dogg said nothing, and Ben just swallowed, scared to death of Uniss right now.

"Soon as I used the soul stream to return, Starlin had me tagged somehow," Uniss said.

"I know. It's been happening to me for a while too," Dogg said. "I tried to warn you, but couldn't get a message through. Then I lost Ben."

"You what? You lost him! Here? Where? Amongst all this? Sun's burst! What else did he get into here?"

Dogg sighed. "Benataa died within acceptable parameters. I felt his passing, and Titarliaa turned up in time to make the crucial shift in the events where they both die."

Uniss paused as if discovering something new. "Dogg, Titarliaa is still here. In fact, he's still killing Flaxon not far from here. He's supposed to be dead already from a fall. Over there … within ten yards of that rock, as he illuminated a group of Flaxon."

Uniss pointed and his complexion turned pale, then he stared at Dogg for a long moment. "We are now completely devoid of markers. Everything now has more tangles than a blind man's fishing tackle."

In the background, the battle continued to thunder on toward its conclusion.

Uniss snapped his focus on Ben. "We have some serious work on our plate now, son, after all your interference. Not another step out of line or the consequences will be dire."

Ben swallowed and choked back angry tears. "The hell with all of this! I tried to follow all the rules you set out—but then I was forced to make

< 169 >

decisions without you guys around!" He paused to swallow again. "Yeah, so I know I made some mistakes and changed some things, but how come you interfered with those men down there, huh?" Ben asked Uniss.

"My hand was forced. Wasn't it, Dogg? It's what we do, Ben, and what you're training for. Or were."

"But that can't be right!" Ben said. "Don't they get a chance like everyone else?"

"Not when they are causing more harm to the Continuum balance by creating unwanted threads," Uniss said.

"How could they be doing that? They are a part of the free will of the Superverse too, aren't they?" said Ben.

"Yes, until they become harmful to the balance of things," Uniss said, turning to Dogg. "We have to go, Dogg. It gets worse. Three and a couple of the other Evercycles want to see us—without Ben."

"Hang on, Uniss!" Ben said.

Before Uniss answered, Ben watched Uniss and Dogg do that long stare at each other they did when they spoke mind to mind. Then Uniss turned squarely to Ben. Suddenly, Ben felt very small.

"Ben," Uniss said, then sighed. "I know you're frustrated and angry … and prob'ly a little scared, too. But I'll state this plainly. If you were told to stay somewhere, that is precisely what you were supposed to do. That was never a negotiable choice at any time—an order you ignored. And the consequences that came of it have turned everything upside down and now things need some extreme actions."

"I was getting shot at!"

"Irrelevant! You're not scheduled to be dead for quite some time yet. Certainly not while our association lasts—something you have jeopardized now."

"Dogg said that Scarzen wasn't supposed to die, either," said Ben.

"Not right then and there. But now that it's happened, the Akashic record will compensate, Ben. But now there are so many unknowns. It makes me think you're not the man for the job."

"But—"

< 170 >

"Quiet! By helping a Scarzen poison the water, you changed the lifeline of hundreds of those soldiers. Many died long before they were supposed to. Nice one. This all translates to *us* explaining to the Citadel Council how everything went so sideways. In short, a whole bunch of new and unpredictable threads have been created. Dogg took you to a parallel present, I surmise, to identify the imbalances that caused the massive catastrophe that plunged the Superverse into darkness before. When you attempted to *help* Benataa—a word I use here only for reference—you caused him to turn into the shot early. Had you said nothing, it would have only nicked him and killed Spanaje at the other end of the corridor. He was supposed to die later in that battle—over there." Uniss pointed. "Alongside Commander Titarliaa."

"Oh."

"Yeah. Oh. For now, mouth shut, and do only what you're told!"

"Uniss," Dogg said. "What is Three up to?"

"Superverse dominance ... a sightseeing trip on Boona 4 ... Damn if I know. She'd love to get her paws on sonny here—that I know for sure. She is going to use this mess for all it's worth. She failed last time, so I reckon now she might be odds-on favorite to dominate the Superverse after all."

Uniss paused a moment.

"Uniss," Dogg said. "Herrex is definitely active now too."

"I should have guessed. Everything else is out of sync, so why not his emergence, too?"

"I am sure I heard him on the wind. Have you been to see Farron yet? I sensed we are being tracked, but I can't see by whom."

"Prob'ly Starlin or one of his cronies, and yes, I saw her briefly. She's looking forward to seeing you regardless of circumstances."

Ben cleared his throat. "Can somebody—"

"Uniss, we could shunt him back to earth the way we used to when we had to do emergency incarnate extractions. It should still work and it won't use the high-end soul stream reinstituted for the last five millennia. They won't be able to track him, and they will never look for him there," said Dogg.

"Get him out of the way for a bit till we get our bearings. It should still work, I suppose," said Uniss.

< 171 >

"We're going to need him, and now that we know how bad they want him, we need to find out why, Uniss. He could be the key to setting everything right again."

Uniss thought for a minute and nodded. "Mmm." He put a hand on Ben's shoulder. "Ben, right now, we have stuff to do and people to see to rectify the situation. We'll contact you soon."

"What? No. Wait a minute!" Ben said. "I want to stay!"

Ignoring Ben's protests, Uniss squeezed his shoulder. Ben instantly dissolved and returned to his mortal home.

"I'm sorry, Uniss. This is all my fault, but you were pretty hard on him, you know," Dogg said.

"We're all feelin' it, Dogg. No apology necessary. I have to know what he can handle, and his part in all this adds up to a whole lot more than we can see right now, that's for sure. There's no time to ease him in. I'm sure Three wants to use him to liberate Herrex somehow. But something far worse is happening, much bigger than either her or Herrex's machinations." Uniss looked to the battlefield. "Now … what to do about this?"

In the fields opposite, Dogg and Uniss saw Commander Titarliaa's force crush the Flaxon, sending what was left in full retreat on flatbed wagons, while others lucky enough to be able to use legs ran alongside.

"I'll go track down young Beetaa—see what his thread reveals," Dogg said. "You?"

"Might stay for Benataa's passing ceremony. Need to clear my head. Maybe I'll watch some matches of carrack … listen to some campfire stories for a while."

Dogg nodded. "Mmm. Ben is not worth the risk of losing. We are going to need him; you'll see," she said.

Uniss looked at Dogg. "You're too attached to him, Dogg. It won't help us, or him."

"I remember a few attachments of yours that more than changed the course of things."

Uniss shrugged. "But none would've shaken the Superverse's foundations, and using my past to strengthen your present case is no case at all. If he steps

< 172 >

over the mark again, I'll have to send him to the Echaa Realms for erasure myself to level the playing field. We're stuck with each other, but Ben made the commitment too. His mettle *will* be tested."

"Everyone's mettle will be tested this time, Uniss. Let's just be sure we are all focused on the real issues and have no personal misunderstandings interfere. See you shortly, then," said Dogg.

With that, she dissolved from that timeline, attempting a soul stream shift to where old Spanaje sat, finishing his story under the big tree with Thorr and Beetaa.

* * *

Dogg arrived successfully on the other side of the old tree where the three still sat in conversation. She opened a phase channel, which took longer than normal, to establish an open channel to Ben's soul mind via his universal translator. In her mind, she saw him as a transparent ghostly figure. "I wanted you to hear their final words. It might help later," Dogg said to him. She turned her focus to the three Scarzen, and Ben saw and heard them through her senses.

"Your otaa died with the greatest honor," Spanaje said to Beetaa. "The enemy suffered a great defeat that day. Afterward, Keeper Malforce himself came to the battleground to pay respects. Mistress of the Mountain Farron accompanied him as well. They personally oversaw the ceremonies of all our fallen. Your otaa was given a lord's honor. It's all some time ago now, and the Flaxon have been our enemy with increased venom ever since."

"Thank you," Beetaa said, still reflecting on Spanaje's words.

"That scar you have on your cheek, sir ... Why have you not had it seen to in your retirement?" asked Thorr.

"I leave it as a reminder," he said in lament. "Now ... you both have things to do, and this old warrior has places to be," he said, standing. Spanaje looked at both young Scarzen thoughtfully. "Remember: all things are a point of view. That is the key to life. Scarzen are guardians of Ludd, protectors of trilix. Our code has its compassion, and your otaa's memory symbolizes that, Beetaa. Consult only with valor and open eyes."

< 173 >

Spanaje left the pair to contemplate past actions and future obligations.

< 174 >

A fter Ben was soul streamed back home to be hidden on his uncle's farm on Earth and had the one dream of Spanaje, a year of his time passed before he heard from Dogg or Uniss. To allay the boredom, he'd gotten a part-time job at the radio shop in town using the skills his father had taught him before he died. One afternoon at quitting time, Ben looked up from the counter, and there stood a perfect life image of Dogg in the doorway. Gob-smacked, he stared at her silently for a moment.

*"Dogg, how did you get off Tora?"* Ben said to her in his head.

*"Hello, Ben,"* he heard her say inside his mind via the universal translator that remained attached to his skin at all times. *I didn't leave Tora, actually. This is an old-tech projection, pre soul stream era. I'm using your universal translator as a homing hub. It's nearly time to return to Tora. When the time comes, we'll bring you to us.*

Ben noticed Floyd Gungster, his boss, staring at Dogg in the doorway.

"That your dog, Ben?" Floyd asked. "No dogs in the shop, young fella."

"Ah, yes, sir, I know."

*"Don't you ever give any warning, Dogg?"*

"I'll be going now if that's okay, sir?" Ben said.

"Righto. Be on time tomorrow. There's a lot to do."

*"Will I?"* he asked in his head, looking at Dogg.

*"In that human's head, you will be,"* Dogg said. *"Come on, you have more important things to do."*

"No worries," Ben said to Floyd.

\* \* \*

Ben hoped that Dogg would bring him to Tora straightaway, but she didn't. Instead, a couple of weeks passed while Dogg met Ben at the front gate of the farmhouse every day before and after work. She ran alongside him as he rode his pushbike between destinations. Each day, they'd stop and sit under Hallot Bridge long enough for Dogg to expand his knowledge of the real workings of both Earth and Tora.

"I never would have guessed everyone's actions were so connected, Dogg, especially mine. There are so many things connected—can't Starlin or Herrex find me here?"

"So far, no. They'll be looking, have no doubt. We'll bring you back as soon as it's safe."

"Gee, Dogg, after all that last trouble on Tora, I thought if everyone is truly responsible for their every action, with most living many lives on many worlds, then why shouldn't we be permitted to remember our previous lives?"

"Because there would be no natural random choices of free will or unfiltered Superverse expansion," said Dogg. "Ultimately, that would cause the complete decline of existence for sentients. As a consequence, for many sola centuries, there's been a huge black market for karmic future—a crime punishable by banishment to the Echaa Realms for complete erasure."

"I thought the likes of Herrex, Three, and Starlin were bad enough, until you told me about the Echaa and why they were created. That just about froze my blood," said Ben. "To have everything you are, were, or could be completely erased so there's not even the smallest sign of you in any corner of the Superverse, that's not just executing someone—that's making their whole meaning irrelevant," said Ben.

"It's something Everoyele Zero instituted after the Citadel Wars to deter individuals helping the likes of Herrex. He vowed to extinguish this existence and rebuild a whole new Superverse under his control and promised great

< 176 >

reward for any who would assist his cause. It's turned out for some a great way to get rid of evidence. Uniss and I believe that's what they intend for you after you have served the purpose of Starlin's superior, Three—Herrex's mother. She has a sinister hand in all of this too, and she, unlike Herrex, has been clever enough to operate freely and in open view—and you have always been part of her plan to liberate Herrex, and Three holds jurisdiction over the Echaa. Now the leading edge of the Superverse present has reestablished a new paradigm and anything could cross our path."

Ben's face turned pale. "Oh, I didn't realize that."

"Yes, the Echaa have served many a darker purpose than just cleaning up the Superverse."

"Maybe that's why, of late, I can't help feeling I'm being watched. It's not like when you're around. It's creepy. A couple times in the weeks before you came, I was sure I heard a jumbled voice whispering to me over my shoulder. It's mostly when I'm riding my bike home late afternoon crossing Plumes Bridge."

"It's likely a didactic message put over multiple frequencies by Herrex or Three's agents—like Starlin, to flush any desirables into the open. Your universal translator picks it up. The translator works on both ethereal and mortal universe metta waves. Your best defense is to do *nothing*."

"The voice I hear sounds like an old fella, older than Uniss. One time, I got the daylights scared out of me when I felt someone touch my shoulder while I pedaled past that bridge."

"You felt physical contact?"

"Yes."

*Oh dear, Herrex couldn't have that kind of reach here, could he?* Dogg thought.

"Ben, I think it's time you learned how to keep your four states of consciousness in check."

"What?"

"The technique will help you to quickly sharpen your intuition for what is real and what is not. Now listen carefully and learn well."

And so his new study with Dogg began. He learned about the true

< 177 >

purpose of the great beings on Earth and beyond, and how to breathe to hear his true heart. Sitting under the willow tree one spring afternoon rounded off the end of learning that foundation.

"So, Ben, that's why on Earth you have had Jesus, the Buddha, and so many other great beings manifested here. Each adds their strength to ensure Herrex stays put."

"I see now why people have had so many misunderstandings and have been misled to follow false prophets so blindly and why the Citadel Wars happened. Herrex and the others churned all that up just to keep mankind off balance so Herrex could make his escape."

"That's right," said Dogg.

"Wow … that must have been bad."

"It was; many suffered unnecessarily." Dogg paused a moment and then nodded to herself. "If Herr—if the enemy has grown so strong that you feel his physical touch, then we must be more careful. And that's why …" Dogg paused to write Herrex's name in the air with light. "That's why, from now on, we must avoid saying the Destroyer's name out loud. Simply refer to him as 'H' when talking about him, okay?"

Ben nodded. "Some of it still seems unfair. Like those Bach archive visuals you showed me of how people have made seemingly right choices that could only turn out horribly wrong—how destinies of so many fell in the negative as a result."

"It's how the Continuum works, Ben. Often, those who present righteousness and moral ethics as their allies are false, only seeking profit from their actions. Many on both Tora and Earth want power for ill-gotten gain. It's profilers like us whose job it is to keep incarnate cycles and traffic traveling the way it should. This is why you must make clear and informed choices. Hatred, cupidity, antipathy, and bewilderment … They are the easiest paths to a large karmic debt. Learn to see that and forgive what is flawed in those around you. A tight jaw toward others only adds to their burden."

"Now I realize that every thought, public or not, and every action, known or not, could pivot a change of events affecting, well, everything."

"That's right. Life is like your game of dominoes. The fall of each single

< 178 >

thought has direct effect on thousands of others that cannot be seen or felt directly."

*If I can keep his realization going, we might just be able to use whatever secret it is he's carrying to straighten the whole mess up yet,* Dogg thought. "I think we are just about there, Ben."

\* \* \*

As Dogg prepared to take next steps with Ben, inside Citadel 3 on the division between realms mortal and ethereal far from Earth and Tora, Evercycle Three, Lord of Chaos, waited for her agent Starlin's next situation update.

Her focus held impatiently on the grapefruit-sized crystal matrix atop a miniaturized spire in the nexus room of her Citadel. This now was her only reliable and untappable source of outside communications since the first cavion fields began to appear across the jurisdiction of all Evercycle Council members. The cavion fields of unknown origin were on the increase, and like the other Evercycles, Three was beginning to have difficulty in freely using her ordinarily omnipotent powers. How such a situation could exist, she didn't know, and there was a small anomaly in her memory—something she sensed the other Evercycles also had. Everything had been wrapped up so well after the Great Event, and yet somehow, something subtle had changed Continuum reality; she knew this as fact.

"It matters not now," she said to herself. "Herrex will be free soon no matter what has passed and set us blind. Then I'll have a new reality constructed—get rid of all the dead wood from the top down."

There was a whirl of energy in her chamber. Then, to express her frustrations and displeasure, she chose to project her image as an aging maiden of Aphrodite from the Citadel gods division once charged with caring for Planet Earth. The communication crystal used her divine will as a power source and was uniquely imprinted to her for contact with both mortal and other sentient-class realms.

\* \* \*

On Tora, Starlin had managed to soul stream into Yorr Fields, looking

< 179 >

for clues as to the troublesome trio's whereabouts, after they had eluded him earlier. He found the remnants of a battle fought many hours previous. A chilling west wind made the scene more depressing. Now, not far from the litter of dead soulless corpses strewn where the Flaxon had engaged the Scarzen, Starlin stood near the stone maze, letting his gray eyes take it all in. He wished he had been there to see the carnage. Mostly, he hoped to find Uniss … and that infuriating Filion—Tula—and most important, the human they called Ben, but they were nowhere to be seen. He removed his black-banded hat by the shade of a large stone boulder, his long brown coat, and other coverings, allowing him to blend in against the stone and long grasses. Afternoon sunlight revealed a tidy crop of dark hair cut in the style reminiscent of his Earth namesake, over the cruel features of a man around fifty standard Earth years. He drew back his sleeve to look at his timeline chronograph to sync his coming communication. It was time to speak to *her*—the one who owned his soul-debt and reason for being. Starlin opened a secure Citadel 3 channel using the scrying crystal all agents from her jurisdiction carried. As the sound of four fine musical notes echoed, the intercosmos signal connection established itself, and he again saw her wild-eyed face in the crystal's fish-eye lens.

"Sorry, my lady, distortion is occurring across Tora's atmosphere and the intercosmos communicom," said Starlin.

"Never mind that! It should have been done by now. Why haven't you delivered what I asked?" Three demanded.

"I tracked the human carrying the key via the bug you implanted on their soul, but those two screwups, Uniss and Tula, as usual couldn't follow orders. They rejected my authority and, by default, yours by refusing to hand the human over."

"Did you give them reason to suspect anything?"

"No, my lady, they were just being belligerent as always," said Starlin.

"Profilers! Nothing but a disrespectful scourge. When I'm in charge that will be the first designation erased. The human must be on the planet surface. It has been locked down by Tyr since there was suggestion of tampering with the planet's metasphere. Tell me, are you suffering any degradation of your

< 180 >

powers? The open channel to your thought processes and sensory pickups has often been lost to me recently."

"I am deeply sorry to hear that, my lady. My soul is open to you willingly." *Could I be free of her at last?* he wondered.

"Don't be so patronizing; we both know you would be in parts unknown the moment freedom was on offer. It isn't, though, and I'll feed you to the Echaa the moment you ever dare employ the notion of actually seeking independence. Besides, you are worthy of being in my presence and you please me from time to time. Serve me well and I'll see you are justly rewarded when it is all done."

"I am, as always, indebted to your good graces and compassion, my lady."

"Well then, ensure a proper outcome. Locate the human and the *Tome of Zharkaa,* then take both to the top of the mount. Throw the human into the soul pool and perform the incantation that will allow Herrex to make use of the human vessel."

"Will Lord Herrex be able to absorb the great force the human carries? You know how strong it is, and Lord Herrex will not be at his … best upon first emergence."

"I'm counting on both occurrences. Both are vital for my coup to be victorious. Avoid unlawful mind reading that leaves tracers for the other Evercycles, especially Seven. They have become a lot stronger since the event. Notify me the moment you have accomplished your task so I may commune directly with Herrex. And, Starlin, don't trust him—guard yourself against his use of great language. Wouldn't want you inadvertently swapping allegiance, would we?"

"As always, my service is in your best interests," he replied, bowing.

"You are an unpopular but loyal instrument, Starlin. Demonstrate some compassion in your thinking, at least enough to get me what I want."

"Without fail, great Three. I go to ensure your success."

< 181 >

O n a bright spring afternoon, Ben and Dogg discussed Citadel histories under the willow tree at the farm. A grasshopper landed on Ben's folded knee as Dogg said, "Starlin is the present Citadel accountant, Ben. He is ruthless, and loyal only to Three, the Lord of Chaos. There were others before him. In bygone ages, the Evercycles themselves dealt with the Continuum through divine power. But after the intercosmos evolved to a certain number of universes to combine and become what we now call the Superverse, everything changed. Then it became necessary to dispatch many specially constructed sentients like Starlin and the profilers like us to keep things running smoothly. An accountant's function is to burrow into the many billions of micro-planes to find and record universal karmic infractions before the problems become unmanageable."

"That sounds difficult."

"It is. It also means that such knowledge makes Starlin one of the most influential forces in central Citadel management. He is supposed to record all debt to be recalibrated so that positive change can result, bringing balance to all Continuum incarnate traffic. But he abuses his office regularly, and because he has the full support of Three and Five, we can never have him removed."

"Knew he was bad news the moment I saw him." Ben broke a stick with his fingers, thinking about how Starlin made him feel.

"One of the worst that no one ever sees doing anything wrong. Starlin reports everything to Evercycle Three first, which is illegal in Citadel protocol. Uniss and I have been trying to prove that for far too long, but have never been able to. Then the others get what she wants them to hear. We weren't helpful to her during the retrial and capture of Herrex and the others after the big event. It's at that point in the timeline that the glitch occurred, and no one can remember quite what happened. That's why the Triporian Alliance sent us to retrace our steps and find you again—all in the hope we can uncover what happened in the moments before the blank occurred and reset the Continuum's balance. Uniss and I know the different Evercycles had personal agendas. We only have fragments of how you were involved in that other present, which is why it's so hard to say what part you've truly played. Now this greater present timeline is locked, as though preventing something from correcting to a true cause. I do know this, Ben. You are a very great deal stronger than you can ever imagine. And when the time comes for you to use whatever it is you're carrying, use it for the good and justice of all things to come."

Ben nodded. "I will, Dogg. So everyone who was there before, who has any real pull, knows something happened, but they don't know what or who really caused it?"

"That's right. Even Lord Zero—oldest of the Evercycles and leader of our intercosmos house and champion of justice for all sentients—is completely at a loss to explain what happened. He has said his insight is fading with no reason he can tell, and unless we find out what happened, the entire Evercycle Council and the Superverse could … well … vanish.

"That's ridiculous."

"No, it's chaos—just the way Three likes it. Starlin has a few bones to pick too—a to-do list, and at the top of it are Uniss, me, and now you. So watch your step. That's why it's time for us to go back, Ben. There is work to be done."

Ben reached out, placing his hand on her shoulder, and then closed his eyes. The soul stream transported the two from the physical space on Earth

< 183 >

back to Tora.

* * *

On Planet Tora inside the Talon West Bunker training facility, Blue Squad had been pressed hard on a harsh training schedule, with a vast array of theoretical assessments for each cadet to complete. Day and night, superior armed, unarmed, and kinetic combat continued on a rotating three-hour cycle. Training in tactics with ambush occurred every other day, as did the building of miscellaneous weaponry. Everyone felt the pressure of a full-scale war coming.

Proximity and compulsory unit member cooperation molded Beetaa and Thorr to become close working allies under all conditions. After a meal one day, the two sat under a thick-trunked stendle tree, playing a game of carrack before afternoon exercises commenced.

"You always favor the flank," said Thorr, looking at the strength of Beetaa's pieces on the octagonal board.

"Yes. Always easier to break your knees from the side than with direct assault," said Beetaa, focused on the game.

"Final assessment's not far away, you know," Thorr said while placing a pyramid down to oppose Beetaa's stacked disc. "There! Counter that if you can."

"I know. But, right now, how do you feel about … that!" said Beetaa, moving a post laterally and removing Thorr's opposing pyramid.

"What! Humph. Your moves are like moonlight. Why do I never see it coming? That makes us five to two. Well played." He paused. "Big decisions soon," Thorr said.

"Uh huh!"

"Any clear plans about your specialization application yet?"

"I'm more concerned about the question of my battle ally. That's at least fifty percent of the equation," Beetaa said, resetting the board.

"Indeed,"

"Spanaje says that choice represents the path to winning respect of the ancestors. Has to be someone who complements my skill. One unwavering—

< 184 >

like Spanaje and my blood otaa were on and off of the consulting ground."

"Any particular leanings?" Thorr asked, eyes square on him.

"Well, among the selections here, I can only think of one I would commit to under all circumstance."

Thorr straightened up in his seat, thinking Beetaa's choice lay elsewhere. "I'm sure they will honor you, whoever your choice is."

"Will you trust me with your life, Thorr, offspring of Traldon?" Beetaa asked.

Thorr shuffled in his seat. "For a minute I thought … Well, I was thinking to ask you the same thing. I have watched you closely in past weeks. I feel that such a union would please the ancestors." Thorr extended a hand. "Yes, my life, mind, and hearts will join with yours willingly."

"So we are agreed?" said Beetaa.

"We are," said Thorr. "From this day, we are committed."

They both stood facing each other.

"Well, that's settled, then," Beetaa said. "I have my blade of bonding to exchange. Do you have yours?"

"I do," answered Thorr.

"We must inform Squad Commander Zaxaa before signing the commandant's ledger."

"There is not long before we shall be assigned. Our blades must be combined before then," said Thorr.

"I say the keeper's bond to you with my soul. Maatulac. And commit again in common tongue: 'May the heads of your enemies always fall swift at your feet. Ancestors bless our union.'"

"I say to you, jikaa arune," replied Thorr. "I am honored by your sentiment; may the same reflect on you."

"I will have my clan informed," said Beetaa.

"I will do the same."

Both took one formal pace back, then bowed deeply with eyes down, as Scarzen custom demanded at a point of such commitment.

Together, they said, "We are one, bound until life's end. Maatulac!

< 185 >

\* \* \*

Later that afternoon, all of Blue Squad sat on meditation cushions on a long veranda inside a small compound, practicing development of kin. Some sat facing in pairs, wrestling in mind-lock skirmishes amidst mental landscapes conjured from memories or imagination to develop their kin will. Between their foreheads and sternums, threads of scarlet and turquoise energy braided and unbraided together in small brilliant flashes of light. On the floor in front of others sat an octagonal-sided block on a tripod. Using kin, each cadet aimed to raise the block and then make it rotate in both directions, a task Beetaa found simple to do. During the course of the exercise, a visitor wearing a black-hooded robe entered the space and stood silently to the side, observing.

Beetaa watched Thorr struggle with the exercise.

"Your kin is not your strong suit," Beetaa said dryly.

Thorr's kin link faltered and his cube fell. "Broz," Thorr muttered to himself. "My enemies don't miss it; they are too occupied with other threats."

Thorr then noticed Beetaa was manipulating his block and talking to him at the same time. Beetaa's cube held stable at the textbook standard of his sternum center, spinning it clockwise. Then, when Beetaa turned from Thorr and placed his view upon it, the block suddenly began to unfold like a paper flower.

"Woo!" said Thorr, raising an eyebrow at the unusual sight.

The cube's material unfolded, wafer thin, spreading four times its size in area to be flat like a sheet of parchment. Then it spun, making a whirring noise.

"Tighten my battle belt. How did you do that?" Thorr asked.

Beetaa's spinning square slowed and dropped, clattering to the deck.

"It was a struggle at first," said Beetaa, apparently unclear as to how he'd accomplished the feat. "Then its state became … *clear*, I suppose. You know, instead of being tethered to my kin, we became one, and then that happened."

Thorr rolled one muscular shoulder and tilted his head in puzzled thought. Across the way, Zaxaa now stood next to the hooded visitor, and

< 186 >

Thorr noticed the two in a quiet exchange. Zaxaa looked directly at Beetaa and went to step forward, but the visitor gently touched Zaxaa's arm, holding him back. Then the visitor whispered something and made a slight respectful bow and left.

"I think you have someone's attention," said Thorr, observing Zaxaa looking straight at both of them.

* * *

That afternoon, Beetaa was summoned to the office of Zaxaa.

"Seems you have been noticed, pup," said the Blue Squad commander, hands clasped on the desk.

Beetaa stood at attention and made no reply.

"You are to report to the Brasheer Lair's high gate via Gantry. Here are your orders of reassignment."

Zaxaa pushed a scrolled parchment across his table to Beetaa, who had a most puzzled look.

"Do you like high-end kin study, Cadet Pinnaraa?"

"I find the prospect interesting, Drillmaster. Isn't Gantry on the east side of Yorr Fields? I've never been over in that part of Ludd before."

"Well, a field trip should put some spring in your step, then."

"I don't understand, Drillmaster."

"When you have the right braids for that, pup, you won't need sad warriors like me to show you how to scratch your pecs. You report immediately. Now get out of here before sentimentality takes over and you find my boot in your butt."

"But, Drillmaster, I have already made bond with an ally. We must see the smith about our blades of bond before either of us leaves here," Beetaa said.

"If I had my druthers, Cadet, I'd send you to my old engineer's regiment. Your skills could be well used on the front line." Zaxaa looked up. "That was a compliment, bone-buster. But it's not my call. Leave here and go and see the smith. I'll make sure of an appropriate arrangement and alert your ally. Who is it?"

"Thorr, offspring of Tralldon."

< 187 >

"Mmm … a strong match. Your bond is noted. I'll bear witness. Be on your toes, Warrior. No march-out parade for you. You're in black ops from now on, so don't get lost beyond the shadows."

Beetaa straightened.

"Some of that drommal dump the Brasheer do can really screw a good Scarzen around," Zaxaa said. "Maatulac. Now, go!"

Beetaa paid respects and left.

\* \* \*

*What an unusual remark coming from Zaxaa,* Beetaa thought, walking back to collect their gear. *Zaxaa never came across as a Scarzen with a sentimental disposition.*

Buried in thought and not paying attention to his direction, Beetaa rounded a corner and stumbled into an oncoming group from the Red Squad.

"Ah! Watch it, cow's breath," said one Red Squad member, a palm shoving Beetaa.

"My apologies," Beetaa said, ignoring the comment and trying to move on.

Another strong arm prevented Beetaa's departure, grabbing his shoulder. Beetaa stalled in step.

"Is that the best you can do, cousin?" said another, pushing from the flank.

Beetaa turned to the familiar voice to see his officious clan cousin Illaa. The atmosphere quickly grew icy. Now completely aware of the rivalry situation, Beetaa took a more active posture.

*Careful,* whispered a little voice inside Beetaa's head.

"Clan feud has no place here, Illaa," Beetaa said, looking him straight in the eye.

Illaa scoffed at the remark. Bolstered by the presence of his other Red Squad comrades, Illaa stepped forward. "You're not in your otaa's chamber now, broz. No one to rescue you now. It's you who must retreat this time," Illaa snorted, pushing Beetaa's chest.

The small circle of Red Squad members now closed around Beetaa.

"I heard Blue Squad needs permission tickets to dump pits before they rise in the morning," Illaa said, laughing in Beetaa's face.

< 188 >

"Come back after further training, *cousin*," Beetaa said. "You've chosen poor ground for victory here. Elevate your inelegance to realize when your mouth precedes your brain."

"Ooo!" the hostile group jeered.

Illaa lunged to take Beetaa by the throat, shouting, "Why you …!"

By reflex, Beetaa rolled a shoulder and merged with Illaa's lunge, bringing a hand up and across the opponent's wrist, anchoring it hard, and stepped wide in a pivot. The result was that Illaa went winding and flailing to the ground for all to see, with Beetaa still gripping Illaa's wrist. Beetaa twisted the wrist sharply and then drove a tight fist into the grounded Illaa's abdomen with gusto, twice. The strike sounded like a sandbag being hit with a heavy hammer.

"Now back off. This is pointless, Illaa," Beetaa said, throwing off Illaa's hand.

Illaa lay gasping, humiliated. Two of the group launched at Beetaa from behind. Very quickly, a skirmish escalated: one against seven. Beetaa fended off a couple of the opposition, shunting them with a kin barrier. Caught off guard a couple of times from the side, he received the same in return. The rising noise of the scuffle carried some distance. Just as all-out war was about to be declared, a loud, commanding voice gripped everyone in the fiery group: "YOU WILL STOP NOW! OR BY THE ANCESTORS, YOU WILL PAY THE PRICE!"

The force of the voice penetrated, stalling some fists and legs midstream. A rolling barrier of dispersion struck the core offenders, bowling them over like skittles. Looking in the direction of the booming voice, all eyes fell upon Drillmaster Zaxaa. He stood with a ball of energy glistening in his right hand, clearly ready to take action. Beetaa suddenly realized the old drillmaster was probably a lot more than an engineer. On his left flank stood Thorr, looking positively bristling with readiness to jump to the defense of his intended battle ally.

"THE NEXT CADET THAT MOVES WITHOUT MY EXPRESS ORDER WILL FIND THEMSELVES IN THE HOLE, AFTER I PERSONALLY TEAR THE REPRODUCTIVES FROM THEIR CHEST!"

< 189 >

Zaxaa bellowed.

Zaxaa and Thorr closed on the group. Beetaa could see Thorr fuming.

"Facility protocol one: Scarzen will not forget themselves in this bunker! That is the law!" said Zaxaa.

"Yeah!" said Thorr, folding his arms, his comment slipping out before he could pull up.

Zaxaa gave him a disapproving side glance. "YOU! Broznick with the 'someone-kicked-my-gonads face'—my office. NOW!" Zaxaa ordered Beetaa.

Beetaa paid respect and left, brushing off the dust.

Zaxaa turned to the others. "This incident will be reported candidly to your commander. I just know he is going to be thrilled to hear how impeccably his cadets fail to uphold bunker protocol when he's not holding their hands. Rest assured, the commandant will be notified. I'll be surprised if some of you aren't charged and reassigned to farming detail for a year or more," Zaxaa stated, as if it was already fact.

Zaxaa walked closer to the offenders and Thorr went to follow. Zaxaa put a hand out.

"Stay," he said to Thorr.

Standing up close to Illaa and speaking in conversational tone, Zaxaa said, "If any of you frakin' broznicks ever jump one of my squad in pack formation again, I will have you in the challenge ring myself. Then you'll find out why battlefield commendation bands are issued, for real! Am I clear, cadets?" He scowled at them.

The group noticed Zaxaa's braids had many commendation bands from several campaigns.

"Ho," they all said meekly.

"I'LL HAVE A LITTLE MORE GUSTO, RED SQUAD!" Zaxaa shouted.

"HO!" they roared, coming to attention.

"Now get in file."

The group clamored for position.

"Out of my sight and to your commander's office! March!"

The battered Red Squad members lined up, then stepped off, marching with discipline. Zaxaa waited till they had turned the corner and then looked

< 190 >

over his shoulder.

"What are you still doing here, Blue 19? Don't you have things to do?" Zaxaa snapped, glaring up at Thorr as he strode past.

Thorr paid respect and headed in the other direction.

\* \* \*

Soon, Zaxaa walked into his office, where Beetaa waited, standing to attention.

"Back so soon, Cadet Pinnaraa?" Zaxaa said, walking past.

He sat in his chair, looking at a ruffled and dust-covered Beetaa. Zaxaa muttered to himself, threading his gnarled fingers together on the table.

"I should charge you, Cadet Pinnaraa—have you sent to the slaa groves to turn compost for the next decade. That what you want?" he said.

"No, Drillmaster!"

"Broz, standing orders require I charge you—today! What should I do here?"

"Drillmaster. I—"

"Did you hold your own, Cadet Pinnaraa? Speak true."

"Sir?" Beetaa replied, unsure of his commander's question.

"Did I fish you out of a shit hole of shame, or did you uphold Blue Squad's honor?"

"Ah, no, Drillmaster. I mean, yes, Drillmaster. Many found their consulting prowess sadly inferior."

*Good,* Zaxaa thought. *Never liked their dropkick of a commander anyway.* "Then, as far as I am concerned, you have been the Brasheer's responsibility since just a bit ago when I gave you your new orders. You're their problem now.

"Yes, Drillmaster," Beetaa said, feeling the noose slacken.

"So, get your scrawny butt out of my bunker before I have you arrested for loitering."

Beetaa held back a smile and paid respect, then turned and went to leave.

"Warrior foot-pad first class Pinnaraa!"

"Drillmaster?"

< 191 >

"Good luck!"

< 192 >

## CHAPTER 15

# GANTRY

The onset of the Winter Bear had started pressing a dull sun's warmth on Beetaa's face as he and two accompanying scouts made their journey aboard military drommal toward Gantry. Beetaa read his orders in silence once more as his drommal plodded on between the two others: *"Travel by Gantry Road approved through Yorr Fields. Rest approved at Gantry settlement. Rest location: Lotus Inn."*

By the time they reached the Yorr Fields, night—and cold—had set in. Snow lay thick in parts, and were it not for a half-moon, the road in darkness would have been difficult. Entering Yorr Fields for the first time, the wondering about their otaa's passing, having happened so close by years earlier, made Beetaa's pulse race. *If only I had time to stop and pay my respects.* As the drommal clomped through patches of snow-covered moss and brittle grass, only occasional creaks of saddle leather and snow crushed under hooves broke the natural silence. Beetaa halted his mount, causing the trailing two to pull up on either side.

"What is it?" one asked.

"Stories … from an old one's memories," replied Beetaa, looking around.

"I don't understand," said the other escort.

"Come, we are losing time," said Beetaa, urging their drommal forward.

Crossing the rolling hills, Beetaa imagined the battle there and the various places Spanaje had described. The trio passed a wood grove in a center field, and by the tree formation, Beetaa felt certain that was the place of the last stand. He tried to identify evidence of the struggle in the evening moonlight. To his right, up the slope, loomed a large cluster of stones. He knew for certain what that must be.

*I will come back here at first opportunity,* he thought.

A little farther on, one of the escorts noticed a small campfire just inside the forest line near the Yorr Pass entrance. Shadowed figures lazily moved around the camp, oblivious to their observers.

"Winter camps are always a dismal affair," said one scout.

They rode on.

\* \* \*

Just past midnight on the outskirts of Gantry settlement, they saw that the roadwork on the approach over the Gantry Bridge, which traversed a steep gully, had been newly constructed. The Scarzen crossed the stone bridge, seeing the shadowed outline of the large west wall and gates of Gantry ahead. Closer, they saw that the robust width of the timbers used to form the main wall sat behind an emerging heavy stonewall that would eventually replace them. Beetaa noted that watchtowers sat at each farthest corner of the western perimeter. Silhouettes of guards could be seen occasionally moving about, illuminated by dull yellow torchlight. Up the steeper slopes to the north, high on a ridge that looked like some prehistoric beast's decaying spine, another watchtower could be seen overlooking the settlement.

*A primitive-looking place,* thought Beetaa. *What earns this place such respect from command?*

Looking at the outlines of guards in the towers, one of Beetaa's companions said, "They offer an easy target. Gantry seems more like an unfinished building site than something safe and dependable to defend."

"Have you been to Gantry before?" asked Beetaa.

"No," said the scout.

"Then don't be so quick to judge. The obvious often conceals quite the opposite. There is something more here than what is in front of your eyes,"

< 194 >

said Beetaa, spurring his drommal on. *Why has this place got such a reputation as a forbidden target anyway?*

Just as Beetaa's drommal plodded to a stop in front of the gates, a short figure holding a lantern stepped out from a hidden nook beside the gate shoulder.

"Halt your beasts right there!" the figure said.

The three Scarzen looked into the face of a round little Celeron man in a bowler hat and town clothes. To the Scarzen, he smelled of strong tobacco and cider brew.

"We have already done so and wish to enter this hamlet. We intend to stay at one Lotus Inn," said Beetaa pleasantly in common tongue.

The Gantry guard lifted his lantern high in one hand, his expression showing apparent surprise at the sight of three unexpected Scarzen travelers.

"That so?" the guard said in a thick midlands accent.

Beetaa saw the pudgy man's face in the yellow light. Then he noticed an old powder firearm with a trumpet muzzle lapped over the other arm. He knew what it was because of the example he had seen hanging as a trophy on Spanaje's den wall.

*Must use that as a club. Looks more dangerous to himself than anyone else!*

Beetaa thought the little Celeron amusing but showed no sign of it.

"No such instructions have come to my post!" the Celeron said with a gruff lisp, trying to sound official.

The escort closest grunted and leaned forward slightly toward the guard. "We are here to lodge at this settlement's Lotus Inn, one night. Come morning, we go to the Brasheer High Gate, which I tell you as a courtesy. Now, let us pass."

The little man narrowed his eyes. "Feisty. You outsiders are all the same. First, I see you are ill informed, Scarzen *warrior* of Talon West. This is Gantry *town,* and we use good manners when making requests here. We ain't been no *settlement* for nearly ten full seasons. By whose authority do you go to Mountain Gate?"

"I will tell you we travel by authority of Zaastaa, Commandant of Talon West training facility. We come on invitation from the Mistress Farron, of

< 195 >

the Brasheer Mountain. Now, should that hat of yours seek a new head, or shall we pass?" said the escort.

"Ah, beg your pardon, sir. That won't be necessary. You are recognized!"

The little man's vernacular changed mid-sentence, shifting to a common Scarzen lilt. Suddenly, the little man began to shimmer and shape shift. Beetaa and the two escorts all moved a hand toward their weapon hilts. The little figure staggered a step back and changed his stance to a more balanced position as a blurred turquoise light saturated him. A swoosh of wind buffeted them, sounding like a large flute's deep note, and then there in the lamplight stood a much taller cloaked figure of average Scarzen height. Beetaa frowned as the hooded figure uncovered his Scarzen face.

"My name is Enoxx. I am the eyes waiting on your arrival. You are on time. The Mistress will be advised," Enoxx said, looking at Beetaa. "Feel welcome. Your quarters are made ready. Arrive at the gates to the Lair of Bach by midday tomorrow. Do not be late."

Enoxx paid respect, whistled, and stepped aside to let them pass. There was a solid shunt sound, and the seam separating the two large wooden gates groaned and cracked open to reveal Gantry town. Beetaa prodded his drommal and proceeded through the gates.

* * *

Some spans inside, one of the escorts looked back to see the gates closing by themselves with an echoed thud. The place they entered lay in silence and low shadows as the single sound of drommal hooves drew attention to their mounts. No one could be seen up the dimly lit wide gravel street.

*The place feels strange, like a thousand eyes pressed upon my back,* thought Beetaa.

"What an odd place," said one escort. "Buildings made of timber … humph. Streets of gravel."

A gust of wind blew tumbleweed across the street in front of them.

*All have taken to their beds. Wait. Who's that?* Beetaa thought.

One scruffy old Celeron male, wearing trousers, braces, and a white long-sleeved shirt, leaned against a failing lamppost across the road. A broad-

< 196 >

brimmed bowler hat obscured his face. Beetaa could feel him watching. *He looks drunk ... or ill.* Then the Celeron lifted his head and stared as the three plodded past. Backlit by a dull splash of illumination from the window behind, the man's eyes made Beetaa feel infiltrated somehow. Some strides down the road, Beetaa took a furtive look back over his shoulder, but the observer had vanished. Now, only the clop of knocking hooves suggested life, until the scent of open fireplaces met their noses when they turned a corner. A bell rang in a distant place nine times.

*This place feels like one of my otutt's dark stories. Our farms have stronger defenses ... or does its spoken formidability come from another source?* Beetaa asked himself.

* * *

South of Gantry town under fading moonlight on the shoulder of the Brasheer Mountain, Dogg and Ben sat near the entrance of the Lair of Bach. A broad, crudely fashioned stairway near them led back down the mountain through the forest and foothills below. Wind blew cold across Ben's shoulders, making him shiver. Snow lay thick around them as they peered down through the darkness at a few specks of amber light from the watchtowers suggesting Gantry's outline.

"Company's coming, and H is stirring stronger every day," said Dogg.

"Who's coming?" Ben asked, still looking down to the town.

"Fragments tell me that it is one whose influence changed your view of existence forever and made victory against H possible. I only hope that events will serve to do the same again. Come, it's time. They'll be expecting us to knock."

Ben looked back over his shoulder to the considerable flat stone shelf stretching away behind them. A shrouded oil light had been secreted in a small carved-out alcove, impossible to see unless close by. He stood and followed Dogg across to the vertical rockface near the light and looked up. His view up the rockface faded quickly with the cloak of night, but Ben saw carved into the vertical stone an obscure-looking array of squiggles, shapes, and other mysterious writings. Overall, the carvings made the shape of a huge

< 197 >

cathedral arch. A seam of glyphic writing divided the arch down the center.

*I should know how to open this,* thought Dogg.

"Looks like someone drew a house plan, Dogg. What is it?"

"Both a warning and a map of the cosmos to many faraway places. It's also a door," said Dogg, moving closer.

"What do you mean?" asked Ben with a frown.

"Wait. I'll try … this," said Dogg, focused on the wall.

She drew her nose from left to right. The dull indentations began to glow bright green in the night light.

"They look like neon stars," Ben said.

"More important, Ben, is which stars are winking. See here." She nudged. "These are known as the Pleiades, and inside them, the Seven Sisters." She gestured to her left. "Here is the Trifid Nebula near Orion. Many battles were fought there in the Citadel Wars." A fragmented memory sparked something in Dogg's mind. "Cluster 47 … Something about a place called Cluster 47?" she murmured.

"What's up? Did we just knock?"

"Oh, nothing … just another fragment. Look here, that's your present home: in Sol. It is your sun's position as seen from Alpha Centauri."

"What's that purple one?" Ben asked, pointing high and to the right.

"When your kind discover that one, it will be called the Medusa Nebula. Over here is the Gemini Cluster; it was my home at one time."

Saying that, her ears dropped. Ben thought she looked sad staring at it for a long moment. Then, without another word, Dogg gestured across the stone face with her nose again. All the illuminated signs on the stone began to pulse. The wind dropped and the stone cracked down the center. Ben felt the earth shudder underfoot. The two halves swung outward, revealing a wide softly lit interior corridor leading into a great cavern.

"Scrape a bone, Dogg! When you knock, it's really something."

"Thank you, I do my best. Ben, inside here, we will be visible. Farron is a very old and dear friend, nothing to be afraid of. Come on," she said, moving forward.

The two passed into the mountain and the doors swung shut behind

< 198 >

them with a *thoom*, leaving no sign of their entry.

* * *

Down in Gantry, the three travelers approached the inn. Lamplight splashed onto the veranda floorboards from a single window next to the door. A sign saying *Madeline's Lotus Inn* swung with a squeak in the wind over the entry. The three drew their mounts to a halt at the hitching post in front and dismounted. Beetaa saw a female Celeron lean out of the main doors, looking in their direction.

"Will you need a stable for your mounts?" she asked in common tongue.

The backlight from inside cast the woman's face in shadow, obscuring any of her facial details.

"We will," said Beetaa.

The woman said nothing more and disappeared back inside. A short moment later, a teenage boy appeared in the doorway in an overcoat and with sloppily laced boots on his feet.

*He looks more asleep than awake*, thought Beetaa.

The woman stuck her head out the door again. "Come inside. Jeb will see to your mounts."

Beetaa's drommal dwarfed the boy. The boy took the reins, but Beetaa said nothing, barely paying the boy a glance as he led the first beast around to the stable.

*Celerons feel as strange as their town.*

Beetaa and the two escorts entered the inn through the front doors, ducking a little under the lintel. Inside, Beetaa straightened up cautiously, thinking it might not be suitable for a Scarzen's head height.

"Watch your head in here," the escort said to Beetaa from behind.

Soft yellow lamplight from several places around the foyer allowed Beetaa to see everything in full detail. He stepped down onto floral-patterned rugs from a short interior landing to the creak of floorboards underfoot.

*Oh, this is pleasant enough. Otutt's account of her travels to the Celeron city Bon fits well here. Far too many furnishings, though. Indefensible in the event of an incursion—the position of the lamps makes starting a fire far too easy.*

< 199 >

They all stepped toward the female, now standing behind a polished redwood counter.

*Furnishings look like the kind you should sit in for a long time. I'd probably disappear inside one of those lounges if I did.*

One of the escorts had to correct a step after kicking up a corner of a smaller rug placed over the other larger coverings. Beetaa stepped up to the counter, removing his gloves, with the other two waiting a step behind.

"Welcome, travelers. I am Madeline, owner of the Lotus Inn."

"We have come from Talon West," said Beetaa. "We need lodgings for one night. I understand you were informed of our coming?"

"Yes, I was," she said, looking at Beetaa with a slight frown as she finished marking the register, dotting it twice with her quill. "But your accent is from Talon East, is it not?"

"Ah, yes. Correct," said Beetaa.

"You have traveled the long way, then."

*She's well informed for an innkeeper.*

A strong smell of wood and dust mixed with burning lamp oil hung in the air.

*What is that scent she wears? Smells like something my otutt has in her kitchen.*

The Celeron woman appeared to be middle aged, and of slender build. Her head barely matched the height of his sternum; she wore her night hat, pink shawl that covered her shoulders, and a crimson floor-length dress.

*Her skin looks as white as a Pujan cow's milk. What strange night attire these Celeron wear.*

She looked up from her pen work, greeting the travelers with a pleasant smile.

"Have we kept you from your bed?" asked Beetaa.

*You're wearing something my otutt wouldn't have across a window.*

"No, thank you. My working hours reach far into the night. This must be your first journey away from the bunker, yes?" she said, looking up at Beetaa. "I have never traveled to the midlands and am finding it ... fascinating."

"Don't worry, Warrior Pinnaraa, meeting new races and experiencing their ways helps set aside preconceptions and broaden perspective ... don't

< 200 >

you think?"

Her comment produced the eerie feeling that she had heard his thoughts. She made a note in the register that Beetaa didn't recognize before she spun it around to face the three visitors.

*Are all Celeron females this terse?* Beetaa thought. *Otutt never said anything about Celeron picking up thoughts—or their directness, either.*

Madeline walked out from behind the counter and over to the front doors.

She slid a heavy bolt across, locking them shut, and then the Scarzen saw a golden light emanate from her hands as they held the bolt and then there was an odd background sound. She turned to them with a quaint smile.

*Strange, she wears no protection out here in hostile territory.*

"You'll be quite safe here. No unwanted guests stay long in Gantry at night."

"We were not afraid out there," said Beetaa. *She speaks with such authority through her thin lips, as though she is in the Scarzen chain of command.*

Beetaa could see by the stray curl, which hung from beneath her flimsy head covering, that her hair was the color of auburn sand.

*Such vibrant green eyes.*

Shortly, the boy who had stabled the drommal reappeared from a door off to the side.

"All done, Mother," he said, not looking at her, but passing the three Scarzen and staring.

"Jeb! Manners," she said, her head tilting with a kind mother's disapproval.

The boy kept moving. "Sorry."

"To bed with you," Madeline said.

Jeb gave a vague nod and the visitors a last glance, then went out through a back door, closing it softly behind.

"Sorry about that," she said, dragging the three Scarzen's attention back. "You two," she said, looking at the escorts. "Down the hall, first on the left. And you, Warrior Pinnaraa, on the right, three down. Breakfast served at six of the morning. Don't be late. They eat fast and leave quickly in these parts."

Beetaa went to speak as she handed each of them their keys from a sideboard.

< 201 >

"If there's any bother, there is a bell on the desk." She pointed to it without looking. "Good night. Dreams bring you peace."

Beetaa nodded, then felt dumb for doing so. The three Scarzen looked at each other, and one escort shrugged. Beetaa pursed his lips, making a click with his tongue, then proceeded down the hall, followed by the others, and entered his room.

\* \* \*

Beetaa's room had a large soft bed in the right corner. *How many do they expect to sleep on this?* He sat on the edge and bounced a little. *Way too soft and it squeaks. No wonder their bodies are soft. The floor looks much better.* Beetaa moved across and looked through the vertical cracks of the window shutter on the wall opposite. *Black as pitch. "Dreams bring you peace." I'm not dead.*

In the hour before waking, the same dream Beetaa had in his lair in Talon East returned. The outline of a hideous face washed over him, saying, *"Kill him."* This time, the impact forced him to wake in fright with a gasp, looking at the end of his bed. Just for an instant, Beetaa felt sure a powerful dark figure stood at the end of his bed. He threw his legs over the side of the bed and stood up. Feeling tense, he noticed the temperature in the room had an unnatural chill, and he went to the sideboard where the water pitcher and basin stood. Dumping some water in the basin, he splashed water on his face.

"You're going brain slack, broz," he said, looking through splayed fingers at his distorted, gaunt face reflected in the polished metal disc on the wall. *Ugly, too.*

To his right, early morning light sifted through the window cracks from outside.

Beetaa collected his weapons from the undisturbed side of the bed, cradled them in one arm, then entered the hall and looked to the foyer at the other end.

*There's the innkeeper ... Madeline.*

He saw her dart past, carrying a tray. Beetaa headed down the passage to the front of the building, smelling the pleasant and enticing aromas of something palatable.

< 202 >

*Time to eat. At least the foreign food smells good. My back's killing me from that soft bed.*

Entering the foyer, Beetaa heard muffled conversation coming from beyond a curtain in the direction Madeline had gone. He walked toward the voices and parted the curtain to see an active dining room. At the other end, Madeline added a tray to a long table where a number of other guests from races across Ludd had already seated themselves.

A tall, long-faced female Minnima merchant sat on the left just inside the door. She looked up from her plate and made eye contact with a smile. He nodded almost imperceptibly, and she gestured to the vacant seat opposite to her. Beetaa nodded and sat.

"Morning," Beetaa said.

"Morning," the merchant replied. "I recommend the corn jacks," she said, using tongs to place two more of the saucer-sized local breakfast favorites on her well-used plate.

"I had no idea Minnima Clan traveled to these parts of Ludd," said Beetaa, accepting the tongs.

"We have conquered the boiling oceans of the west, Warrior, so passing through Gantry to Wuden for textile trade in the north presents no challenge. After Wuden, I return to Hoch for our Crossing of the Moons celebrations that highlight female dominance for the last twenty generations."

"Yes, a merchant in my home bunker spoke of that happening. I hope to visit Hoch one day."

"The most beautiful city in all of Ludd. Not as imposing as one of your bunkers, I'll grant, but a majestic presence nonetheless," said the merchant in diplomatic tone.

"My otutt praises the potency of Minnima apothecary and empathic skill. She states they are second to none in Ludd."

*Chatty, for a Scarzen,* thought the merchant. "Where are you headed?" she asked.

"Just on a routine field trip," said Beetaa. *Otutt said foreign allies like to chat; maybe I can learn something. She seems forthright enough.* He looked to the end of the table. *The others look like travelers from the Celeron city of Bon.*

< 203 >

*They always have such well-crafted traveling clothes for non-Scarzen.* Two of them stared with blank faces at Beetaa. *Something behind that feigned neutrality.*

Peripherally, Beetaa noticed three other merchants dressed in garb of the western regions. Beetaa squeezed the customary false smile. *Lame drommal sellers.*

One looked at their friend and busied themselves in their meal. Just then, Beetaa's two escorts walked in and gauged the breakfast setting. Beetaa gestured for them to sit. Madeline passed them with another tray. Her son, Jeb, then entered the room, dressed for the day behind her.

"Get it while it's hot," she said, placing the tray in between Beetaa and the Minnima merchant.

Seeing a vacant seat, Jeb sat down beside the Minnima merchant and quickly focused on a tray of fried duck eggs and peppered green tomatoes. After taking his first breakfast sample, Jeb looked across the table directly into Beetaa's bright orange eyes. He took in the Scarzen's facial detail before asking, "Do you like duck eggs, master warrior?"

Remembering the tutorials on foreign custom, Beetaa produced a gentle curl of a smile. The young man smiled back and passed the clean spoon from the tray to Beetaa.

"Thank you," Beetaa said, very relaxed.

Madeline entered the dining room with a jug of hot goat's milk blended with wild apple juice. She set it down between Beetaa and the others.

"This will help chase the meal down," Madeline said.

"It's been a long time since I visited your Talon East," the merchant said. "The pearl-black defense walls are an imposing sight."

One of the escorts raised an eyebrow, listening in, but said nothing. The merchants at the other end of the table whispered amongst themselves in unintelligible murmurs.

"They are as beautiful as they are impregnable. How do you know our bunkers so well?" asked Beetaa, passing the peppered tomatoes to the escort on his right.

"Not your other clan's bunker. Just yours. Your braids are bound in reverse with a purple thong," the merchant replied. "Talon West warriors use green

< 204 >

and red like your two friends there. I once traded jewelry set with Scarzen polished glass-stone from Talon South. It was good business in my region, Celeron, and across the oceans for a time. But it has slowed in Ludd of late."

"And why have your travels brought you here?" asked Beetaa.

"Oh, now I trade sellenor. Been delivering eggs and juveniles to Master of Scouts Paxx at Talon East for two years now."

All three Scarzen focused in on her with that answer. Beetaa noticed her comment even stirred the interest of the others at the end of the table, stalling them in their private mutterings.

"Your name, good merchant?" Beetaa asked.

"Ranken Yosh. Merchant, at Scarza's service," she said, not extending her hand as custom, required in many parts of Ludd. Instead, she paid Scarzen respect in just the acceptable gesture, placing her right hand on her heart and saying, "Maatulac."

"Jikaa," Beetaa responded with the hint of a respectful laugh.

"Honorable," the escort next to Beetaa said to him. "Time to go."

"Yes. I am aware." Beetaa nodded, then turned his attention back to the merchant. "Good to have met you, Merchant Yosh. And you, young Jeb of Gantry. Perhaps our paths will cross again."

"Good to have met you too, sir," Jeb replied.

* * *

Entering the foyer, Beetaa saw Madeline standing behind the registry desk and walked across, intending to thank her for the hospitality.

"Bed and breakfast meet your needs?" she asked as they all approached.

"More than satisfactory," replied Beetaa.

"Happy to hear it. Your drommal can remain in the stable till your business is done up the Mountain. The debt is taken care of."

"For myself, that would be appreciated. However, my clan will not be going on farther. They return to Talon West this day."

Madeline crimped her lips in thought. "I'll have them brought around to the hitch post out front," she said.

Her guests bid good day and left the inn.

< 205 >

\* \* \*

Walking out into the sunshine to see Gantry in daytime, the town's main street presented many of the rustic wood and stone buildings bearing signs on the façades for their various purposes. Some windows even had marbled glass panes backed by curtains. They could feel a gentle westbound breeze on their faces.

*Expensive items for a trader town*, Beetaa thought. *Obtained from the far north in the Chou region, no doubt.*

Beetaa and the others headed east up the street, passing a cobbler, a coach and coffin builder, and a blacksmith. The latter looked to be already hard at work, slamming a hammer over an anvil. Directly across the road stood a general store with a rocking chair out front. A sign on a building corner pointed back across to a side street, directing to the town cooper's shop. They turned south along a street, walking past a shop called "Known & Unknown Curiosities." The town weapon-smith's shop lodged right next door. As they passed by, the sights in the window made the scout on Beetaa's left stop humming a traditional Scarzen campfire tune when a heavy laminated recurve bow caught his eye.

"I'd like a look in there some time," he said.

Then Beetaa noticed signs here and there on a corner post or window frame that wouldn't have stood out for eyes uninterested in odd things.

"What are those strange small runes carved on the lampposts and building shoulders?" Beetaa asked.

"It is not common tongue script, nor is it Cellonese," said one scout.

"They're even on the boardwalk here and there—look," said Beetaa.

"Never considered them before. Perhaps some superstitious ritual laid down by the townsfolk."

A small gusts of wind passed by as they continued on. Most Gantry citizens appeared to be dressed in a mixture of Minnima and Celeron town garb. All were much shorter than the Scarzen and went about their daily business passing them as though they did not exist.

*Lovely smell of freshly baked bread. So very pleasant.*

Beetaa saw the old town miller hard at work dragging sacks of grain

< 206 >

to a wagon. The stocky man in clothes covered in grain dust cast them a suspicious glance. In his pause, he wiped a hand on his apron before putting his head back down to continue his task. The trio left the town of Gantry behind at a steady jog via a back pasture.

< 207 >

## CHAPTER 16
## STRANGE LIAISONS

till some considerable distance away from Beetaa's advancing position, the enormous conical shape of the Brasheer Mountain loomed. Beetaa could see its summit disappear into a thin cloud cover while the rest of the Lyran Range forged off to the west.

*So good to be away from so many confused town smells,* Beetaa thought.

The mountain was forested from the bottom to almost two-thirds of its height. Thick woods gave way to an alpine section and then a stony, weather-beaten ascent. Arriving at the base of the foothills, they found a wide shallow stream flowing past at a steady rate. Resting for a moment, Beetaa took a deep breath with eyes closed. *Hmmm, freedom.* On the other bank, dead tree limbs and fallen trees lined the banks. *The stream travels east to west. It appears the stream follows the foothills off toward Yorr Fields.*

They crossed the stream and headed upward until the beginnings of a trodden path emerged, meandering up through the thicker forest of beech and cypress pine. Another three hours of climbing a steep incline brought them to the one and only path leading to the Brasheer Lair. Beetaa could see ahead in the distance a marker in the shape of a stone obelisk, similar to those in Talon East. One of the escorts walked up beside Beetaa.

"From that marker, the path to the gates begins," the escort said. "It will take you to the entrance of the Lair of Bach. Do not waste time. They will be waiting."

The other escort handed Beetaa a small map of the area, showing the important waypoints from Gantry to the Lair of Bach. Beetaa bid them farewell and continued alone up through the natural cutting.

* * *

It took considerably longer than Beetaa had first anticipated to reach the obelisk. The steeper ascent, though well trodden, was hard going and slippery at times. It wound up around thick beech and pine trunks across a ridge that fell away steeply on either side. The ground lay thick with forest debris and mossy stone. Beetaa arrived at the landing of the obelisk, breathing hard.

*Thank Naught for the resting place. Now … what does this obelisk say?*

He saw many languages of Ludd etched upon it. The top line, written in common tongue, read: *Only Scarzen with Naught's grace are welcome past this point.* Then, in smaller script underneath, a line said: *Consider your next steps carefully.*

Beetaa smiled. *Someone has a sense of humor. Or perhaps it's a deliberate warning.*

As Beetaa trudged past the obelisk's shoulder, he looked back for a moment and stopped with a shudder. *Ooo!* On the high side of the stone, Beetaa saw a petrified body melted to the obelisk, the figure's arms up in a defensive posture. The face had a ghoulish, distorted expression.

"Guess it was a warning," Beetaa said out loud.

He looked up the rise and marched on.

* * *

Ahead of Beetaa inside the Brasheer Lair, a tall hooded figure greeted Ben and Dogg.

"You are both expected. Welcome, Master Tula. I am Taal," the Brasheer warrior said. "Allow me to show you to your lodgings. Mistress Farron will see you shortly."

"Dogg, can they see me? I mean, really see me?" Ben asked.

"As I told you, yes. You are in Farron's house. The moment we stepped

< 209 >

inside, all façades were lifted, Ben. Deception would be most improper here—*and* lethal, should we not be received as allies. This is no ordinary Scarzen stronghold. Think and speak with care."

*Great,* Ben thought. *Now there's nowhere to hide.*

"There never was," Dogg said.

\* \* \*

Some time later, with Dogg lying at his feet, Ben lay on a firm bunk—more suited to a Scarzen—in what Dogg called his "new place of awakening." The space was carved out of the solid stone and about the size of an average dining room. Oil lamps burned in the corners above his head height, and the place smelled clean but of natural earth. Wide awake, Ben looked up at all the story circles carved into the reddish stone ceiling of his room. The sight made him wonder how long Scarzen had been at war.

"That one is the Battle at Yorr Pass—the original," said Dogg, looking at him with one open eye.

*Uh-oh!*

Ben's eyes stopped on one part of the picture. His forehead crimped into a frown, and he felt cold for a moment as he ran his eyes along the story. He looked upon a picture of a Scarzen being struck by a rocket, with a Scarzen boy sticking halfway out of a nook, a hand stretched out in warning.

*Cripes!*

Ben closed his eyes, thinking about people from Earth to get his mind off the picture. First his mum and Sally, then Aunty Murl. But when Ann's face appeared, his mindscape stuck.

*How come you're so different? I wish you were here.* His body tingled whenever he thought of her. *Girls are so confusing.* He rubbed his stomach. *Damn butterflies whenever you're in my head. Feels like your hand's inside my chest. Girls shouldn't be that pretty, smart, and stubborn. Makes a fella nervous the way she looks me straight in the eyes. Sweetest thing to look at, though.* He smiled. *That long black wavy hair and those big beautiful*

"Ben!"

The door was open and Dogg now stood in the gap, causing Ben to sit

< 210 >

bolt upright and his daydream to dissolve.

"What?" he said, shooting her a look in frustration.

"Come. It's time for you to meet Mistress Farron."

Ignoring Dogg for a moment, Ben twisted his lips in a thoughtful pose before throwing his legs over the side of the bunk, and then he sat there, scratching his head.

"Everything okay?" asked Dogg.

Ben stood and took a big breath, just staring at her for a moment. "Mmm, nope. Private stuff," he said through his shirt as he pulled it on over his head.

"I left you a gift on the table there," Dogg said, gesturing to it.

Ben looked to the small table and chair in the corner of the room. He saw a faded dark blue hat that had the faintest shimmer of energy. It sat on top of a folded, shiny black leather coat. A pair of heavy black mid-shin boots sat on the floor below.

"Am I goin' to be breaking horses or riding motocross? Looks pretty high-grade clobber. What's wrong with the grays you gave me?"

"We thought it was time you had some proper intergalactic travel attire befitting a real profiler apprentice."

Ben walked over to the table. "Okay, ah … thanks."

"Try on the headwear," said Dogg. "Gently now, it's sensitive gear."

Ben frowned at her comment and placed the hat on his crown with both hands. It dropped to cover his ears. "It's a bit sloppy on," said Ben.

"Try the other things, adjustments can be made," said Dogg.

He hauled on the ankle-length black duster. "I'll need it shortened, or to get a lot taller. Looks like my Uncle Tom's boundary coat, only fancier," he said, examining it with his arms out. "Same black buttons down one side too. His is brown heavy leather, though. Thought this was the same at first. But it's heaps different—just as thick but much lighter, and his doesn't have this silky shimmer." Ben looked up. "Aw! Is this Scarzen slaa thread, Dogg?"

"It is called the Coat of Elements and has protective properties. It is a gift from Farron to aid you in your quests."

"Well, it's comfortable. Please thank her. What's this odd inside pocket near my hip for?"

< 211 >

"You should thank her yourself—and that pocket is actually a weapon hitch. Now, sit and try on your new boots. They'll keep your feet warm, amongst other things."

The boots looked and felt strong. Each foot went in with a *fump*. "Aw, are they always going to tingle like that? What are these made of?"

"As absurd as it will sound, they are Boots of Healing and saved the previous owner's life many times. They are my gift, from me to you."

"So where is the other owner now?"

"Dead, swallowed by a Goolock—the boots couldn't bring them back from that one, I'm afraid. The boots will attune themselves to your body's physics and then imprint into your soul core values to defend you against normal knife wounds, blunt-force trauma, incorporeal nasties—that kind of thing."

"Oh, you just made me feel so much safer, Dogg."

"Thank you."

"Wasn't that kind of compliment, Dogg."

"That's alright, dear. They are made of rare leather from an ethereal creature called a Stoateling. The gold stitch down the center seams in front of the calf straps is selrick yarn and the soles are yuba hide. They are lined with Chi-ling down."

"They fit perfect."

"They will grow along with you, sort of a wear-for-life kind of footwear. The coat is a gift from Mistress Farron, the boots are from me, but the hat, as always, is here by his own choosing."

"Eh?" Ben said. He pulled the hat off his head, looking at it closely. *How does a hat go anywhere by itself ... and since when is a hat a 'he?'* "I know Uniss says that nothing's as it seems, and I thought this hat had a funny shine to it when I first looked, but it seems like an ordinary used drover's hat to me, Dogg. Seen a few miles by the looks." Hat in hand, he looked at himself, stretching his arms out in front. "Reckon I'm ready for anything now, Dogg. Thanks. But you can keep the hat; it's a bad fit."

"I'll give him a bad fit," a gruff male voice murmured.

Ben looked about for the voice's owner.

< 212 >

"It's not your average hat," Dogg said. "In fact, 'hat' isn't the term a Jenaoin likes to be called by, Ben."

"A what?"

"Try him on one more time," she said.

"You're creeping me out, Dogg. Hats aren't him or her," Ben remarked, placing the hat on his head again.

This time, the hat slipped down over his eyebrows and his ears, nearly to the bridge of his nose.

"Dogg?"

"Yes, Ben."

"It's gotten bigger. Am I supposed to get a job as a lamp shade?"

"Roland. A comfortable fit, if you please," Dogg said politely.

"Humph. I should clip his ears instead," the mysterious male voice said.

Ben flinched when, by itself, the hat jiggled and shrunk to a perfect fit, even keeping its broad brim.

"Dogg?"

"Yes, Ben?"

"The hat's alive."

"Oh, Roland is a lot more than alive, Ben."

The hat began to wobble on his head and then …

"Alive? Of course I'm alive, cranium vacuum! And if we're going to be a team, you'd better stop calling me *it*. I have a name, Sparky."

"Shit!" Ben exclaimed, ducking. He tried to swat the hat off his head as though evading something from above. "Ah!"

The hat stayed stuck fast to his crown. Ben gripped the hat in both hands and tried to rip it off his head.

"Roland, it's Ben," Dogg said. "We talked about this before you agreed to the transfer. Don't you remember?"

"Remember what?" said Roland.

As Ben struggled to remove Roland from his crown amidst grunts of frustration and hard breathing, Roland began to think.

"This isn't funny, Dogg!" Ben said.

Try as Ben might, Roland wouldn't budge, and the two staggered around

< 213 >

the room in a clumsy dance and tug-of-war that Dogg thought looked decidedly comical.

"The soul stream transfer is the last thing I remember, but it wasn't normal," Roland said. "I barely remember why I came."

Ben ran over to the wall and head-butted Roland's crown into the wall. "Get … off … my … head!" he shouted.

"But you remember me, don't you, Roland?" Dogg asked.

Ben straightened up, dizzy. "Bugger, that broke my head—don't know about his."

"Yes, Tula, I know you!" Roland bellowed in his gruff British accent, in both Ben's head and ears. "But things are jumbled, I'm afraid. Don't even fully remember why I've agreed to be paired with this … this … man, and what I do remember is hard to hold onto. Hey! Little Earth human, hold still! You might as well pull your own head off. I'm going nowhere, so get your grubby mitts off my brim! You'll stretch my electro-membrane!"

*Oh no!* Dogg thought. *It's as if they're meeting for the first time—but then, I suppose they are in a way.*

Ben turned, struck his shin, and stumbled over the edge of his bed, with an "Ow!" before face-planting into his pillow—with Roland still in place. Ben felt the pressure from the living hat around his head slacken, though it still felt securely fixed on his crown. He stood, arms by his sides and his mouth in a twist of frustration.

"Breaking in a new mortal! I'm too old for this, Tula—especially if it's for the second time. I remember that much," Roland said with the voice of a hard but tired old man. "Pull me down to where we can talk mouth to mouth, lad."

*Bloody hat sounds like an English sergeant,* thought Ben. "Dogg?"

"Yes, Ben?"

"A talking hat just kicked my butt and speaks as if it's in charge."

"'He,' Ben. Roland is a 'he'—Jenaoin, to be specific. He's here for your protection."

Ben reached up once more, thinking to tug the hat down fast.

"Not that way, boy, unless you intend pulling your own head off!" said

< 214 >

Roland. "Uncivil behavior is no way to start a relationship."

Ben used a gentle two-handed grip to pull Roland down, and he slid off without effort.

"See what a little less angst gets you. That's it. Let's look at each other crown to crown," said Roland.

Now looking at the hat's crown, Ben's eyes widened in amazement as he saw a shift of energy pass across the hat's blue felt surface. It squirmed in his hands ever so slightly, as though waking, and then shivered. Ben felt not fear but a chill of excitement when two large energy swirls manifest to form sapphire-blue, owl-shaped eyes that filled the upper indents of the crown. The uneven ridge down the center formed a rudimentary nose bridge, and under that manifested a generous mouth, showing a sliver of orange-pink energy swirling inside.

"What?" said Roland. "Stuck for something to say? What about 'Sorry for pulling at you with my clammy human mitts?'"

"I'll never see hats the same again," Ben said, looking to Dogg in amazement. *Stern-lookin' bugger. Got a face like old Bertrand Wallace at Broken Hill General Store. All it needs is a moustache.*

"If you'd stop shouting, I'd be grateful," Roland said, "and if I'm going to accept you as my fitting, you'll use my name or there's no more to be said."

"Strike a light, Dogg. You never said anything about living, talking hats."

"Roland isn't a talking hat, Ben. As I said, he's a Jenaoin. Roland, do you have any memory of Ben or his older self from before you entered the soul stream?"

Roland looked at Ben hard for a moment. "Only enough to know that we are supposed to work together and fix what happened after the Great Event."

"Do you remember what happened? After all, your race has a higher connection to the Evercycles than even mine."

Ben watched Roland's expression become one of concentration.

"Pointing my focus at the matter only produces a scramble of dwindling fragments, Tula. I'm sure I was fine before I left. Did the time stamps match when you both arrived?"

"At first," Dogg said, "but now everything is as though our other present

< 215 >

and this one have braided together, and the effect is draining my abilities and those of Uniss. Sequences that were well recorded as fact have proven skewed in many cases and Ben's physiology has had a reaction to contamination of Scarzen blood."

"Oh, yes. I see: the orange eyes—not a normal human pattern design at all. I'll put it on the to-do list. I sense his life core is substantially different, far more potent than any ordinary human design, I'm certain. Do you feel well, Ben?" Roland asked, looking at him curiously.

"Well, they always said I was a round peg in a square hole back home, but I prob'ly feel better than I ever have," said Ben.

"Indeed, a gas giant's worth more than that, I'll wager," Roland said.

"Can you tell what is hidden?" asked Dogg.

"It's at least a greater-class four-evolution design. Beyond that, no, but there is no dual occupancy of the skin vessel, I can detect that much. We should get him to a bridgeport facility and have this sorted before we engage with a force as potent as Herrex."

"Ah, watch saying his name aloud, Roland. He's already gained too much power as it is," Dogg said. "And your idea would be too risky now, I'm afraid. Our last attempt saw our soul streams collide and almost cross-braid and become fused during transition."

"Oh dear."

"It's now so unstable for any of us to off-world jump, even for a Filion independent, that I fear we could become lost amongst the ghosts of the Gray Realm forever. We are stuck until the cause can be found. Uniss and I are positive that H, with Three's help, has something to do with it, and certainly there's been interference from Starlin, who is trapped here too."

"Starlin. Now there is one headache we could do without. My metta senses tell me you are correct." Roland spun in Ben's hands toward Dogg. "Does his age match the original timeline of our original meeting?"

"I believe so, but the truth of anything is hard to gauge now. We should treat this present as the only present and work with what we can examine as circumstances unfold."

"I concur. What about the reader? Do you still have contact with them?"

< 216 >

"Well, yes. Can't you detect them? They are right next to you."

Roland's face took on a startled expression. "No—I mean, I could sense another presence but nothing that substantial."

"So there is a tear in the metta veil now too. The reader has been ordered to follow whoever is riding the crest of our present. Their account could be invaluable later on."

"Let's hope they can keep up, then. I will update management as soon as I'm able. I'll also timestamp the next sixty seconds as the true present record so we can trace our steps in the event memory degrades further and reference is lost." Roland spun back to face Ben.

"Well, if this is our first meeting, can I know something about you?" Ben asked Roland.

"My string pattern is of Jenaoin command class," Roland said. "I was raised from bonnet to mature crown in the star system called Medusa Cluster. It's a long way from your Planet Earth."

"You look just like the hat Uniss wears," Ben said.

"Naught's beard, never! Don't you know that the first sign of bad manners toward a Jenaoin is to compare crown and brim? Especially one from a different lodge. Each Jenaoin is unique, complete with a full, independent incarnate Akashic record and special intercosmos travel permissions. There are Jenaoin and then there are decoys we taught you about when your race was learning to tie on a loincloth—called hats. Sure, both have a crown and a fitment cavity. Just like humans have a head and bum, but that's where the likeness finishes, see?"

"Sorry," said Ben.

"All Jenaoin have families called 'lodges,' Ben," said Dogg. "Roland belongs to the Medusa Selva Lodge. Trever, Uniss's Jenaoin, belongs to Harnax Lodge."

"That's right," said Roland. "We combine efforts sometimes. That doesn't mean we want to hang out on the same rack. I took this assignment because Tula said, she said … ah, well, I'm supposed to be here to help educate you, I think. So far, the gray cells of yours I've observed are not filling me with hope of too many great strides."

< 217 >

"Hey!" Ben said. "Where I come from, a fella doesn't get slapped by a hat unless another fella's got hold of one. So gimme a break." Agitated, Ben rolled his eyes back to Dogg.

"Then learn to discriminate, Sparky," Roland said. "Most hats on Earth and Tora are just mock-ups, see. Inanimate, poor likenesses; few Jenaoin agents there now, since the Great Event passed."

"I get it. So now what?" asked Ben.

"Our agreement, of course. You've got a head too. So use it, low watt."

"Okay, okay! Geez, keep your ... brim on, Roland. Dogg, are we really stuck with each other?"

"No, Ben, you're not. Roland has many talents that will assist you, especially now, but you must agree to the union, which is for the term of this full cycle."

"Crap, sounds like a marriage," said Ben, frowning.

"It's much more than that. Every Jenaoin is very choosy about whose head they accept. Take it as a great compliment that such a highly decorated Jenaoin commander such as Roland agreed to this fitting—again."

"Surely, I'd remember if I had a talking hat, Dogg," said Ben. "Especially one that has something to do with my far future."

"Which none of us can remember or focus on now. Nothing is as it was or even as it is supposed to be, Ben. I do know that Roland will watch out for you—that he is a trusted friend with much knowledge. Where he comes from, he is regarded as a Top Hat in fighter command. That's the best hat standard in the galaxy."

"Damn straight!" Roland said. "Don't expect me to carry the load all the time either, Sparky. I'm like your lawyer: I advise you, then you use free will. Anything that goes brim-up is your responsibility. Got it?"

"You always going to be this rude?" Ben asked. "Or is this just a bad day?"

"Only when the woods is seriously green or thick, Sparky. You appear to be both." Roland looked at Dogg hard, then back to Ben for a long moment. Then his voice softened a little. "Look here, Sparky. There are a lot of things that are coming your way if what Tula says is correct. And some of it is nothing to tap-dance about. Truth. I see your head's got potential

< 218 >

and your heart is good too. But your head's fuzzed by too many things back where you come from. Like Ann Mac—"

Ben shoved his hand over Roland's mouth in haste to muffle his words. Roland continued to make unintelligible overtures, then stopped talking and frowned.

"Mind-tapping without permission is strictly not allowed, Mr. Jenaoin!" Ben said, then removed his hand.

"If I don't know what's broken, I can't fix it, now, can I?" Roland said. "Your present train of thought won't cut it if we're going to be on the front line together."

Another figure appeared at the door and they all turned.

"Master Tula," a Brasheer said, "the Mistress requests you and the apprentice meet her in the speaking chamber at once."

"Very well," Dogg said. "Please inform her we are on our way."

The Brasheer bowed slightly and left.

"Well, what's it to be, Ben?" asked Dogg.

Ben looked at her and then to Roland.

"Well, it does get cold and I guess I can use all the help I can get. I've never partnered with a friend like you before, Roland."

"Humph. I never accepted a human before you, either."

"Well, then I … I guess we could try to sort this out together."

"Try!" Roland's mouth crumpled. "Losers try, lad! We either do or we die along the way. Now, give me permission to hear and thought-speak to you, and we can get the birth of this new timeline underway."

Ben looked at Dogg and then focused back on Roland. "Alright then, let's go."

"Good! Then place me where I should be and the contract is sealed. After you, Tula," said Roland.

All agreed, the three left to meet with the Mistress Farron Bach.

\* \* \*

Outside the Lair of Bach, with a stiff breeze pushing through the trees behind, Beetaa stood in front of the gates. On either side of the entrance,

< 219 >

at the cliff face, stood two hooded figures dressed in the same robes as the Brasheer warrior seen at Gantry, their faces completely obscured. They turned and bowed when Beetaa stepped toward them. Beetaa replied in kind, arms spread out with palms forward and open, in peace.

"I am Beetaa Pinnaraa. My presence is requested on orders from Talon West."

"The escorts?" asked the Brasheer on the left in a husky tone.

"They have returned."

The Brasheer looked at each other. Beetaa saw a fine silver vapor of energy pass the two-stride gap between them, which he recognized as a mind-exchange. There was a heavy shunt of stone from behind the cliff face between them.

"Welcome, Apprentice," said the Brasheer on the right.

Both Brasheer turned, then passed a hand in front of the stonewall. The seam between the two great doors separated, and the stone doors opened inward.

"Leave your world behind," said one and then both walked in.

Beetaa followed through the arched entry and heard the stone door close behind with a *thoomb*. Walking along the lamplit wide passage, unfamiliar smells and sounds stimulated every sense. Beetaa noticed the same runes carved into the walls as those seen in Gantry. As they advanced, different passages broke away from the main thoroughfare at random.

*Quite a catacomb, this place.*

"This stonework is exquisite. It must have taken an age," Beetaa said as they passed one particularly elaborate wall.

Neither Brasheer made reply. In fact, even to Beetaa's trained ears, their every movement was silent. Somewhere in the distance, a strange faint droning sound could be heard. *Chanting of the Articles of War maybe. So many corridors and stairwells, who could say where their origin lies?*

Alien smells of spice, cordite, and chemicals flowed past on soft currents of air. Beetaa followed around a corner and stepped through a large archway into an antechamber preceding an enormous natural cathedral space. There, whispers from an unknown source crept from shadow to ear, which pressed

< 220 >

upon him as though they were searching hands.

"Wait here," said the forward escort.

Then, before Beetaa could bow in respect, both Brasheer activated their blur ability and dissolved into the dim light, leaving a heavy silence to settle upon the new inductee. Standing there, he realized there was a force of nature in this place, and it had its focus squarely on him.

*Now what?*

\* \* \*

Dogg and Ben arrived at Mistress Farron's speaking chamber from the south wing of the Bach Lair.

"Follow me," said Dogg.

Farther in, Ben noticed a softly lit space with cavernous natural ceilings and a large fireplace over to the left. One figure sat in a high-backed chair, and another figure could be seen on the edge of shadow to the right, near the fireplace.

*A homey place, in a kind of medieval knights' keep sort of way. Hate the feeling of being watched like this. What's all the hiding for, anyway?*

*"Think a lot softer, Sparky, or I'm sure you'll find out,"* Ben heard Roland say in his head.

*"Cripes. Now there are two of you listening to my head."*

Dogg looked across her shoulder. *"Shh, both of you. Farron is sitting by the fire."*

*"Hang on. I know the fella in that hat near the fire,"* Ben thought, as they drew closer. Then he smiled. "Uniss," Ben said to himself.

*"Come, Ben."* Dogg said. *"Don't speak here till you're spoken to."* She padded toward the center of the room, leading the way. *"An audience with Mistress Farron has no equal on this world. Few on this world even know she really exists, let alone have spoken to her. We have known each other for an age."*

*"She looks like an empress sitting there. Cripes, she's as tall as the ones in the bunker, only with silver-gray hair,"* Ben thought.

*"Farron Bach is no ordinary sentient, Sparky,* Roland chimed in. *She is a Honan lord who has taken the form of half Scarzen to fulfill her role as leader*

< 221 >

*of the Scarzen Brasheer. On the Superverse tier of power, the Honan stand as the first tier of command under the Evercycle Council along with Tula's Filion race."*

*"And where does your race stand then?"* Ben asked.

*"Next in line under them; our opposite is the Echaa."*

*"Oh, I didn't realize you had that much clout …"*

*"Few ever do."*

*"So do all Honan like Mistress Farron have faces a bit like an elf?"*

*"Only when they choose to walk as mortals."*

*"But, Roland, she looks like a Scarzen too, with her braids and such."*

*"Scarzen hair is never glossy silver, Sparky. Look at her eyes when you're close. They're sapphire-blue—not orange—and full of the wisdom of ages."*

They stopped some steps away from Farron, who turned her focus on them.

"Well, Tula," Farron said, arms resting on her chair. "Again we meet in interesting times. I found myself unable to respond to your metta-wave hails, some parlor game of H, no doubt. He has been stirring more of late."

"As always I know you'll bring light to a darkened space," Dogg replied.

Farron acknowledged Dogg's compliment with a short nod, then said, "Roland, it feels a millennium has passed. I hope the soul stream transfer left you without distortion on arrival. This world's present has developed some unstable fields associated with the cavion seal the Citadel Council has enforced lately. I see you agreed to participate in discovering what has sullied such a triumphant victory at the conclusion of the Great Event."

Roland's front brim slouched down in respect. "Whatever my circumstance, whenever the Abbess of Bach needs Roland's service, she will never be refused, as promised. Though I know I left with full memory of my part to play, like those I have arrived with, my memory is vague, other than what the humans would say is a 'gut feeling.' Being here and accepting my present fitting is key to discovering the answer."

"Indeed, I understand your dilemma, Commander," Farron said. "It affects me, too."

"A Honan affected by a Continuum timeline fault? Unheard of," said Roland.

< 222 >

"Yes," said Farron. "But not before I discovered a rift in a parallel present associated with the Great Event that collided and braided this present with a future Superverse potential into one locked present. It appears as though someone very powerful intends to turn back time for some alternate victory. I only know because I managed to log and isolate the event in a sealed archive that exists in my private quarters inside the Bach Fortress. Being inaccessible to any Continuum anomalous interference, the research file wasn't erased along with everyone else's pivotal memories of what has reshaped and locked this present reality after the Great Event. But, like you, all my ability to put the facts together has been … interfered with."

"I see. Regardless, Mistress, I will serve in my fullest capacity," said Roland.

"There's no place for retired, memory-fractured worn brims on this rack," another voice cut in from near the fireplace.

"Drop the feud, Trev. No place for it here," said Uniss to the Jenaoin on his crown, still gazing into the fire.

Roland's face twisted toward Uniss and Trever with a grimace, but he said nothing and spun back to Farron, who ignored the interplay.

"And how does your new fitting please you, Roland?" Farron asked.

"As mortals go, he's not the most flexible mind I've covered, but I sense a very deep well of potential and know he is one of the keys to setting things right."

Ben frowned. *"Well, thanks, I think,"* Ben said, mind to mind. *"How old must someone be to know all that stuff? And she speaks like my old aunt Ethol, who was ninety when I saw her last."*

"And all my other abilities function perfectly," Farron said. "Including hearing loud thoughts of young human men. Come forward."

Wide-eyed, Ben shuffled uncomfortably, feeling Farron's gaze upon him. *Cripes.* He felt she could see straight through him. She tapped her lip thoughtfully with one finger.

"This is all very strange to you, yes?" she asked Ben.

"Yes, ma'am."

"But it does not give you pause for concern?"

"No, ma'am."

< 223 >

"You may call me 'Mistress Farron.'" A small smile started at the corner of her mouth. "It's been awhile since I have talked to such a curious one, Tula."

"He was assigned from witness protection and came with a black file," Dogg said.

"Yes. I know. We will speak of that later. Ben Blochentackle, you are among friends. How do you measure the sum of your experience so far?"

Roland's eyes and crown tilted down as though watching Ben from above as he looked at the ground, searching for a focused answer.

"I … cannot measure the depth of something I have no comparison for, Mistress. I know it's kicked my shins pretty hard, though, and there's more to come."

Farron looked at Dogg. "Much more. I have scant memory of you from before, but seeing you tells me you just might have the right stuff we'll need. No preincarnate history at all?" Farron asked.

Uniss shook his head. "Like Tula said, all files were back-locked and my memory is as bent as everyone else's. He's got a mind of his own, I can tell you that much, and he's important to this whole mess, that's for certain—and someone high up stuck him with a soul tracker at birth."

"A soul tracker," Farron said, eyeing Ben in deep thought. "Such a thing is only sanctioned for very special packages."

"It all had Three's mark on it, confirmed when I found Starlin lurking and looking for an opportunity to snatch the lad away," Uniss said. "In the end, he tried taking Ben from us in the open. He wanted him that badly."

"And Uniss extracted the tracker and pulled it into himself," Dogg said, still clearly upset at the risk Uniss had taken. "Could have turned his soul to fuzz, risking such a thing."

Uniss stepped away from the fire. "That was the price. Ben's the key to something pivotal about the Great Event and our way forward. The only way we are going to find out what is to retrace the timeline."

"And keep H from achieving a comeback," said Trever.

"Yes, it's a full schedule. We'll see to both of them as we go, then. On another subject, any Echaa activity?" Farron said.

"Unknown, but Starlin is trapped planetside and that's madness enough,"

< 224 >

Uniss said. "Soon as he gets tired of lookin' for Ben, he's going to go looking to aid H."

"That's not good news." Farron looked to Ben. "I'll keep him here and boost his education. Roland, ensure wisdom and maturity are his motivating force, lest he be corrupted." She looked to a shadowed corner. "Atacuss, bring in our final guest."

A thin-framed Brasheer stepped into the light, paid respect without a word, and moved toward the other end of the chamber.

"Take a moment to make yourselves comfortable," Farron said. "I need a word with Tula."

Ben went to tip his hat.

*"Just bow,"* Ben heard Roland say.

Following instruction, he paid respects using a Scarzen salute and went over to join Uniss at the fireplace, leaving Dogg and Farron to a more private chat.

\* \* \*

"Hello, Uniss," Ben said as the smell of burning embers met his nose.

Uniss nodded. "G'day, young fella."

The expression on Uniss's face was one of concern, something Ben rarely saw from Uniss. Ben watched as Uniss picked up a log from a short stack at the side of the fireplace and dropped it into the flames. Preoccupied with something, Uniss nodded to himself. He swung a glance at Ben's new companion.

"Roland, good to see you made it okay," Uniss said.

"Good tidings to you, Uniss," Roland said before shifting his focus to Uniss's Jenaoin companion. "Hello, Trever, I see the change in Continuum dynamics hasn't dulled your temperament," Roland said in a dry tone.

"It's a talent of mine," Trever replied, tipping his crown.

"So, Ben ... that was a good answer to Mistress Farron, young fella. You did well," said Uniss.

"Didn't know it was a test," said Ben.

"Just *being* is a test, Ben. To the Honan lords like Farron, everything is

< 225 >

interconnected and you just showed her where you fit in," Uniss said.

"I thought we were never supposed to interfere," Ben said. "But we seem to be doing it a lot."

"No, son, *you're* not supposed to interfere, 'less I say so—until you know the rules anyway. Farron is happy with you, and since she seems to be the one with the least loss of memory of past events, let's leave it at that."

"But all those guys you executed in Yorr Fields? Isn't that interfering?" Ben whispered.

"You still don't get it, do you?" Uniss said. "It would have been a crime against universal law for me not to. Because of *your* actions in the maze, life-cycle timelines were skewed, and brand-new Continuum threads emerged. Since the timeline could not be stabilized, I was forced to work with the new one, and so now we have this reality and not the one previously archived. Now, listen well," Uniss said, "Farron has friends in some pretty high places on the Continuum, so stay on the ball and in her good books. Are we clear?"

"And if I fail?" Ben asked.

"Then, young fella, your career as a profiler will come to a sudden end. Farron is Evercycle Zero's direct representative—my superior, you might say. Her word is final. Pleased you said the right thing?"

Ben said nothing; instead, he looked across at Farron still in conversation with Dogg, trying to fathom their exchange.

Just then, all heads turned to see Farron's aide return with another Scarzen warrior. Farron's personal guard escorted Beetaa Pinnaraa to stand within a short distance. Stopping, Beetaa paid respect. Farron, still seated, nodded and gestured for him to sit with Dogg to her right. Beetaa sat, trying to hide a sense of awe. Farron looked at Beetaa in her regal manner, considering the young Scarzen carefully. Beetaa noticed a young Flaxon male standing next to the fire along with an older Flaxon of darker skin tone.

*Flaxon? Here? What mischief is this?*

"Why have you come?" asked Farron, her voice smooth and firm.

*By order, of course,* Beetaa thought, then frowned. He finally said, "I have been summoned for service, Great Mistress. That is all I know."

"That is true. There is much at stake in your future here." She leaned

< 226 >

forward and held Beetaa's gaze. "Identify your blood otaa."

"You already know, Mistress," Beetaa replied without thinking. The answer jumped out of his mouth with the same alacrity that he would have answered Spanaje.

"That's right. I do," she said, relaxing back into her seat. "Your blood otaa graced these very halls. His potential had great reach, far more than that of a masterful Brasheer. He could have led the Scarzen into a new era, but chose instead to participate in lesser things."

"My otaa was … is held—"

Farron raised a hand. "No need. His honor is not in doubt here. But your future is." She looked around at the others. "Everyone's is." Her gaze fell back on Beetaa. "Your blood otaa's memory holds high honor in this place. I see that Benataa's rebellious fire still resides in his pup."

"I meant no disrespect, Great Mistress. I did not expect to be amongst alien of Scarza in this sacred place. I have also been separated from my mirror. Our bond is new," said Beetaa.

"That will be rectified in time. All paths are now uncertain, and your choices today open the way to uncharted future," she said.

"Is this why I've been called before such … mixed company?" Beetaa remarked, throwing a visible sneer at Ben and Uniss.

"Watch your tongue, foot-pad!" Farron's eyes flashed bright orange in disapproval. "From now on, choose your comments wisely, or transition without honor you shall see. Then stand before your ancestors if you can!"

Beetaa fidgeted.

"You are here *only* because you show potential for the future that is now disturbingly unpredictable!" Farron said.

As she spoke, Ben thought he felt the ground shudder underfoot.

"Your blood otaa Benataa and several of his clan before him were apprenticed to me. I personally educated them in the manner of all things."

*No Scarzen lives that long,* Beetaa thought.

Farron sat forward with a menacing look. "Who said I was *all* Scarzen, pup?"

"But, Great Mistress, I always understood that—"

< 227 >

"You understand *nothing* beyond the confines of your bunker and clan, that is clear! There are forces at work in this world beyond your comprehension, Warrior Pinnaraa. Even your ancient mystic Nur clan of Scarza's old world would comprehend what is happening in this present."

*"The Nur—who are they, Roland?"* Ben asked Roland in thought.

*"The Nur were part of another time in Scarzen evolution. Their powers of kin and intuitive reach regarding this world have never been equaled. They were ultimately crushed by the very forces we are dealing with now,"* Roland answered.

"The Nur were seeing the truth in what was to come long before Scarzen were considering braids as a sign of rank," Farron snapped, looking across at Ben. "Nur chronicles record that one from a world beyond shall unite with a clan native. Together, they shall liberate all beings from this world and beyond from being forgotten. Together, they shall put down a revolt of the second coming of great manipulator."

"Herr—I mean, H," said Ben.

"At the very least—and you need not fear saying his name in this stronghold," Farron said, her view swinging back to Beetaa. "My lifespan will see me well beyond your life and many of your descendants, Scarzen. My race was mapping existence on either side of the mortal-ethereal divide long before your species had evolved a second heart. You will follow orders as I dictate them to the letter, pup. Am I clear?"

Beetaa straightened. "Ho!"

*"Command authority goes only one way, Sparky,"* Roland whispered in Ben's head. *"Ears open, voice mute, and mind set to receive and respond, see?"*

Ben nodded slightly.

Farron relaxed back in her chair, easing the tension. "Now that we have that clear, we can move on. You, Warrior Pinnaraa, are here to play your part and to have your potential tested. The two here that resemble Flaxon are in fact of two different races." She gestured to Ben. "His future is interlocked with your own; you will treat him as clan in good favor. The other, as of now, is your immediate superior. You shall address him as Commander Uniss."

Both Ben and Beetaa braced a little at that comment. Farron raised one eyebrow and eyed them both. "Ben, come here!" she ordered.

< 228 >

"Weak at the knees" didn't quite do justice to how Ben felt, now looking squarely into Beetaa's bright ember-orange eyes. He approached and stood within arms' reach of the young Scarzen, who had dropped his eyes to the ground.

"Ben, you know more of the greater picture," Farron said. "You will teach him as much about it as you can. He in turn will teach you the ways of the Scarzen. Look at me, both of you. You are both here in this life because of something in the far past. *Together*, you must help to right a wrong from that time. Your collaboration is key to saving this world at the very least."

"Mistress, I am newly committed to a battle ally!" Beetaa said. "The Scarzen *Book of Right Action* prohibits interplay with another ally unless exceptional circumstances prevail. He barely looks capable of having the strength to lift a spoon to feed himself—*and* he reeks of the smell of Flaxon. Each time I look at him, I see one of them. I demand the Scarzen right to have his heart tested—combat-tested."

"You'll get more than you bargain for, young Scarzen," Dogg said, taking Beetaa by surprise.

A breath later, Beetaa turned squarely to Ben. The aggression from him was palpable, making Ben want to jump as far out of the way as he could. But, before he could move, a shower of green light fell all around him to the ground, and he heard Roland say in his head, *"Stand your ground, Sparky, and look him in the eyes!"*

"Now, any Scarzen, even a young impetuous one like you, should know how to choose a battlefield," Roland said to Beetaa. "This isn't it! We Jenaoin abhor bad manners. But, if you feel the need to breathe your last, raise your ends of peace."

The surprise of Roland's action froze the moment for both Ben and Beetaa. Neither individual knew what to do next. Beetaa looked from Farron to Ben and then to Roland. Ben stayed locked on Beetaa, outwardly solid, inwardly jelly.

"Seems to me that squabbles amongst allies only help the enemy," Dogg said. "Whaddaya think? Roland, please turn off your faux-matter field."

The field around Ben dispersed, and Beetaa took a breath, then relaxed.

< 229 >

"Warrior Pinnaraa, if you know your history, you know who I am," Farron said. "This human is my apprentice and under the direct mentorship of Commander Uniss. Give Ben a chance to prove his worth and work with him, and I give you my word, if he proves incompetent, I will remove him myself."

"My apology, Mistress. I was unaware of the gravity of my situation," Beetaa said. "One and all, I beg pardon."

"No harm done. Understandable in some ways," said Farron. "Ben's world is beyond the stars you see in the night skies. He bears you no ill will. Am I correct, Apprentice Ben?"

Ben took a relieved swallow. "I'll do my best, Mistress," he said.

Beetaa considered Ben for a couple of moments. "Please accept my apology … human. I shall serve the objective as ordered," Beetaa said to Ben, paying respect.

Ben stood dumb for a moment.

*"Say 'accepted,' Sparky,"* Ben heard Roland say in his head.

"Accepted," Ben said.

"Herrex, Lord of Balance, will be our first objective to neutralize," Farron said. "He gathers force as each day passes. His presence on this world is no longer dormant. More of this, you will learn later. Share as much information and skills as you can. Your mission plan shall be presented shortly."

"Who is this lord?" asked Beetaa. "Studying the histories, I have not seen any reference."

"You will know him in Scarzen history as 'the Dark Star,'" Farron said.

"World destroyer," Ben said under his breath.

"Quite so," replied Farron. "Good to see you have been listening to your mentors."

Ben nodded.

"Long before either of you knew life in this form, Herrex attempted to overthrow those responsible for existence, called the Evercycle Council," Farron said. "Herrex wanted to generate a second parallel Superverse where he alone ruled. In short, his actions plunged the entire Superverse into a catastrophic war. It divided power in both mortal and ethereal worlds. Many advanced

< 230 >

races were lost. Herrex sent countless great sentient beings, irreplaceable in Superverse evolution, to the Echaa Realms for erasure, never to reincarnate again. All that remains of them is an index file number. Herrex will have this world erased too if he resurrects into whole form.

"Only because of the skills of Uniss and Tula here, and the gallant support of those from the Jenaoin Empire—such as Roland and Trever—Herrex was caught and incarcerated on your Earth, Ben, and here on Tora, Beetaa. Humans and Scarzen were given the task, along with a small group of lesser gods, to be caretakers on the inside."

"Seeing to it that Herrex remained ineffective," Uniss said.

"But I never understood … Herrex doesn't appear in Earth history or the Bible or in any belief system text that Dogg told me," remarked Ben.

"Of course not! All your ancestors' memories were altered to suit the need prior to reincarnation," Farron said.

"Sort of like now," said Ben.

"Yes," said Farron. "It's one reason there are many religions and inventions on your planet. They are all part of a larger collective consciousness showing the same perspective from many points of view. It has kept Herrex in check until now. Be assured he and those assisting him will use present circumstance to every advantage to see him brought back into being. Your last incarnation, for instance, Ben Blochentackle, I believe you lived a demonic cycle. It's the only reason the likes of Three would be so persistent in wanting you for her uses. Her jurisdiction is chaos and covers the evolution of demon realm sentients."

"What? I don't believe it. I'm no demon," Ben said, shaking his head.

"A short while ago, Ben Blochentackle, you thought hats didn't talk, either, did you?" Farron said. "Before the Continuum's anomalous breakdown occurred, and knowing of your intended arrival, Ben and Beetaa, I traced your birth parents' life cycles and the calculated insemination of your births. Benjamin, yours was most unusual in its reincarnate signature. Someone had tampered with it, which is an offence punishable by erasure. I was able to procure a security-sealed file annexed to your Akashic records. It shows that both of you …" She pointed to Ben and Beetaa. "… held significant

< 231 >

positions in Three's armies. You were bound to the House of Three, Lord of Chaos, and marched under her son Herrex's command for a time. After Herrex's overthrow, you both chose redemption and turned evidence against the Lord of Balance. After that, your soul signatures disappeared and were placed in witness protection."

"Struth!" Ben and Uniss said in unison, then looked at each other.

"Now Three's manipulations make sense," Uniss said.

"Zero, the original Evercycle," Farron said, "passed a decree. Zero ordered you hidden in reincarnate witness protection with the help of Seven, Lord of Reincarnation. Neither Uniss, Tula, nor even myself is permitted access to your full background without the combined consent of Zero and Nine, the Lord of Harmony."

Ben went to speak, but Roland slapped him on the forehead with the front of his brim.

"So they could even be used as double agents, should it get that far," Roland said.

"That's one scenario," said Farron. "Herrex now lives in the ideas, thoughts, and actions of many on Ben's world and, it appears, on Tora too. Coiled in the back of unsuspecting minds … growing like a parasite."

"How does that force our hand here?" asked Dogg.

Farron nodded. "I have learned that Trabonus, Regent of Flaxor, has been attempting with some success to resurrect Herrex himself. Herrex is clearly manipulating the little dictator, but it is a real threat nonetheless."

"So, stopping Trabonus is the first solid step," said Uniss, reading into her words.

"If Herrex re-forms, the Council will be thrown into chaos, and existence as we know it would cease. The Citadel Wars could be a normal progression all over again."

"But, if Herrex knows we are here, intending to stop him, won't he come after us?" asked Ben.

"I'm counting on it," said Farron, glaring at him. "And all the other snakes in the grass we've yet to see."

"You're still technically the Abbess of Bach. Any chance of help from

< 232 >

there?" said Uniss.

"As I have said, I need Nine and Zero's consent. Nine is in parts unknown, and my clearance has been downgraded since my station here. Other than that, the Angel of Archives, Mortilan, might offer some shade of assistance. But she is sealed in the heart of Bach's central vault and would need to be awakened. By all accounts, Ben and Beetaa must have provided or carried something very special to the Evercycle Council. Only six percent of the opposition was given clemency. The rest were sent to the Echaa Realms for erasure.

"So we were bad guys who flipped sides," Ben said with a nervous laugh.

"At one time, Ben," Farron said, "I suspect the very worst, given your records' archive-security level. Right now, however, you are just plain 'Apprentice Ben.'"

"Well, what if I wanted to find out who I was?" Ben asked, frowning.

"Any attempt to do so would be futile, not to mention the price you would pay," Farron said. "Even if it were possible, it would certainly be a nightmare of the worst kind for you and us. The realizations of your past lives and actions could bring back old desires. Leave it be. You must both focus on other things here." Farron threw Dogg and Uniss a glance, realizing there would be private questions later. "Now, Starlin. As the Council's chief accountant for karmic burden, he had access to archives as interim administrator in Bach for a time after the war. As those acquainted with him know, he is not to be trusted. I know he was trading information for Three, who used it for extortion against several gods and leaders of master mortal races, such as the Varian, but we could never prove it."

"Give me ten standard minutes without Three backing him, and he'll tell you every venomous act and dirty thing he's ever done," said Dogg.

"Business before fantasy pleasures, Tula," Farron said. "Starlin's duties included recovering all lesser karmic debts by individuals entering a new cycle. His territory crossed a myriad of threads on the Continuum, including Tora's populace. Many we know received punishment far above the crime's weight. As an agent of Three, mayhem motivates his darker vices. He rejoices in the suffering of others."

< 233 >

"Humph!" said Dogg. "It was like putting the cat in charge of guarding the cream."

"It has been done, Tula. Three sanctions his every action, which all but makes him untouchable," Farron said, frowning.

Trever harrumphed atop Uniss's head. "Someone long ago should have ripped Starlin a new ar—"

"Trev!" Uniss snapped.

"A new accounts book, I intended to say," Trever said.

"Not in the centuries I've known you," said Roland.

"So what are your orders, Mistress?" asked Beetaa, ignoring the interplay.

"Firstly, you two will commence your training in the development of arcane skills under the guidance of Quinn, Brasheer Master Battle-Mage. Waste no waking moment to absorb all Quinn has to teach you. That knowledge will help keep you both safe and Herrex where he belongs for as long as possible."

"Earth, too?" Ben asked.

"Yes, Earth, too," Farron replied. "There is much to do. We will speak again later. Atacuss, my aide, will take you through the necessary details. Uniss, Tula, and I must see to other things."

The same Brasheer who had been standing in the shadows of a corner again stepped into view. Drawing his hood back, he exposed a handsome Scarzen face of middle age. Then Atacuss approached.

"Come with me," he said.

Beetaa and Ben paid respects, and Atacuss led them to other parts of the Lair.

"Still some fire under old Roland's brim," Trever said with a tone of respect, watching him leave with Ben.

"Yep," said Uniss. "Good to have 'im here."

* * *

After Beetaa and Ben departed, Farron spoke final words to the remaining three.

"Herrex has a fingernail dug into this present, I can feel it," she said.

< 234 >

"Those two bring mixed tidings to the affair, and with Starlin on the hunt, you'll need to watch them close."

"Why don't the Evercycles just shut Earth and Tora down now? Surely Herrex is still weak enough to be dispersed," said Trever.

"The Continuum is in flux, Trever," Farron said. "Actions that should have occurred have not. You know that Evercycles are the foundation of existence itself. They know existence may only be moved around, not created or destroyed. The best any could do with Herrex was incarcerate him."

"Feed 'im to the Echaa on Tyr's leash, then. He wouldn't come back from that," Trever said.

"Nah, mate," Uniss said, shaking his head. "Can't do that. Herrex is an Evercycle, part of the Superverse dark-matter construct."

"Uniss is correct," Farron said. "Herrex could be subdued, possibly a couple of trillion years even. It could also signal his rebirth. No one knows what the final chemistry would be, and I have a suspicion the Echaa are not as well in hand as the Council would have us believe."

"If Herrex found a way to use the Echaa against us … there is nothing that would stop him," said Dogg.

"So now what?" said Uniss.

"The first step is to shut down Trabonus's efforts. That buys us time. Are your abilities still diminishing?" Farron asked everyone.

"Yes," Uniss.

"Mine, too," said Dogg.

"I'm still okay," Trever said. "At least, I feel okay."

"Okay. Very well, first things first," said Farron. "Uniss, see if you can find out what Starlin is up to. Tula, see how far Trabonus has advanced to his goal. I can't see the outcomes beyond a short distance now. Last news said all bridgeports between ethereal and mortal planes are static. That means we are on our own here. I need to speak to Malforce in Talon East to gauge the strength of the Scarzen armies. I think we are in for a ground war."

"What about me?" asked Trever.

"Do as you and other Jenaoin have always done: protect your fitting at all times."

< 235 >

"Got it!" said Trever.

"Now, leave me. I need to meditate on this further."

Everyone left and went their separate ways. The game was on.

< 236 >

## CHAPTER 17
## SHRINKING NET

On the same windswept day that Ben made new acquaintances in the Brasheer Mountain, a Grand Circle of all Scarza's high keepers was convened in Talon East. A Scarzen Grand Circle rarely met. Such a thing was only spared for matters of the utmost importance. Prior to the keepers arriving, security in the bunker doubled, and all diplomatic and foreign visitors were asked to leave because of an outbreak of Scarzen flu and scale rash. To prevent any undetected spies from mapping the bunker's general layout, all short walls were reset every three hours, closing off standard thoroughfares and opening new pathways. With the bunker cleansed of any non-Scarzen eyes, a feast was presented for the honored guests. The Grand Circle then convened on the third day of Targ's moon in Talon East's Hall of Ceremonies.

There, all keepers sat around an ornately carved wooden table shaped into a nine. In front of each sat a drinking vessel and a small dome-shaped stone, called an "approval stone." The table was centered in a grand polished glass-stone chamber, where high walls displayed hung baskets of colorful orchids. Any outsider would have felt the power of those gathered in that space, each leader a formidable foe in their own right. Commander Titarliaa, head of bunker security and newly promoted to viceroy of Talon East, sat on High Keeper Malforce's right, acting as meeting arbiter.

All officer attachés accompanying their keepers sat on comfortable bench seats at the sides with independent mini-tables to hold a beverage and parchment. Attendants stood in corner positions of the room to provide service when needed. Prior to the meeting's beginning, loose chatter echoed as everyone awaited the signal. Viceroy Titarliaa tapped a crystal bell that swung delicately from a pyramid glass-stone frame on the table. Guards then sealed the hall shut, and Viceroy Titarliaa addressed the collective:

"In Scarzen history, a great feast always precedes going into a great war. Talon East bids you all dine well as we gather force and momentum for victory!"

All keepers except Malforce knocked the table with their approval stone to calls of "Hear, hear!"

"On Keeper Malforce's orders, shortly after your arrival, you received a sealed scroll. Each has a Talon East ring seal confirming the information is drafted by Keeper Malforce's hand. Would you each now exchange that scroll with the peer on your right to confirm that the information is exactly the same for all?"

Moments later, nods and a tap of approval stones signaled united agreement, and Titarliaa handed the meeting over to High Keeper Malforce.

"Navigators of Scarza," Malforce said. "We are here under grave circumstance. Until recently, a tolerance existed between Flaxor, their allies in the north, and ourselves. That peace has been abused, hiding a conspiracy to assault Scarza as a whole. No doubt you have heard rumors. Detail of the truth will have a bitter taste and will guarantee your support, I am certain. This circle has been called to decide appropriate consultation measures to put our enemy down before any momentum to their advantage can be gained."

Malforce relaxed back into his chair.

"Questions? Statements?" asked Titarliaa, looking around the table.

"What is the primary threat? And how far advanced is it?" asked High Keeper of Talon South, Jallanaa.

Malforce looked to Viceroy Titarliaa and nodded for him to proceed.

"As you know, some time back, we reacquired the Tears from the Flaxon capital of Weirawind at some considerable cost," Titarliaa replied. "Agents

< 238 >

returned with intelligence reporting the Flaxon being on the right track to unlock the formula that would stabilize our trilix crystal to *rebuild* their population."

"Yes, ancient history. The Tears were recovered, so?" Jallanaa said.

*Naught's beard, even in these times, Jallanaa plays his political card,* Malforce thought, wanting things to move on.

"Keeper Jallanaa," Titarliaa said. "The Flaxon have used the byproduct of that information from those events to take steps to poison all Scarzen main water supplies, using trilix as the catalyst."

"What!" Jallanaa said. "Malforce, how long have you known of this?"

"Keeper Jallanaa, if you'll allow me to continue?" Titarliaa said, forcing Jallanaa to silence. "Recently, Flaxon command sent a pair of Quall assassins here with two objectives: one, acquire further information on trilix by stealing Alchemist Ereedaa's personal notes; and, two, assassinate Alchemist Ereedaa. Evidently, the Flaxon have information on Ereedaa's importance in trilix research. Ereedaa was assassinated, and the Quall escaped from the bunker confines, but we soon captured them. We know all this from an open confession by the Quall."

A few grumbles of dissatisfaction welled up over that comment. All listened in grim silence as Titarliaa continued.

"We have confirmed the Flaxon intend placing the reactive agent on trilix in underground streams that feed the drinking water supply. This is a dishonorable plan even for Flaxon."

"Why would the Quall be so… helpful toward us? I, for one, have only ever crushed them under my boot," said Jallanaa.

"The Quall we discovered were in fact held to ransom and acting under duress. They have given their bond of service to Scarza with Keeper Malforce's endorsement," said the viceroy. "Keeper Malforce in return has agreed to assist them in the recovery of their elder, Makayass, who is the hostage held by the Flaxon as insurance. So we have good reason to go and consult with Flaxor in the extreme—and we now have double agents to get very close to Regent Trabonus." Titarliaa took a breath. "Navigators, the aim of Regent Trabonus is to wipe our clans from the face of Ludd."

< 239 >

"I believe this threat real enough that we must cut down the Flaxon menace or our clan will potentially perish in a pool of our own gut throwing," said Malforce.

A servant began topping off each of the keepers' drinking vessels, forcing them to consider something as simple as drinking water to be so threatening to their existence.

"I'll have my step into the beyond as the ancestors intended," said Keeper Keenas. "Have you spoken to others? Who beyond Scarza would declare themselves as allies?"

"We have sent envoys to both the Minnima and Celeron capitals," Titarliaa said. "Queen Yazmin's Minnima army will stand with Scarza; the Celeron are more likely to take a diplomatic path, as always. They prefer parley and back-room agreements to open battle."

A swell of voices raised in acknowledgement.

"In this, we must think beyond ourselves," said Malforce. "Should the Flaxon succeed, they'll not stop until Ludd is in their grip."

"Humph! Celeron! Merchants and politicians!" Jallanaa grumbled. "If it's not in their personal interests, they never fight on the front line. They give us sellenor at a discount, and we watch their backs."

"You grizzle because they are on your border and you cannot press them to your will," said Keenas.

"Finger-pointing gets us nowhere. Time is short," said Malforce.

"Yes, I could speak with Celeron King Karnor if that will help your emotional bruises, Jallanaa," said Keenas.

Jallanaa looked at Keenas with distain. "The Flaxon have not endeared themselves of late in that region. Once Karnor knows the position, we will have his aid."

A couple of the keepers sat silent while others spoke with vigor to their peers. Titarliaa tapped the bell, breaking the rumble of conversation.

"The first step proposed is the assassination of Regent Trabonus …" Titarliaa said, "a task our new agents the Quoll are well suited to and they have already supplied sound planning for such a coup."

"Just a moment," said Norstaa, Keeper of the Northern Region. "What

< 240 >

EARTH'S SECRET TRILOGY: BOOK TWO — WAR AND LIES

about the witch and her ghouls—Mistress Farron and her almighty Brasheer? Where are they in all this? She could dance a cloud over Flaxor and it would be done in a blink with no trace or blame."

Jallanaa gave a short guttural laugh. "Why don't you just walk on up there yourself and instruct her to do just that?"

As Norstaa gave a snort of anger, Jallanaa folded a piece of parchment and passed it to an attendant.

"Don't mock me, Jallanaa!" Norstaa said.

"Oh … threats?" Jallanaa said. "Please, Norstaa, spare us the dramatics. We all know your sad tidings over her rejection. Not enough oomph in your kin, eh?"

"There's nothing wrong with my oomph, Jallanaa," snapped Norstaa.

"So you say," Jallanaa said.

Norstaa pounded the table with a fist. "You sit in your southern forests, your back covered by the Minnima border and bows and spear-throwers. We stand at the frontier. I'll have any Scarzen's head on a plate who calls me coward!"

The rising tension broke when a security officer opened the door from the hall. Four sentinels entered, ready to subdue any hostility. Malforce waved them back. Jallanaa remained unfazed by Norstaa, just smirking at winning the verbal match.

*Both a miracle from the same chest. You'd think after all this time they would bury their aging grievances,* thought Malforce.

Malforce watched Norstaa, uncomfortable with the silence, sit back with a sour sneer aimed at Jallanaa. Malforce stood and showed open palms in a placating gesture, wanting focus returned to the real problem.

"Should we do the enemy's work for them? The very thing we would have happen to them must not befall us. We must remain united," Malforce said. "None of us controls the Brasheer Mistress. She will do as she will but always acts in the clan's best interest."

"Does she know?" asked Keeper Keenas.

"I have no doubt she is aware. She hears most things before they reach even our ears. It is best not to force a hand where she is concerned. In the

< 241 >

interests of all, I will arrange an audience to advise her of our present position."

Jallanaa gave a short laugh. "You could go with Malforce, Norstaa."

Norstaa narrowed his eyes and grumbled.

"If we could return to the matter of the regent, that would be more constructive," Malforce said.

"Why not just crush the Flaxon as a whole?" asked Daylin, Keeper of the Western Shores Bunker.

"The regent's removal will help to throw their command into chaos and turn their focus elsewhere. They will have an internal power struggle in the hurried attempt to establish a new leader," said Malforce.

"Then they will seek justice," said Daylin.

"And we will goad their wound with a gathering threat near the Flaxon border. One of their generals will stand as champion, wanting leadership of Flaxor. This has been their way in the past," said Titarliaa.

"And if the assassins are unsuccessful—or worse, captured—in the act?" asked Jallanaa.

"Either way, keepers of Scarza, honorable battle is coming—only with more vigor in the second instance. The Chou Empire of the north will want to strengthen their chances by offering the Flaxon support ... only to pull out at the last moment as is their common tactic when odds are clear. The Flaxon will then consult with us *alone*," said Titarliaa.

*Yes, and none in Ludd will miss the Flaxon's meddling ways once they are crushed,* Malforce thought.

"So, while being on our guard and preparing, everything must appear business as usual," said Malforce. "The Flaxon are a collective of small fiefdoms united through a religious underbelly—what do they call it?"

Titarliaa raised a hand. "Ah ... I believe they call it a church, my Keeper," he said, sitting forward. "If I may?"

Malforce bid him carry on.

"As you know, their priests provide a rigid framework of belief. Only the regent is above reproach, being the physical representative of a one god protocol. Their church teaches that their salvation lies in the conversion of all to one way of accepting life, and death. If the church zealots are allowed

< 242 >

to steer the Flaxon's will unchecked, they are quite a force. Our first task is fragmentation by turning church against state through poisonous dialogue and doubt in their regent. That will be something our Celeron allies will delight in perpetuating."

"If they are so well protected by their god and their heaven is so appealing, why do Flaxon fear death so, and why does their regent aim to live in that moldy meat sack of a body for eternity?" asked Keenas.

"Flaxon customs are not my interest. What of their latest weapon development?" asked Jallanaa.

"Intelligence is still to come back on that, but we do know they have made some improvements to their mass throwing weapons—something they call a *rocket*. Simple examples have been seen starting at Yorr Pass years ago. Our armorers are working on protection layers to help," Titarliaa said.

"Scarzen don't need armor," said Daylin.

"We do when our enemy develops a projectile stronger than our armor-piercing arrow racks and capable of piercing our warriors' slaa battle garments! Your warriors' kin fields will only hold so long against such a thing," snapped Malforce.

They all sat, slapped to silence for several breaths. Suddenly, the doors to the main hall burst open again ... and everyone stared at those entering. Flanked by two Brasheer bodyguards, and dressed in an exquisite black slaa-thread gown, Mistress Farron walked into the room. Every movement other than hers and her bodyguards' stalled as Farron made her way to the head of the table. Malforce stood, followed by the others. Everyone greeted her in standard military fashion.

"I see unnecessary debate still infests Scarza's navigators," Farron said.

Her bodyguards retreated a short distance to the rear, a purple hood and gown shrouding all detail of their face and body. She stood there, clearly in charge, surveying all at the table with her ice-blue eyes.

A long pause later, she acknowledged their respect: "Maatulac, sit."

*Why does she come now? Does she think we cannot take care of our own concerns? We need no matriarchal otutt here!* thought Norstaa, the last to sit down, almost missing his chair.

< 243 >

Still standing, Farron gave her bodyguards a nod and they retreated further. "It's good to see you too, Norstaa," Farron said. "Thinking as vociferously as always, I see."

The Brasheer bodyguards brought to Farron an elegant high-backed chair bearing strange runes, which she had said in the past were 'numbers.' Ten symbols in gold inlay adorned the head of the backrest. After a deliberate pause, Farron sat down.

"Scarza is at a crossroads for its future, and I wanted to be certain you are targeting your true nemesis," Farron said as one bodyguard placed a beverage to her right.

"As always, you are well informed, Mistress," said Malforce. "You needn't have pained yourself with a visit. We have the matter in hand."

"Perhaps. Until you all realize the enemy you seek to overcome is a ruse—a puppet of something much more powerful. The threat I speak of, you have not fought before," she said. "This time, you know not who you truly intend to consult with."

"What, have the Flaxon grown a second set of marbles?" said Norstaa.

"Mock me again, Norstaa, and being unable to produce offspring will be the least of your concerns," Farron said.

Norstaa's proud posture slumped just enough to show subservience.

"Scarzen hearts in battle have no equal, Norstaa. That is fact on this world," Farron said. "This situation is different. You stand in opposition to something beyond this world. Hear this explanation and ignore it at your peril. Before I begin, all below the rank of keeper are to wait outside."

Eyes flashed from one individual to another at the unprecedented command.

"Viceroy Titarliaa, if you please," said Malforce.

Seeing Malforce make the first move, the others—several reluctantly— followed suit. The room cleared of all non-essential clan, and Farron glanced back to one of the bodyguards, who moved immediately to secure the exit doors. She then cupped her hands on the table as though concealing something secret. When her hands opened, palms facing up, an expanding blue energy field mushroomed quickly and expanded to encapsulate all

< 244 >

seated. Jallanaa straightened from his normally relaxed pose, and Keenas looked around apprehensively.

"Do not be alarmed," Farron said. "This is only to ensure absolute security. No part of what I am about to tell you may be discussed outside this space. Is that clear?"

"Ho," all replied.

Farron nodded and began: "Long before Scarzen were civilized or could carve the glass-stone, the end of a great war in the stars was coming to a close. At its conclusion, the leader of the defeated force—a god force told in your newborn tales as 'the Dark Star'—was captured and put on trial. There, he was called 'Herrex.'"

"The tales were real?" asked Keenas.

"Very. For their crimes against the sky worlds and those of stone and air, Herrex's form was divided in two, then imprisoned. One half, the body so to speak, was turned into crystal and laid to rest on this world we call 'Tora,' in your catacombs. Yes, Herrex's body is the crystal you guard so closely. The other part, Herrex's everlasting soul, was placed in another world a very great distance from ours, called 'Earth.'"

Looks of confusion appeared on several faces as Farron continued. Some thought the drommal cheese had slid off her corn bread.

"The commander in chief of the force that defeated the Dark Star is called Zero; you recognize him by the name of 'Naught' and this symbol." She pointed over her shoulder to a glowing gold circle embedded into the crest of her chair. "This symbol represents his house. Zero knew that our enemy the Dark Star, like himself an eternal being along with eight others called Evercycles, was indestructible. Thus, to imprison the Dark Star—Herrex—in the sky worlds, Zero used the combined strengths of all the uncorrupted Evercycles to collide two immense physical masses together amongst the stars to make Tora and Earth.

"The story you have for trilix's discovery and its properties was injected into the minds of your ancestors, mixing truth and illusion to create one reality. It was done to ensure that your guardianship of it was uncompromising. As with all the best-laid plans, random choice leads to unpredictable outcomes.

< 245 >

Gravity of circumstance beyond your control has pulled you all into the most dire of unfolding events."

Farron paused to take a sip of her beverage. Some of the keepers murmured amongst themselves about her story.

"The third-generation leader of the Brasheer, Zharkaa, stumbled across a fragment of Herrex's pure body in the Brasheer Mountain—a fragment not completely crystallized. The instant Zharkaa touched it, Herrex's incorporeal form invaded Zharkaa's own afterlife body. Zharkaa went insane from attempting to repel Herrex in a mind war and to resist the growing forces inside him, and from there, the Dark Scarzen began to reemerge."

Farron stopped, watching several keepers whisper thoughts of concern to one another.

"Fortunately," Farron continued, "complete resurrection for Herrex failed in the last moments due to intervention by a young apprentice named Benataa Pinnaraa. He discovered Zharkaa during the final ritual. A faction struggle broke out. Fortunately, the one you call Tula, myself, and another were close by investigating a connected problem. We assaulted the Brasheer lair with one Brasheer faction led by Benataa's otaa, Soraxas.

At the mention of Benataa's name, many keepers again whispered to each other.

"I always knew there was more to Benataa than met the eye," said Jallanaa.

"Silence, please," Farron said. "All will be explained. Benataa saw Zharkaa reading from a secret tome in which he had recorded all the voice instructions from Herrex. Zharkaa was approached by Soraxas and asked to hand over the tome for the keepers to rule on what should be done about the arcane influence. Zharkaa refused, and a confrontation ensued. Zharkaa attempted to produce a cavion field, we think, possibly assisted by Herrex in some small way, to repel the resistance until the ritual was complete. Then Zharkaa sealed himself behind a repel field, defended by his unit of Dark Scarzen. It was Tula who broke the field defense and charged Zharkaa direct, putting herself in great jeopardy, her companion—Uniss—and I struck down Zharkaa's unit of Dark Scarzen liborators and halted the process."

"Such a fantastic tale, Mistress. Why were we never told?" asked Norstaa.

< 246 >

"For your own world's safety. Mortally wounded, Zharkaa vanished in the last moments of the struggle—along with his tome. That book, until recently, was thought lost. A short while ago, a part of the tome re-emerged—in the hands of the Regent Trabonus."

"Naught's beard!" Keenas said. "We must take it from the broznick at all costs. That Flaxon should have been turned to cornmeal decades ago. He would be a plague on Ludd should he receive such an ally."

"I'm sure we all agree," Farron said. "The partial tome, thankfully, has been wrested from Trabonus by Tula herself."

"Then we are safe from this threat!" Keenas said.

Farron shook her head. "While Tula extracted the original tome, my spies tell me that Trabonus copied the parts he was studying, and aims to use that information—as soon as he is able to piece the puzzle together. Herrex is attempting another resurrection through manipulation of a mortal puppet."

As concerned murmurs arose again, Farron gave them some moments to digest her story.

"You should all know also that a rogue coven of the Dark Scarzen still exists today," Farron said.

"What!" several said, including Malforce.

"Their faction is alive and well," Farron said. "They have been biding their time, waiting for such a circumstance to arise."

"I have seen that written in the Nur chronicles of Ajaa," said Keenas.

"They have been taking newborns to bolster their numbers for years," said Farron.

All the listeners gasped at that, and Norstaa almost choked on his wine.

"I thought the loss of so many offspring was because the ancestors were angry with our lack of conquering Ludd," said Norstaa.

"I have lost an offspring after a gray sleep. This can't be," remarked Daylin. "I thought what I remembered was a dream."

"No, your mind was manipulated to think it was so. Expect more to be taken. Don't forget, they are directly influenced by Herrex now," Farron said.

"Then … can we be victorious?" asked Jallanaa.

"Nothing is certain, not even in the heavens. The power of Herrex,

< 247 >

even depleted, is beyond anything you can comprehend. Some things have arisen that may stem the tide of Herrex's full ability return—but Trabonus still knows enough to continue with his mission."

"What swift steps can we take to crush the Flaxon?" asked Malforce.

"This is a war we will take to the very gates of Weirawind," Farron said. "Your enemy has upgraded technology. Your scale will not be enough to turn their firepower. We must upgrade in turn. Do we still have sky-world siege weaponry?"

"Yes," Malforce said, "but after what happened during unification, as you commanded, the clans dismantled them. There are a few units kept as reminders, but they haven't been used since before my otaa's time. One of the old ones still lives who might remember how to reassemble them."

"See to it, and order your armorers to produce as much of this armor as they can." Farron gestured to one of her Brasheer, who placed on the table a scroll containing armor-building plans for both warrior and drommal. "Navigators, there is much to be done." Farron looked around the table. "Keep the reasoning to your subordinates simple. Tell them there is a great army rising against us, spearheaded by the Flaxon, who must be consulted with in the extreme." Farron stood from her chair. "Navigators of Scarza, you are about to prove Naught's choice in you over all the great warriors of the heavens to keep this monster where he belongs justified. Take up this fight. Let your ancestors see what it is to be Scarzen!"

"Ho," all replied.

"God or not, by Naught's beard, Herrex has met his nemesis, and damn the afterlife if any oppose our course!" shouted Keenas.

"To your tasks, then," Farron said. "Malforce, I would speak to you on another matter."

Malforce paid respect. Farron stood, opened her palms, and looked to the ceiling. The force field surrounding them evaporated, and without paying the others any more mind, she left.

A short time later, after much discussion among the keepers, Malforce stood at the head of the table.

"Then we are agreed," Malforce said. "Coordinate via sellenor messenger."

< 248 >

"Well, we know where the Mistress stands," said Norstaa.

The circle paid mutual respects and left the Hall of Ceremonies to prepare for war.

\* \* \*

Far to the north inside Weirawind city castle, as if some quirk of fate kept time with Farron's words, Regent Trabonus sat sullen faced, poring over his personal notes after losing the *Tome of Zharkaa.*

*Have no fear, Great Herrex! I'll not be denied my right at your side. You shall yet be set free.*

Trabonus sighed and glanced past the notes on his desk to a signed funds release; he gave his brother Waldon, still the chief magistrate, permission to continue with his obsession against the Scarzen.

*Yes, build your new weapons factory, brother Waldon, research new ways to kill my enemy. Your wait will not be long.*

\* \* \*

Carrying a festering hatred fifty seasons beyond the loss of his son Waldon the Younger, Waldon the Elder sat at his desk in his new private office, amidst his new special-weapons factory. A sweaty-faced Flaxon sergeant stood at attention in front of the desk.

"I don't care what he thinks, Sergeant," Waldon said with an embittered expression. "Tell him anything beyond the north wall falls under *my* jurisdiction. Now shut the door on your way out before I have you used for targeting practice."

"Yes, Magistrate."

As the sergeant snapped a salute and left, Waldon lifted an ear to the sound of smithies' hammers and the cranking of machinery nearby.

*Finally on schedule. That old bell caster Screwman better come through. The blacksmiths, fletchers, and gunsmiths are waiting.*

Turning in his chair to peer out the window overlooking the factory floor, Waldon gazed at the platforms being built for rolling rocket-carriages.

*These'll put some pepper down those Scarzen gullets.*

< 249 >

A knock at the door shifted Waldon's attention.

"Come."

In walked Waldon's factory engineer.

"Good news, I hope, Saxby," Waldon said.

"Yes, sir. We've finally got the ratios of the spark's powder mix right. Once we found phlogiston to be impotent and combined the sulfur, charcoal, and saltpeter correctly, everything changed. Now your delivery platforms are reliable, each houses three rear-door-loading rocket cylinders that'll have our enemies' parts covering the hills, sir. The main rocket can be launched with reasonable accuracy, estimated to five hundred spans. The two smaller side mounts we tested were accurate to one hundred and seventy-five spans. Screwman has redesigned all rocket heads to splinter on impact, or at a general preset distance. As you can see by the one almost completed below, the spring recoil wheelbase will carry the more formidable larger rocket mounted through the center easily over most terrain."

"Excellent. Wouldn't want anyone to miss out, would we?"

"No, sir. A few rockets have shown the occasional flaw, but the ordnance is one hundred percent acceptable for general stockpiling here."

"Anything else?"

"Yes. The older wooden wheel hub-and-spoke design has been replaced with a lighter twist-flat metal-forged spoke arrangement. The sides and deck of the platforms are now covered in fine-mail meshing as requested. We are now using wider bound-over yew tree wood molded wheel hoops that'll add traction. Flak blankets have been made to protect the pulling animals from projectiles and blades while in harness. Now, here you can see …" Saxby placed a set of plans down on the desk. "This newer breach-loading infantry shooter designed by Screwman—that I've taken the liberty of calling the 'Screwman'—will replace all older smoothbore small arms. Screwman deserves the kudos, sir. It will help with morale in the factory, too. His miniaturized version of the cannon barrel for the infantry's shoulder arm has improved accuracy considerably. They load faster and are easier and cheaper to produce."

"Fabulous. That will keep the regent's purser off my back."

< 250 >

Outside, whistles blew for lunch.

"Right, off you go," Waldon said. "Eat well. A job well done, Saxby."

As Saxby left, Waldon spun in his chair to again look at the progress of his weapons.

*All Scarzen will fall for what they have done to me, very soon.*

< 251 >

Leaving Talon West after graduation—more than a month after Beetaa had departed for Brasheer Mountain—Thorr felt despondent without Beetaa standing beside him to go to battle. That gap was broadened with Thorr's posting to a nomadic guerilla field unit.

"Welcome to Poison Myst, Warrior," Commander Tazorr said to Thorr. "From tomorrow, we will be operating in the northeast delta. Says here you demonstrate outstanding combat and strategic potential—have a reputation for jumping in."

"Don't like standing around, sir."

"Here, independence occurs with my sanction. Our potency results from a team effort. So what's this womp rat shit about refusing to take a battlefield ally in my unit?"

"I already have a registered alliance, sir. I've presented a formal request to that effect and to work in tandem until my battle ally, who's temporarily transferred to the Brasheer, returns."

"The Brasheer," snorted Tazorr, furrowing his brow. "Wake up, broz! Nobody transfers 'temporarily' to the Brasheer."

"You did, sir."

"Humph. What's the would-be ghoul's name—this ally of yours?"

"Pinnaraa, sir. Beetaa Pinnaraa."

"That so? Any connection to Benataa Pinnaraa?"

"His blood otaa, sir."

"Mmm. Okay, we'll float your skills where needed during your assessment."

"Your wisdom as an older commander of Talon East is appreciated, sir. I understand you participated in crushing the Flaxon at Yorr Pass under Viceroy Titarliaa's command."

"That's right, and if I hear one more slack's joke about my retirement being overdue, the culprit has his chest cavity turned inside out, clear?"

"Abundantly, sir."

"Good. We've received an assignment for a stealth mission to support a couple of Quall assassins in the Flaxon hot zone. We rendezvous with those Quall near the hot springs in the redwood hills at sunset. That's only ten leaps out from Weirawind, so stay sharp."

* * *

Hours before sunset, Thorr's unit pressed north into the redwood hills of Flaxor.

*If my mouth were any drier, a cactus would die in it,* Thorr mused, jumping over a fallen log following two other unit members. *Bah, stop complaining, mud-guts! They'll feel the same. Tazorr sets a cracking pace, I'll give him that.*

Under the cover of individual blur fields, the unit moved across the landscape in pairs. Thorr found himself matched with an older warrior named Ajax, out on point. They all filtered through the hills and valleys, ghostlike, stopping every few hours for new bearings.

*The color and smell of this place reminds me of Otutt's hot-baked rolls back home. Where's a good chaw of kambaa root when I need one?*

"When's the next food stop?" Thorr asked Ajax via their close-proximity mind-link.

"Stop grumbling. No one's listening. There's no wildlife in these hills, less you want a gut full of raider ants or the odd slitherer. Keep moving."

"How far?"

"That information, Tazorr will tell."

Dust puffed up under pounding steps as the unit progressed. Soon,

< 253 >

one hill seemed the same as the next, moving against constant wind gusts and blowing debris as the hours of forced marching passed. Finally, Tazorr ordered the pace to be slowed.

"In the distance—the ruffled tops of the redwoods. That's it," Tazorr said.

*Good,* thought Thorr, feeling both hearts pounding. *Rest and food will be welcome.*

* * *

Now in Flaxon territory, the unit approached the stand of redwoods from three points. Thorr and Ajax had seen two distant Flaxon patrols already. Shortly, the unit arrived at the grove. They set camp and a watch as last light ushered in the cold.

*Least the trees break the wind in here,* thought Thorr.

Inside the knot of trees, Thorr recognized the last remnants of a once mighty forest. There were signs of previous Flaxon activity, in the form of aging cut timber. It reminded him of how close they were getting to the enemy stronghold.

Thorr looked up, back against one of the huge trunks. *These stendles must be forty spans high and more.* The forest cluster had a small natural clearing in the middle where the ground was strewn in leaf litter. Away to his right, small pools of hot mud bubbled, bringing popping sounds to his ears when the wind dropped. *Smells of damp rot.* Tazorr ordered sentries to take position in some tall redwoods at opposite ends to set an elevated watch. He gave permission for a covered campfire, but only dry rations. Thorr's stomach rumbled upon hearing that.

*Not even a hot nettle grass brew?*

"Humph."

*Better be some real action at the end of this.*

* * *

By early evening, the wind had dropped. The stone-cowled small fire occasionally flickered in the breeze, illuminating close tree trunks with wobbling shadows. While three gray figures, including Thorr, sat as decoy

< 254 >

near the fire, others remained out of sight at different vantage points.

"Love these clear nights," Thorr said softly.

A night bird called in the distance, and Thorr slumped back against one of the large trunks and closed both eyes to sleep before his watch. Soon, though, Thorr heard something scurrying around in the shadows a short distance away and opened one lazy eyelid, dropping it again just as quickly.

Two slender bluish hands slipped silently around the rough tree trunk closest to the fire. Slowly, the side profile and pale bluish face of a Quall peered round. His huge eyes focused on the large Scarzen snoozing close by. He went to move, then stopped as the big one had a little snore.

The Quall, Sooza, eyed the sleeping warrior warily. *Bush pig!* He looked to the opposite side of the camp, the direction that his brother, Cezanne, now closed from. *Safe ... no traps. And this one's breathing sounds like lifting steam.*

On the other side of the fire, one of the Scarzen stood up.

*Where do you go?* Sooza thought. *Time to be introduced ...*

Using his chameleon skill, Sooza matched his skin with the reddish-brown tree bark.

*Very careful, Sooza,* he urged himself, sliding around the trunk. Then, cheekily, he sat down next to the sleeping Thorr.

Thorr stirred with a snuffle and bumped Sooza's arm with an elbow. Immediately, Thorr's eyes cracked open. Faster than Sooza expected, Thorr spun about, driving a heavy flat hand hard toward the trunk of the tree. Sooza sprung out of the way, easily evading the crushing palm. Thorr's hand smashed into the tree, and the sounds turned all Scarzen heads. Blades were quickly drawn. Negating his chameleon skill, Sooza opened his four arms, his face showing a big smile.

"Sooza is a fr-friend of Scar-Scarzen," he said, ducking one of Thorr's vicious swings.

"Come here, flea!" Thorr grumbled, straightening from semi-crouch to full height.

A blade sped across the gap over the fire, biting into the tree trunk millispans from Sooza's head with a *thunk*.

"Do me no harm, please! I am Sooza, an ally."

< 255 >

"Allies don't sneak about, imp!" said Thorr.

"Stand down, Warrior!" Tazorr ordered in his low gravelly voice. "They are expected."

Sooza let out a breath. "All Quall sneak about after first steps, Warrior," Sooza said to Thorr. "Just as Scarzen kill from first crawl. But you will not kill Sooza today, yes!" He smiled at Thorr then turned to his right. "As the stone-voiced one said, we are expected," Sooza said.

There was silence. Sooza began to feel his entry should have been less of a surprise. Thorr said nothing, but held Sooza in an inescapable hard fixed stare.

"Scarzen are fierce, brave, deadly," Sooza said. "Quall are deadly too. Keeper Malforce had sent us here for joint venture."

"First, Scarzen need no friends. Second, you're exactly where I expected you'd be!" Tazorr growled.

The Scarzen unit commander walked into the firelight, dragging Sooza's brother by the scruff of the neck—already gagged and arms bound.

"Next time you plan a festive entry, recognize others might not get the joke," Tazorr said, flinging Cezanne roughly to the ground. "My unit's always hungry and you could have topped the menu. Now, prove what you say or I'll let the pups loose to play."

Sooza looked at Thorr, who gestured with both hands, ready to ring the quall's neck. For a moment, Sooza's mood darkened at seeing his brother treated with such indignity. He suppressed any threatening remark when he sensed many other Scarzen closing and surrounding them from the shadows. He relaxed his posture, changing his skin pigment back to its natural pale blue and then smiled.

"Then we will make good allies, yes?" Sooza said. "Yes! I have proof, here."

Now looking at the Scarzen commander, Sooza slowly reached for an inside vest pocket and produced a fold of parchment bearing Keeper Malforce's seal.

Sooza sensed Thorr relax upon seeing the parchment. The big Scarzen still looked pensive for a long moment, noticing just how many black throwing blades the small Quall carried on his person.

< 256 >

*Little insect is a walking blade store.*

"Time to be more civil, then. Come, sit," Tazorr said, untying Cezanne's arms and gag, then gestured for them to move toward the fire.

\* \* \*

The commander and the Quall sat in close proximity. Tazorr accepted the sealed order from Sooza and stowed it in a pocket of his own. Others, including Thorr, stayed within earshot.

"What is your news, Master Assassin?" asked Tazorr.

Sooza looked at Tazorr with a neutral expression. "Our objective is dangerous, Commander," he said. "We will need great caution."

"The target stands high in the Flaxon royal court, this I know, but who is it exactly?"

"Regent Trabonus himself," Sooza said.

Tazorr shifted. *That's an unexpected target*, Tazorr thought, tilting his head. "How do you propose to remove the mark?" Tazorr asked. "It is reported the regent is paranoid of assassination after two failed attempts and is well guarded."

"Quall do not fail! We know a weakness. We have a quiet method," Sooza said, drawing his shouldered purse around to the front. He undid the flap and produced a small metal pot and a rough amber crystal bowl. He looked around at the staring cluster of curious individuals, then without a word placed the items on the ground. Next, he pulled out two small pouches.

"Lovers are known to play deadly games," Sooza said. "The regent is famous for excesses with females. His weakness is there."

Tazorr nodded in understanding, then said, "How long will it take to prepare? Getting close won't be easy."

"Several hours to distill the compound. During the course of that time, no one must disturb or interfere in any way. It takes masterful focus to arrange the potent mix," Sooza said.

"Very well," Tazorr said.

The commander gestured to the others, ushering them away. The warriors dispersed, disappearing back into the night shadows. Sooza laid out all the

< 257 >

components on the open flap of his shoulder purse, including a measuring spoon and small mortar and pestle.

"A few fragments of gray spore into a little pile," Sooza murmured, breaking up the head of a fungus.

Then, with one of his many knives, Sooza shaved shards from a slender pink root.

"Some blood of the north into the bowl," Sooza said.

"An interesting collection of forest flora you have," said Tazorr.

"Not to trifle with," Cezanne muttered, sitting next to his brother.

From a small wrapped piece of cloth, Sooza added a small, narrow fish jawbone, which had tiny serrated teeth.

"This ensures no return," Sooza said, handling it delicately and appearing to show it respect.

"What is that?" asked Tazorr.

Sooza nodded slightly, contemplating an answer. "I will make Black Sky. This, we call the chorser fish; 'chorser' in Quall tongue means 'beyond dead.'"

Sooza began grinding it to dust. The stirring of the stone rod made scratching sounds as he worked the mortar and pestle in his lap.

The commander gave him a questioning look. "Where our ancestors lived in the old stories, many died handling and eating this fish. This," Tazorr said as he pointed at the clump of shavings of the pink root, "ancients call Corgg's Kiss. In the right quantities, a male can satisfy a female endlessly, but no more offspring will follow."

"You have had training in the ways of earth and sky?" Sooza asked.

"My otutt was a healer in our bunker. I learned a thing or two when I was young.

Many become addled after a single use of Corgg's Kiss—permanently. But the union will show the pair the heavens, and such is our need for offspring that the risk is worth it.

"It's very popular amongst the tribes in the far northwest too," said Sooza. "Their populations, sadly, are now not very big, either." He had a half chuckle at that, then went on: "But when mixed with fish bone and some other items the goddess gives the land, Corgg's Kiss becomes sleeping

< 258 >

death, leaving only a small pungent odor for a very short while after contact with the skin. Other than that, it is invisible. Although …" he stalled, "a faint black line does appear on the inside of the lips. We will administer the gift while the regent sleeps."

"There is a black market for this poison amongst those in elite families of the Flaxon and Celeron who have unhappy unions," said Cezanne. "Sometimes the target and careless murderer die together."

"Of course," Sooza confirmed with a nod. "That is because the fools do not respect it, seeking self-gratification instead of wanting a professional to do it for a reasonable fee."

Sooza finished grinding the fish bone, then picked up the piece of cloth on which all the ingredients lay and shook all of it into the small pot.

"There." He looked at his brother. "You must not touch it from the beginning if you are to be safe."

Sooza added some orange fungi and odd-looking grass strips to the mixture with a small amount of water from a skin that Cezanne handed him. Sooza then picked up the pot and placed it at the base of the fire near the coals. Using a slender spoon, he stirred the ingredients slightly. He then placed a thin, round metal sheet over the pot: a lid with three tiny holes punched in the center for steam to escape. After a few scants, the pot began to puff some steam through the lid. The aroma smelled of damp rotting rags to Tazorr.

"Now we wait," Sooza said, using a stick to pull the concoction back a little from the heat.

\* \* \*

From a seated position against a tree trunk, Thorr watched Commander Tazorr and the Quall engage, still puzzled as to how the little slimeball had crept up so close.

*That's the first and last you'll do that, bug eyes. Scarzen don't get snuck up on and live long after.* "It's in the damn manual," Thorr grumbled, softly balling one fist into the other cupped hand. *Gotta learn me that step.* He saw a rodent scurry away nearby like the silence of a passing cloud.

< 259 >

\* \* \*

At the campfire, Tazorr shifted gears to tactics.

"How will you penetrate the stronghold, Sooza?"

Sooza did not answer for a moment, not being accustomed to hearing his name from beyond his clan, especially from a Scarzen.

Cezanne broke in: "We are known to the controllers of Weirawind." His thin lips twisted into a shallow smile. "We have been there several times to ply our trade. We have scouted many alternatives for entry and escape."

"We could do it by daylight if we had to," said Sooza. "Because they are still expecting us to bring back news of the ... what do you call it? The responsibility, yes, that's it."

Tazorr nodded at hearing that information.

"But we must not be searched," said Sooza. "That is their way if we pass through open gates. No, for this task we must infiltrate unseen."

The lid on the pot began to tinkle, with a wisp of steam puffing out the side. Sooza pulled some of the coals away to slow the temperature.

"How do you propose to administer the message, then?" Tazorr asked. "Sounds near impossible."

"For you, maybe," said Sooza. "Big clumsy feet."

"Watch your tone, my four-armed rogue. My lack of patience for such humor among allies is very limited!" Tazorr said, giving the Quall a predatory glare.

"As I said," Sooza continued, ignoring the threat, "the regent will receive it in his sleep. I will be the primary in this task. Should I fail—and that has never happened—then my brother will see the job through. He is young, but highly effective. The regent will be long dead by the mid-sun after next."

"You had better be as good as your word."

Sooza twisted his lips and looked away. He began to make another retort, but thought better of it, instead saying, "We go in tomorrow night. Also, I was instructed to give you this by the Keeper Malforce."

Sooza pulled a second sealed parchment from his inside vest pocket and handed it to Tazorr, who accepted it with a frown. Upon examining it, Tazorr saw the ring seal of Malforce himself over the pressed red wax blot

< 260 >

that sealed the message. Tazorr broke the seal and read the note to himself:

> *Keeper's advice.*
> *Commander Tazorr's Eyes Only, Myst Unit 7*
>
>
> *With primary objective met, destroy all Weirawind munitions storage locatable. Zero tolerance for those defending the target is acceptable. After securing the release of the Quall Elder Makayass, head at all speed for the western forests, meet with Keeper Keenas. He will be expecting you. Viceroy Titarliaa's 9$^{th}$ Fighting Battalion shall arrive on moons' ends. You shall receive further orders from him.*
>
> *Good hunting!*
> *Malforce*

Tazorr grimaced. *That's four days away,* he thought. *It will press us hard.*

Tazorr cleared his throat while folding the parchment, then he pressed it into the embers of the fire.

"It seems things are going to get interesting," said Tazorr. "Ajax, Thorr!" he called to the nearby warriors in the shadows.

In tandem with Thorr, a tall, motley-faced Scarzen officer moved quickly to his side.

"Yes, Ruhe."

The Quall picked up the term "scout patrol" in the Scarzen tongue. Ajax and Thorr paid respects with a nod and left.

Tazorr watched them leave silently and swiftly. He covered the remnants of the burning message with burning coals and looked at the Quall.

"Do your job right. We'll do our part," Tazorr said to Sooza.

"We will not miss our mark," replied Sooza.

"I have some things to sort. We will speak again before break of camp,"

< 261 >

Tazorr said, then rose. He dusted his hands, giving both Quall a final look of consideration before leaving them to their task.

* * *

Cezanne shuffled closer to his brother, drawing a sharpening disc from his vest. He pulled a black blade from his belt and began honing the edge. Speaking in their native tongue, Cezanne asked, "What is our true potential in this mark, brother?"

"Even if it was ten percent, I would still go," said Sooza in a bitter voice. "After seeing our elder with a chain around his neck like some perimeter dog, I would give my life to see the regent's forfeit. You must remember to keep your head on this one, Cezanne. There will be no margin for impatience."

"I understand," said Cezanne, his head tilted down.

Sooza looked to the simmering pot. "You should get some rest. I will watch this."

Cezanne ran the stone along the knife in a contemplative manner one last time, then nodded and said, "Maybe we'll get lucky and the sky bourn will smile on us." He then turned away and moved to the base of an unoccupied tree trunk and sat. Reaching into the lining of his vest, Cezanne pulled out a slender bone flute, folded his legs, and rested his back gently against the trunk. His top two arms held the instrument, using three fingers of each hand to cover the offset holes. His bottom two palms formed a semi-sphere in front of his abdomen. The sound of the flute was soft and melodious, a striking contrast to his life's vocation. Cezanne's musical spirit filled the air, prompting many thoughts of quieter meditative times away from the Scarzen battlefield.

Eventually, the melody stopped and Sooza finished preparing the Black Sky. Once the mixture was distilled, Sooza carefully poured it into the crystal dish. Upon contact with the crystal, the liquid turned from a murky brown to the color of mushroom gray. Sooza nodded with satisfaction. *The message is ready.*

< 262 >

# CHAPTER 19
# ARCANE THINGS TO COME

Inside the Lair of Bach, Ben felt that his life's weird-o-meter clearly had a far greater range than he'd ever imagined. After leaving the parley with Mistress Farron, Atacuss presented Beetaa with a long shoulder bag that Ben assumed must be his personal belongings. Then he and Beetaa followed Atacuss along a side passage deeper into the catacombs. All the while, Ben wondered how long it would take to get accustomed to having a living being ride around upon his head, always tapped into his every thought. He didn't know whether the shiver up his spine meant he was excited about all this, or if it was like the feeling after jumping from a plane with a parachute that didn't open, face-plant planetside imminent.

*Guess this is what important folks back home mean when they say, "Careful what you wish for,"* Ben thought to himself—at least he hoped it was to himself.

*"Don't worry, Sparky, you're up for this. I feel it in my brim,"* Roland said in his mind.

*"Tell that to the angry Scarzen next to me; he doesn't think so."*

*"You'll gain his trust and teach him a few things along the way, Sparky. But you're right in thinking that you're up to your neck in something really important,"* Roland said.

Ben sighed, realizing his thoughts would never be his own again. They passed small stone nooks and hollows where cloaked individuals experimented with energy or studied obscure texts.

"This place isn't like your bunkers at all," Ben whispered to Beetaa. "I haven't seen any guards in this place."

"What do you know of our bunkers?" said Beetaa.

Atacuss spoke over one shoulder. "That is unnecessary here. We have other means of protection far more potent. Intruders do not fare well here."

Atacuss stopped in front of a strong metal-framed door. It had a heavy latch bolt that he drew back with a *slap-crack* before pushing the creaking door inward.

"This is your space during your stay," Atacuss said. "Rest now. Shortly, you will be summoned to Master Quinn's chamber."

Ben followed Beetaa past Atacuss into a sparsely furnished stonewalled space that smelled a tad musty but adequate for two Scarzen-sized occupants. The back wall had basic shelves cut into the stone and two stone slabs at Ben's hip height, serving as beds with a Scarzen in mind. Each slab was covered with the same brown thick mattress padding he'd rested on earlier. Each bed had a heavy patchwork quilt lying rolled up on the end. In one corner of the room stood a solid rustic table large enough to seat them both, with a bench seat either side. Inkwells and two parchment stacks had been laid out to one side. *I'll need a booster seat to work there,* Ben thought. As the two surveyed their living quarters, the door shut with a bump behind them. They both turned to see that Atticus had left.

"He was the dark silent type," Ben said, looking to spark light conversation.

Beetaa made no response, sitting on one bed, clearly preoccupied with something.

*"He looks concerned about something other than you, Sparky,"* Roland said in his head.

Ben shrugged and walked to the other platform, then removed his coat.

"Guess this one's mine, then." Ben sat, looking about. "Thought it would be much colder and damp inside a mountain," he said.

"It's the natural heat from underground. There is much underground pressure and hot water in these mountains. We use the same thing in my bunker," Beetaa said, lying back on his bed slab. He looked at Ben curiously.

< 264 >

"Why do you have eyes like a Scarzen? Do all—what are you called again—humans? Do all humans have our eyes?"

"No, I, ah, I inherited these in a mishap awhile back. They are nothing special."

"Look beside you, Ben," Roland said, "I brought you something to help you in your travels."

Knowing the bed surface had been empty when he sat down, Ben saw, lying in an elegant swirl, a glittering silver-and-gold whip of fine braid.

"Struth!" Ben said.

Beetaa sat up. "That wasn't there when we came in."

"No, it was not," said Roland. "It is my offering of respect for one charged with such a task."

Roland lifted from Ben's head and hovered across to settle on the table, facing him.

"Ben, when a Jenaoin takes a new fitting, it is customary to bring a gift that represents trust in the binding commitment for them both."

*No stockman's whip ever looked like that on the farm,* Ben thought, figuring that Roland wouldn't hear his thoughts since he'd left his head.

"Only one exists in the entire Superverse," stated Roland aloud.

Ben looked at Roland, realizing that the Jenaoin could hear his thoughts whether on his head or not. Ben touched a finger on the whip's braiding and felt an icy sizzle up his arm, and the whip glowed with a soft golden light. In nervous reflex, Ben pulled his hand back.

"It's okay, Sparky, I pre-imprinted your soul signature into its matrix. It now will recognize only you. Anyone else attempting to pick it up will get a nasty surprise."

Roland slung an impassive look to Beetaa. Ben picked up the whip by the grip as the other two looked on. The whip unraveled like a long limp snake with a *throp* as its weight and tip touched the ground. Ben stood, holding the grip up.

"Looks longer than a big black snake. Leaded on the tip, too; that's gotta hurt. Uncle Tom would have liked this one heaps, Roland!"

Ben examined the grip to see that both hilt and pommel had a four-

< 265 >

sided face of precious-looking stones. He loosely weighed the weapon, and suddenly felt the grip mold to the exact fit of his hand.

"Looks a lot heavier than it is, Roland."

Ben lifted the whip up and down gently, feeling its weight. He ran a thumb over one of the four encrusted jewels on the splayed hilt. The stone began to light up, and he thought he heard it make a sound.

"Careful there, Sparky. It reacts to will and intention. Now that it recognizes its new owner, your life force acts like a key. Should a hand other than yours attempt to hold it, the effect of the stone you last touched would be applied to the unwelcome instantly. There is more to it than its physical sting, which I assure you *is* considerable."

Ben slowed his examination of the whip. "Does it come with a manual?" he asked, twisting the back of the pommel.

The limp length of braid snapped out rigid from the grip, mutating into a fine jewel-handled impaler of just over three feet in length.

"Scrape a bone, Roland. This is seriously hard-core good!" Ben said with a big smile, holding the whip's tip high with both hands locked around the grip. "What do you think, my Scarzen friend? Have you ever seen anything like it?"

"My name is Beetaa, and, no, I have not. It is an … extraordinary end of peace."

"A what?" Ben asked.

"It is the weapon of choice used to consult with an enemy," said Beetaa.

"I had not anticipated that happening," Roland said and chuckled. "Ha! Farron is a clever one."

"What do you mean?" asked Ben.

"The coat, Sparky! The coat that Farron gave you: it was made by the same Tengu master armorer—Shogun Buko's armorer in fact—who designed and produced your whip. Because both are from a matching set of arms and armor, the combined potential of them is raised significantly. And this raises your effectiveness in combat considerably."

"Wow," Ben whispered.

"You now hold the mesh Whip of Medusa. It has been in my care for many

< 266 >

of your human generations. The whip has had three previous distinguished owners. They were all of noble heart. Only someone with a heart steered by the light of compassion may wield this weapon. That said, I sense corruption in your soul core that will need to be rooted out if the whip's potency is to operate at peak. The purer the user's chivalry, the stronger its effect. My previous fittings distinguished themselves on many battlefields with it, and they never had the Coat of Elements to enhance its power. It is my gift to you until our task is done. I will educate you in its use. For now, all you need to know is each stone in the grip represents an element. Pressing any of the stones while using correct commands will apply its effect. The blue stone is for water or ice; the red is for transformation by fire. The white is for light and air. The one that looks like the eye of a beast is for earth and decay. Most importantly, the shiny black stone in the pommel is called the 'Eye of Fracture.' Hitting that will cause the Medusa Effect and the power of all four stones to come into full application. I suggest studying that effect last."

Ben nodded. "This'd make Batman jealous."

"Who?" asked both Roland and Beetaa together.

"Oh … right. Let's stay in the real world, shall we?" said Roland. "There are many combinations of the four stones. This means your attitude plays a big role in the kinds of effects you can manifest. You will need to improve your meditation significantly. Beetaa, perhaps, can help you with that. The whip's consequences cannot be reversed, even by the gods."

"Such a weapon needs a truly masterful hand," said Beetaa, looking at the young human and the Jenaoin.

Roland swiveled to Beetaa. "Well put, Apprentice Brasheer. Ben will benefit from your aid. Under the circumstances, you both could be each other's lifeline one day. If my memory of Scarzen Code Number 5 serves correct, a true ally's heart wears no clothes," he stated, swinging them both a direct look.

Before another word could be said, the door swung open with a creak. Farron's aide Atacuss stood in the gap. "Master Quinn will see you now."

Roland lifted from the table and landed on Ben's head. He looked up, still adjusting to his new mentor's ways.

< 267 >

"Any more surprises?" Ben asked.

"Only that you need a haircut and decontamination."

Ben rolled his eyes, and the three followed Atacuss out and into the hallway for a meeting with the one called Quinn.

\* \* \*

Atacuss led them deeper into the catacombs along a winding, less well-kept passage. The passage ended with a heavily built bronze-studded iron-plate door. The thick bolts top and bottom had unclasped chunky iron padlocks hanging off each deadbolt. Above Ben's eye line, embossed into a brass-looking plate, were three symbols Ben didn't recognize.

"What does that say?" he asked Atacuss.

"It is written in Brasheer's cipher and represents the Three Pillars of Existence. The first symbol represents vibration, the second, non-vibration, and the last, void."

Beetaa pointed at the other standard Scarzen Chicaa written from right to left underneath. "*Quinn's Laboratory of elemental infusion. Deadly hazards. Stay away!*"

"Knock twice, then wait!" said Atacuss, punctuating the words from behind, leering at the two newcomers. Beetaa knocked twice. At first, silence was the response. Then a deep *whoosh* from behind the door was heard, and a flash of light from under its base caught Ben's eye. *"Frankenstein's hangout,"* he thought to Roland, who said nothing in reply.

Footsteps approached the door on the other side, and several bolts slid back before the door cracked ajar. Through the hand-span gap, Ben was surprised to see an old man's bearded face peer around. The man harrumphed at seeing Atacuss and unhooked one last line of defense, then swung the door ajar.

"Time lost is unrecoverable, state your business," he said with a raspy voice, walking away from them.

Under a high cavernous ceiling, the inner space revealed an uneven walled area covered in benches and shelves stacked with all manner of curiosity. Some containers advertised their contents by labels in Chicaa while others

< 268 >

looked to be a need-to-know lucky dip. A long, sturdy workbench stretched down the center of the main space, sectioned off with loose-bound texts and oddities Ben could only guess at. A large, apparently stuffed, raven sat on a perch to the side of it. There were lots of strange scents that neither Ben nor Beetaa had smelled before. They both took in a deliberate sniff of the pleasant, the sweet, and the pungent.

*Great wizard's cave,* thought Ben to himself. Looking about, he saw liquids bubbling in small pots on spindly cast-metal frames. *"Look at that, Roland. Wow!"*

On the closest bench, a suspended long blue flame with no apparent fuel source heated several beakers.

*"Where's the gas pipe feeding the flame, Roland?"*

*"I'm sure Quinn will tell you when the time's right, Sparky."*

"So why is my work interrupted, hmm?" asked the tall, wizened-faced man.

*"Him and Gandalf could be brothers, Roland."*

*"Who?"*

*"You know, from* The Lord of the ... *never mind. It's the whole 'silver-streaky beard and hair pulled back in a long ponytail tied off in sections' thingy and the robes. Okay, maybe he's more like a wizardy Viking."*

*"Quiet, just listen."*

Ben looked around with an awkward smile, trying not to laugh. Beetaa stood neutral-faced, waiting for the next command.

"Sir, these are the new apprentices from Talon West," said Atacuss, "whom Mistress has sent."

Distractedly, Quinn looked to his bench, clearly more concerned about something else. "Hold that thought," Quinn said, raising one finger.

Ben looked at Beetaa with a *What now?* expression. Beetaa ignored Ben's deliberate glance and remained focused on Quinn.

Atacuss turned to Beetaa and Ben, and quietly said, "Master Quinn is a Celeron citizen. Their ways have a discipline of their own. He is a truly powerful alchemist, you will—"

"Be with you momentarily," Quinn said, examining something bubbling

< 269 >

in a jar.

In one hand, the wizard held up a small clay pot, in the other an apple. He placed the apple on a small triangular stand and poured two drops of a caramel-looking liquid in the top center of the apple. A tiny wisp of smoke twisted its way up, accompanied by a sizzle. Then the apple turned an amber color, and soon spider-webbing formed before it shattered to broken crystals. Quinn sucked on his bottom lip in frustration.

"Balf, needs more air," he muttered. "Less fire, too."

Atacuss cleared his throat to draw Quinn's attention.

Quinn looked up from his experiment. "Ah ... ho, you're still here."

Quinn walked across, one hand behind his back while looking at the two apprentices.

"Now, what was it again? I'm very busy, Atacuss."

"These are the two apprentices you were informed about, sir," said Atacuss with a gesture to them.

"What? No, I don't need any, thank you," said Quinn, shaking his head and about to turn away. "Take them back."

"Master Quinn," Atacuss pressed, "these are the two that the Mistress spoke to you about days ago."

Quinn pulled his head back in surprise and his face took on a pinched look. "Really, is that now?"

"It is."

Quinn turned to Beetaa, asking, "You're the pup of Benataa Pinnaraa, then?"

"I am."

"Your otaa's history and glory on the battlefield precedes you with much fanfare. Mmm, you have his eyes," Quinn said, nodding as if recalling something from the past. "Welcome."

They both paid Scarzen respect.

"And you. You are not Celeron." Quinn looked at Ben closer. "A Flaxon—horu?" He frowned. "No, I suppose not, but the untrustworthy features look is remarkably similar, except for those eyes. They are not Flaxon at all. Who might you be, then? It's most rare that Mistress would give consent to any

< 270 >

other than Scarzen to be here."

"He is called 'human,' sir," Atacuss said. "He is the one who has come from the world across the void to assist with the mission. He is named 'Ben.'"

"Ben!" Quinn drew his chin in sharply, stiffening his jaw in poised thought. "Ha-ha. 'Ben' means 'shovel' in Cellonese. Hope it bodes a better meaning where you come from. Mistress led me to believe ... well, I never thought for a scant that ... This will be interesting indeed."

Quinn suddenly noticed Roland, whose eyes had become more defined. He exhaled with delight and slowly raised a hand toward Roland in wonder.

"Is this your familiar, young Ben?" Quinn asked. "Could I—"

"Steady on, Sparky. Unauthorized contact will result in discomfort," said Roland.

Quinn withdrew his hand. "Apologies," said Quinn. "Being from beyond the mortal coil, obviously you are the far more interesting guest that Mistress referred to."

"He is addressed as 'Roland,'" Atacuss said. "His clan is called 'Jenaoin.' He acts as advisor and guardian to this apprentice called Ben."

Quinn dropped his gaze to Ben and back up to Roland.

"It is my honor to meet you both—all three, I mean," Quinn said. "Recently, Mistress Farron has made conversation of some old Scarzen stories involving beings of your origin, Roland, who helped guide the Scarzen out of the dark age. Now I begin to see why."

"We assist many races," said Roland. "The honor to meet is equaled, Great Mage."

"Honorables, time presses," Atacuss said. "The apprentices must begin as soon as possible."

"Yes, yes, of course." Quinn focused back on the two apprentices. "Well, if you have half the potential your father had ..." he pointed to Beetaa, "... your development will prove inspiring."

"It seems my otaa's presence was greatly felt here. I knew little of him," Beetaa said.

"Yes, well, I was very young when all that happened."

"I don't understand," said Beetaa.

< 271 >

"I know. I am sure Mistress will say more when opportunity is better suited. There was quite a stir over all that. Yes, quite a stir."

Ben saw Beetaa's expression turn to puzzlement. *More skeletons, by the looks*, Ben thought to himself.

"And I am sent a human with a guardian from beyond the stars. Your path will be interesting indeed, Apprentice Ben. Very well," Quinn said pleasantly. "Atacuss, tell Mistress all is well."

"I shall let Mistress know."

Atacuss paid respects, turned, and left the three to their beginnings.

"Let's begin, shall we? We have much to unlock," Quinn said.

< 272 >

# CHAPTER 20
# DANGEROUS PARTNERS

In Flaxor, dense clouds dropped soaking rain on Weirawind castle. Regent Trabonus sat in the castle's west wing in his generations-old private library chamber, still poring over transcribed notes from the *Tome of Zharkaa*. Losing the original manuscript to a masterful thief recently had been infuriating. But the loss ultimately served to double his resolve to resurrect the one called "Herrex," who had been calling to him amidst murky dreams of things he'd done and wanted to do. Being a true maniacal autocrat, it didn't take much for Trabonus to be manipulated into seeing it was his duty to represent the rulers of creation on Tora—and this god Herrex was going to see him get what he deserved. Trabonus sat hunched over his worktable, chewing on a last morsel of grub blue-vein cheese. He read on, quill in hand, with eyes bloodshot from lack of sleep and too much ale. Still in his grubby calico nightshirt and slippers, the silhouette of his sweaty overweight mass pressed through his feeble coverings via penetrating yellow lamp light. The flame above the notes wavered in a small draft as his finger traced a line on one page. He farted, and three insects circling the flame dropped dead on the page. With a grunt, he swept them away with the back of one meaty hand.

*I'll never see the way in at this rate!* "Damn Scarzen symbols. Such sequences turn a brain to soup." *Why should being recognized by the gods stretch a Flaxon so?* He looked up as though speaking directly to the Herrex. "You said I am, after all, the best of us here, Lord Herrex? I've endured several moons of your ramblings." Trabonus frowned and thumped the table. *You could damn well give me a sign at least.* He gripped a pen in frustration. "Show some gratitude for the effort, damn you," he muttered into the silence, feeling a slipper fall from his foot.

The euphoria of the dreams during his slumber had vanished in recent weeks. Now the voices only came to repeat their message, reciting the same thing over and over, giving him a headache. Trabonus held his head with both hands, hearing the same superior voice in the castle corridors in his waking hours. He looked up again, waiting for something to come. Nothing.

"Crutch rot." *Always the same dream. Your hand moving the symbols in the tome around* ... "Changing the order all the time!" he said aloud in a strained voice. "I'm giving you what you want, aren't I? Give me what I am due, damn you!" He looked down at the page and muttered the words to himself: "'To the heavens we will bring you. Help us through, help us through, and receive a special reward or two.' Right ... I don't think so." He sighed and continued: "'Lies convicted us to bring the end. Speak the words, use the key. Rule with me, let me walk within you.'" Trabonus looked up and shook his head. "Well, voices in my head no longer count." Then he read the rest: "'Let us be one, the embodiment of the true force of creation. Be untouchable. Stand alone, show your fire!'"

He thumped the page back on the table. In truth, of late, the dreams had been changing and leaving him more testy than usual, and he began to rant:

"I want no more Scarzen faces or their screaming war cries jumping at me from dark places. Do you hear!" he protested, remembering last night's dream. Unlike the others, this one had started with a well-manicured hand, its pointer finger moving steadily down the pages he now researched. In silence, it continued from one page to the next. The finger would stop here and there to move the strange symbols around on the page. Then, at one point, the hand stopped and tapped a finger at a particular symbol on the page: naught. The hand's appearance mutated, suddenly becoming the hard-skinned hand of a Scarzen. As the memory of it became totally vivid in his

< 274 >

mind, Trabonus envisioned the menacing hand slowly lift away from the page and point a finger at him. He flinched and felt a shiver of repulsiveness when he smelled the change in the ozone around him. *Keep your head, Trabonus. You are being tested, that's all,* he thought, trying to reassure himself.

But an irrational fear saturated his reality as he now relived the dream. He stood, feeling his heart begin to race, and then backed away from his desk, stopping with a cry of fright when he bumped into something behind. He spun to see, up close, an enormous emaciated Scarzen face with big, sunken orange eyes hovering.

"Back, vermin! Get back!" Trabonus shouted, hallucinating. "You are not real! Torment me no longer!"

Seeing only endless cloud and mist around the threat, he went to flee. Then his head spun and it all changed—as visions often do. There was the Scarzen hand again over his notes on the desk pointing to a page. It wagged a boney finger and flicked pages out of the way before stopping near the end. Then Trabonus saw the finger push the script upon the page into a different order and then tap the page for him to look. Trabonus's eyes opened like saucers as the realization struck him—he knew the secret of the mysterious writing. Then the hand morphed into the Scarzen face once more. Its eyes had changed from orange to hideous ink-black pits. In a wink, it closed on him, snatching his breath away and forcing him to backpedal in terror.

"Gods, you can't be what I'm after!" He turned tail and ran, or felt that's what he was doing, feeling the chase as the foreboding horror clawed at his mind. In a fit of panic, he looked over his shoulder, only to see gnarled taloned fingers outstretched to snatch at him. "Get away! Get away from me!" he screamed.

In his delirium, he tripped on something quite obscure and fell face upon the ground in a sprawl, then felt the giant hand descend, grab him by the torso, and snatch him up. Trabonus struggled, feeling the grip crushing him. Then the hand shook him violently, as a child might shake a rag doll, and dropped him to the ground, exhausted. Lifting his head, Trabonus saw distorted snarling Scarzen faces coming toward him from all around—ugly, rotting faces that drew near and spoke in low unintelligible tones. Trabonus

< 275 >

scrambled to his feet, and one spat in his face with a sneer while the rest mocked him with ghoulish laughter. Then, with the sound of rushing wind, they were sucked away by some unseen vacuum into the black, and natural light returned to show the *real* space around him in a shambles.

"My lord. Forgive me. Please forgive me," Trabonus whispered.

Heavy silence pressing on him, Trabonus opened his eyes and found himself in a huddle on the floor. Knees shaking with exhaustion, he forced himself to stand and heard a whispering call from the shadows on his right: *"Open the gate. Do as I ask."*

Then, not quite close enough to touch, came a vision of Trabonus's father—Straxus II—whom he'd murdered many years past. His father's face, although ghostly, looked gentle and comforting. The sight of him made Trabonus's blood run cold. The ghostly figure stepped forward and reached out with both hands to hold Trabonus's face with a look of forgiveness and compassion. Nervously, Trabonus offered a hand, but as he went to touch the face, it dissolved, as though being blown away by a gentle breath of air in a soft *woosh.*

Standing there, not sure of being in a nightmare or the living day, Trabonus heard one last time the voice of the one he called lord: *"Open the gate, fool. This cannot wait."*

Trabonus wiped his nose on the back of his sleeve with a snuffle, angry with regret. He took a last look at his notes, and then a sound deep breath. "Right then." Tapping his finger on the page, Trabonus stepped back from the desk and shrugged his shoulders. He cleared his throat, then craned his neck, bolstering some courage, and looked to the ceiling. With full intent, he spoke the words from memory with gusto: "From vibration and the non-material, through me I invite you to enter. In my heart, I welcome Herrex, Lord of Balance, to reside within me. I am your servant. My body is your host. Take my eyes and limbs as yours and be set free!"

Trabonus chanted the invocation three times with the commitment of a true believer. He raised the tempo each time, then stopped in the ensuing silence and waited. Long moments passed and nothing happened other than a moth passing by the table lamp. His shoulders slumped, partly relieved

< 276 >

and strangely disappointed. He leaned on the desk in front of him, beads of sweat dotting his brow.

*Gods be damned, I'm finished in this folly. I'll find another way. Who needs the gods anyway?*

Just as his mental tension relaxed, the lamp flame on his desk began to dance. Trabonus felt a breath of stale wind envelop the space, and he coughed to clear his throat. Suddenly, a chill of the winter north wind wrapped around him, and the lamp flame went out with a puff, leaving Trabonus in total, silent darkness.

"Crutch rot," he muttered after a nervous swallow.

He lifted a finger to call for his servant to re-light the lamp. His voice evaporated, though, when a pinhead of suspended light appeared just out of arms' reach at face height. It appeared to Trabonus to be spinning as it grew to something the size of a dinner plate. Suddenly, the bead of light shot small light darts all around, some sticking in the walls and on Trabonus. The ground beneath his feet started to shudder. The bead of light grew to the size of a large circular window that developed a deep purple center, which swirled with a ringing sound.

*Gods aid me. Is that a … tunnel?* He heard a snap. *Wait!* he thought, peering into the darkening purple void. *In the distance … something comes from inside it!*

Trabonus felt his stomach churn when a crisp ocean-salt fresh wind poured forth, blowing the remnants of a once thick head of silvery hair rearward and coating his face in cold.

*What mischief now?*

He closed his eyes, wanting to stop what was happening, and then he forced another look. When he did, Trabonus saw, coming closer from within the tunnel, a spirit-like figure with the gentlest, most beautiful face he had ever seen.

*Yes yes yes yes! It's finally worked. I am going to be a god!* Trabonus stretched out his arms in full welcome, mimicking the ghostly figure's actions. As the ghostly figure's smoky hands cupped his face, Trabonus thought, *You feel like the morning mist settling on my cheeks.*

< 277 >

With the contact, every fiber of his being experienced an indescribable euphoria. He looked into the being's angelic face and opened his mouth to speak, and as he did—with speed faster than thought—the ghostly being dove down his throat. Trabonus snapped his mouth shut with a gulp and winced as if swallowing something horrid. Then he felt a mighty blow within, as though being punched hard in the chest, only from the inside out. He stumbled and staggered backward.

*Mother's breast! What welcome is this?*

Trabonus shook his head with blurry vision. It quickly cleared and he focused forward—only to see …

"Me?" he whispered.

A perfect ghostly replica of himself stood there, staring at him.

"What is this treachery? What have you done?" Trabonus demanded.

He watched the ghostly figure turn solid and begin feeling itself, as if making sure all the arms and legs were there.

"Bravo!" the duplicate Trabonus said, filling his lungs with air.

The real Trabonus, who now felt infinitely more ghostly than the new arrival, sensed the weight of the imposter's gaze.

With a villainous smile, the doppelganger spoke: "My dear fellow, you were sensational! A little sloppy on the uptake, but for a crude design, you performed superbly. I feel almost in your debt!" The duplicate paused for a moment, staring intently at the regent. "Note, I said 'almost!' Wait a moment. Something isn't right." He looked about, reaching out with his senses. "The present on this thread is altered, and not by me. Mother, you naughty wench, what have you done this time?" he wondered. "No matter, deal with that later. I'm back. Oh, what shall I do first?"

Trabonus just stood there in shock, watching the duplicate take a deep lungful of air again and crack his neck from side to side as if he wasn't even there.

"This feels positively like physical utopia. I love it!" The twin snorted a laugh and refocused on the bleary-eyed Trabonus. "But my manners! Allow me to introduce myself and offer gratitude: Herrex, Eighth Evercycle, late of Citadel 8, visionary of the Superverse. Heartfelt thanks to you for your

< 278 >

selfless service to my Superverse! You may bow now; grovel if you must. Just be quick about it; I'm on a tight schedule."

Herrex waited for his view of an acceptable response from the mortal. Trabonus's fear, on the other hand, had given way to total outrage at being duped. He stared at Herrex as though something was stuck in his throat.

*The cretin is clearly overwhelmed at being so privileged,* Herrex thought. "Never mind, then," Herrex said, and drew breath to issue his next command.

"Has your brain been left in a bucket somewhere?" snapped Trabonus. "Is this how I am repaid after all my sacrifice?" Trabonus spoke the next words through gritted teeth: "Respectfully, Lord Herrex, we seem to be on unequal footing. I liberated you. You owe me, and if you're a god of any real standing, you'll fulfill your promise and give me everything I deserve—now!"

Herrex's expression soured. *I never realized how basic mortals like these could actually be. I'll have to see their design recycled along with the rest of the unwanted rubbish.* "Oh, I intend dispensing the full account you are owed. Are you ready?" Herrex said.

Now Trabonus felt a true blast of fear surge through his fading existence. "Well, now, perhaps a small sample first. You-you told me … me …"

"Told you what?" Herrex said, closing the gap between them with a deliberate stride. Mocking Trabonus's whine, Herrex repeated some of his earlier whisperings: "'To the heavens we will bring you. Help us through, help us through, *and* receive a special reward or two.' Huh. Yes, I suppose that's mostly true." Herrex winked at Trabonus. "Fine print! Mortals never ask about the fine print. It's all a point of view, my innocent friend. Never mind. You shall ensure your name and body be remembered here as the personification of a true force of creation, even a visionary ruler," Herrex said with a grin. Leaning forward, he knocked Trabonus on the head with one knuckle. "Quick, quick then, little spark. Off you go! The Echaa will see to your every need," Herrex finished, still wearing a smirk. "And hey, don't bother to write!"

Then Herrex clapped his hands sharply twice, just for effect. He waved a good-bye, and the ghostly figure of Trabonus atomized and evaporated in a swirl. Then Herrex slapped both hands together in triumph and turned to

< 279 >

the partitioned doorway. He took in the general details of his surroundings.

*This all felt so different on the other side.* A movement spied from the corner of his eye caused him to step back at the sight of his new host body in a mirror to his left. "Oh. Colliding realms! What a pile of feces I've crawled into!"

Hurriedly, he tore his nightshirt off to survey his new vessel. Standing there naked, things looked even worse. He looked at a pendulous flabby potbelly with a crust of yellow dirt in the navel. A hairy, mole-littered, sunken chest, skinny bleached white legs, and ugly, saggy bits not worth boasting about below finished the view.

*Who approved this species?* "Yes. Well," he said aloud. "Any glove for a needy hand!"

Herrex's attention was caught in the mirror by a bushy-eyebrowed pale face peering sheepishly around the partition. He spun about to face the mortal being with a scowl. The regent's footman, who had just summoned enough courage to see about all the racket, gasped at the sight of his naked regent.

"Are you ... all right, my lord?" said the footman. "Oh ... what has happened to my lord's eyes?

"What?" said Herrex, impatient to be rid of the mortal.

"They always seemed so ... brown, sir."

Herrex pressed his icy-blue gaze upon the man. The servant's face went pale and he looked like he was about to faint.

"Do you serve me?" asked Herrex, stone-faced.

"With all my heart, sir."

In the far corner of the room, Herrex noted a freestanding bath. He pointed to it. "Then fill that up with something appropriate to sanitize this body, and get me some clean attire to cover it up."

"But, sir, it's only midyear. Your royal wash isn't due for—"

"Was I not clear?" Herrex snapped. "Are all mortals here so void of intelligence? Do as I say before I make you dust."

With eyes wide and head bowed, the footman began to slowly back away out of sight. "Yes, my lord, as you wish, my lord!"

Herrex heard quick steps follow as the footman strode away, leaving the

< 280 >

chamber and closing the door with a *clunk*. He looked back to the mirror momentarily, then thought to do some exploring of his own. He strode toward the wall, expecting to pass through unimpeded, but hit the rough stone nose first, making a dull slap.

*Ahh, caw!* He stepped back, bent over, and held his face. *Ahh, caw!* Feeling harsh mortal pain for the first time, Herrex looked in the mirror again. Blood soon trickled from a cut on his eyebrow, joining with a bleeding and battered nose.

"What a limiting skin-slack sack of festering discharge!" He harrumphed. "Mortal limitations! This will take some getting used to."

He went and sat in the chair by the desk, then picked up a dirty shirt off the floor and used it to blot the blood on his face. He relaxed and closed his eyes to focus on his surroundings. He cast his mind far and wide across the lands and suddenly stopped.

"Ah, so you are still here," he said, a picture of Uniss in his head. "This will work out nicely. Ready for step two. Prepare to subjugate all necessary assets, then leave this world and set things right." *This time, things get done my way.*

< 281 >

## CHAPTER 21
# DIFFERENT TOOLS

In the Bach Lair, weeks of study passed for Beetaa and Ben without contact from the outside world. Though their differences at times frustrated them both, it was with the occasional mediation from Roland that the two odd bedfellows became comfortable and trusting friends. Both were curious about each other's worlds, and at times of rest, they exchanged information and colorful descriptions of their homelands.

"I don't get it," said Beetaa, pushing a bowl of hot-baked corn bread across to Ben. "Why would a culture play sport—a poor excuse for war, it seems to me—if it wasn't connected to the battlefield?"

"Sport isn't war, Beetaa. It's about teamwork, being competitive, and showing a strong spirit."

"So it *is* war, then? Never mind—as long as your pukecko game picks up. I'm starving for some sound competition."

*"Ben. We are out of time for banter right now,"* said Roland. *"It's time for your next lesson."*

\* \* \*

Roland educated Ben in wider Superverse history and the use of the Medusa Whip through steady practice and firm guidance.

"You're showing some aptitude, Ben, but you must wield your will with more focus. Don't hurl it so brashly," Roland said. "Kin is sophisticated. It reflects your heart's true intention."

"Yeah, well, sometimes 'kin me' is out to lunch and I just want to swing like Spider-Man," said Ben. He threw another stroke of his whip and split a thick piece of timber down the center that Roland had sunk vertically into the ground for practice. "Every time Beetaa is teaching me those foundation skills for the Labyrinth of Shadows, I see just how much kin I don't have. This makes me feel like I've got something worthwhile instead of looking like a wuss."

"Scarzen kin is innate, and you certainly possess more than I ever expected from any human, but it is raw and lacks direction. Give it time, Ben," Roland said.

"Well, all I know is I apply my thimble full of kinetics, and he bounces me across the floor with a barrier field like a ping-pong ball."

"A ping-pong in Ludd is a pregnant bull fly. Beetaa would find that amusing. Look, Ben, that is the Scarzen way. Doesn't Beetaa's head swirl at your teaching him mathematics and English writing?"

"Yeah, so?"

"That is unique for them. For Beetaa, having a language that doesn't exist in Ludd, either spoken or written, has many advantages for future Scarzen secret communications. Believe me, you are giving him something very special. Now, quit beating yourself up, and let's join everyone for some good food and conversation."

* * *

Much later, in a converted chamber space not far from Quinn's room, Beetaa and Ben engaged in a friendly contest of what Beetaa called "pukecko for humans." Ben stood opposite him, holding the chool and considering his next attempt.

"Come, Ben. Show me some human courage. You must be able to pass me by now."

*Easy for you to say, Gumby, with all your height, strength, and speed. I'll never reach the top third of the repel marker,* Ben thought, looking to where

< 283 >

Beetaa expected him to jump.

Ben heard Beetaa genuinely laugh and then he clapped his hands. "Let's go, little frog. You'll never go to war this way." He tossed a provocative kinetic barrier at Ben's feet. "Come on, little frog, jump."

Beetaa tossed a second barrier, and Ben jumped unconsciously, tapping into a deep reservoir of force he didn't know he had. His foot hit the high mark on the repel platform more than twice his own height, which shot him across to the vertical hole over the makeshift bunker and slammed the chool in. He fell with a thump at Beetaa's feet.

"Take that, Magilla Gorilla," he said, oddly out of breath.

"Naught's beard, little frog! Where did you get those legs?"

"I don't know. Strike, I thought my head was going to pop," said Ben with one hand on his forehead.

"I would say the effects of being exposed to Scarzen blood has finally made some changes," said Farron, stepping out of the shadows. *And something far more unnatural to humans,* she thought. "Changes we shall have to monitor closely."

"What Scarzen blood?" Beetaa asked. "When?"

"That is perhaps history for another time," Farron said. "Right now, Roland and I wish to speak to Ben privately. He will join you with Master Quinn later."

As they all left the chamber, Ben could feel Beetaa's eyes and mind upon him.

* * *

To Ben and Beetaa, their teacher Quinn was often aloof, unless it had to do with dimension travel theory, chemistry, or metaphysics. In this learning environment, however, Ben blossomed, and as his confidence grew, so did his ability to assert himself. He developed an appreciation for all things alchemical and metaphysical, which gave him and Beetaa more diverse things to discuss. Ben also knew after hearing Farron's comment about him and Scarzen blood that Beetaa was eager to know the connection.

Home on Earth seemed far away to Ben in those times, except for thoughts

< 284 >

of Ann, whom Ben recognized as someone special. One day, during one of Farron's experiments to unlock the instability question over soul stream transition with Dogg and Quinn, she found that Ben's signature alone was not affected by the anomaly.

"I have a hazardous first assignment for you, Ben," she said, standing in her speaking chamber.

"What is it?"

"Tula and I would like your permission to perform an individual short-range soul stream transition from one end of my chamber to another."

Ben couldn't say why, but by this point, such a thing excited him more than anything—and it would be his first jump, alone. He agreed and earned kudos with Beetaa for showing such courage. Fitted with a small modified Jenaoin time-space transition modulator from Farron—courtesy of some tinkering by Roland—clipped to his collar, Ben took his short journey. Via an unusual gold-and-silver metta wave neither Farron or Tula had seen before, Ben reappeared exactly where expected, unfuzzy.

"Yes!" he shouted, feeling all his bits where they should be.

After several experiments with Ben proved 100 percent stable, Farron decided it was time to make a more significant jump. Knowing that every race's home world had regenerative properties in the atmosphere for an incarnate's soul core, and also noting the slow degradation of Ben's soul core, she decided his next jump would be to Earth.

"We must control transition from this end for the time being, Ben," she told him. "The window of your experience there could be different than we register here. Lose the modulator and we have no way to retrieve you. Stay in the proximity of your family home. You never know who's watching. The data you bring back may help us unlock the problem here. Here, take these glasses, and if anyone asks, tell them your eyes have been light sensitive lately but improving. Can't have them panicking over bright orange eyes, now, can we?"

"I understand," he said, as those on Tora watched him evaporate on his way back to Earth.

< 285 >

\* \* \*

Back home on Earth, everyone treated him as though he'd always been about. A few curious questions arose about his new glasses, which he dealt without too much struggle—young folks always had their stuff, after all. Besides, the glasses went with what his mother determined was his whole new rebellious look. First chance he got, he called Ann, who almost cycled her legs off getting to the farm to see if it was really him. For Ann, after knowing something so fantastic could exist around Ben, the more she heard, the more she wanted to know.

Sitting under the old willow one day, Ann asked, "But why doesn't anyone here miss you like me?

"You miss me? Really?"

"Ben, you know what I mean."

"It's the way the Superverse works. See, in their minds, I'm never away, Ann. I've learned that reality is flexible. Dogg said because I've chosen to train as a profiler, that path affords some advantages, and being allied with Zero's house comes with protections other mortals don't experience. You miss my absences because you know both sides of the coin now—and can't tell a soul. That burden will afford you some concessions too, provided you keep the secret Dogg said. Remember, if you do tell, you will only cause trouble for yourself. It's part of the debt to knowing the true reality of things. Everyone else remembers seeing me in all kinds of places and situations—all as real as this experience you are having now."

Ann had to think hard on all of it at first. "Well, Benny, I always thought you were special and a lot of fun. Make sure you write all your adventures down. They will make great stories. You could be the first human author of the Superverse, you know."

"Just remember never to speak to anyone of what you know and everything will be fine, Ann."

And Ann did dutifully keep their secret.

\* \* \*

Now and then, because of his new situation, and because he was acting

< 286 >

as a transition guinea pig, Ben found some adjustments difficult while visiting Earth.

"Dogg, it does my head in at times to see sister Sal on one visit running around at age seven, and on the next only a month later, she's a couple of years older," he told Dogg in Farron's speaking chamber one afternoon. "It all seems out of sync. You never age in front of me—or Roland, Beetaa, or Uniss. Will Mum and Sal forget me? Will I watch them grow old and die?"

"No to the first question, Ben. Of course they won't forget you, since you never truly leave there in their experience. Time is a paradox as a rule when, like us now, you stand on the border crossing of the space-time intercosmic threshold," said Dogg. "It is both a boon and a responsibility that you adjust to it."

*That doesn't make me feel any more comfortable,* Ben thought.

"But it's the truth," Dogg said, listening. "Time to grow and adapt, Ben."

"You know, sometimes you hearing my thoughts is a real pain in the butt."

"Those who have our best interests at heart are often so accused."

"Then I have to make sure Mum, Sal, and the others are all right—in that life anyway."

"Hmm," Dogg said. "Okay, I have an idea. I can arrange for them to have some … 'investments' built—which you will have to manage until I say otherwise, mind you. And bear in mind the consequences in such manipulations of the threads."

"What have you got in mind?"

"Some future technologies just around the bend, in their timeline. Don't worry, I'll tell you what and when."

"Thanks, Dogg. I'll do my bit. You'll see."

"You'd better. Your end now means more than any of us dare hope, my gut tells me."

"If you are going to do what I think you are, what will Uniss think of such unscheduled good fortune manipulations?" asked Roland. "Ben's … unexpected independence hasn't exactly ingratiated him. This could tip the scale."

"Not now. Ben is too pivotal. Let me worry about Uniss, Roland. That's

< 287 >

mine to sort."

"Still no luck stabilizing the soul stream transition yet?" asked Roland.

"No, every time Farron identifies one instability in the soul stream transition port, the corridor matrix for sentient transfers destabilizes on the very next cycle. Uniss reports other Citadel agents soul streaming in now and then. Every one of them so far has soul stream bounced back off-world seconds after they arrive. Farron thinks their soul cores are unlike Ben's and degrade very fast, disallowing all four states of consciousness to unify."

"*Crap, I hope that's not going to happen to me,*" thought Ben with a shiver.

"Well, if it is a soul stream bounce, going fuzzy is inevitable," said Dogg.

"Not a fate any of us want, being stuck in the in-betweens," said Roland.

"Let's hope she finds an answer soon," said Dogg.

\* \* \*

Day and night passed without notice inside the mountain as they prepared and looked for answers to contain Herrex and open the soul stream transition port again. Occasionally, news of outside goings-on caught Beetaa's and Ben's ears when invited to fireside chats with Farron. In those chats, she expanded their knowledge about the intercosmos as a whole.

"Just as there are energy forms using vibration, there are others that function in non-vibration, such as faux matter and what some call 'dark matter,'" she told them. "Ben, your coat, for instance, has some extraordinary properties that assist you, but also some drawbacks."

"What do you mean, Mistress?"

"Your coat comes from an ethereal dominated by the Tengu race and made by a master armorer there. The Tengu are a race similar in nature to the Scarzen of Tora. Your coat can, for example, protect you from elemental and even some physical force attacks. It will slow your aging process and regenerate your soul core by as much as half when you are on your home world. However, the longer you wear your Coat of Elements away from there, the more critically it will affect you If you were to remove the coat on, say … a Maxalon intercosmos jump ship in mortal space. Then be warned, your aging process would accelerate considerably."

< 288 >

Listening in his chair, Ben's face fell and he felt his coat sleeve. "Crap. No free lunch."

"Never. Now you know why I told you: taking it off has consequences. It's time for you both to see Quinn. Study hard. Much is happening outside you will need to be prepared for."

* * *

Studying in Quinn's chamber seemed to Ben like having the best fantasy chemistry set and experimental workshop in the world. Initially, Quinn had insisted that he and Beetaa remember the names of every ingredient and oddity on his shelves along with their properties of change, as Quinn called them. They had to observe in silence as he worked on various experiments. Sometimes, when the old mage fiddled with his enchanted clocks or devices from *the cabinet*, unintended surprises fascinated everyone. The most accurate time, Ben noted, was kept by Mac, Quinn's pet raven, the one they originally thought stuffed. Mac turned out to be very alive and no birdbrain at all. In fact, Ben and Beetaa learned that if Mac was standing back when Quinn was experimenting, they'd best do the same. This day, the three stood around his main workbench.

"Pay attention here," Quinn said. "Today's lesson continues with the use of kin." He lifted a hand as though weighing something up. "Note how I use kin to shape this small tree using only heated honey as the medium."

He waved a hand as though conducting music, and honey strings laced together to form branch and leaf. Finished, the three-dimensional sculpture stood suspended in the air about two feet in height, its glistening branches and leaves all beautifully formed.

Suddenly, Mac squawked, "Duck and cover, bird, duck and cover!"

The honey tree shuddered and sprayed hot honey everywhere, mostly over Quinn. Ben and Beetaa started to laugh, but Roland, dripping with a large splash of the sticky muck, wasn't impressed.

"Hat feathers! My felt will never recover!"

It took them weeks to get the sticky mess off all the surfaces, and days for Quinn to get it out of his hair and beard.

< 289 >

* * *

It had taken weeks, but eventually, Ben felt more and more uncomfortable and aware of Beetaa's furtive stares. Finally, he couldn't stand it anymore.

"Okay, mate. What's scratching you the wrong way?" Ben asked.

"Where is Roland?" Beetaa asked.

"He's with Dogg and Farron in her chambers. Why?"

"Tell me about your eyes."

"What?"

"Your eyes. They've changed again—darker somehow. Farron said we could speak of it later—and it's much later."

"Look, mate ... I ..."

Ben felt insecure and looked at his glasses sitting on the study table. He wished he had them on. He stood and moved to a metal mirror next to the bookshelf to look closer.

*Shit. What the hell!* He touched the side of one eye, looking at it seriously. "I don't know," Ben said. "I'll ask Master Quinn. That wasn't there yesterday."

"You know what I'm asking about. Stop evasive tactics. Tell me about the incident of being splashed with Scarzen blood."

Ben sighed and turned toward Beetaa. "Beetaa, it's not a big deal, and you know what Mistress said: I can't talk about it."

"When did this incident happen? Come, we are allies; trust is imperative. You can tell *me*," Beetaa said, walking up beside Ben. "What did you call us—'roommates'? Wasn't that it? Roommates shouldn't have any secrets, should they?"

"Beetaa. Strike, come on, mate. I ..." Ben's words stalled when he felt the now subtle familiar application of Beetaa's mind-lock. *Crap, in a closed room with an annoyed Scarzen. Not good.* "I told you, no! Now back off," Ben said, attempting to push Beetaa back.

"Quinn mumbled something about a Scarzen battle zone?" Beetaa said, angered and feeling deceived. "What did he mean?"

Beetaa parried Ben's extended arm and a furious unexpected flurry of evasive combative countermeasures erupted. The pace of the exchange took them both by surprise. As Ben ducked and rolled to evade Beetaa's driving

< 290 >

knife hand, both individuals felt a force wedge between them. It flung them to opposite ends of the room with a crash.

"What's going on here? Pugilism is reserved for other areas of the lair!"

They both looked to see Quinn standing in the doorway, palms extended as though holding both of them apart, a purple aura emitting from both his hands. Ben straightened up, wiping a bloody lip with the back of his hand. He looked at Beetaa, who appeared to be favoring his right side.

"No, Master Quinn. No problem," said Ben. "Beetaa was just instructing me on some finer points of labyrinth boxing. I tripped."

Quinn looked at both of them, sensing Ben's cover-up. He also noted the change of hue in the human's eyes. "Another such incident and your Mistress will hear of it. See that you confine such roughhouse interplay to the designated area. Now, come with me. We have things to do."

They followed Quinn out the door and on to his chambers.

* * *

"Take a stool," Quinn said, pointing to a cleared space on the central table in his lab.

He joined them, and the three sat at the bench as if having a drink in a bar.

"You've both been bored of late, judging by what just happened, I think," said Quinn, gathering some things close by.

Beetaa and Ben both looked a little sheepish.

"Why must we build a masterful life foundation?" Quinn asked.

"Without it, we can't see the bigger picture," Ben said.

Quinn gave a slightly frustrated grimace and a shake of the head. "Mmm. Thought that's what you'd say. No, Ben. It's so you can always find your way back when the way is lost."

Beetaa sat up straight with a puzzled look.

"Look here, you are both bright young prospects. You have shown discipline in the tasks set before you. But if you are going to wield the elements well, you have to think of the universe as being able to hear, see, and breathe—as the tide responds to the moons. Everything is intrinsically connected, from

< 291 >

what motivates the stars to shine to what stimulates germination of seed into tree. Dealing with the elements, you have to appreciate the interplay. Look here."

Quinn pulled over a glass beaker, an elm leaf, a small jug of water, a wad of cotton, some liquid spirit, and a match.

"There are four basic elements, yes?" Quinn asked.

Ben murmured the items as Quinn recited: "Earth, water, fire, and air! A Brasheer masters these basic elements. He is the gravity that transforms them." Quinn gestured to the items on the bench. "Earth symbolically represents all that is solid and can carry a load, like this jug. Water represents formlessness and strength through suppleness. Fire is transformation through rising temperature. And air is the lifeblood of the other three; without it, the others are inert." Quinn pulled a stone from his pocket and set it on the table. "To create stone, we need correct ratios for all four elements, yes?"

"Yes," both pupils replied.

"Good. Water represents cohesion." He pointed to the jug. "The air element is used to bind the other three. Kin represents air and is the catalyst for that which keeps a stone together or tears it apart," Quinn said, pouring water from the jug into the beaker. Air is in water, yet has different qualities necessary to fire—water's opposite. Earth is dense and restrictive, and can hold both fire and water. Like water, a flame can penetrate solid masses. Uncontrolled, it defuses quickly and dies. Fire is corruption, and if used wisely, few things can resist it. Air has the ability to move things, which implies mass and resistance. So, in air, we see that it can in its own way behave like …?"

"Earth! Ben said.

"Good," confirmed Quinn. "And when earth transforms, it mirrors …?"

"Fire," said Beetaa.

"Yes. In realms smaller than the best spyglass can aid us to see, there are strings.

"Strings?" Ben said.

"Strings, yes—one tiny happening looped around the next, ever in a state of flux," said Quinn. With that, he picked up the wad of cotton with

< 292 >

a pair of tongs and doused it with the spirit. "Water holds the chemical you now smell, made from earth," he said, referring to the dripping wad, then he struck the match and applied the flame. There was a *woof* of flame. "With air driving the first two elements, the result is a released byproduct of all the elements involved. The wad supports the flame as long as the liquid remains held by the cloth, and the air supports the continuance."

Beetaa and Ben looked at each other, unsure of Quinn's point.

"What if we took the flame like this?" Quinn asked.

Saying that, Quinn waved the palm of his hand gently under the burning wad. The flame separated from it and danced about one hand span above Quinn's bare palm, with no sign of burning him.

"What's holding it up?" asked Beetaa quietly.

"Ah-ha!" said Quinn, grasping the flame. Then, with a backhanded movement, he threw a small flaming ball against a space on the wall.

*Splat!*

"A Brasheer uses what is around him. He cannot conjure out of nothing. If you always know *the* something that exists therein, you can make the elements dance for you."

For a flash, Beetaa thought about his blood otaa and the size of the fireball that Spanaje had described in the story of Yorr Pass.

"Was my blood otaa as powerful as they say?" asked Beetaa.

Quinn nodded. "Benataa could have been a light this world would have never forgotten. But other choices have him remembered differently." He took a step back in pause. "Enough of the melancholy! Knowledge is the key that separates cupidity, antipathy, and bewilderment from the truth."

Those were Quinn's final words that day, and they were to be the keys to a treasury of knowledge and ability that both Beetaa and Ben would not have imagined possible.

< 293 >

**CHAPTER 22**
## BOO!

While his other allies were researching answers inside the Brasheer Mountain, Uniss searched for clues about Herrex's activities and anyone allied to his course. One gray cloudy evening near the Mustard Fields, with the deserted Fort Cragg visible on the foothills behind, Uniss sat in front of a small campfire, mind-talking with his Jenaoin companion, Trever.

*"How could I have been so stupid, Trev? It was staring me in the face from the moment Three set us up. If we'd have given Ben to Starlin, we'd all be done dinners now. She's going to let Herrex run interference while she walks in through the back door to take the Superverse."*

*"I don't know, Uniss. Something is nigglin' at my crown about who's pullin' whose leg,"* said Trever. *"I feel it in my hat band that whatever happened before the Great Event to throw stars in all our eyes has had a hand in all this too. Something Herrex said at his trial, but every time I try to remember what he said then, it all goes to space dust. What if Three and her cronies like Starlin don't know somethin's wrong? What if they are just playin' the hand they been dealt?"*

*"I can't answer that, mate. None of the Evercycles responded to my hails before the lockdown here. Sooner Furron fixes the soul stream issue, sooner I can get off this rock and do some proper digging. Not having the soul stream really limits our capability."*

*"Well, Lord Herrex has some cards to play of his own, is all I'm sayin'—that's as sure as every Jenaoin has a brim,"* said Trever.

*"I'll bet none of 'em figured on the Echaa making an independent move, though, Trev. All this imbalance has created just the right avenue for uncontrollable nasties like them to do hell-raising damage to everyone. It's not a win, but it may buy us some time."*

Into his hand, Uniss poured some raw trilix crystal from a pouch he carried. As the blue crystal came into contact with his hand, Uniss's palm began to glow with a brilliant blue light. He stared at the small pile of crystals before slowly letting them all trickle to the ground, forming a small pyramid on the ground.

Smiling, Uniss said, "Nothing created, nothing destroyed, eh, Herrex?"

From the shadows, he heard a stick crack under the weight of a foot. Lifting his head slowly, Uniss straightened his back. *"Bad company, Trev."*

Trever furtively scanned for thermal and ethereal bio signatures. *"Uniss, one directly behind. Others in the shadows left and right front. Flaxon, by the feel of them, and one mortal ethereal combine—something mighty powerful,"* Trever said.

"Yeah, mate," Uniss said aloud. *"Real big. It's Herrex—got to be. Steady as we go on this, Trev. Be ready to turn it up full on my word."*

Uniss remained seated. Slowly, he glanced behind. Then, from out of the shadows in front of him, three Flaxon in brown and crimson robes appeared. Two had unusual-looking shackles in their hands; the other seemed to be carrying a nightstick of sorts. Uniss recognized it as an ethereal weapon and reached furtively for his god-cutter blade inside his coat.

"Easy on the hostility, Unity," said a voice from the shadows—Herrex, both Uniss and Trever knew. "It will be more bother than you're counting on."

"Herrex," Uniss said. "So, you are out."

"How could you have ever doubted me, Unity?"

All the faces of the encircling men remained hard and grim. No one spoke a word.

"I take it you fellers aren't here for a friendly chat and a brew, then?" Uniss said.

< 295 >

"So, who paid your fare and donated their vessel this time, Herrex?" Uniss looked beyond the men to the shadows. "You sucker another poor slob into delusions of grandeur like last time?"

Uniss heard Herrex laugh.

"It was an honest trade, Unity. I always keep my word. He got everything he asked for—and more. Nothing like an already delusional ego groomed with a touch of celestial magic and some great special effects to sweeten the fall. Now, Profiler, it's your turn."

Herrex emerged from out of the shadows—in the unexpected form of Lord Trabonus, assisted by a servant holding him by the elbow.

"Not feelin' the best, old mate?" Uniss asked. "Skin-walking a little different in practice, I take it. Ah, and I see you banged your beak." Uniss winced. "Aw, bugger. Bet that hurt. Wish I was there to see you dance." Uniss showed Herrex a toothy grin.

*"Gotta stall him, Trev. He's weak but not to be played with. We need a way out,"* Uniss said mind to mind.

"This body will serve its purpose," said Herrex. "Tell your little Jenaoin friend to keep his eyes to himself or I guarantee every one of his race will be exterminated the moment I'm off-world."

Uniss saw a possible way out and shifted his weight. "Where'd you send the spark? These fellas know how your promotion scheme works?" Uniss asked and went to stand.

"Don't get up, Unity," Herrex said.

Uniss turned sideways on and Trever's eyes and crown shifted in a slight twist to face the Lord of Balance. The eyes of the Jenaoin made Herrex's henchmen edgy as Trev swung a glare from one to the other.

"Gods, wh-what is that—some demon form?" one of the henchmen sputtered, a wave of fear touching him.

"Nothing to be concerned about. Right, Unity?" Herrex said, stone cold, as they watched him.

"Aw, you know us. just a pair of passive conformists," Uniss said.

"How good of you to light the way, Unity, holding a little piece of myself in the palm of your hand," Herrex said. "Made me a trifle sentimental."

< 296 >

"Save it, Herrex. Now what?"

"I want the location of the bridgeport sub-gate here on Ludd."

"What sub-gate?" Uniss asked. "I think the transition's made you a little loopy, old fella. If there were a sub-gate, I would have used it a long way back. As you prob'ly know, we're all stuck here. But, since you're lookin' for a way off this rock, that tells me it isn't you stuffing around with the plumbing."

"Don't try to deny it. I know one exists. Give me its location and things will go better for you."

Uniss began to crush the pile of trilix under his heel.

"Don't help and I guarantee the suffering for all will be immense," said Herrex.

Uniss, knowing revenge was high on Herrex's to do list, relaxed. "I thought you'd be pleased to see I was right."

"About what?" sneered Herrex.

"You being the same sly, deranged shitbag you were when we put you here."

"It was all of you who missed what was really going on. None of you were worth trusting—and before I have you erased, I'll ensure you see just how naïve you have been." Herrex stepped closer. "We could have been quite a force."

"What, this your idea of a sales pitch? Man, you have to work on your delivery."

"Oh, I think you'll find my delivery more than up to the task," Herrex spat.

"You're trapped in a mortal body and stuck on this world, Herrex, and that's as far as you'll get."

"Not once I step through that sub-gate that you're going to tell me the location of."

"Not going to happen. The Council will know of your emergence—and by now, Tyr's making ready to turn this rock and everything on it into a barren, lifeless mass."

"I doubt that," said Herrex. "Tyr has—"

In that instant, Uniss stood and spun to face Herrex, attempting to hurl

< 297 >

a barrier—but nothing happened. Uniss drew his blade, advancing at Herrex, and Trever hurled bursts of electromagnetic shock waves multiplying into chain lightning to shut Herrex down. Herrex countered, stretching out a hand with splayed fingers that developed a defensive energy field. The bolts of energy from Trever froze, then reversed in an explosion, jumping from one enemy to the next. Trever was blown from Uniss's head, disappearing into the darkness as Uniss cut down one of the henchmen who put himself between Herrex and Uniss. Blinded by the charge, Uniss visibly turned gray. His entire being began to wither and dry up like a husk. He fought with all his will against the power draining him of life. He fell to one knee, weak and faint.

"TAKE HIM!" bellowed Herrex.

One henchman rushed in from behind and cracked Uniss over the head with the ethereal rod. Uniss folded forward, falling face-first into the dirt. He attempted to get back up, but was struck again. Uniss felt a last knock on his head before everything went black.

Herrex knelt down beside him and placed a hand over the trilix lying on the ground near Uniss's leg. Immediately, the crystal gravitated toward his palm. The reputation of trilix's fatal qualities were well known to the bystanders. Aghast, the onlookers expected a horrendous and painful death for Herrex. Instead, the opposite occurred. The devilish blue crystal invigorated their regent. Herrex stood and took a deep breath as though he had been filled with life. For a moment, the hue of his complexion changed from a sickly bedraggled old man to someone in their prime. The Flaxon took this miracle as further sign of the regent's true divinity. Several knelt before him, heads bowed.

*Finally ... rejuvenation!* Herrex thought.

Then, suddenly, the majority of Herrex's new vitality evaporated, returning him to frailty.

"No! Damn you, no!" he said. "I must have all of this world's trilix, do you hear? Every skerrick."

Herrex looked down at Uniss lying unconscious on the ground.

"And you, Agent of Zero. You are going to help me get it. Bind him. Put

< 298 >

him in my cells in Weirawind where we can interrogate him at my leisure."

Uniss's legs and hands were shackled, and two of the henchmen then manhandled him into a limp standing position. Standing in front of his prisoner, Herrex clapped his hands. They all disappeared in a flash of light, leaving only a small, extinguished campfire to show some trace.

* * *

Hours later, Trever awoke, knocked about and caught up between the limbs of a needle tree on the clearing's edge. He looked to where they had all struggled earlier, and gasped.

"Uniss, where …? Oh no! Must find Dogg … and tell Farron that the Dark Star himself is now manifest and walks on Tora. The Superverse is at war!"

With some effort, Trever hovered away, heading for the Brasheer Mountain.

< 299 >

**CHAPTER 23**
# HUNTING

Far north of Uniss's camp, and unknown to anyone, Tazorr's two-warrior scouting party closed on Weirawind. Ajax and Thorr sped through the forest quick and silent using the blur skill. Wind was dead calm now. Ajax and Thorr had heard one Flaxon patrol below the ridge that Ajax had chosen before they saw them and passed without detection. That had been a small company of twenty horsemen on the Victory Road. Now, just ahead, Thorr spied another unit patrol moving through the forest on their left, and he alerted Ajax. They maintained their mind-link and maintained battle formation.

"*I see them,*" Thorr heard Ajax's voice echo in his head.

"*We could strike and head on without losing time,*" said Thorr, running four strides to the side of Ajax.

"*Our orders are specific,*" said Ajax. "*We must find access and a possible escape route for the assassins. No time for hunting Flaxon—yet. The grass is thick underfoot and the ground hilly. Weirawind is near, so move.*"

At a strong pace, the two continued.

*Wish he was a little more talkative at times,* Thorr thought to himself, checking his stride. *Tazorr said his skill set was very specialized and didn't have a broad scope. Humph. Clearly, interaction isn't amongst them. Pure genius with an end of peace, though, if Tazorr's right: few can match his precision under*

< 300 >

*pressure. Want to see that.*

"*Keep the pace, shield,*" Ajax ordered in Thorr's mind. "*Focus on our task.*"

Thorr grunted an acknowledgment, wondering if Ajax had perhaps heard his thoughts, maybe because Thorr had been too lax about keeping them to himself. Ajax, many cycles older than Thorr, was a closed book to most. Over the past weeks, though, Thorr had managed to glean some personal backstory, but details remained vague. He'd had a life partner who had died some years back at the Battle of Sojaa against the Chou. Between them, Ajax and their mirror had taken down forty or so of the enemies, it was said. After that, Ajax remained in the field, seeking only an honorable death to join his mirror and their ancestors. He'd accept no unit protégés till Thorr came along, and then only because Ajax said he knew something of Thorr's otaa that made him nod. "Don't make me clean up after you, pup," was how their relationship had started. Thorr felt happy to be the silent partner from then on and learned a lot from Ajax, the "Ghost," as Thorr's unit referred to him. He cut right of a standing broad dead tree trunk.

*Beetaa, you would like this warden's maverick, ruthless ways. He is a great tactician and has taught me much about efficient consult and ambush. We have devastated our enemy several times since I have been apprenticed to him, though Ajax had to save my backside on a couple of occasions due to ... overexuberance on my part. He did not cause me loss of face, though. Were we not bound, Ajax would make a fine battle ally.*

As the two sped along, instinctively alternating their marathon heart and lungs with their auxiliaries to ward off fatigue, Ajax's lanky frame loped through the forest ahead of Thorr. At one point, Thorr saw him surprise a wild razor boar sleeping in the grass. It caused the animal to start with a grunt and a squeal, followed by a charging scream. The massive ball of aggression charged Ajax from a blind side. Ajax leapt into the air, drawing both his long knives wide like the wings of a bird of prey. In his descent, Ajax landed atop the beast's shoulders with a well-timed step. Plunging both knives through either side of the rib cage up to the hilt and without a pause in momentum, Ajax stepped off the boar's rump, withdrawing his knives with a sharp jerk. The predator was dead before it fell. Their objective's

< 301 >

watchtower lights could now be seen in the mid distance.

\* \* \*

In Weirawind, the city bell chimed one hour past midnight, and with it came the change of guard. On the northern parapets, a persistent cold wind kept soldiers active, and the night sky suggested rain.

Corporal Jenson pulled his collar up with a shiver. *A mug of mead and a kip in the cot will be damn welcome this night,* he thought. *Quicker I get these new boots off, the better. Bloody blisters will cripple me if I don't get them off soon.*

Just then, Jenson saw below the staff sergeant who'd ordered the change of footwear that afternoon. *Pig's arse!* Jenson yelled inside his head.

Eyes forward, Jenson marched past the other guard on shift. The about-face saw them meet near a cannon emplacement. Both men glanced at each other with disciplined, expressionless masks as their shoulders passed, almost touching. Jenson took six more steps and halted, stamping his right boot down sharply by his left. His hobnail boots made a metal-to-stone clap, then a scrape as his left foot slid back and he about-faced. A fine point of pain seared through his ankle, causing him to grit his teeth. Motionless, he peered out into the night eastward, scanning with his eyes—unaware the enemy was staring back from the nearby hills.

\* \* \*

After barely breaking a sweat during a run of some hours, Ajax and Thorr now sat concealed in a thicket of young trees in the hills overlooking Weirawind. They surveyed the area of the east wall, looking for possible entry.

"Many guards march behind the parapets at regular intervals," said Thorr.

"Flaxon protocol makes them a ready target," said Ajax.

"They'll make a good test of a Scarzen's skill at close quarter in large numbers, then?" said Thorr.

"I've fought them many times en masse in the past. As individual warriors, most lack integrity. Do you see? Seems most now carry fire barrels instead of the longbows of the past."

Thorr nodded, still studying the details. "The city is spread over a sizable

< 302 >

expanse. Ground undulates. The defensive walls enclosing the city are thick. Their fortifications look robust, but void of any individual character. How high do you think their walls?"

"About twenty standard spans," Ajax said. "See the enclosed emplacements every forty spans?"

"The emplacements look like they're smiling," said Thorr.

"From each of those cavities lie in wait not one but two cannons with muzzles bigger than your fist. Each covers a thirty-five-degree radius. Formidable in daylight. See the vague outlines of the murder holes running vertically down the wall? Originally used for archers. Now I suspect a garrison with firearms use them, which will make our task slower," said Ajax with a wince.

"What about a distraction to draw them out?" Thorr asked, looking beyond the main defensive wall. "Their agricultural fields are unfortified on the east side. We could burn them easily. Draw them out."

"Take too long and is in no way inconspicuous," Ajax said, then looked skyward at the moon's position. "Come on. We need a closer look."

Quietly, they moved down close to the northern wall using their blur skill, looking for any potential entry. They stopped near the northeastern corner. There, Ajax saw in the dim light a possibility.

*"There, to the left,"* Ajax said within Thorr's mind. *"That round grated airway. That will lead to the inside."*

*"Hope we don't have to keep maintaining this blur skill. My brain is starting to hurt,"* thought Thorr, hand on his forehead.

Ajax saw a tiny suggestion of light blink occasionally through the grate from inside. Ajax pointed. *"There."*

*"Where will it lead?"* Thorr asked.

Ajax looked farther along the wall to the west, where the city's smaller northern rear gate stood set into the stonework. Guards could be seen at attention on either side. A signal fire burning in an open metal basket flickered nearby. They both kept low, still applying blur to their physical image. They moved closer to their objective like two dull gray clouds, stopping unseen in the dark shadows of the wall next to the round air grate. The grate reached

< 303 >

to Ajax's shoulder height.

"*Let's see,*" said Ajax, grabbing at the bars to peer inside.

"*Wait,*" Thorr replied.

Suddenly, voices and marching steps could be heard coming from around the corner in the short distance. Ajax moved swiftly to see while Thorr watched the other direction. Peering around the corner of the wall, Ajax saw the dull flicker of lamplight fluttering as a perimeter patrol approached.

"*Don't need this,*" Ajax said.

Thorr took cover, as did Ajax. Both moved several strides away from the grate to a depression in part of some older wall stonework, and backed in. Their blur skill allowed them to blend in with night shadows as though they were a part of the wall itself.

"*Be ready,*" Ajax said.

As the perimeter guard approached, rounding the corner in marching formation, the torchlight exposed vague details of the block stonewall. Ajax and Thorr stood so still that the five soldiers who marched past remained oblivious of a death threat close enough to reach out and touch them.

*Gotcha, broz,* thought Thorr.

Ajax waited until the soldiers were twenty or so spans farther on and broke off to approach the grate again.

"*Watch them,*" Ajax told Thorr as he went to work on the grate.

Ajax drew an instrument from his utility belt, consisting of two pieces of flat metal. One piece had a hooked fork with a sharpened wheel inserted in between the prongs. The other was shaped into a narrow half-moon spoon. The two pieces snapped together at a locating pin toward the head of the instrument. Clipped together, they made a cutter typical of Scarzen design. Ajax reached up and with practiced skill applied the assembled cutter to the base of one iron rod. He worked it back and forth with vigor, and the motion made a small tweeting sound.

*Come on. Give up.*

It soon sliced through the thumb-thick iron rod with a final tiny snap.

*That's got it.*

He checked back to the gate once to see the five guards who'd passed

< 304 >

them scants ago now just disappearing inside the rear gate, and he went back to work on the next rod.

*Two more turns.*

There came a small cracking sound at the rod's base.

*That's two.*

He smiled and fumbled with the tool. It slipped from his hand, striking a flat stone at his boot with a sound.

*Turds.*

Its clang and clatter broke the night's silence. Ajax watched the direction of the guards while bending down to feel with one hand. He found the tool at his feet.

"Keep going," whispered Thorr, finding it easier to speak at the moment than use the mind-link.

Quickly, Ajax moved on to the other bars, repeating the process on the top and bottom of each one. The job finished, Ajax left the severed rods in place. They would look uncut from any upward view and too high for any Flaxon to notice walking past in the daylight. Ajax put the tool away. Thorr tapped him on the shoulder. There seemed to be new activity near the gate.

*"Someone's taking interest,"* said Thorr via mind-link.

They both froze in position while one guard stood staring in their direction. The guard farthest away walked up behind the other and said something. Thorr saw a short, unintelligible exchange between the two. The guards' mutterings seemed to take a long time.

*"Should I remove the problem?"* Thorr asked.

*"Too much torchlight. Night watch above might catch a glimpse of the exchange,"* said Ajax before creeping forward.

"We're done here; retreat that direction," Ajax whispered. "Let's go."

They retreated east to a stream at the base of the hills and crossed over undetected. Once back undercover, Thorr stayed behind on watch while Ajax returned to inform Tazorr of their findings.

* * *

Some hours on, back in the grove, Ajax relayed the information to Tazorr.

< 305 >

After a discussion with the Quall, Tazorr laid down a plan for a coordinated assault the following night. They arrived at Thorr's position in the north hills overlooking Weirawind at sunup, where a light breeze cut from the west.

Tazorr and Ajax crouched in a concealed position next to Thorr. The others lay low close behind.

"No interest in our work since Ajax left, Commander," said Thorr. "It's easy to see the city guard on the battlements now."

Tazorr nodded. "It's been thirty years since my last sighting of this place. It was only a growing township then. Nothing more than some isolated watchtowers around some basic fortification with one large garrison there in the northeast corner. Some of the stonework had been started for this main defensive wall. But I didn't expect this."

"So they've been busy," said Thorr.

"That's a fact. It's a fully energized city now by the looks. Main gates face east, not north as before. Now blockhouses—containing cannon—divide the parapets at regular intervals. That part of the old original stronghold wall. Looks like they worked it into the newer structure along the connecting eastern wall. I'll have to send a full report on this."

"We go in right there, sir," Ajax said, pointing out the breach that had been created in the middle of the previous night.

The round stone grate, small but visible from their vantage point, satisfied Tazorr as a good entry point.

"Well done, pups. Very tidy, very tidy indeed. I think we can get their attention through there."

Tazorr stared at the city in thought. *The city must measure about five thousand standard spans square, an impressive effort for Flaxon. Boring but tough stonework ... looks a fortress of medium strength. Our engineer units could have it breached easily in two days for a frontal attack.*

As he looked beyond the walls to the central city, one building stood out on raised ground. Made of white stone, it looked to be the largest and newest building in the area. A huge monolith had been erected in front of the southern face.

*The regent's personal castle. Has to be, from what Sooza described. All eyes*

< 306 >

*could see that spire from anywhere inside the city. Humph. Just in case anyone might forget where those in charge live.*

"The place seems divided into four main areas, sir," said Thorr. "You'll note all main roads end at the regent's castle, which acts as a central nexus for the four points of the city. There's a large coliseum still in construction over there in the southwestern corner. It's the only significant untidy blot on the orderly cityscape. Workers have been scrambling about the upper levels like ants for hours. A good place to herd them if need be, I thought."

Tazorr glanced back over his shoulder momentarily. "Yes. I think you might be right. Well observed," he said.

"Apart from the garrison in that northeastern corner we can see, given the size of the place, there must be others," Thorr said.

"Mmm. The Quall say their elder is being held in either the central city garrison, possibly that compound there east of the castle," Tazorr said and pointed. "Or the one in that northeast corner. For some reason, our Celeron spies say the Flaxon shuttle key prisoners between military compounds— possibly to avoid assassination, as the Quall reputation for infiltration and illumination of a target is well respected. Logic would dictate that, being larger than the others, the northeast corner garrison must hold the city's main defense. So it will be well filled with their warriors."

Tazorr moved his attention to the rear of the city, westward. There, he saw a separate new industrial-looking facility. *Those chimneys suggest metalwork … smithy shops of some kind possibly. At the least, it looks constructed for the purpose of industry. And it's not far west of the rear gate. Those heavy cannon in the blockhouses on the parapet are a worry … their radius sweep of these hills. Could easily pound us close to this very position. It's a long way, too, on foot under fire even aided by their weapons' inaccuracy. Any incursion or escape would definitely have to be by night.*

Tazorr nodded to himself and looked to the northwest, where the head of the Urd River descended from the north hills and ran parallel with the city.

*They've re-dammed and put in an aqueduct to siphon water directly into the city. That won't please the Celeron. Three villages were submerged after that dam went in last time. Their farmland and freshwater supply must be cut to a trickle.*

< 307 >

"What has your interest, sir?" asked Thorr.

"The dam. They've rebuilt it after we were ordered to take it down years ago. Last time, a Celeron envoy reported the Flaxon, making everyone downstream pay tax—be the first thing I'd hit if it were me."

A thin tree line marked the downward course of the water flow. In the far distance, he could see the position on the Urd where the natural watercourse filled the low lands—now blocked by the dam that the Flaxon had rebuilt twenty years ago.

"You two!" Tazorr called, gesturing to two warriors behind him. "I want some mischief down there, in that industrial building along the outside of the north wall," he said, pointing. "And don't spare the casualties."

With the order given, faces formed an expression of satisfaction at the mission. "Yes, Ruhe," they both replied.

"Bring back anything of value for the keeper's eyes. Wait until the night's eleventh hour, then do your worst."

"Ho," they said, paying respects before moving off.

Turning to Ajax and Thorr, Tazorr instructed: "We wait for nightfall. You two will breach the wall and spearhead the assault. Once inside, get the rear gate open. By Naught's beard, they'll have stories to tell after this."

\* \* \*

That afternoon in the targeted facility, Magistrate Waldon stood, hands on hips, looking out his office window over his now finished weapons factory. Within the walls of his new facility, an artillery and small-arms forge churned out all his latest designs. Six specialized smithy shops lined the northern side of the factory. Inside the facility, only the magistrate's personal command unit was permitted—called the 1st Mobile Artillery Force and dubbed the MAF. Waldon ordered many soldiers to work in the factory alongside the weapon smithies to ensure knowledge of their weapons in the field.

*Three more months and we'll be right to crush them fully,* he thought. *I'm so sick of Trahonor's grumbling about the treasury running low all the time. Damn his position. How does he expect me to destroy the Scarzen without profits to make the weapons?* He looked at his ledger of the huge stockpiled gunpowder

< 308 >

stores. He looked out the window again at all the covered munitions boxes. *Good thing Saxby and that alchemist Binks finally got it right. That stack would make a hell of a hole if it blew.*

He rubbed his neck unconsciously, remembering how the only thing that saved his neck in their last argument was the fact that he was the regent's brother. The munitions and weapons factory had appealed to the regent at first, but as time dragged on and results came slow, Trabonus's enthusiasm faded.

*The fool seems possessed all of a sudden. All that new foppish look and pretense can't hide who he really is. God, he's even bathing regularly and wearing rose water. Bah. Keep your head here, Waldon. First the Scarzen, then the regency.*

He examined a set of plans for the new cannon.

*Screwman's new upgrades of the projectiles for the cast-iron smoothbore cannon have worked wonders. Might even raise his Flaxon class if all this goes well.*

There was a knock at his door.

"Enter." Waldon turned. "Yes, Saxby, what is it?"

"Bell caster Screwman sends his thanks. As ordered, sir, all new cannon and small-arms barrels have Cedric Screwman's namesake embossed as Waldon Technology Screwshot Armaments. Casting the new molds and relining the in-service old smoothbore cannon to accept the new more powerful munitions have made all the difference."

"Yes, smart thing—inserting a wrought-iron inner cage that way," said Waldon. "It looks a lot like the large eel trap we use, only composed of three flat iron straps, wound in a hollow braid."

"Yes, sir, it does. He pressed a flat ring of bronze over the ends to make the cage and slotted the lot inside the original bore. Clever bastard achieved a cold forge by firing a proof charge through the cage, which had the effect of tightening both outer and inner barrels together. It creates a spiral striation. The new MKII breach-load doors at the rear work like a treat too, and while they're only safe for one hundred and fifty rounds, it takes little time to replace a door in the field."

"Excellent."

"Apart from better barrel strength reliability and distance, most importantly

< 309 >

we have improved the trajectory prediction for a projectile by up to seventy-three percent. What has made the greater accuracy possible is how Screwman has designed the projectile to spin. Like this smaller dummy example I left beside your desk." Saxby picked up the dummy round. "See here. Screwman has made the back with ribbing that produces a spiral effect post-firing. It results in a much more stable shot. Captain Soams feels very confident our weapons will meet expectations in the field now. The big news is, sir, that after His Lordship Trabonus saw the latest test fire, he ordered all blockhouses and near defenses around the city wall to have the new cannon emplacements put in immediately. He signed the order this morning," said Saxby, placing it on Waldon's desk.

Waldon looked at the document. "Ha. He has also approved my order for the iron-cladding squares to be riveted to the outer defensive walls. Well done, Saxby! At this rate, we will be impregnable in no time. Ensure that the work begins around the entry gates and below each blockhouse first."

"The check pattern will give the city walls a royal jackboard look."

"Use whatever labor you need for increased production. Put more children into the mines and furnaces where necessary."

"You realize that taking child labor from the fields will increase military supplies, but harm agriculture, sir. Food supply will drop by a third after one season. If food and ale drop, the working class could see the Rents Court in a darker light, sir."

*And right on time, I hope.* "No sacrifice, no return, Saxby. Let me worry about the regent's office. Now, get cracking—we have an army to build and a land to take control of." *And ... I intend to rule it all.*

< 310 >

# EPILOGUE

" Well, Reader, that's how it went. Two presents and a past got rolled into one unstable fixed point, the hand of more than the gods stirring the pot. Factions on either side of the mortal-ethereal Continuum geared for war, with none of them really prepared for the catastrophic shock wave of events that would swallow us all.

"And front and center was Ben, our apprentice with the mystery background, who had begun showing there was a whole lot more to him than what you got from a handshake. At about that time, it made me realize that he was like gravity: stuff just kept happening around him as he gathered momentum to shake the Superverse by the tail. What he ended up doing to wrap this mess up knocked the wind out of even me.

"Oh yeah, and I had a front row seat of sorts—and nothin' good to happen there while Herrex tested his land legs and the Scarzen gathered to hit his house hard. Even a few of the little guys came out of the woods with sticks bigger than they should carry and somehow got payback and gave Herrex's shins a proper bruising.

"So there's a lot more to tell about the life and times of Commander Ben Bloch and his intercosmos crew—and that, dear Reader, includes you."

—END: BOOK TWO—

## Next in the Citadel 7 Series *Earth's Secret* Trilogy …

### *Book Three: A Test of Good and Evil*

The concluding volume of Citadel 7's opening trilogy keeps the heroes in a pressure-cooker even as the existence of the Superverse hangs in the balance! Ben's life and understanding of reality have been changed forever. From the moment he arrived on Planet Tora with Uniss and Dogg, he's faced more life-threatening experiences than he can keep track of. Now the ante has been upped again. Uniss has been kidnapped and tortured by the worst of their enemies. He will surely perish if Ben and the others can't mount a successful rescue. Then there's Dogg, who nearly died at the Battle of Yorr Pass as the Scarzen and Flaxon race war erupted, all driven by Lord Herrex and Agent Starlin's nefarious machinations. Herrex and Starlin, though, both have much more in mind than mere domination of this off-the-grid prison planet.

Now, Lord Herrex and Ben's destinies converge in a cataclysmic confrontation—and nobody's survival is certain. Underneath it all, something even more sinister is at work, and Ben discovers that he is somehow the key to either victory or oblivion for the entire Superverse. But even as *A Test of Good and Evil* charges toward its conclusion, a sudden twist unfolds at the bitter end—keeping in step with what Citadel 7 readers have come to expect from Yuan Jur's multiple Cygnus award-winning series: "Nothing's as it seems!"

< 312 >